The Gadfly

Ethel L. Voynich

The Gadfly

Copyright © 2014 by Bibliotech Press
All rights reserved.

Contact:
BibliotechPress@gmail.com

The present edition is a reproduction of 1912 publication of this work. Minor typographical errors may have been corrected without note, however, for an authentic reading experience the spelling, punctuation, and capitalization have been retained from the original text.

ISBN: 978-1-61895-141-0

"What have we to do with Thee, Thou Jesus of Nazareth?"

AUTHOR'S PREFACE.

MY most cordial thanks are due to the many persons who helped me to collect, in Italy, the materials for this story. I am especially indebted to the officials of the Marucelliana Library of Florence, and of the State Archives and Civic Museum of Bologna, for their courtesy and kindness.

PART I

CHAPTER I

Arthur sat in the library of the theological seminary at Pisa, looking through a pile of manuscript sermons. It was a hot evening in June, and the windows stood wide open, with the shutters half closed for coolness. The Father Director, Canon Montanelli, paused a moment in his writing to glance lovingly at the black head bent over the papers.

"Can't you find it, carino? Never mind; I must rewrite the passage. Possibly it has got torn up, and I have kept you all this time for nothing."

Montanelli's voice was rather low, but full and resonant, with a silvery purity of tone that gave to his speech a peculiar charm. It was the voice of a born orator, rich in possible modulations. When he spoke to Arthur its note was always that of a caress.

"No, Padre, I must find it; I'm sure you put it here. You will never make it the same by rewriting."

Montanelli went on with his work. A sleepy cockchafer hummed drowsily outside the window, and the long, melancholy call of a fruitseller echoed down the street: "Fragola! fragola!"

"'On the Healing of the Leper'; here it is." Arthur came across the room with the velvet tread that always exasperated the good folk at home. He was a slender little creature, more like an Italian in a sixteenth-century portrait than a middle-class English lad of the thirties. From the long eyebrows and sensitive mouth to the small hands and feet, everything about him was too much chiseled, overdelicate. Sitting still, he might have been taken for a very pretty girl masquerading in male attire; but when he moved, his lithe agility suggested a tame panther without the claws.

"Is that really it? What should I do without you, Arthur? I should always be losing my things. No, I am not going to write any more now. Come out into the garden, and I will help you with your work. What is the bit you couldn't understand?"

They went out into the still, shadowy cloister garden. The seminary occupied the buildings of an old Dominican monastery, and two hundred years ago the square courtyard had been stiff and trim, and the rosemary and lavender had grown in close-cut bushes between the straight box edgings. Now the white-robed monks who had tended them were laid away and forgotten; but the scented herbs flowered still in the gracious mid-summer evening, though no man gathered their blossoms for simples any more. Tufts of wild parsley and columbine filled the cracks between the flagged footways, and the well in the middle of the courtyard was given up to ferns and matted stonecrop. The roses had run wild, and their straggling suckers trailed across the paths; in the box borders flared great red poppies; tall foxgloves drooped above the tangled grasses; and the old vine, untrained and barren of fruit, swayed from the branches of the neglected medlar-tree, shaking a leafy head with slow and sad persistence.

In one corner stood a huge summer-flowering magnolia, a tower of dark foliage, splashed here and there with milk-white blossoms. A rough wooden bench had been placed against the trunk; and on this Montanelli sat down. Arthur was studying philosophy at the university; and, coming to a difficulty with a book, had applied to "the Padre" for an explanation of the point. Montanelli was a universal encyclopaedia to him, though he had never been a pupil of the seminary.

"I had better go now," he said when the passage had been cleared up; "unless you want me for anything."

"I don't want to work any more, but I should like you to stay a bit if you have time."

"Oh, yes!" He leaned back against the tree-trunk and looked up through the dusky branches at the first faint stars glimmering in a quiet sky. The dreamy, mystical eyes, deep blue under black lashes, were an inheritance from his Cornish mother, and Montanelli turned his head away, that he might not see them.

"You are looking tired, carino," he said.

"I can't help it." There was a weary sound in Arthur's voice, and the Padre noticed it at once.

"You should not have gone up to college so soon; you were tired out with sick-nursing and being up at night. I ought to have insisted on your taking a thorough rest before you left Leghorn."

"Oh, Padre, what's the use of that? I couldn't stop in that miserable house after mother died. Julia would have driven me mad!"

Julia was his eldest step-brother's wife, and a thorn in his side.

"I should not have wished you to stay with your relatives," Montanelli answered gently. "I am sure it would have been the worst possible thing for you. But I wish you could have accepted the invitation of your English doctor friend; if you had spent a month in his house you would have been more fit to study."

"No, Padre, I shouldn't indeed! The Warrens are very good and kind, but they don't understand; and then they are sorry for me,—I can see it in all their faces,—and they would try to console me, and talk about mother. Gemma wouldn't, of course; she always knew what not to say, even when we were babies; but the others would. And it isn't only that——"

"What is it then, my son?"

Arthur pulled off some blossoms from a drooping foxglove stem and crushed them nervously in his hand.

"I can't bear the town," he began after a moment's pause. "There are the shops where she used to buy me toys when I was a little thing, and the walk along the shore where I used to take her until she got too ill. Wherever I go it's the same thing; every market-girl comes up to me with bunches of flowers—as if I wanted them now! And there's the church-yard—I had to get away; it made me sick to see the place——"

He broke off and sat tearing the foxglove bells to pieces. The silence was so long and deep that he looked up, wondering why the Padre did not speak. It was growing dark under the branches of the magnolia, and everything seemed dim and indistinct; but there was light enough to show the ghastly paleness of Montanelli's face. He was bending his head down, his right hand tightly clenched upon the edge of the bench. Arthur looked away with a sense of awestruck wonder. It was as though he had stepped unwittingly on to holy ground.

"My God!" he thought; "how small and selfish I am beside him! If my trouble were his own he couldn't feel it more."

Presently Montanelli raised his head and looked round. "I won't press you to go back there; at all events, just now," he said in his most caressing tone; "but you must promise me to take a thorough rest when your vacation begins this summer. I think you had better get a holiday right away from the neighborhood of Leghorn. I can't have you breaking down in health."

"Where shall you go when the seminary closes, Padre?"

"I shall have to take the pupils into the hills, as usual, and see them settled there. But by the middle of August the subdirector will be back from his holiday. I shall try to get up into the Alps for a little change. Will you come with me? I could take you for some long mountain rambles, and you would like to study the Alpine mosses and lichens. But perhaps it would be rather dull for you alone with me?"

"Padre!" Arthur clasped his hands in what Julia called his "demonstrative foreign way." "I would give anything on earth to go away with you. Only—I am not sure——" He stopped.

"You don't think Mr. Burton would allow it?"

"He wouldn't like it, of course, but he could hardly interfere. I am eighteen now and can do what I choose. After all, he's only my step-brother; I don't see that I owe him obedience. He was always unkind to mother."

"But if he seriously objects, I think you had better not defy his wishes; you may find your position at home made much harder if——"

"Not a bit harder!" Arthur broke in passionately. "They always did hate me and always will—it doesn't matter what I do. Besides, how can James seriously object to my going away with you—with my father confessor?"

"He is a Protestant, remember. However, you had better write to him, and we will wait to hear what he thinks. But you must not be impatient, my son; it matters just as much what you do, whether people hate you or love you."

The rebuke was so gently given that Arthur hardly coloured under it. "Yes, I know," he answered, sighing; "but it is so difficult——"

"I was sorry you could not come to me on Tuesday evening," Montanelli said, abruptly introducing a new subject. "The Bishop of Arezzo was here, and I should have liked you to meet him."

"I had promised one of the students to go to a meeting at his lodgings, and they would have been expecting me."

"What sort of meeting?"

Arthur seemed embarrassed by the question. "It—it was n-not a r-regular meeting," he said with a nervous little stammer. "A student had come from Genoa, and he made a speech to us—a-a sort of—lecture."

"What did he lecture about?"

Arthur hesitated. "You won't ask me his name, Padre, will you? Because I promised——"

"I will ask you no questions at all, and if you have promised secrecy of course you must not tell me; but I think you can almost trust me by this time."

"Padre, of course I can. He spoke about—us and our duty to the people—and to—our own selves; and about—what we might do to help——"

"To help whom?"

"The contadini—and——"

"And?"

"Italy."

There was a long silence.

"Tell me, Arthur," said Montanelli, turning to him and speaking very gravely, "how long have you been thinking about this?"

"Since—last winter."

"Before your mother's death? And did she know of it?"

"N-no. I—I didn't care about it then."

"And now you—care about it?"

Arthur pulled another handful of bells off the foxglove.

"It was this way, Padre," he began, with his eyes on the ground. "When I was preparing for the entrance examination last autumn, I got to know a good many of the students; you remember? Well, some of them began to talk to me about—all these things, and lent me books. But I didn't care much about it; I always wanted to get home quick to mother. You see, she was quite alone among them all in that dungeon of a house; and Julia's tongue was enough to kill her. Then, in the winter, when she got so ill, I forgot all about the students and their books; and then, you know, I left off coming to Pisa altogether. I should have talked to mother if I had thought of it; but it went right out of my head. Then I found out that she was going to die——You know, I was almost constantly with her towards the end; often I would sit up the night, and Gemma Warren would come in the day to let me get to sleep. Well, it was in those long nights; I got thinking about the books and about what the students had said—and wondering—whether they were right and—what—Our Lord would have said about it all."

"Did you ask Him?" Montanelli's voice was not quite steady.

"Often, Padre. Sometimes I have prayed to Him to tell me what I must do, or to let me die with mother. But I couldn't find any answer."

"And you never said a word to me. Arthur, I hoped you could have trusted me."

"Padre, you know I trust you! But there are some things you can't talk about to anyone. I—it seemed to me that no one could help me—not even you or mother; I must have my own answer straight from God. You see, it is for all my life and all my soul."

Montanelli turned away and stared into the dusky gloom of the magnolia branches. The twilight was so dim that his figure had a shadowy look, like a dark ghost among the darker boughs.

"And then?" he asked slowly.

"And then—she died. You know, I had been up the last three nights with her——"

He broke off and paused a moment, but Montanelli did not move.

"All those two days before they buried her," Arthur went on in a lower voice, "I couldn't think about anything. Then, after the funeral, I was ill; you remember, I couldn't come to confession."

"Yes; I remember."

"Well, in the night I got up and went into mother's room. It was all empty; there was only the great crucifix in the alcove. And I thought perhaps God would help me. I knelt down and waited—all night. And in the morning when I came to my senses—Padre, it isn't any use; I can't explain. I can't tell you what I saw—I hardly know myself. But I know that God has answered me, and that I dare not disobey Him."

For a moment they sat quite silent in the darkness. Then Montanelli turned and laid his hand on Arthur's shoulder.

"My son," he said, "God forbid that I should say He has not spoken to your soul. But remember your condition when this thing happened, and do not take the fancies of grief or illness for His solemn call. And if, indeed, it has been His will to answer you out of the shadow of death, be sure that you put no false construction on His word. What is this thing you have it in your heart to do?"

Arthur stood up and answered slowly, as though repeating a catechism:

"To give up my life to Italy, to help in freeing her from all this slavery and wretchedness, and in driving out the Austrians, that she may be a free republic, with no king but Christ."

"Arthur, think a moment what you are saying! You are not even an Italian."

"That makes no difference; I am myself. I have seen this thing, and I belong to it."

There was silence again.

"You spoke just now of what Christ would have said——" Montanelli began slowly; but Arthur interrupted him:

"Christ said: 'He that loseth his life for my sake shall find it.'"

Montanelli leaned his arm against a branch, and shaded his eyes with one hand.

"Sit down a moment, my son," he said at last.

Arthur sat down, and the Padre took both his hands in a strong and steady clasp.

"I cannot argue with you to-night," he said; "this has come upon me so suddenly—I had not thought—I must have time to think it over. Later on we will talk more definitely. But, for just now, I want you to remember one thing. If you get into trouble over this, if you—die, you will break my heart."

"Padre——"

"No; let me finish what I have to say. I told you once that I have no one in the world but you. I think you do not fully understand what that means. It is difficult when one is so young; at your age I should not have understood. Arthur, you are as my—as my—own son to me. Do you see? You are the light of my eyes and the desire of my heart. I would die to keep you from making a false step and ruining your life. But there is nothing I can do. I don't ask you to make any promises to me; I only ask you to remember this, and to be careful. Think well before you take an irrevocable step, for my sake, if not for the sake of your mother in heaven."

"I will think—and—Padre, pray for me, and for Italy."

He knelt down in silence, and in silence Montanelli laid his hand on the bent head. A moment later Arthur rose, kissed the hand, and went softly away across the dewy grass. Montanelli sat alone under the magnolia tree, looking straight before him into the blackness.

"It is the vengeance of God that has fallen upon me," he thought, "as it fell upon David. I, that have defiled His sanctuary, and taken the Body of the Lord into polluted hands,—He has been very patient with me, and now it is come. 'For thou didst it secretly, but I will do this thing before all Israel, and before the sun; THE CHILD THAT IS BORN UNTO THEE SHALL SURELY DIE.'"

CHAPTER II

MR. JAMES BURTON did not at all like the idea of his young stepbrother "careering about Switzerland" with Montanelli. But positively to forbid a harmless botanizing tour with an elderly professor of theology would seem to Arthur, who knew nothing of the reason for the prohibition, absurdly tyrannical. He would immediately attribute it to religious or racial prejudice; and the Burtons prided themselves on their enlightened tolerance. The whole family had been staunch Protestants and Conservatives ever since Burton & Sons, ship-owners, of London and Leghorn, had first set up in business, more than a century back. But they held that English gentlemen must deal fairly, even with Papists; and when the head of the house, finding it dull to remain a widower, had married the pretty Catholic governess of his younger children, the two elder sons, James and Thomas, much as they resented the presence of a step-mother hardly older than themselves, had submitted with sulky resignation to the will of Providence. Since the father's death the eldest brother's marriage had further complicated an already difficult position; but both brothers had honestly tried to protect Gladys, as long as she lived, from Julia's merciless tongue, and to do their duty, as they understood it, by Arthur. They did not even pretend to like the lad, and their generosity towards him showed itself chiefly in providing him with lavish supplies of pocket money and allowing him to go his own way.

In answer to his letter, accordingly, Arthur received a cheque to cover his expenses and a cold permission to do as he pleased about his holidays. He expended half his spare cash on botanical books and pressing-cases, and started off with the Padre for his first Alpine ramble.

Montanelli was in lighter spirits than Arthur had seen him in for a long while. After the first shock of the conversation in the garden he had gradually recovered his mental balance, and now looked upon the case more calmly. Arthur was very young and inexperienced; his decision could hardly be, as yet, irrevocable. Surely there was still time to win him back by gentle persuasion and reasoning from the dangerous path upon which he had barely entered.

They had intended to stay a few days at Geneva; but at the first sight of the glaring white streets and dusty, tourist-crammed promenades, a little frown appeared on Arthur's face. Montanelli watched him with quiet amusement.

"You don't like it, carino?"

"I hardly know. It's so different from what I expected. Yes, the lake is beautiful, and I like the shape of those hills." They were standing on Rousseau's Island, and he pointed to the long, severe outlines of the Savoy side. "But the town looks so stiff and tidy, somehow—so Protestant; it has a self-satisfied air. No, I don't like it; it reminds me of Julia."

Montanelli laughed. "Poor boy, what a misfortune! Well, we are here for our own amusement, so there is no reason why we should stop. Suppose we take a sail on the lake to-day, and go up into the mountains to-morrow morning?"

"But, Padre, you wanted to stay here?"

"My dear boy, I have seen all these places a dozen times. My holiday is to see your pleasure. Where would you like to go?"

"If it is really the same to you, I should like to follow the river back to its source."

"The Rhone?"

"No, the Arve; it runs so fast."

"Then we will go to Chamonix."

They spent the afternoon drifting about in a little sailing boat. The beautiful lake produced far less impression upon Arthur than the gray and muddy Arve. He had grown up beside the Mediterranean, and was accustomed to blue ripples; but he had a positive passion for swiftly moving water, and the hurried rushing of the glacier stream delighted him beyond measure. "It is so much in earnest," he said.

Early on the following morning they started for Chamonix. Arthur was in very high spirits while driving through the fertile valley country; but when they entered upon the winding road near Cluses, and the great, jagged hills closed in around them, he became serious and silent. From St. Martin they walked slowly up the valley, stopping to sleep at wayside chalets or tiny mountain villages, and wandering on again as their fancy directed. Arthur was peculiarly sensitive to the influence of scenery, and the first waterfall that they passed threw him into an ecstacy which was delightful to see; but as they drew nearer to the snow-peaks he passed out of this rapturous mood into one of dreamy exaltation that Montanelli had not seen before. There seemed to be a kind of mystical relationship between him and the mountains. He would lie for hours motionless in the dark, secret, echoing pine-forests, looking out between the straight, tall trunks into the sunlit outer world of flashing peaks and barren cliffs. Montanelli watched him with a kind of sad envy.

"I wish you could show me what you see, carino," he said one day as he looked up from his book, and saw Arthur stretched beside him on the moss in the same attitude as an hour before, gazing out with wide, dilated eyes into the glittering expanse of blue and white. They had turned aside from the high-road to sleep at a quiet village near the falls of the Diosaz, and, the sun being already low in a cloudless sky, had mounted a point of pine-clad rock to wait for the Alpine glow over the dome and needles of the Mont Blanc chain. Arthur raised his head with eyes full of wonder and mystery.

"What I see, Padre? I see a great, white being in a blue void that has no beginning and no end. I see it waiting, age after age, for the coming of the Spirit of God. I see it through a glass darkly."

Montanelli sighed.

"I used to see those things once."

"Do you never see them now?"

"Never. I shall not see them any more. They are there, I know; but I have not the eyes to see them. I see quite other things."

"What do you see?"

"I, carino? I see a blue sky and a snow-mountain—that is all when I look up into the heights. But down there it is different."

He pointed to the valley below them. Arthur knelt down and bent over the sheer edge of the precipice. The great pine trees, dusky in the gathering shades of evening, stood like sentinels along the narrow banks confining the river. Presently the sun, red as a glowing coal, dipped behind a jagged mountain peak, and all the life and light deserted the face of nature. Straightway there came upon the valley something dark and threatening—sullen, terrible, full of spectral weapons. The perpendicular cliffs of the barren western mountains seemed like the teeth of a monster lurking to snatch a victim and drag him down into the maw of the deep valley, black with its moaning forests. The pine trees were rows of knife-blades whispering: "Fall upon us!" and in the gathering darkness the torrent roared and howled, beating against its rocky prison walls with the frenzy of an everlasting despair.

"Padre!" Arthur rose, shuddering, and drew back from the precipice. "It is like hell."

"No, my son," Montanelli answered softly, "it is only like a human soul."

"The souls of them that sit in darkness and in the shadow of death?"

"The souls of them that pass you day by day in the street."

Arthur shivered, looking down into the shadows. A dim white mist was hovering among the pine trees, clinging faintly about the desperate agony of the torrent, like a miserable ghost that had no consolation to give.

"Look!" Arthur said suddenly. "The people that walked in darkness have seen a great light."

Eastwards the snow-peaks burned in the afterglow. When the red light had faded from the summits Montanelli turned and roused Arthur with a touch on the shoulder.

"Come in, carino; all the light is gone. We shall lose our way in the dark if we stay any longer."

"It is like a corpse," Arthur said as he turned away from the spectral face of the great snow-peak glimmering through the twilight.

They descended cautiously among the black trees to the chalet where they were to sleep.

As Montanelli entered the room where Arthur was waiting for him at the supper table, he saw that the lad seemed to have shaken off the ghostly fancies of the dark, and to have changed into quite another creature.

"Oh, Padre, do come and look at this absurd dog! It can dance on its hind legs."

He was as much absorbed in the dog and its accomplishments as he had been in the after-glow. The woman of the chalet, red-faced and white-aproned, with sturdy arms akimbo, stood by smiling, while he put the animal through its tricks. "One can see there's not much on his mind if he can carry on that way," she said in patois to her daughter. "And what a handsome lad!"

Arthur coloured like a schoolgirl, and the woman, seeing that he had understood, went away laughing at his confusion. At supper he talked of nothing but plans for excursions, mountain ascents, and botanizing expeditions. Evidently his dreamy fancies had not interfered with either his spirits or his appetite.

When Montanelli awoke the next morning Arthur had disappeared. He had started before daybreak for the higher pastures "to help Gaspard drive up the goats."

Breakfast had not long been on the table, however, when he came tearing into the room, hatless, with a tiny peasant girl of three years old perched on his shoulder, and a great bunch of wild flowers in his hand.

Montanelli looked up, smiling. This was a curious contrast to the grave and silent Arthur of Pisa or Leghorn.

"Where have you been, you madcap? Scampering all over the mountains without any breakfast?"

"Oh, Padre, it was so jolly! The mountains look perfectly glorious at sunrise; and the dew is so thick! Just look!"

He lifted for inspection a wet and muddy boot.

"We took some bread and cheese with us, and got some goat's milk up there on the pasture; oh, it was nasty! But I'm hungry again, now; and I want something for this little person, too. Annette, won't you have some honey?"

He had sat down with the child on his knee, and was helping her to put the flowers in order.

"No, no!" Montanelli interposed. "I can't have you catching cold. Run and change your wet things. Come to me, Annette. Where did you pick her up?"

"At the top of the village. She belongs to the man we saw yesterday—the man that cobbles the commune's boots. Hasn't she lovely eyes? She's got a tortoise in her pocket, and she calls it 'Caroline.'"

When Arthur had changed his wet socks and came down to breakfast he found the child seated on the Padre's knee, chattering volubly to him about her tortoise, which she was holding upside down in a chubby hand, that "monsieur" might admire the wriggling legs.

"Look, monsieur!" she was saying gravely in her half-intelligible patois: "Look at Caroline's boots!"

Montanelli sat playing with the child, stroking her hair, admiring her darling tortoise, and telling her wonderful stories. The woman of the chalet, coming in to clear the table, stared in amazement at the sight of Annette turning out the pockets of the grave gentleman in clerical dress.

"God teaches the little ones to know a good man," she said. "Annette is always afraid of strangers; and see, she is not shy with his reverence at all. The wonderful thing! Kneel down, Annette, and ask the good monsieur's blessing before he goes; it will bring thee luck."

"I didn't know you could play with children that way, Padre," Arthur said an hour later, as they walked through the sunlit pasture-land. "That child never took her eyes off you all the time. Do you know, I think——"

"Yes?"

"I was only going to say—it seems to me almost a pity that the Church should forbid priests to marry. I cannot quite understand why. You see, the training of children is such a serious thing, and it means so much to them to be surrounded from the very beginning with good influences, that I should have thought the holier a man's vocation and the purer his life, the more fit he is to be a father. I am sure, Padre, if you had not been under a vow,—if you had married,—your children would have been the very——"

"Hush!"

The word was uttered in a hasty whisper that seemed to deepen the ensuing silence.

"Padre," Arthur began again, distressed by the other's sombre look, "do you think there is anything wrong in what I said? Of course I may be mistaken; but I must think as it comes natural to me to think."

"Perhaps," Montanelli answered gently, "you do not quite realize the meaning of what you just said. You will see differently in a few years. Meanwhile we had better talk about something else."

It was the first break in the perfect ease and harmony that reigned between them on this ideal holiday.

From Chamonix they went on by the Tete-Noire to Martigny, where they stopped to rest, as the weather was stiflingly hot. After dinner they sat on the terrace of the hotel, which was sheltered from the sun and commanded a good view of the mountains. Arthur brought out his specimen box and plunged into an earnest botanical discussion in Italian.

Two English artists were sitting on the terrace; one sketching, the other lazily chatting. It did not seem to have occurred to him that the strangers might understand English.

"Leave off daubing at the landscape, Willie," he said; "and draw that glorious Italian boy going into ecstasies over those bits of ferns. Just look at the line of his eyebrows! You only need to put a crucifix for the magnifying-glass and a Roman toga for the jacket and knickerbockers, and there's your Early Christian complete, expression and all."

"Early Christian be hanged! I sat beside that youth at dinner; he was just as ecstatic over the roast fowl as over those grubby little weeds. He's pretty enough; that olive colouring is beautiful; but he's not half so picturesque as his father."

"His—who?"

"His father, sitting there straight in front of you. Do you mean to say you've passed him over? It's a perfectly magnificent face."

"Why, you dunder-headed, go-to-meeting Methodist! Don't you know a Catholic priest when you see one?"

"A priest? By Jove, so he is! Yes, I forgot; vow of chastity, and all that sort of thing. Well then, we'll be charitable and suppose the boy's his nephew."

"What idiotic people!" Arthur whispered, looking up with dancing eyes.

"Still, it is kind of them to think me like you; I wish I were really your nephew——Padre, what is the matter? How white you are!"

Montanelli was standing up, pressing one hand to his forehead. "I am a little giddy," he said in a curiously faint, dull tone. "Perhaps I was too much in the sun this morning. I will go and lie down, carino; it's nothing but the heat."

After a fortnight beside the Lake of Lucerne Arthur and Montanelli returned to Italy by the St. Gothard Pass. They had been fortunate as to weather and had made several very pleasant excursions; but the first charm was gone out of their enjoyment. Montanelli was continually haunted by an uneasy thought of the "more definite talk" for which this holiday was to have been the opportunity. In the Arve valley he had purposely put off all reference to the subject of which they had spoken under the magnolia tree; it would be cruel, he thought, to spoil the first delights of Alpine scenery for a nature so artistic as Arthur's by associating them with a conversation which must necessarily be painful. Ever since the day at Martigny he had said to himself each morning; "I will speak to-day," and each evening: "I will speak to-morrow;" and now the holiday was over, and he still repeated again and again: "To-morrow, to-morrow." A chill, indefinable sense of something not quite the same as it had been, of an invisible veil falling between himself and Arthur, kept him silent, until, on the last evening of their holiday, he realized suddenly that he must speak now if he would speak at all. They were stopping for the night at Lugano, and were to start for Pisa next morning. He would at least find out how far his darling had been drawn into the fatal quicksand of Italian politics.

"The rain has stopped, carino," he said after sunset; "and this is the only chance we shall have to see the lake. Come out; I want to have a talk with you."

They walked along the water's edge to a quiet spot and sat down on a low stone wall. Close beside them grew a rose-bush, covered with scarlet hips; one or two belated clusters of creamy blossom still hung from an upper branch, swaying mournfully and heavy with raindrops. On the green surface of the lake a little boat, with white wings faintly fluttering, rocked in the dewy breeze. It looked as light and frail as a tuft of silvery dandelion seed flung upon the water. High up on Monte Salvatore the window of some shepherd's hut opened a golden eye. The roses hung their heads and dreamed under the still September clouds, and the water plashed and murmured softly among the pebbles of the shore.

"This will be my only chance of a quiet talk with you for a long time," Montanelli began. "You will go back to your college work and friends; and I, too, shall be very busy this winter. I want to understand quite clearly what our position as regards each other is to be; and so, if you——" He stopped for a moment and then continued more slowly: "If you feel that you can still trust me as you used to do, I want you to tell me more definitely than that night in the seminary garden, how far you have gone."

Arthur looked out across the water, listened quietly, and said nothing.

"I want to know, if you will tell me," Montanelli went on; "whether you have bound yourself by a vow, or—in any way."

"There is nothing to tell, dear Padre; I have not bound myself, but I am bound."

"I don't understand———"

"What is the use of vows? They are not what binds people. If you feel in a certain way about a thing, that binds you to it; if you don't feel that way, nothing else can bind you."

"Do you mean, then, that this thing—this—feeling is quite irrevocable? Arthur, have you thought what you are saying?"

Arthur turned round and looked straight into Montanelli's eyes.

"Padre, you asked me if I could trust you. Can you not trust me, too? Indeed, if there were anything to tell, I would tell it to you; but there is no use in talking about these things. I have not forgotten what you said to me that night; I shall never forget it. But I must go my way and follow the light that I see."

Montanelli picked a rose from the bush, pulled off the petals one by one, and tossed them into the water.

"You are right, carino. Yes, we will say no more about these things; it seems there is indeed no help in many words——Well, well, let us go in."

CHAPTER III

THE autumn and winter passed uneventfully. Arthur was reading hard and had little spare time. He contrived to get a glimpse of Montanelli once or oftener in every week, if only for a few minutes. From time to time he would come in to ask for help with some difficult book; but on these occasions the subject of study was strictly adhered to. Montanelli, feeling, rather than observing, the slight, impalpable barrier that had come between them, shrank from everything which might seem like an attempt to retain the old close relationship. Arthur's visits now caused him more distress than pleasure, so trying was the constant effort to appear at ease and to behave as if nothing were altered. Arthur, for his part, noticed, hardly understanding it, the subtle change in the Padre's manner; and, vaguely feeling that it had some connection with the vexed question of the "new ideas," avoided all mention of the subject with which his thoughts were constantly filled. Yet he had never loved Montanelli so deeply as now. The dim, persistent sense of dissatisfaction, of spiritual emptiness, which he had tried so hard to stifle under a load of theology and ritual, had vanished into nothing at the touch of Young Italy. All the unhealthy fancies born of loneliness and sick-room watching had passed away, and the doubts against which he used to pray had gone without the need of exorcism. With the awakening of a new enthusiasm, a clearer, fresher religious ideal (for it was more in this light than in that of a political development that the students' movement had appeared to him), had come a sense of rest and completeness, of peace on earth and good will towards men; and in this mood of solemn and tender exaltation all the world seemed to him full of light. He found a new element of something lovable in the persons whom he had most disliked; and Montanelli, who for five years had been his ideal hero, was now in his eyes surrounded with an additional halo, as a potential prophet of the new faith. He listened with passionate eagerness to the Padre's sermons, trying to find in them some trace of inner kinship with the republican ideal; and pored over the Gospels, rejoicing in the democratic tendencies of Christianity at its origin.

One day in January he called at the seminary to return a book which he had borrowed. Hearing that the Father Director was out, he went up to Montanelli's private study, placed the volume on its shelf, and was about to leave the room when the title of a book lying on the table caught his eyes. It was Dante's "De Monarchia." He began to read it and soon became so absorbed that when the door opened and shut he did not hear. He was aroused from his preoccupation by Montanelli's voice behind him.

"I did not expect you to-day," said the Padre, glancing at the title of the book. "I was just going to send and ask if you could come to me this evening."

"Is it anything important? I have an engagement for this evening; but I will miss it if———"

"No; to-morrow will do. I want to see you because I am going away on Tuesday. I have been sent for to Rome."

"To Rome? For long?"

"The letter says, 'till after Easter.' It is from the Vatican. I would have let you know at once, but have been very busy settling up things about the seminary and making arrangements for the new Director."

"But, Padre, surely you are not giving up the seminary?"

"It will have to be so; but I shall probably come back to Pisa, for some time at least."

"But why are you giving it up?"

"Well, it is not yet officially announced; but I am offered a bishopric."

"Padre! Where?"

"That is the point about which I have to go to Rome. It is not yet decided whether I am to take a see in the Apennines, or to remain here as Suffragan."

"And is the new Director chosen yet?"

"Father Cardi has been nominated and arrives here to-morrow."

"Is not that rather sudden?"

"Yes; but——The decisions of the Vatican are sometimes not communicated till the last moment."

"Do you know the new Director?"

"Not personally; but he is very highly spoken of. Monsignor Belloni, who writes, says that he is a man of great erudition."

"The seminary will miss you terribly."

"I don't know about the seminary, but I am sure you will miss me, carino; perhaps almost as much as I shall miss you."

"I shall indeed; but I am very glad, for all that."

"Are you? I don't know that I am." He sat down at the table with a weary look on his face; not the look of a man who is expecting high promotion.

"Are you busy this afternoon, Arthur?" he said after a moment. "If not, I wish you would stay with me for a while, as you can't come to-night. I am a little out of sorts, I think; and I want to see as much of you as possible before leaving."

"Yes, I can stay a bit. I am due at six."

"One of your meetings?"

Arthur nodded; and Montanelli changed the subject hastily.

"I want to speak to you about yourself," he said. "You will need another confessor in my absence."

"When you come back I may go on confessing to you, may I not?"

"My dear boy, how can you ask? Of course I am speaking only of the three or four months that I shall be away. Will you go to one of the Fathers of Santa Caterina?"

"Very well."

They talked of other matters for a little while; then Arthur rose.

"I must go, Padre; the students will be waiting for me."

The haggard look came back to Montanelli's face.

"Already? You had almost charmed away my black mood. Well, good-bye."

"Good-bye. I will be sure to come to-morrow."

"Try to come early, so that I may have time to see you alone. Father Cardi will be here. Arthur, my dear boy, be careful while I am gone; don't be led into doing anything rash, at least before I come back. You cannot think how anxious I feel about leaving you."

"There is no need, Padre; everything is quite quiet. It will be a long time yet."

"Good-bye," Montanelli said abruptly, and sat down to his writing.

The first person upon whom Arthur's eyes fell, as he entered the room where the students' little gatherings were held, was his old playmate, Dr. Warren's daughter. She was sitting in a corner by the window, listening with an absorbed and earnest face to what one of the "initiators," a tall young Lombard in a threadbare coat, was saying to her. During the last few months she had changed and developed greatly, and now looked a grown-up young woman, though the dense black plaits still hung down her back in school-girl fashion. She was dressed all in black, and had thrown a black scarf over her head, as the room was cold and draughty. At her breast was a spray of cypress, the emblem of Young Italy. The initiator was passionately describing to her the misery of the Calabrian peasantry; and she sat listening silently, her chin resting on one hand and her eyes on the ground. To Arthur she seemed a melancholy vision of Liberty mourning for the lost Republic. (Julia would have seen in her only an overgrown hoyden, with a sallow complexion, an irregular nose, and an old stuff frock that was too short for her.)

"You here, Jim!" he said, coming up to her when the initiator had been called to the other end of the room. "Jim" was a childish corruption of her curious baptismal name: Jennifer. Her Italian schoolmates called her "Gemma."

She raised her head with a start.

"Arthur! Oh, I didn't know you—belonged here!"

"And I had no idea about you. Jim, since when have you——?"

"You don't understand!" she interposed quickly. "I am not a member. It is only that I have done one or two little things. You see, I met Bini—you know Carlo Bini?"

"Yes, of course." Bini was the organizer of the Leghorn branch; and all Young Italy knew him.

"Well, he began talking to me about these things; and I asked him to let me go to a students' meeting. The other day he wrote to me to Florence——Didn't you know I had been to Florence for the Christmas holidays?"

"I don't often hear from home now."

"Ah, yes! Anyhow, I went to stay with the Wrights." (The Wrights were old schoolfellows of hers who had moved to Florence.) "Then Bini wrote and told me to pass through Pisa to-day on my way home, so that I could come here. Ah! they're going to begin."

The lecture was upon the ideal Republic and the duty of the young to fit themselves for it. The lecturer's comprehension of his subject was somewhat vague; but Arthur listened with devout admiration. His mind at this period was curiously uncritical; when he accepted a moral ideal he swallowed it whole without stopping to think whether it was quite digestible. When the lecture and the long discussion which followed it were finished and the students began to disperse, he went up to Gemma, who was still sitting in the corner of the room.

"Let me walk with you, Jim. Where are you staying?"

"With Marietta."

"Your father's old housekeeper?"

"Yes; she lives a good way from here."

They walked for some time in silence. Then Arthur said suddenly:

"You are seventeen, now, aren't you?"

"I was seventeen in October."

"I always knew you would not grow up like other girls and begin wanting to go to balls and all that sort of thing. Jim, dear, I have so often wondered whether you would ever come to be one of us."

"So have I."

"You said you had done things for Bini; I didn't know you even knew him."

"It wasn't for Bini; it was for the other one"

"Which other one?"

"The one that was talking to me to-night—Bolla."

"Do you know him well?" Arthur put in with a little touch of jealousy. Bolla was a sore subject with him; there had been a rivalry between them about some work which the committee of Young Italy had finally intrusted to Bolla, declaring Arthur too young and inexperienced.

"I know him pretty well; and I like him very much. He has been staying in Leghorn."

"I know; he went there in November———"

"Because of the steamers. Arthur, don't you think your house would be safer than ours for that work? Nobody would suspect a rich shipping family like yours; and you know everyone at the docks——"

"Hush! not so loud, dear! So it was in your house the books from Marseilles were hidden?"

"Only for one day. Oh! perhaps I oughtn't to have told you."

"Why not? You know I belong to the society. Gemma, dear, there is nothing in all the world that would make me so happy as for you to join us—you and the Padre."

"Your Padre! Surely he——"

"No; he thinks differently. But I have sometimes fancied—that is—hoped—I don't know——"

"But, Arthur! he's a priest."

"What of that? There are priests in the society—two of them write in the paper. And why not? It is the mission of the priesthood to lead the world to higher ideals and aims, and what else does the society try to do? It is, after all, more a religious and moral question than a political one. If people are fit to be free and responsible citizens, no one can keep them enslaved."

~ 17 ~

Gemma knit her brows. "It seems to me, Arthur," she said, "that there's a muddle somewhere in your logic. A priest teaches religious doctrine. I don't see what that has to do with getting rid of the Austrians."

"A priest is a teacher of Christianity, and the greatest of all revolutionists was Christ."

"Do you know, I was talking about priests to father the other day, and he said——"

"Gemma, your father is a Protestant."

After a little pause she looked round at him frankly.

"Look here, we had better leave this subject alone. You are always intolerant when you talk about Protestants."

"I didn't mean to be intolerant. But I think Protestants are generally intolerant when they talk about priests."

"I dare say. Anyhow, we have so often quarreled over this subject that it is not worth while to begin again. What did you think of the lecture?"

"I liked it very much—especially the last part. I was glad he spoke so strongly about the need of living the Republic, not dreaming of it. It is as Christ said: 'The Kingdom of Heaven is within you.'"

"It was just that part that I didn't like. He talked so much of the wonderful things we ought to think and feel and be, but he never told us practically what we ought to do."

"When the time of crisis comes there will be plenty for us to do; but we must be patient; these great changes are not made in a day."

"The longer a thing is to take doing, the more reason to begin at once. You talk about being fit for freedom—did you ever know anyone so fit for it as your mother? Wasn't she the most perfectly angelic woman you ever saw? And what use was all her goodness? She was a slave till the day she died—bullied and worried and insulted by your brother James and his wife. It would have been much better for her if she had not been so sweet and patient; they would never have treated her so. That's just the way with Italy; it's not patience that's wanted—it's for somebody to get up and defend themselves———"

"Jim, dear, if anger and passion could have saved Italy she would have been free long ago; it is not hatred that she needs, it is love."

As he said the word a sudden flush went up to his forehead and died out again. Gemma did not see it; she was looking straight before her with knitted brows and set mouth.

"You think I am wrong, Arthur," she said after a pause; "but I am right, and you will grow to see it some day. This is the house. Will you come in?"

"No; it's late. Good-night, dear!"

He was standing on the doorstep, clasping her hand in both of his.

"For God and the people——"

Slowly and gravely she completed the unfinished motto:

"Now and forever."

Then she pulled away her hand and ran into the house. When the door had closed behind her he stooped and picked up the spray of cypress which had fallen from her breast.

CHAPTER IV

ARTHUR went back to his lodgings feeling as though he had wings. He was absolutely, cloudlessly happy. At the meeting there had been hints of preparations for armed insurrection; and now Gemma was a comrade, and he loved her. They could work together, possibly even die together, for the Republic that was to be. The blossoming time of their hope was come, and the Padre would see it and believe.

The next morning, however, he awoke in a soberer mood and remembered that Gemma was going to Leghorn and the Padre to Rome. January, February, March—three long months to Easter! And if Gemma should fall under "Protestant" influences at home (in Arthur's vocabulary "Protestant" stood for "Philistine")———No, Gemma would never learn to flirt and simper and captivate tourists and bald-headed shipowners, like the other English girls in Leghorn; she was made of different stuff. But she might be very miserable; she was so young, so friendless, so utterly alone among all those wooden people. If only mother had lived——

In the evening he went to the seminary, where he found Montanelli entertaining the new Director and looking both tired and bored. Instead of lighting up, as usual, at the sight of Arthur, the Padre's face grew darker.

"This is the student I spoke to you about," he said, introducing Arthur stiffly. "I shall be much obliged if you will allow him to continue using the library."

Father Cardi, a benevolent-looking elderly priest, at once began talking to Arthur about the Sapienza, with an ease and familiarity which showed him to be well acquainted with college life. The conversation soon drifted into a discussion of university regulations, a burning question of that day. To Arthur's great delight, the new Director spoke strongly against the custom adopted by the university authorities of constantly worrying the students by senseless and vexatious restrictions.

"I have had a good deal of experience in guiding young people," he said; "and I make it a rule never to prohibit anything without a good reason. There are very few young men who will give much trouble if proper consideration and respect for their personality are shown to them. But, of course, the most docile horse will kick if you are always jerking at the rein."

Arthur opened his eyes wide; he had not expected to hear the students' cause pleaded by the new Director. Montanelli took no part in the discussion; its subject, apparently, did not interest him. The expression of his face was so unutterably hopeless and weary that Father Cardi broke off suddenly.

"I am afraid I have overtired you, Canon. You must forgive my talkativeness; I am hot upon this subject and forget that others may grow weary of it."

"On the contrary, I was much interested." Montanelli was not given to stereotyped politeness, and his tone jarred uncomfortably upon Arthur.

When Father Cardi went to his own room Montanelli turned to Arthur with the intent and brooding look that his face had worn all the evening.

"Arthur, my dear boy," he began slowly; "I have something to tell you."

"He must have had bad news," flashed through Arthur's mind, as he looked anxiously at the haggard face. There was a long pause.

"How do you like the new Director?" Montanelli asked suddenly.

The question was so unexpected that, for a moment, Arthur was at a loss how to reply to it.

"I—I like him very much, I think—at least—no, I am not quite sure that I do. But it is difficult to say, after seeing a person once."

Montanelli sat beating his hand gently on the arm of his chair; a habit with him when anxious or perplexed.

"About this journey to Rome," he began again; "if you think there is any—well—if you wish it, Arthur, I will write and say I cannot go."

"Padre! But the Vatican———"

"The Vatican will find someone else. I can send apologies."

"But why? I can't understand."

Montanelli drew one hand across his forehead.

"I am anxious about you. Things keep coming into my head—and after all, there is no need for me to go———"

"But the bishopric——"

"Oh, Arthur! what shall it profit me if I gain a bishopric and lose——"

He broke off. Arthur had never seen him like this before, and was greatly troubled.

"I can't understand," he said. "Padre, if you could explain to me more—more definitely, what it is you think———"

"I think nothing; I am haunted with a horrible fear. Tell me, is there any special danger?"

"He has heard something," Arthur thought, remembering the whispers of a projected revolt. But the secret was not his to tell; and he merely answered: "What special danger should there be?"

"Don't question me—answer me!" Montanelli's voice was almost harsh in its eagerness. "Are you in danger? I don't want to know your secrets; only tell me that!"

"We are all in God's hands, Padre; anything may always happen. But I know of no reason why I should not be here alive and safe when you come back."

"When I come back——Listen, carino; I will leave it in your hands. You need give me no reason; only say to me, 'Stay,' and I will give up this journey. There will be no injury to anyone, and I shall feel you are safer if I have you beside me."

This kind of morbid fancifulness was so foreign to Montanelli's character that Arthur looked at him with grave anxiety.

"Padre, I am sure you are not well. Of course you must go to

Rome, and try to have a thorough rest and get rid of your sleeplessness and headaches."

"Very well," Montanelli interrupted, as if tired of the subject; "I will start by the early coach to-morrow morning."

Arthur looked at him, wondering.

"You had something to tell me?" he said.

"No, no; nothing more—nothing of any consequence." There was a startled, almost terrified look in his face.

A few days after Montanelli's departure Arthur went to fetch a book from the seminary library, and met Father Cardi on the stairs.

"Ah, Mr. Burton!" exclaimed the Director; "the very person I wanted. Please come in and help me out of a difficulty."

He opened the study door, and Arthur followed him into the room with a foolish, secret sense of resentment. It seemed hard to see this dear study, the Padre's own private sanctum, invaded by a stranger.

"I am a terrible book-worm," said the Director; "and my first act when I got here was to examine the library. It seems very interesting, but I do not understand the system by which it is catalogued."

"The catalogue is imperfect; many of the best books have been added to the collection lately."

"Can you spare half an hour to explain the arrangement to me?"

They went into the library, and Arthur carefully explained the catalogue. When he rose to take his hat, the Director interfered, laughing.

"No, no! I can't have you rushing off in that way. It is Saturday, and quite time for you to leave off work till Monday morning. Stop and have supper with me, now I have kept you so late. I am quite alone, and shall be glad of company."

His manner was so bright and pleasant that Arthur felt at ease with him at once. After some desultory conversation, the Director inquired how long he had known Montanelli.

"For about seven years. He came back from China when I was twelve years old."

"Ah, yes! It was there that he gained his reputation as a missionary preacher. Have you been his pupil ever since?"

"He began teaching me a year later, about the time when I first confessed to him. Since I have been at the Sapienza he has still gone on helping me with anything I wanted to study that was not in the regular course. He has been very kind to me—you can hardly imagine how kind."

"I can well believe it; he is a man whom no one can fail to admire—a most noble and beautiful nature. I have met priests who were out in China with him; and they had no words high enough to praise his energy and courage under all hardships, and his unfailing devotion. You are fortunate to have had in your youth the help and guidance of such a man. I understood from him that you have lost both parents."

"Yes; my father died when I was a child, and my mother a year ago."

"Have you brothers and sisters?"

"No; I have step-brothers; but they were business men when I was in the nursery."

"You must have had a lonely childhood; perhaps you value Canon Montanelli's kindness the more for that. By the way, have you chosen a confessor for the time of his absence?"

"I thought of going to one of the fathers of Santa Caterina, if they have not too many penitents."

"Will you confess to me?"

Arthur opened his eyes in wonder.

"Reverend Father, of course I—should be glad; only——"

"Only the Director of a theological seminary does not usually receive lay penitents? That is quite true. But I know Canon Montanelli takes a great interest in you, and I fancy he is a little anxious on your behalf—just as I should be if I were leaving a favourite pupil—and would like to know you were under the spiritual guidance of his colleague. And, to be quite frank with you, my son, I like you, and should be glad to give you any help I can."

"If you put it that way, of course I shall be very grateful for your guidance."

"Then you will come to me next month? That's right. And run in to see me, my lad, when you have time any evening."

Shortly before Easter Montanelli's appointment to the little see of Brisighella, in the Etruscan Apennines, was officially announced. He wrote to Arthur from Rome in a cheerful and tranquil spirit; evidently his depression was passing over. "You must come to see me every vacation," he wrote; "and I shall often be coming to Pisa; so I hope to see a good deal of you, if not so much as I should wish."

Dr. Warren had invited Arthur to spend the Easter holidays with him and his children, instead of in the dreary, rat-ridden old place where Julia now reigned supreme. Enclosed in the letter was a short note, scrawled in Gemma's childish, irregular handwriting, begging him to come if possible, "as I want to talk to you about something." Still more encouraging was the whispered communication passing around from student to student in the university; everyone was to be prepared for great things after Easter.

All this had put Arthur into a state of rapturous anticipation, in which the wildest improbabilities hinted at among the students seemed to him natural and likely to be realized within the next two months.

He arranged to go home on Thursday in Passion week, and to spend the first days of the vacation there, that the pleasure of visiting the Warrens and the delight of seeing Gemma might not unfit him for the solemn religious meditation demanded by the Church from all her children at this season. He wrote to Gemma, promising to come on Easter Monday; and went up to his bedroom on Wednesday night with a soul at peace.

He knelt down before the crucifix. Father Cardi had promised to receive him in the morning; and for this, his last confession before the Easter communion, he must prepare himself by long and earnest prayer. Kneeling with clasped hands and bent head, he looked back over the month, and reckoned up the miniature sins of impatience, carelessness, hastiness of temper, which had left their faint, small spots upon the whiteness of his soul. Beyond these he could find nothing; in this month he had been too happy to sin much. He crossed himself, and, rising, began to undress.

As he unfastened his shirt a scrap of paper slipped from it and fluttered to the floor. It was Gemma's letter, which he had worn all day upon his neck. He picked it up, unfolded it, and kissed the dear scribble; then began folding the paper up again, with a dim consciousness of having done something very ridiculous, when he noticed on the back of the sheet a postscript which he had not read before. "Be sure and come as soon as possible," it ran, "for I want you to meet Bolla. He has been staying here, and we have read together every day."

The hot colour went up to Arthur's forehead as he read.

Always Bolla! What was he doing in Leghorn again? And why should Gemma want to read with him? Had he bewitched her with his smuggling? It had been quite easy to see at the meeting in January that he was in love with her; that was why he had been so earnest over his propaganda. And now he was close to her—reading with her every day.

Arthur suddenly threw the letter aside and knelt down again before the crucifix. And this was the soul that was preparing for absolution, for the Easter sacrament—the soul at peace with God and itself and all the world! A soul capable of sordid jealousies and suspicions; of selfish animosities and ungenerous hatred—and against a comrade! He covered his face with both hands in bitter humiliation. Only five minutes ago he had been dreaming of martyrdom; and now he had been guilty of a mean and petty thought like this!

When he entered the seminary chapel on Thursday morning he found Father Cardi alone. After repeating the Confiteor, he plunged at once into the subject of his last night's backsliding.

"My father, I accuse myself of the sins of jealousy and anger, and of unworthy thoughts against one who has done me no wrong."

Farther Cardi knew quite well with what kind of penitent he had to deal. He only said softly:

"You have not told me all, my son."

"Father, the man against whom I have thought an unchristian thought is one whom I am especially bound to love and honour."

"One to whom you are bound by ties of blood?"

"By a still closer tie."

"By what tie, my son?"

"By that of comradeship."

"Comradeship in what?"

"In a great and holy work."

A little pause.

"And your anger against this—comrade, your jealousy of him, was called forth by his success in that work being greater than yours?"

"I—yes, partly. I envied him his experience—his usefulness. And then—I thought—I feared—that he would take from me the heart of the girl I—love."

"And this girl that you love, is she a daughter of the Holy Church?"

"No; she is a Protestant."

"A heretic?"

Arthur clasped his hands in great distress. "Yes, a heretic," he repeated. "We were brought up together; our mothers were friends—and I—envied him, because I saw that he loves her, too, and because—because——"

"My son," said Father Cardi, speaking after a moment's silence, slowly and gravely, "you have still not told me all; there is more than this upon your soul."

"Father, I——" He faltered and broke off again.

The priest waited silently.

"I envied him because the society—the Young Italy—that I belong to————"

"Yes?"

"Intrusted him with a work that I had hoped—would be given to me, that I had thought myself—specially adapted for."

"What work?"

"The taking in of books—political books—from the steamers that bring them—and finding a hiding place for them—in the town———"

"And this work was given by the party to your rival?"

"To Bolla—and I envied him."

"And he gave you no cause for this feeling? You do not accuse him of having neglected the mission intrusted to him?"

"No, father; he has worked bravely and devotedly; he is a true patriot and has deserved nothing but love and respect from me."

Father Cardi pondered.

"My son, if there is within you a new light, a dream of some great work to be accomplished for your fellow-men, a hope that shall lighten the burdens of the weary and oppressed, take heed how you deal with the most precious blessing of God. All good things are of His giving; and of His giving is the new birth. If you have found the way of sacrifice, the way that leads to peace; if you have joined with loving comrades to bring deliverance to them that weep and mourn in secret; then see to it that your soul be free from envy and passion and your heart as an altar where the sacred fire burns eternally. Remember that this is a high and holy thing, and that the heart which would receive it must be purified from every selfish thought. This vocation is as the vocation of a priest; it is not for the love of a woman, nor for the moment of a fleeting passion; it is FOR GOD AND THE PEOPLE; it is NOW AND FOREVER."

"Ah!" Arthur started and clasped his hands; he had almost burst out sobbing at the motto. "Father, you give us the sanction of the Church! Christ is on our side——"

"My son," the priest answered solemnly, "Christ drove the moneychangers out of the Temple, for His House shall be called a House of Prayer, and they had made it a den of thieves."

After a long silence, Arthur whispered tremulously:

"And Italy shall be His Temple when they are driven out——"

He stopped; and the soft answer came back:

"'The earth and the fulness thereof are mine, saith the Lord.'"

CHAPTER V

THAT afternoon Arthur felt the need of a long walk. He intrusted his luggage to a fellow-student and went to Leghorn on foot.

The day was damp and cloudy, but not cold; and the low, level country seemed to him fairer than he had ever known it to look before. He had a sense of delight in the soft elasticity of the wet grass under his feet and in the shy, wondering eyes of the wild spring flowers by the roadside. In a thorn-acacia bush at the edge of a little strip of wood a bird was building a nest, and flew up as he passed with a startled cry and a quick fluttering of brown wings.

He tried to keep his mind fixed upon the devout meditations proper to the eve of Good Friday. But thoughts of Montanelli and Gemma got so much in the way of this devotional exercise that at last he gave up the attempt and allowed his fancy to drift away to the wonders and glories of the coming insurrection, and to the part in it that he had allotted to his two idols. The Padre was to be the leader, the apostle, the prophet before whose sacred wrath the powers of darkness were to flee, and at whose feet the young defenders of Liberty were to learn afresh the old doctrines, the old truths in their new and unimagined significance.

And Gemma? Oh, Gemma would fight at the barricades. She was made of the clay from which heroines are moulded; she would be the perfect comrade, the maiden undefiled and unafraid, of whom so many poets have dreamed. She would stand beside him, shoulder to shoulder, rejoicing under the winged death-storm; and they would die together, perhaps in the moment of victory—without doubt there would be a victory. Of his love he would tell her nothing; he would say no word that might disturb her peace or spoil her tranquil sense of comradeship. She was to him a holy thing, a spotless victim to be laid upon the altar as a burnt-offering for the deliverance of the people; and who was he that he should enter into the white sanctuary of a soul that knew no other love than God and Italy?

God and Italy——Then came a sudden drop from the clouds as he entered the great, dreary house in the "Street of Palaces," and Julia's butler, immaculate, calm, and politely disapproving as ever, confronted him upon the stairs.

"Good-evening, Gibbons; are my brothers in?"

"Mr. Thomas is in, sir; and Mrs. Burton. They are in the drawing room."

Arthur went in with a dull sense of oppression. What a dismal house it was! The flood of life seemed to roll past and leave it always just above high-water mark. Nothing in it ever changed—neither the people, nor the family portraits, nor the heavy furniture and ugly plate, nor the vulgar ostentation of riches, nor the lifeless aspect of everything. Even the flowers on the brass stands looked like painted metal flowers that had never known the stirring of young sap within them in the warm spring days. Julia, dressed for dinner, and waiting for visitors in the drawing room which was to her the centre of existence, might have sat for a fashion-plate just as she was, with her wooden smile and flaxen ringlets, and the lap-dog on her knee.

"How do you do, Arthur?" she said stiffly, giving him the tips of her fingers for a moment, and then transferring them to the more congenial contact of the lap-dog's silken coat. "I hope you are quite well and have made satisfactory progress at college."

Arthur murmured the first commonplace that he could think of at the moment, and relapsed into uncomfortable silence. The arrival of James, in his most pompous mood and accompanied by a stiff, elderly shipping-agent, did not improve matters; and when Gibbons announced that dinner was served, Arthur rose with a little sigh of relief.

"I won't come to dinner, Julia. If you'll excuse me I will go to my room."

"You're overdoing that fasting, my boy," said Thomas; "I am sure you'll make yourself ill."

"Oh, no! Good-night."

In the corridor Arthur met the under housemaid and asked her to knock at his door at six in the morning.

"The signorino is going to church?"

"Yes. Good-night, Teresa."

He went into his room. It had belonged to his mother, and the alcove opposite the window had been fitted up during her long illness as an oratory. A great crucifix on a black pedestal occupied the middle of the altar; and before it hung a little Roman lamp. This was the room where she had died. Her portrait was on the wall beside the bed; and on the table stood a china bowl which had been hers, filled with a great bunch of her favourite violets. It was just a year since her death; and the Italian servants had not forgotten her.

He took out of his portmanteau a framed picture, carefully wrapped up. It was a crayon portrait of Montanelli, which had come from Rome only a few days before. He was unwrapping this precious treasure when Julia's page brought in a supper-tray on which the old Italian cook, who had served Gladys before the harsh, new mistress came, had placed such little delicacies as she considered her dear signorino might permit himself to eat without infringing the rules of the Church. Arthur refused everything but a piece of bread; and the page, a nephew of Gibbons, lately arrived from England, grinned significantly as he carried out the tray. He had already joined the Protestant camp in the servants' hall.

Arthur went into the alcove and knelt down before the crucifix, trying to compose his mind to the proper attitude for prayer and meditation. But this he found difficult to accomplish. He had, as Thomas said, rather overdone the Lenten privations, and they had gone to his head like strong wine. Little quivers of excitement went down his back, and the crucifix swam in a misty cloud before his eyes. It was only after a long litany, mechanically repeated, that he succeeded in recalling his wandering imagination to the mystery of the Atonement. At last sheer physical weariness conquered the feverish agitation of his nerves, and he lay down to sleep in a calm and peaceful mood, free from all unquiet or disturbing thoughts.

He was fast asleep when a sharp, impatient knock came at his door. "Ah, Teresa!" he thought, turning over lazily. The knock was repeated, and he awoke with a violent start.

"Signorino! signorino!" cried a man's voice in Italian; "get up for the love of God!"

Arthur jumped out of bed.

"What is the matter? Who is it?"

"It's I, Gian Battista. Get up, quick, for Our Lady's sake!"

Arthur hurriedly dressed and opened the door. As he stared in perplexity at the coachman's pale, terrified face, the sound of tramping feet and clanking metal came along the corridor, and he suddenly realized the truth.

"For me?" he asked coolly.

"For you! Oh, signorino, make haste! What have you to hide? See, I can put——"

"I have nothing to hide. Do my brothers know?"

The first uniform appeared at the turn of the passage.

"The signor has been called; all the house is awake. Alas! what a misfortune—what a terrible misfortune! And on Good Friday! Holy Saints, have pity!"

Gian Battista burst into tears. Arthur moved a few steps forward and waited for the gendarmes, who came clattering along, followed by a shivering crowd of servants in various impromptu costumes. As the soldiers surrounded Arthur, the master and mistress of the house brought up the rear of this strange procession; he in dressing gown and slippers, she in a long peignoir, with her hair in curlpapers.

"There is, sure, another flood toward, and these couples are coming to the ark! Here comes a pair of very strange beasts!"

The quotation flashed across Arthur's mind as he looked at the grotesque figures. He checked a laugh with a sense of its jarring incongruity—this was a time for worthier thoughts. "Ave Maria, Regina Coeli!" he whispered, and turned his eyes away, that the bobbing of Julia's curlpapers might not again tempt him to levity.

"Kindly explain to me," said Mr. Burton, approaching the officer of gendarmerie, "what is the meaning of this violent intrusion into a private house? I warn you that, unless you are prepared to furnish me with a satisfactory explanation, I shall feel bound to complain to the English Ambassador."

"I presume," replied the officer stiffly, "that you will recognize this as a sufficient explanation; the English Ambassador certainly will." He pulled out a warrant for the arrest of Arthur Burton, student of philosophy, and, handing it to James, added coldly: "If you wish for any further explanation, you had better apply in person to the chief of police."

Julia snatched the paper from her husband, glanced over it, and flew at Arthur like nothing else in the world but a fashionable lady in a rage.

"So it's you that have disgraced the family!" she screamed; "setting all the rabble in the town gaping and staring as if the thing were a show? So you have turned jail-bird, now, with all your piety! It's what we might have expected from that Popish woman's child——"

"You must not speak to a prisoner in a foreign language, madam," the officer interrupted; but his remonstrance was hardly audible under the torrent of Julia's vociferous English.

"Just what we might have expected! Fasting and prayer and saintly meditation; and this is what was underneath it all! I thought that would be the end of it."

Dr. Warren had once compared Julia to a salad into which the cook had upset the vinegar cruet. The sound of her thin, hard voice set Arthur's teeth on edge, and the simile suddenly popped up in his memory.

"There's no use in this kind of talk," he said. "You need not be afraid of any unpleasantness; everyone will understand that you are all quite innocent. I suppose, gentlemen, you want to search my things. I have nothing to hide."

While the gendarmes ransacked the room, reading his letters, examining his college papers, and turning out drawers and boxes, he sat waiting on the edge of the bed, a little flushed with excitement, but in no way distressed. The search did not disquiet him. He had always burned letters which could possibly compromise anyone, and beyond a few manuscript verses, half revolutionary, half mystical, and two or three numbers of Young Italy, the gendarmes found nothing to repay them for their trouble. Julia, after a long resistance, yielded to the entreaties of her brother-in-law and went back to bed, sweeping past Arthur with magnificent disdain, James meekly following.

When they had left the room, Thomas, who all this while had been tramping up and down, trying to look indifferent, approached the officer and asked permission to speak to the prisoner. Receiving a nod in answer, he went up to Arthur and muttered in a rather husky voice:

"I say; this is an infernally awkward business. I'm very sorry about it."

Arthur looked up with a face as serene as a summer morning. "You have always been good to me," he said. "There's nothing to be sorry about. I shall be safe enough."

"Look here, Arthur!" Thomas gave his moustache a hard pull and plunged head first into the awkward question. "Is—all this anything to do with—money? Because, if it is, I——"

"With money! Why, no! What could it have to do——"

"Then it's some political tomfoolery? I thought so. Well, don't you get down in the mouth—and never mind all the stuff Julia talks. It's only her spiteful tongue; and if you want help,—cash, or anything,—let me know, will you?"

Arthur held out his hand in silence, and Thomas left the room with a carefully made-up expression of unconcern that rendered his face more stolid than ever.

The gendarmes, meanwhile, had finished their search, and the officer in charge requested Arthur to put on his outdoor clothes. He obeyed at once and turned to leave the room; then stopped with sudden hesitation. It seemed hard to take leave of his mother's oratory in the presence of these officials.

"Have you any objection to leaving the room for a moment?" he asked. "You see that I cannot escape and that there is nothing to conceal."

"I am sorry, but it is forbidden to leave a prisoner alone."

"Very well, it doesn't matter."

He went into the alcove, and, kneeling down, kissed the feet and pedestal of the crucifix, whispering softly: "Lord, keep me faithful unto death."

When he rose, the officer was standing by the table, examining Montanelli's portrait. "Is this a relative of yours?" he asked.

"No; it is my confessor, the new Bishop of Brisighella."

On the staircase the Italian servants were waiting, anxious and sorrowful. They all loved Arthur for his own sake and his mother's, and crowded round him, kissing his hands and dress with passionate grief. Gian Battista stood by, the tears dripping down his gray moustache. None of the Burtons came out to take leave of him. Their coldness accentuated the tenderness and sympathy of the servants, and Arthur was near to breaking down as he pressed the hands held out to him.

"Good-bye, Gian Battista. Kiss the little ones for me. Good-bye, Teresa. Pray for me, all of you; and God keep you! Good-bye, good-bye!"

He ran hastily downstairs to the front door. A moment later only a little group of silent men and sobbing women stood on the doorstep watching the carriage as it drove away.

CHAPTER VI

ARTHUR was taken to the huge mediaeval fortress at the harbour's mouth. He found prison life fairly endurable. His cell was unpleasantly damp and dark; but he had been brought up in a palace in the Via Borra, and neither close air, rats, nor foul smells were novelties to him. The food, also, was both bad and insufficient; but James soon obtained permission to send him all the necessaries of life from home. He was kept in solitary confinement, and, though the vigilance of the warders was less strict than he had expected, he failed to obtain any explanation of the cause of his arrest. Nevertheless, the tranquil frame of mind in which he had entered the fortress did not change. Not being allowed books, he spent his time in prayer and devout meditation, and waited without impatience or anxiety for the further course of events.

One day a soldier unlocked the door of his cell and called to him: "This way, please!" After two or three questions, to which he got no answer but, "Talking is forbidden," Arthur resigned himself to the inevitable and followed the soldier through a labyrinth of courtyards, corridors, and stairs, all more or less musty-smelling, into a large, light room in which three persons in military uniform sat at a long table covered with green baize and littered with papers, chatting in a languid, desultory way. They put on a stiff, business air as he came in, and the oldest of them, a foppish-looking man with gray whiskers and a colonel's uniform, pointed to a chair on the other side of the table and began the preliminary interrogation.

Arthur had expected to be threatened, abused, and sworn at, and had prepared himself to answer with dignity and patience; but he was pleasantly disappointed. The colonel was stiff, cold and formal, but perfectly courteous. The usual questions as to his name, age, nationality, and social position were put and answered, and the replies written down in monotonous succession. He was beginning to feel bored and impatient, when the colonel asked:

"And now, Mr. Burton, what do you know about Young Italy?"

"I know that it is a society which publishes a newspaper in Marseilles and circulates it in Italy, with the object of inducing people to revolt and drive the Austrian army out of the country."

"You have read this paper, I think?"

"Yes; I am interested in the subject."

"When you read it you realized that you were committing an illegal action?"

"Certainly."

"Where did you get the copies which were found in your room?"

"That I cannot tell you."

"Mr. Burton, you must not say 'I cannot tell' here; you are bound to answer my questions."

"I will not, then, if you object to 'cannot.'"

"You will regret it if you permit yourself to use such expressions," remarked the colonel. As Arthur made no reply, he went on:

"I may as well tell you that evidence has come into our hands proving your connection with this society to be much more intimate than is implied by the mere reading of forbidden literature. It will be to your advantage to confess frankly. In any case the truth will be sure to come out, and you will find it useless to screen yourself behind evasion and denials."

"I have no desire to screen myself. What is it you want to know?"

"Firstly, how did you, a foreigner, come to be implicated in matters of this kind?"

"I thought about the subject and read everything I could get hold of, and formed my own conclusions."

"Who persuaded you to join this society?"

"No one; I wished to join it."

"You are shilly-shallying with me," said the colonel, sharply; his patience was evidently beginning to give out. "No one can join a society by himself. To whom did you communicate your wish to join it?"

Silence.

"Will you have the kindness to answer me?"

"Not when you ask questions of that kind."

Arthur spoke sullenly; a curious, nervous irritability was taking possession of him. He knew by this time that many arrests had been made in both Leghorn and Pisa; and, though still ignorant of the extent of the calamity, he had already heard enough to put him into a fever of anxiety for the safety of Gemma and his other friends. The studied politeness of the officers, the dull game of fencing and parrying, of insidious questions and evasive answers, worried and annoyed him, and the clumsy tramping backward and forward of the sentinel outside the door jarred detestably upon his ear.

"Oh, by the bye, when did you last meet Giovanni Bolla?" asked the colonel, after a little more bandying of words. "Just before you left Pisa, was it?"

"I know no one of that name."

"What! Giovanni Bolla? Surely you know him—a tall young fellow, closely shaven. Why, he is one of your fellow-students."

"There are many students in the university whom I don't know."

"Oh, but you must know Bolla, surely! Look, this is his handwriting. You see, he knows you well enough."

The colonel carelessly handed him a paper headed: "Protocol," and signed: "Giovanni Bolla." Glancing down it Arthur came upon his own name. He looked up in surprise. "Am I to read it?"

"Yes, you may as well; it concerns you."

He began to read, while the officers sat silently watching his face. The document appeared to consist of depositions in answer to a long string of questions. Evidently Bolla, too, must have been arrested. The first depositions were of the usual stereotyped character; then followed a short account of

Bolla's connection with the society, of the dissemination of prohibited literature in Leghorn, and of the students' meetings. Next came "Among those who joined us was a young Englishman, Arthur Burton, who belongs to one of the rich shipowning families."

The blood rushed into Arthur's face. Bolla had betrayed him! Bolla, who had taken upon himself the solemn duties of an initiator—Bolla, who had converted Gemma—who was in love with her! He laid down the paper and stared at the floor.

"I hope that little document has refreshed your memory?" hinted the colonel politely.

Arthur shook his head. "I know no one of that name," he repeated in a dull, hard voice. "There must be some mistake."

"Mistake? Oh, nonsense! Come, Mr. Burton, chivalry and quixotism are very fine things in their way; but there's no use in overdoing them. It's an error all you young people fall into at first. Come, think! What good is it for you to compromise yourself and spoil your prospects in life over a simple formality about a man that has betrayed you? You see yourself, he wasn't so particular as to what he said about you."

A faint shade of something like mockery had crept into the colonel's voice. Arthur looked up with a start; a sudden light flashed upon his mind.

"It's a lie!" he cried out. "It's a forgery! I can see it in your face, you cowardly——You've got some prisoner there you want to compromise, or a trap you want to drag me into. You are a forger, and a liar, and a scoundrel——"

"Silence!" shouted the colonel, starting up in a rage; his two colleagues were already on their feet. "Captain Tommasi," he went on, turning to one of them, "ring for the guard, if you please, and have this young gentleman put in the punishment cell for a few days. He wants a lesson, I see, to bring him to reason."

The punishment cell was a dark, damp, filthy hole under ground. Instead of bringing Arthur "to reason," it thoroughly exasperated him. His luxurious home had rendered him daintily fastidious about personal cleanliness, and the first effect of the slimy, vermin-covered walls, the floor heaped with accumulations of filth and garbage, the fearful stench of fungi and sewage and rotting wood, was strong enough to have satisfied the offended officer. When he was pushed in and the door locked behind him he took three cautious steps forward with outstretched hands, shuddering with disgust as his fingers came into contact with the slippery wall, and groped in the dense blackness for some spot less filthy than the rest in which to sit down.

The long day passed in unbroken blackness and silence, and the night brought no change. In the utter void and absence of all external impressions, he gradually lost the consciousness of time; and when, on the following morning, a key was turned in the door lock, and the frightened rats scurried past him squeaking, he started up in a sudden panic, his heart throbbing furiously and a roaring noise in his ears, as though he had been shut away from light and sound for months instead of hours.

The door opened, letting in a feeble lantern gleam—a flood of blinding light, it seemed to him—and the head warder entered, carrying a piece of bread and a mug of water. Arthur made a step forward; he was quite convinced that the man had come to let him out. Before he had time to speak, the warder put the bread and mug into his hands, turned round and went away without a word, locking the door again.

Arthur stamped his foot upon the ground. For the first time in his life he was savagely angry. But as the hours went by, the consciousness of time and place gradually slipped further and further away. The blackness seemed an illimitable thing, with no beginning and no end, and life had, as it were, stopped for him. On the evening of the third day, when the door was opened and the head warder appeared on the threshold with a soldier, he looked up, dazed and bewildered, shading his eyes from the unaccustomed light, and vaguely wondering how many hours or weeks he had been in this grave.

"This way, please," said the cool business voice of the warder. Arthur rose and moved forward mechanically, with a strange unsteadiness, swaying and stumbling like a drunkard. He resented the warder's attempt to help him up the steep, narrow steps leading to the courtyard; but as he reached the highest step a sudden giddiness came over him, so that he staggered and would have fallen backwards had the warder not caught him by the shoulder.

"There, he'll be all right now," said a cheerful voice; "they most of them go off this way coming out into the air."

Arthur struggled desperately for breath as another handful of water was dashed into his face. The blackness seemed to fall away from him in pieces with a rushing noise; then he woke suddenly into full consciousness, and, pushing aside the warder's arm, walked along the corridor and up the stairs almost steadily. They stopped for a moment in front of a door; then it opened, and before he realized where they were taking him he was in the brightly lighted interrogation room, staring in confused wonder at the table and the papers and the officers sitting in their accustomed places.

"Ah, it's Mr. Burton!" said the colonel. "I hope we shall be able to talk more comfortably now. Well, and how do you like the dark cell? Not quite so luxurious as your brother's drawing room, is it? eh?"

Arthur raised his eyes to the colonel's smiling face. He was seized by a frantic desire to spring at the throat of this gray-whiskered fop and tear it with his teeth. Probably something of this kind was visible in his face, for the colonel added immediately, in a quite different tone:

"Sit down, Mr. Burton, and drink some water; you are excited."

Arthur pushed aside the glass of water held out to him; and, leaning his arms on the table, rested his forehead on one hand and tried to collect his thoughts. The colonel sat watching him keenly, noting with experienced eyes the unsteady hands and lips, the hair dripping with water, the dim gaze that told of physical prostration and disordered nerves.

"Now, Mr. Burton," he said after a few minutes; "we will start at the point where we left off; and as there has been a certain amount of unpleasantness between us, I may as well begin by saying that I, for my part, have no desire to be anything but indulgent with you. If you will behave properly and reasonably, I assure you that we shall not treat you with any unnecessary harshness."

"What do you want me to do?"

Arthur spoke in a hard, sullen voice, quite different from his natural tone.

"I only want you to tell us frankly, in a straightforward and honourable manner, what you know of this society and its adherents. First of all, how long have you known Bolla?"

"I never met him in my life. I know nothing whatever about him."

"Really? Well, we will return to that subject presently. I think you know a young man named Carlo Bini?"

"I never heard of such a person."

"That is very extraordinary. What about Francesco Neri?"

"I never heard the name."

"But here is a letter in your handwriting, addressed to him. Look!"

Arthur glanced carelessly at the letter and laid it aside.

"Do you recognize that letter?"

"No."

"You deny that it is in your writing?"

"I deny nothing. I have no recollection of it."

"Perhaps you remember this one?"

A second letter was handed to him, and he saw that it was one which he had written in the autumn to a fellow-student.

"No."

"Nor the person to whom it is addressed?"

"Nor the person."

"Your memory is singularly short."

"It is a defect from which I have always suffered."

"Indeed! And I heard the other day from a university professor that you are considered by no means deficient; rather clever in fact."

"You probably judge of cleverness by the police-spy standard; university professors use words in a different sense."

The note of rising irritation was plainly audible in Arthur's voice. He was physically exhausted with hunger, foul air, and want of sleep; every bone in his body seemed to ache separately; and the colonel's voice grated on his exasperated nerves, setting his teeth on edge like the squeak of a slate pencil.

"Mr. Burton," said the colonel, leaning back in his chair and speaking gravely, "you are again forgetting yourself; and I warn you once more that this kind of talk will do you no good. Surely you have had enough of the dark cell not to want any more just for the present. I tell you plainly that I shall use strong measures with you if you persist in repulsing gentle ones. Mind, I have proof—positive proof—that some of these young men have been engaged in smuggling prohibited literature into this port; and that you have been in communication with them. Now, are you going to tell me, without compulsion, what you know about this affair?"

Arthur bent his head lower. A blind, senseless, wild-beast fury was beginning to stir within him like a live thing. The possibility of losing command over himself was more appalling to him than any threats. For the first time he began to realize what latent potentialities may lie hidden beneath the culture of any gentleman and the piety of any Christian; and the terror of himself was strong upon him.

"I am waiting for your answer," said the colonel.

"I have no answer to give."

"You positively refuse to answer?"

"I will tell you nothing at all."

"Then I must simply order you back into the punishment cell, and keep you there till you change your mind. If there is much more trouble with you, I shall put you in irons."

Arthur looked up, trembling from head to foot. "You will do as you please," he said slowly; "and whether the English Ambassador will stand your playing tricks of that kind with a British subject who has not been convicted of any crime is for him to decide."

At last Arthur was conducted back to his own cell, where he flung himself down upon the bed and slept till the next morning. He was not put in irons, and saw no more of the dreaded dark cell; but the feud between him and the colonel grew more inveterate with every interrogation. It was quite useless for Arthur to pray in his cell for grace to conquer his evil passions, or to meditate half the night long upon the patience and meekness of Christ. No sooner was he brought again into the long, bare room with its baize-covered table, and confronted with the colonel's waxed moustache, than the unchristian spirit would take possession of him once more, suggesting bitter repartees and contemptuous answers. Before he had been a month in the prison the mutual irritation had reached such a height that he and the colonel could not see each other's faces without losing their temper.

The continual strain of this petty warfare was beginning to tell heavily upon his nerves. Knowing how closely he was watched, and remembering certain dreadful rumours which he had heard of prisoners secretly drugged with belladonna that notes might be taken of their ravings, he gradually became afraid to sleep or eat; and if a mouse ran past him in the night, would start up drenched with cold sweat and quivering with terror, fancying that someone was hiding in the room to listen if he talked in his sleep. The gendarmes were evidently trying to entrap him into making some admission which might compromise Bolla; and so great was his fear of slipping, by any inadvertency, into a pitfall, that he was really in danger of doing so through sheer nervousness. Bolla's name rang in his ears night and day, interfering even with his devotions, and forcing its way in among the beads of the rosary instead of the name of Mary. But the worst thing of all was that his religion, like the outer world, seemed to be slipping away from him as the days went by. To this last foothold he clung with feverish tenacity, spending several hours of each day in prayer and meditation; but his thoughts wandered more and more often to Bolla, and the prayers were growing terribly mechanical.

His greatest comfort was the head warder of the prison. This was a little old man, fat and bald, who at first had tried his hardest to wear a severe expression. Gradually the good nature which peeped out of every dimple in his chubby face conquered his official scruples, and he began carrying messages for the prisoners from cell to cell.

One afternoon in the middle of May this warder came into the cell with a face so scowling and gloomy that Arthur looked at him in astonishment.

"Why, Enrico!" he exclaimed; "what on earth is wrong with you to-day?"

"Nothing," said Enrico snappishly; and, going up to the pallet, he began pulling off the rug, which was Arthur's property.

"What do you want with my things? Am I to be moved into another cell?"

"No; you're to be let out."

"Let out? What—to-day? For altogether? Enrico!"

In his excitement Arthur had caught hold of the old man's arm. It was angrily wrenched away.

"Enrico! What has come to you? Why don't you answer? Are we all going to be let out?"

A contemptuous grunt was the only reply.

"Look here!" Arthur again took hold of the warder's arm, laughing. "It is no use for you to be cross to me, because I'm not going to get offended. I want to know about the others."

"Which others?" growled Enrico, suddenly laying down the shirt he was folding. "Not Bolla, I suppose?"

"Bolla and all the rest, of course. Enrico, what is the matter with you?"

"Well, he's not likely to be let out in a hurry, poor lad, when a comrade has betrayed him. Ugh!" Enrico took up the shirt again in disgust.

"Betrayed him? A comrade? Oh, how dreadful!" Arthur's eyes dilated with horror. Enrico turned quickly round.

"Why, wasn't it you?"

"I? Are you off your head, man? I?"

"Well, they told him so yesterday at interrogation, anyhow. I'm very glad if it wasn't you, for I always thought you were rather a decent young fellow. This way!" Enrico stepped out into the corridor and Arthur followed him, a light breaking in upon the confusion of his mind.

"They told Bolla I'd betrayed him? Of course they did! Why, man, they told me he had betrayed me. Surely Bolla isn't fool enough to believe that sort of stuff?"

"Then it really isn't true?" Enrico stopped at the foot of the stairs and looked searchingly at Arthur, who merely shrugged his shoulders.

"Of course it's a lie."

"Well, I'm glad to hear it, my lad, and I'll tell him you said so. But you see what they told him was that you had denounced him out of—well, out of jealousy, because of your both being sweet on the same girl."

"It's a lie!" Arthur repeated the words in a quick, breathless whisper. A sudden, paralyzing fear had come over him. "The same girl—jealousy!" How could they know—how could they know?

"Wait a minute, my lad." Enrico stopped in the corridor leading to the interrogation room, and spoke softly. "I believe you; but just tell me one thing. I know you're a Catholic; did you ever say anything in the confessional———"

"It's a lie!" This time Arthur's voice had risen to a stifled cry.

Enrico shrugged his shoulders and moved on again. "You know best, of course; but you wouldn't be the only young fool that's been taken in that way. There's a tremendous ado just now about a priest in Pisa that some of your friends have found out. They've printed a leaflet saying he's a spy."

He opened the door of the interrogation room, and, seeing that Arthur stood motionless, staring blankly before him, pushed him gently across the threshold.

"Good-afternoon, Mr. Burton," said the colonel, smiling and showing his teeth amiably. "I have great pleasure in congratulating you. An order for your release has arrived from Florence. Will you kindly sign this paper?"

Arthur went up to him. "I want to know," he said in a dull voice, "who it was that betrayed me."

The colonel raised his eyebrows with a smile.

"Can't you guess? Think a minute."

Arthur shook his head. The colonel put out both hands with a gesture of polite surprise.

"Can't guess? Really? Why, you yourself, Mr. Burton. Who else could know your private love affairs?"

Arthur turned away in silence. On the wall hung a large wooden crucifix; and his eyes wandered slowly to its face; but with no appeal in them, only a dim wonder at this supine and patient God that had no thunderbolt for a priest who betrayed the confessional.

"Will you kindly sign this receipt for your papers?" said the colonel blandly; "and then I need not keep you any longer. I am sure you must be in a hurry to get home; and my time is very much taken up just now with the affairs of that foolish young man, Bolla, who tried your Christian forbearance so hard. I am afraid he will get a rather heavy sentence. Good-afternoon!"

Arthur signed the receipt, took his papers, and went out in dead silence. He followed Enrico to the massive gate; and, without a word of farewell, descended to the water's edge, where a ferryman was waiting to take him across the moat. As he mounted the stone steps leading to the street, a girl in a cotton dress and straw hat ran up to him with outstretched hands.

"Arthur! Oh, I'm so glad—I'm so glad!"

He drew his hands away, shivering.

"Jim!" he said at last, in a voice that did not seem to belong to him. "Jim!"

"I've been waiting here for half an hour. They said you would come out at four. Arthur, why do you look at me like that? Something has happened! Arthur, what has come to you? Stop!"

He had turned away, and was walking slowly down the street, as if he had forgotten her presence. Thoroughly frightened at his manner, she ran after him and caught him by the arm.

"Arthur!"

He stopped and looked up with bewildered eyes. She slipped her arm through his, and they walked on again for a moment in silence.

"Listen, dear," she began softly; "you mustn't get so upset over this wretched business. I know it's dreadfully hard on you, but everybody understands."

"What business?" he asked in the same dull voice.

"I mean, about Bolla's letter."

Arthur's face contracted painfully at the name.

"I thought you wouldn't have heard of it," Gemma went on; "but I suppose they've told you. Bolla must be perfectly mad to have imagined such a thing."

"Such a thing——?"

"You don't know about it, then? He has written a horrible letter, saying that you have told about the steamers, and got him arrested. It's perfectly absurd, of course; everyone that knows you sees that; it's only the people who don't know you that have been upset by it. Really, that's what I came here for—to tell you that no one in our group believes a word of it."

"Gemma! But it's—it's true!"

She shrank slowly away from him, and stood quite still, her eyes wide and dark with horror, her face as white as the kerchief at her neck. A great icy wave of silence seemed to have swept round them both, shutting them out, in a world apart, from the life and movement of the street.

"Yes," he whispered at last; "the steamers—I spoke of that; and I said his name—oh, my God! my God! What shall I do?"

He came to himself suddenly, realizing her presence and the mortal terror in her face. Yes, of course, she must think———

"Gemma, you don't understand!" he burst out, moving nearer; but she recoiled with a sharp cry:

"Don't touch me!"

Arthur seized her right hand with sudden violence.

"Listen, for God's sake! It was not my fault; I——"

"Let go; let my hand go! Let go!"

The next instant she wrenched her fingers away from his, and struck him across the cheek with her open hand.

A kind of mist came over his eyes. For a little while he was conscious of nothing but Gemma's white and desperate face, and the right hand which she had fiercely rubbed on the skirt of her cotton dress. Then the daylight crept back again, and he looked round and saw that he was alone.

CHAPTER VII

IT had long been dark when Arthur rang at the front door of the great house in the Via Borra. He remembered that he had been wandering about the streets; but where, or why, or for how long, he had no idea. Julia's page opened the door, yawning, and grinned significantly at the haggard, stony face. It seemed to him a prodigious joke to have the young master come home from jail like a "drunk and disorderly" beggar. Arthur went upstairs. On the first floor he met Gibbons coming down with an air of lofty and solemn disapproval. He tried to pass with a muttered "Good evening"; but Gibbons was no easy person to get past against his will.

"The gentlemen are out, sir," he said, looking critically at Arthur's rather neglected dress and hair. "They have gone with the mistress to an evening party, and will not be back till nearly twelve."

Arthur looked at his watch; it was nine o'clock. Oh, yes! he would have time—plenty of time———

"My mistress desired me to ask whether you would like any supper, sir; and to say that she hopes you will sit up for her, as she particularly wishes to speak to you this evening."

"I don't want anything, thank you; you can tell her I have not gone to bed."

He went up to his room. Nothing in it had been changed since his arrest; Montanelli's portrait was on the table where he had placed it, and the crucifix stood in the alcove as before. He paused a moment on the threshold, listening; but the house was quite still; evidently no one was coming to disturb him. He stepped softly into the room and locked the door.

And so he had come to the end. There was nothing to think or trouble about; an importunate and useless consciousness to get rid of—and nothing more. It seemed a stupid, aimless kind of thing, somehow.

He had not formed any resolve to commit suicide, nor indeed had he thought much about it; the thing was quite obvious and inevitable. He had even no definite idea as to what manner of death to choose; all that mattered was to be done with it quickly—to have it over and forget. He had no weapon in the room, not even a pocketknife; but that was of no consequence—a towel would do, or a sheet torn into strips.

There was a large nail just over the window. That would do; but it must be firm to bear his weight. He got up on a chair to feel the nail; it was not quite firm, and he stepped down again and took a hammer from a drawer. He knocked in the nail, and was about to pull a sheet off his bed, when he suddenly remembered that he had not said his prayers. Of course, one must pray before dying; every Christian does that. There are even special prayers for a departing soul.

He went into the alcove and knelt down before the crucifix. "Almighty and merciful God——" he began aloud; and with that broke off and said no more. Indeed, the world was grown so dull that there was nothing left to pray for—or against. And then, what did Christ know about a trouble of this kind—Christ, who had never suffered it? He had only been betrayed, like Bolla; He had never been tricked into betraying.

Arthur rose, crossing himself from old habit. Approaching the table, he saw lying upon it a letter addressed to him, in Montanelli's handwriting. It was in pencil:

"My Dear Boy: It is a great disappointment to me that I cannot see you on the day of your release; but I have been sent for to visit a dying man. I shall not get back till late at night. Come to me early to-morrow morning. In great haste,

"L. M."

He put down the letter with a sigh; it did seem hard on the Padre.

How the people had laughed and gossiped in the streets! Nothing was altered since the days when he had been alive. Not the least little one of all the daily trifles round him was changed because a human soul, a living human soul, had been struck down dead. It was all just the same as before. The water had plashed in the fountains; the sparrows had twittered under the eaves; just as they had done yesterday, just as they would do to-morrow. And as for him, he was dead—quite dead.

He sat down on the edge of the bed, crossed his arms along the foot-rail, and rested his forehead upon them. There was plenty of time; and his head ached so—the very middle of the brain seemed to ache; it was all so dull and stupid—so utterly meaningless——

The front-door bell rang sharply, and he started up in a breathless agony of terror, with both hands at his throat. They had come back—he had sat there dreaming, and let the precious time slip away—and now he must see their faces and hear their cruel tongues—their sneers and comments—If only he had a knife———

He looked desperately round the room. His mother's work-basket stood in a little cupboard; surely there would be scissors; he might sever an artery. No; the sheet and nail were safer, if he had time.

He dragged the counterpane from his bed, and with frantic haste began tearing off a strip. The sound of footsteps came up the stairs. No; the strip was too wide; it would not tie firmly; and there must be a noose. He worked faster as the footsteps drew nearer; and the blood throbbed in his temples and roared in his ears. Quicker—quicker! Oh, God! five minutes more!

There was a knock at the door. The strip of torn stuff dropped from his hands, and he sat quite still, holding his breath to listen. The handle of the door was tried; then Julia's voice called:

"Arthur!"

He stood up, panting.

"Arthur, open the door, please; we are waiting."

He gathered up the torn counterpane, threw it into a drawer, and hastily smoothed down the bed.

"Arthur!" This time it was James who called, and the door-handle was shaken impatiently. "Are you asleep?"

Arthur looked round the room, saw that everything was hidden, and unlocked the door.

"I should think you might at least have obeyed my express request that you should sit up for us, Arthur," said Julia, sweeping into the room in a towering passion. "You appear to think it the proper thing for us to dance attendance for half an hour at your door——"

"Four minutes, my dear," James mildly corrected, stepping into the room at the end of his wife's pink satin train. "I certainly think, Arthur, that it would have been more—becoming if——"

"What do you want?" Arthur interrupted. He was standing with his hand upon the door, glancing furtively from one to the other like a trapped animal. But James was too obtuse and Julia too angry to notice the look.

Mr. Burton placed a chair for his wife and sat down, carefully pulling up his new trousers at the knees. "Julia and I," he began, "feel it to be our duty to speak to you seriously about——"

"I can't listen to-night; I—I'm not well. My head aches—you must wait."

Arthur spoke in a strange, indistinct voice, with a confused and rambling manner. James looked round in surprise.

"Is there anything the matter with you?" he asked anxiously, suddenly remembering that Arthur had come from a very hotbed of infection. "I hope you're not sickening for anything. You look quite feverish."

"Nonsense!" Julia interrupted sharply. "It's only the usual theatricals, because he's ashamed to face us. Come here and sit down, Arthur." Arthur slowly crossed the room and sat down on the bed. "Yes?" he said wearily.

Mr. Burton coughed, cleared his throat, smoothed his already immaculate beard, and began the carefully prepared speech over again:

"I feel it to be my duty—my painful duty—to speak very seriously to you about your extraordinary behaviour in connecting yourself with—a—law-breakers and incendiaries and—a—persons of disreputable character. I believe you to have been, perhaps, more foolish than depraved—a——"

He paused.

"Yes?" Arthur said again.

"Now, I do not wish to be hard on you," James went on, softening a little in spite of himself before the weary hopelessness of Arthur's manner. "I am quite willing to believe that you have been led away by bad companions, and to take into account your youth and inexperience and the—a—a—imprudent and—a—impulsive character which you have, I fear, inherited from your mother."

Arthur's eyes wandered slowly to his mother's portrait and back again, but he did not speak.

"But you will, I feel sure, understand," James continued, "that it is quite impossible for me to keep any longer in my house a person who has brought public disgrace upon a name so highly respected as ours."

"Yes?" Arthur repeated once more.

"Well?" said Julia sharply, closing her fan with a snap and laying it across her knee. "Are you going to have the goodness to say anything but 'Yes,' Arthur?"

"You will do as you think best, of course," he answered slowly, without moving. "It doesn't matter much either way."

"Doesn't—matter?" James repeated, aghast; and his wife rose with a laugh.

"Oh, it doesn't matter, doesn't it? Well, James, I hope you understand now how much gratitude you may expect in that quarter. I told you what would come of showing charity to Papist adventuresses and their——"

"Hush, hush! Never mind that, my dear!"

"It's all nonsense, James; we've had more than enough of this sentimentality! A love-child setting himself up as a member of the family—it's quite time he did know what his mother was! Why should we be saddled with the child of a Popish priest's amourettes? There, then—look!"

She pulled a crumpled sheet of paper out of her pocket and tossed it across the table to Arthur. He opened it; the writing was in his mother's hand, and was dated four months before his birth. It was a confession, addressed to her husband, and with two signatures.

Arthur's eyes travelled slowly down the page, past the unsteady letters in which her name was written, to the strong, familiar signature: "Lorenzo Montanelli." For a moment he stared at the writing; then, without a word, refolded the paper and laid it down. James rose and took his wife by the arm.

"There, Julia, that will do. Just go downstairs now; it's late, and I want to talk a little business with Arthur. It won't interest you."

She glanced up at her husband; then back at Arthur, who was silently staring at the floor.

"He seems half stupid," she whispered.

When she had gathered up her train and left the room, James carefully shut the door and went back to his chair beside the table. Arthur sat as before, perfectly motionless and silent.

"Arthur," James began in a milder tone, now Julia was not there to hear, "I am very sorry that this has come out. You might just as well not have known it. However, all that's over; and I am pleased to see that you can behave with such self-control. Julia is a—a little excited; ladies often—anyhow, I don't want to be too hard on you."

He stopped to see what effect the kindly words had produced; but Arthur was quite motionless.

"Of course, my dear boy," James went on after a moment, "this is a distressing story altogether, and the best thing we can do is to hold our tongues about it. My father was generous enough not to divorce your mother when she confessed her fall to him; he only demanded that the man who had led her astray should leave the country at once; and, as you know, he went to

China as a missionary. For my part, I was very much against your having anything to do with him when he came back; but my father, just at the last, consented to let him teach you, on condition that he never attempted to see your mother. I must, in justice, acknowledge that I believe they both observed that condition faithfully to the end. It is a very deplorable business; but——"

Arthur looked up. All the life and expression had gone out of his face; it was like a waxen mask.

"D-don't you think," he said softly, with a curious stammering hesitation on the words, "th-that—all this—is—v-very—funny?"

"FUNNY?" James pushed his chair away from the table, and sat staring at him, too much petrified for anger. "Funny! Arthur, are you mad?"

Arthur suddenly threw back his head, and burst into a frantic fit of laughing.

"Arthur!" exclaimed the shipowner, rising with dignity, "I am amazed at your levity!"

There was no answer but peal after peal of laughter, so loud and boisterous that even James began to doubt whether there was not something more the matter here than levity.

"Just like a hysterical woman," he muttered, turning, with a contemptuous shrug of his shoulders, to tramp impatiently up and down the room. "Really, Arthur, you're worse than Julia; there, stop laughing! I can't wait about here all night."

He might as well have asked the crucifix to come down from its pedestal. Arthur was past caring for remonstrances or exhortations; he only laughed, and laughed, and laughed without end.

"This is absurd!" said James, stopping at last in his irritated pacing to and fro. "You are evidently too much excited to be reasonable to-night. I can't talk business with you if you're going on that way. Come to me to-morrow morning after breakfast. And now you had better go to bed. Good-night."

He went out, slamming the door. "Now for the hysterics downstairs," he muttered as he tramped noisily away. "I suppose it'll be tears there!"

The frenzied laughter died on Arthur's lips. He snatched up the hammer from the table and flung himself upon the crucifix.

With the crash that followed he came suddenly to his senses, standing before the empty pedestal, the hammer still in his hand, and the fragments of the broken image scattered on the floor about his feet.

He threw down the hammer. "So easy!" he said, and turned away. "And what an idiot I am!"

He sat down by the table, panting heavily for breath, and rested his forehead on both hands. Presently he rose, and, going to the wash-stand, poured a jugful of cold water over his head and face. He came back quite composed, and sat down to think.

And it was for such things as these—for these false and slavish people, these dumb and soulless gods—that he had suffered all these tortures of shame and passion and despair; had made a rope to hang himself, forsooth, because one priest was a liar. As if they were not all liars! Well, all that was done with; he was wiser now. He need only shake off these vermin and begin life afresh.

There were plenty of goods vessels in the docks; it would be an easy matter to stow himself away in one of them, and get across to Canada, Australia, Cape Colony—anywhere. It was no matter for the country, if only it was far enough; and, as for the life out there, he could see, and if it did not suit him he could try some other place.

He took out his purse. Only thirty-three paoli; but his watch was a good one. That would help him along a bit; and in any case it was of no consequence—he should pull through somehow. But they would search for him, all these people; they would be sure to make inquiries at the docks. No; he must put them on a false scent—make them believe him dead; then he should be quite free—quite free. He laughed softly to himself at the thought of the Burtons searching for his corpse. What a farce the whole thing was!

Taking a sheet of paper, he wrote the first words that occurred to him:

"I believed in you as I believed in God. God is a thing made of clay, that I can smash with a hammer; and you have fooled me with a lie."

He folded up the paper, directed it to Montanelli, and, taking another sheet, wrote across it: "Look for my body in Darsena." Then he put on his hat and went out of the room. Passing his mother's portrait, he looked up with a laugh and a shrug of his shoulders. She, too, had lied to him.

He crept softly along the corridor, and, slipping back the door-bolts, went out on to the great, dark, echoing marble staircase. It seemed to yawn beneath him like a black pit as he descended.

He crossed the courtyard, treading cautiously for fear of waking Gian Battista, who slept on the ground floor. In the wood-cellar at the back was a little grated window, opening on the canal and not more than four feet from the ground. He remembered that the rusty grating had broken away on one side; by pushing a little he could make an aperture wide enough to climb out by.

The grating was strong, and he grazed his hands badly and tore the sleeve of his coat; but that was no matter. He looked up and down the street; there was no one in sight, and the canal lay black and silent, an ugly trench between two straight and slimy walls. The untried universe might prove a dismal hole, but it could hardly be more flat and sordid than the corner which he was leaving behind him. There was nothing to regret; nothing to look back upon. It had been a pestilent little stagnant world, full of squalid lies and clumsy cheats and foul-smelling ditches that were not even deep enough to drown a man.

He walked along the canal bank, and came out upon the tiny square by the Medici palace. It was here that Gemma had run up to him with her vivid face, her outstretched hands. Here was the little flight of wet stone steps leading down to the moat; and there the fortress scowling across the strip of dirty water. He had never noticed before how squat and mean it looked.

Passing through the narrow streets he reached the Darsena shipping-basin, where he took off his hat and flung it into the water. It would be found, of course, when they dragged for his body. Then he walked on along the water's edge, considering perplexedly what to do next. He must contrive to hide on some ship; but it was a difficult thing to do. His only chance would be to get on to the huge old Medici breakwater and walk along to the further end of it. There was a low-class tavern on the point; probably he should find some sailor there who could be bribed.

But the dock gates were closed. How should he get past them, and past the customs officials? His stock of money would not furnish the high bribe that they would demand for letting him through at night and without a passport. Besides they might recognize him.

As he passed the bronze statue of the "Four Moors," a man's figure emerged from an old house on the opposite side of the shipping basin and approached the bridge. Arthur slipped at once into the deep shadow behind the group of statuary and crouched down in the darkness, peeping cautiously round the corner of the pedestal.

It was a soft spring night, warm and starlit. The water lapped against the stone walls of the basin and swirled in gentle eddies round the steps with a sound as of low laughter. Somewhere near a chain creaked, swinging slowly to and fro. A huge iron crane towered up, tall and melancholy in the dimness. Black on a shimmering expanse of starry sky and pearly cloud-wreaths, the figures of the fettered, struggling slaves stood out in vain and vehement protest against a merciless doom.

The man approached unsteadily along the water side, shouting an English street song. He was evidently a sailor returning from a carouse at some tavern. No one else was within sight. As he drew near, Arthur stood up and stepped into the middle of the roadway. The sailor broke off in his song with an oath, and stopped short.

"I want to speak to you," Arthur said in Italian. "Do you understand me?"

The man shook his head. "It's no use talking that patter to me," he said; then, plunging into bad French, asked sullenly: "What do you want? Why can't you let me pass?"

"Just come out of the light here a minute; I want to speak to you."

"Ah! wouldn't you like it? Out of the light! Got a knife anywhere about you?"

"No, no, man! Can't you see I only want your help? I'll pay you for it?"

"Eh? What? And dressed like a swell, too———" The sailor had relapsed into English. He now moved into the shadow and leaned against the railing of the pedestal.

"Well," he said, returning to his atrocious French; "and what is it you want?"

"I want to get away from here——"

"Aha! Stowaway! Want me to hide you? Been up to something, I suppose. Stuck a knife into somebody, eh? Just like these foreigners! And where might you be wanting to go? Not to the police station, I fancy?"

He laughed in his tipsy way, and winked one eye.

"What vessel do you belong to?"

"Carlotta—Leghorn to Buenos Ayres; shipping oil one way and hides the other. She's over there"—pointing in the direction of the breakwater—"beastly old hulk!"

"Buenos Ayres—yes! Can you hide me anywhere on board?"

"How much can you give?"

"Not very much; I have only a few paoli."

"No. Can't do it under fifty—and cheap at that, too—a swell like you."

"What do you mean by a swell? If you like my clothes you may change with me, but I can't give you more money than I have got."

"You have a watch there. Hand it over."

Arthur took out a lady's gold watch, delicately chased and enamelled, with the initials "G. B." on the back. It had been his mother's—but what did that matter now?

"Ah!" remarked the sailor with a quick glance at it. "Stolen, of course! Let me look!"

Arthur drew his hand away. "No," he said. "I will give you the watch when we are on board; not before."

"You're not such a fool as you look, after all! I'll bet it's your first scrape, though, eh?"

"That is my business. Ah! there comes the watchman."

They crouched down behind the group of statuary and waited till the watchman had passed. Then the sailor rose, and, telling Arthur to follow him, walked on, laughing foolishly to himself. Arthur followed in silence.

The sailor led him back to the little irregular square by the Medici palace; and, stopping in a dark corner, mumbled in what was intended for a cautious whisper:

"Wait here; those soldier fellows will see you if you come further."

"What are you going to do?"

"Get you some clothes. I'm not going to take you on board with that bloody coatsleeve."

Arthur glanced down at the sleeve which had been torn by the window grating. A little blood from the grazed hand had fallen upon it. Evidently the man thought him a murderer. Well, it was of no consequence what people thought.

After some time the sailor came back, triumphant, with a bundle under his arm.

"Change," he whispered; "and make haste about it. I must get back, and that old Jew has kept me bargaining and haggling for half an hour."

Arthur obeyed, shrinking with instinctive disgust at the first touch of second-hand clothes. Fortunately these, though rough and coarse, were fairly clean. When he stepped into the light in his new attire, the sailor looked at him with tipsy solemnity and gravely nodded his approval.

"You'll do," he said. "This way, and don't make a noise." Arthur, carrying his discarded clothes, followed him through a labyrinth of winding canals and dark narrow alleys; the mediaeval slum quarter which the people of Leghorn call "New Venice." Here and there a gloomy old palace, solitary among the squalid houses and filthy courts, stood between two noisome ditches, with a forlorn air of trying to preserve its ancient dignity and yet of knowing the effort to be a hopeless one. Some of the alleys, he knew, were notorious dens of thieves, cut-throats, and smugglers; others were merely wretched and poverty-stricken.

Beside one of the little bridges the sailor stopped, and, looking round to see that they were not observed, descended a flight of stone steps to a narrow landing stage. Under the bridge was a dirty, crazy old boat. Sharply ordering Arthur to jump in and lie down, he seated himself in the boat and began rowing towards the harbour's mouth. Arthur lay still on the wet and leaky planks, hidden by the clothes which the man had thrown over him, and peeping out from under them at the familiar streets and houses.

Presently they passed under a bridge and entered that part of the canal which forms a moat for the fortress. The massive walls rose out of the water, broad at the base and narrowing upward to the frowning turrets. How strong, how threatening they had seemed to him a few hours ago! And now——

He laughed softly as he lay in the bottom of the boat.

"Hold your noise," the sailor whispered, "and keep your head covered! We're close to the custom house."

Arthur drew the clothes over his head. A few yards further on the boat stopped before a row of masts chained together, which lay across the surface of the canal, blocking the narrow waterway between the custom house and the fortress wall. A sleepy official came out yawning and bent over the water's edge with a lantern in his hand.

"Passports, please."

The sailor handed up his official papers. Arthur, half stifled under the clothes, held his breath, listening.

"A nice time of night to come back to your ship!" grumbled the customs official. "Been out on the spree, I suppose. What's in your boat?"

"Old clothes. Got them cheap." He held up the waistcoat for inspection. The official, lowering his lantern, bent over, straining his eyes to see.

"It's all right, I suppose. You can pass."

He lifted the barrier and the boat moved slowly out into the dark, heaving water. At a little distance Arthur sat up and threw off the clothes.

"Here she is," the sailor whispered, after rowing for some time in silence. "Keep close behind me and hold your tongue."

He clambered up the side of a huge black monster, swearing under his breath at the clumsiness of the landsman, though Arthur's natural agility rendered him less awkward than most people would have been in his place. Once safely on board, they crept cautiously between dark masses of rigging and machinery, and came at last to a hatchway, which the sailor softly raised.

"Down here!" he whispered. "I'll be back in a minute."

The hold was not only damp and dark, but intolerably foul. At first Arthur instinctively drew back, half choked by the stench of raw hides and rancid oil. Then he remembered the "punishment cell," and descended the ladder, shrugging his shoulders. Life is pretty much the same everywhere, it seemed; ugly, putrid, infested with vermin, full of shameful secrets and dark corners. Still, life is life, and he must make the best of it.

In a few minutes the sailor came back with something in his hands which Arthur could not distinctly see for the darkness.

"Now, give me the watch and money. Make haste!"

Taking advantage of the darkness, Arthur succeeded in keeping back a few coins.

"You must get me something to eat," he said; "I am half starved."

"I've brought it. Here you are." The sailor handed him a pitcher, some hard biscuit, and a piece of salt pork. "Now mind, you must hide in this empty barrel, here, when the customs officers come to examine to-morrow morning. Keep as still as a mouse till we're right out at sea. I'll let you know when to come out. And won't you just catch it when the captain sees you—that's all! Got the drink safe? Good-night!"

The hatchway closed, and Arthur, setting the precious "drink" in a safe place, climbed on to an oil barrel to eat his pork and biscuit. Then he curled himself up on the dirty floor; and, for the first time since his babyhood, settled himself to sleep without a prayer. The rats scurried round him in the darkness; but neither their persistent noise nor the swaying of the ship, nor the nauseating stench of oil, nor the prospect of to-morrow's sea-sickness, could keep him awake. He cared no more for them all than for the broken and dishonoured idols that only yesterday had been the gods of his adoration.

PART II
THIRTEEN YEARS LATER

CHAPTER I

ONE evening in July, 1846, a few acquaintances met at Professor Fabrizi's house in Florence to discuss plans for future political work. Several of them belonged to the Mazzinian party and would have been satisfied with nothing less than a democratic Republic and a United Italy. Others were Constitutional Monarchists and Liberals of various shades. On one point, however, they were all agreed; that of dissatisfaction with the Tuscan censorship; and the popular professor had called the meeting in the hope that, on this one subject at least, the representatives of the dissentient parties would be able to get through an hour's discussion without quarrelling.

Only a fortnight had elapsed since the famous amnesty which Pius IX. had granted, on his accession, to political offenders in the Papal States; but the wave of liberal enthusiasm caused by it was already spreading over Italy. In Tuscany even the government appeared to have been affected by the astounding event. It had occurred to Fabrizi and a few other leading Florentines that this was a propitious moment for a bold effort to reform the press-laws.

"Of course," the dramatist Lega had said, when the subject was first broached to him; "it would be impossible to start a newspaper till we can get the press-law changed; we should not bring out the first number. But we may be able to run some pamphlets through the censorship already; and the sooner we begin the sooner we shall get the law changed."

He was now explaining in Fabrizi's library his theory of the line which should be taken by liberal writers at the moment.

"There is no doubt," interposed one of the company, a gray-haired barrister with a rather drawling manner of speech, "that in some way we must take advantage of the moment. We shall not see such a favourable one again for bringing forward serious reforms. But I doubt the pamphlets doing any good. They will only irritate and frighten the government instead of winning it over to our side, which is what we really want to do. If once the authorities begin to think of us as dangerous agitators our chance of getting their help is gone."

"Then what would you have us do?"

"Petition."

"To the Grand Duke?"

"Yes; for an augmentation of the liberty of the press."

A keen-looking, dark man sitting by the window turned his head round with a laugh.

"You'll get a lot out of petitioning!" he said. "I should have thought the result of the Renzi case was enough to cure anybody of going to work that way."

"My dear sir, I am as much grieved as you are that we did not succeed in preventing the extradition of Renzi. But really—I do not wish to hurt the sensibilities of anyone, but I cannot help thinking that our failure in that case was largely due to the impatience and vehemence of some persons among our number. I should certainly hesitate——"

"As every Piedmontese always does," the dark man interrupted sharply. "I don't know where the vehemence and impatience lay, unless you found them in the strings of meek petitions we sent in. That may be vehemence for Tuscany or Piedmont, but we should not call it particularly vehement in Naples."

"Fortunately," remarked the Piedmontese, "Neapolitan vehemence is peculiar to Naples."

"There, there, gentlemen, that will do!" the professor put in. "Neapolitan customs are very good things in their way and Piedmontese customs in theirs; but just now we are in Tuscany, and the Tuscan custom is to stick to the matter in hand. Grassini votes for petitions and Galli against them. What do you think, Dr. Riccardo?"

"I see no harm in petitions, and if Grassini gets one up I'll sign it with all the pleasure in life. But I don't think mere petitioning and nothing else will accomplish much. Why can't we have both petitions and pamphlets?"

"Simply because the pamphlets will put the government into a state of mind in which it won't grant the petitions," said Grassini.

"It won't do that anyhow." The Neapolitan rose and came across to the table. "Gentlemen, you're on the wrong tack. Conciliating the government will do no good. What we must do is to rouse the people."

"That's easier said than done; how are you going to start?"

"Fancy asking Galli that! Of course he'd start by knocking the censor on the head."

"No, indeed, I shouldn't," said Galli stoutly. "You always think if a man comes from down south he must believe in no argument but cold steel."

"Well, what do you propose, then? Sh! Attention, gentlemen! Galli has a proposal to make."

The whole company, which had broken up into little knots of twos and threes, carrying on separate discussions, collected round the table to listen. Galli raised his hands in expostulation.

"No, gentlemen, it is not a proposal; it is merely a suggestion. It appears to me that there is a great practical danger in all this rejoicing over the new

Pope. People seem to think that, because he has struck out a new line and granted this amnesty, we have only to throw ourselves—all of us, the whole of Italy—into his arms and he will carry us to the promised land. Now, I am second to no one in admiration of the Pope's behaviour; the amnesty was a splendid action."

"I am sure His Holiness ought to feel flattered——" Grassini began contemptuously.

"There, Grassini, do let the man speak!" Riccardo interrupted in his turn. "It's a most extraordinary thing that you two never can keep from sparring like a cat and dog. Get on, Galli!"

"What I wanted to say is this," continued the Neapolitan. "The Holy Father, undoubtedly, is acting with the best intentions; but how far he will succeed in carrying his reforms is another question. Just now it's smooth enough and, of course, the reactionists all over Italy will lie quiet for a month or two till the excitement about the amnesty blows over; but they are not likely to let the power be taken out of their hands without a fight, and my own belief is that before the winter is half over we shall have Jesuits and Gregorians and Sanfedists and all the rest of the crew about our ears, plotting and intriguing, and poisoning off everybody they can't bribe."

"That's likely enough."

"Very well, then; shall we wait here, meekly sending in petitions, till Lambruschini and his pack have persuaded the Grand Duke to put us bodily under Jesuit rule, with perhaps a few Austrian hussars to patrol the streets and keep us in order; or shall we forestall them and take advantage of their momentary discomfiture to strike the first blow?"

"Tell us first what blow you propose?"

"I would suggest that we start an organized propaganda and agitation against the Jesuits."

"A pamphleteering declaration of war, in fact?"

"Yes; exposing their intrigues, ferreting out their secrets, and calling upon the people to make common cause against them."

"But there are no Jesuits here to expose."

"Aren't there? Wait three months and see how many we shall have. It'll be too late to keep them out then."

"But really to rouse the town against the Jesuits one must speak plainly; and if you do that how will you evade the censorship?"

"I wouldn't evade it; I would defy it."

"You would print the pamphlets anonymously? That's all very well, but the fact is, we have all seen enough of the clandestine press to know——"

"I did not mean that. I would print the pamphlets openly, with our names and addresses, and let them prosecute us if they dare."

"The project is a perfectly mad one," Grassini exclaimed. "It is simply putting one's head into the lion's mouth out of sheer wantonness."

"Oh, you needn't be afraid!" Galli cut in sharply; "we shouldn't ask you to go to prison for our pamphlets."

"Hold your tongue, Galli!" said Riccardo. "It's not a question of being afraid; we're all as ready as you are to go to prison if there's any good to be got by it, but it is childish to run into danger for nothing. For my part, I have an amendment to the proposal to suggest."

"Well, what is it?"

"I think we might contrive, with care, to fight the Jesuits without coming into collision with the censorship."

"I don't see how you are going to manage it."

"I think that it is possible to clothe what one has to say in so roundabout a form that——"

"That the censorship won't understand it? And then you'll expect every poor artisan and labourer to find out the meaning by the light of the ignorance and stupidity that are in him! That doesn't sound very practicable."

"Martini, what do you think?" asked the professor, turning to a broad-shouldered man with a great brown beard, who was sitting beside him.

"I think that I will reserve my opinion till I have more facts to go upon. It's a question of trying experiments and seeing what comes of them."

"And you, Sacconi?"

"I should like to hear what Signora Bolla has to say. Her suggestions are always valuable."

Everyone turned to the only woman in the room, who had been sitting on the sofa, resting her chin on one hand and listening in silence to the discussion. She had deep, serious black eyes, but as she raised them now there was an unmistakable gleam of amusement in them.

"I am afraid," she said; "that I disagree with everybody."

"You always do, and the worst of it is that you are always right," Riccardo put in.

"I think it is quite true that we must fight the Jesuits somehow; and if we can't do it with one weapon we must with another. But mere defiance is a feeble weapon and evasion a cumbersome one. As for petitioning, that is a child's toy."

"I hope, signora," Grassini interposed, with a solemn face; "that you are not suggesting such methods as—assassination?"

Martini tugged at his big moustache and Galli sniggered outright. Even the grave young woman could not repress a smile.

"Believe me," she said, "that if I were ferocious enough to think of such things I should not be childish enough to talk about them. But the deadliest weapon I know is ridicule. If you can once succeed in rendering the Jesuits ludicrous, in making people laugh at them and their claims, you have conquered them without bloodshed."

"I believe you are right, as far as that goes," Fabrizi said; "but I don't see how you are going to carry the thing through."

"Why should we not be able to carry it through?" asked Martini. "A satirical thing has a better chance of getting over the censorship difficulty than a serious one; and, if it must be cloaked, the average reader is more likely to find out the double meaning of an apparently silly joke than of a scientific or economic treatise."

"Then is your suggestion, signora, that we should issue satirical pamphlets, or attempt to run a comic paper? That last, I am sure, the censorship would never allow."

"I don't mean exactly either. I believe a series of small satirical leaflets, in verse or prose, to be sold cheap or distributed free about the streets, would be very useful. If we could find a clever artist who would enter into the spirit of the thing, we might have them illustrated."

"It's a capital idea, if only one could carry it out; but if the thing is to be done at all it must be well done. We should want a first-class satirist; and where are we to get him?"

"You see," added Lega, "most of us are serious writers; and, with all respect to the company, I am afraid that a general attempt to be humorous would present the spectacle of an elephant trying to dance the tarantella."

"I never suggested that we should all rush into work for which we are unfitted. My idea was that we should try to find a really gifted satirist—there must be one to be got somewhere in Italy, surely—and offer to provide the necessary funds. Of course we should have to know something of the man and make sure that he would work on lines with which we could agree."

"But where are you going to find him? I can count up the satirists of any real talent on the fingers of one hand; and none of them are available. Giusti wouldn't accept; he is fully occupied as it is. There are one or two good men in Lombardy, but they write only in the Milanese dialect——"

"And moreover," said Grassini, "the Tuscan people can be influenced in better ways than this. I am sure that it would be felt as, to say the least, a want of political savoir faire if we were to treat this solemn question of civil and religious liberty as a subject for trifling. Florence is not a mere wilderness of factories and money-getting like London, nor a haunt of idle luxury like Paris. It is a city with a great history———"

"So was Athens," she interrupted, smiling; "but it was 'rather sluggish from its size and needed a gadfly to rouse it'——"

Riccardo struck his hand upon the table. "Why, we never thought of the Gadfly! The very man!"

"Who is that?"

"The Gadfly—Felice Rivarez. Don't you remember him? One of Muratori's band that came down from the Apennines three years ago?"

"Oh, you knew that set, didn't you? I remember your travelling with them when they went on to Paris."

"Yes; I went as far as Leghorn to see Rivarez off for Marseilles. He wouldn't stop in Tuscany; he said there was nothing left to do but laugh, once the insurrection had failed, and so he had better go to Paris. No doubt he agreed with Signor Grassini that Tuscany is the wrong place to laugh in. But I am nearly sure he would come back if we asked him, now that there is a chance of doing something in Italy."

"What name did you say?"

"Rivarez. He's a Brazilian, I think. At any rate, I know he has lived out there. He is one of the wittiest men I ever came across. Heaven knows we had nothing to be merry over, that week in Leghorn; it was enough to break one's heart to look at poor Lambertini; but there was no keeping one's countenance when Rivarez was in the room; it was one perpetual fire of absurdities. He had a nasty sabre-cut across the face, too; I remember sewing it up. He's an odd creature; but I believe he and his nonsense kept some of those poor lads from breaking down altogether."

"Is that the man who writes political skits in the French papers under the name of 'Le Taon'?"

"Yes; short paragraphs mostly, and comic feuilletons. The smugglers up in the Apennines called him 'the Gadfly' because of his tongue; and he took the nickname to sign his work with."

"I know something about this gentleman," said Grassini, breaking in upon the conversation in his slow and stately manner; "and I cannot say that what I have heard is much to his credit. He undoubtedly possesses a certain showy, superficial cleverness, though I think his abilities have been exaggerated; and possibly he is not lacking in physical courage; but his reputation in Paris and Vienna is, I believe, very far from spotless. He appears to be a gentleman of—a—a—many adventures and unknown antecedents. It is said that he was picked up out of charity by Duprez's expedition somewhere in the wilds of tropical South America, in a state of inconceivable savagery and degradation. I believe he has never satisfactorily explained how he came to be in such a condition. As for the rising in the Apennines, I fear it is no secret that persons of all characters took part in that unfortunate affair. The men who were executed in Bologna are known to have been nothing but common malefactors; and the character of many who escaped will hardly bear description. Without doubt, SOME of the participators were men of high character——"

"Some of them were the intimate friends of several persons in this room!" Riccardo interrupted, with an angry ring in his voice. "It's all very well to be particular and exclusive, Grassini; but these 'common malefactors' died for their belief, which is more than you or I have done as yet."

"And another time when people tell you the stale gossip of Paris," added Galli, "you can tell them from me that they are mistaken about the Duprez expedition. I know Duprez's adjutant, Martel, personally, and have heard the whole story from him. It's true that they found Rivarez stranded out there. He had been taken prisoner in the war, fighting for the Argentine Republic, and had escaped. He was wandering about the country in various disguises, trying to get back to Buenos Ayres. But the story of their taking him on out of charity is a pure fabrication. Their interpreter had fallen ill and been obliged to turn back; and not one of the Frenchmen could speak the native languages; so they offered him the post, and he spent the whole three years with them, exploring the tributaries of the Amazon. Martel told me he believed they never would have got through the expedition at all if it had not been for Rivarez."

"Whatever he may be," said Fabrizi; "there must be something remarkable about a man who could lay his 'come hither' on two old campaigners like Martel and Duprez as he seems to have done. What do you think, signora?"

"I know nothing about the matter; I was in England when the fugitives passed through Tuscany. But I should think that if the companions who were with a man on a three years' expedition in savage countries, and the comrades who were with him through an insurrection, think well of him, that is recommendation enough to counterbalance a good deal of boulevard gossip."

"There is no question about the opinion his comrades had of him," said Riccardo. "From Muratori and Zambeccari down to the roughest mountaineers they were all devoted to him. Moreover, he is a personal friend of Orsini. It's quite true, on the other hand, that there are endless cock-and-bull stories of a not very pleasant kind going about concerning him in Paris; but if a man doesn't want to make enemies he shouldn't become a political satirist."

"I'm not quite sure," interposed Lega; "but it seems to me that I saw him once when the refugees were here. Was he not hunchbacked, or crooked, or something of that kind?"

The professor had opened a drawer in his writing-table and was turning over a heap of papers. "I think I have his police description somewhere here," he said. "You remember when they escaped and hid in the mountain passes their personal appearance was posted up everywhere, and that Cardinal— what's the scoundrel's name?—Spinola, offered a reward for their heads."

"There was a splendid story about Rivarez and that police paper, by the way. He put on a soldier's old uniform and tramped across country as a carabineer wounded in the discharge of his duty and trying to find his company. He actually got Spinola's search-party to give him a lift, and rode the whole day in one of their waggons, telling them harrowing stories of how he had been taken captive by the rebels and dragged off into their haunts in the mountains, and of the fearful tortures that he had suffered at their hands. They showed him the description paper, and he told them all the rubbish he could think of about 'the fiend they call the Gadfly.' Then at night, when they were asleep, he poured a bucketful of water into their powder and decamped, with his pockets full of provisions and ammunition———"

"Ah, here's the paper," Fabrizi broke in: "'Felice Rivarez, called: The Gadfly. Age, about 30; birthplace and parentage, unknown, probably South American; profession, journalist. Short; black hair; black beard; dark skin; eyes, blue; forehead, broad and square; nose, mouth, chin———' Yes, here it is: 'Special marks: right foot lame; left arm twisted; two ringers missing on left hand; recent sabre-cut across face; stammers.' Then there's a note put: 'Very expert shot; care should be taken in arresting.'"

"It's an extraordinary thing that he can have managed to deceive the search-party with such a formidable list of identification marks."

"It was nothing but sheer audacity that carried him through, of course. If it had once occurred to them to suspect him he would have been lost. But the air of confiding innocence that he can put on when he chooses would bring a man through anything. Well, gentlemen, what do you think of the proposal?

Rivarez seems to be pretty well known to several of the company. Shall we suggest to him that we should be glad of his help here or not?"

"I think," said Fabrizi, "that he might be sounded upon the subject, just to find out whether he would be inclined to think of the plan."

"Oh, he'll be inclined, you may be sure, once it's a case of fighting the Jesuits; he is the most savage anti-clerical I ever met; in fact, he's rather rabid on the point."

"Then will you write, Riccardo?"

"Certainly. Let me see, where is he now? In Switzerland, I think. He's the most restless being; always flitting about. But as for the pamphlet question——"

They plunged into a long and animated discussion. When at last the company began to disperse Martini went up to the quiet young woman.

"I will see you home, Gemma."

"Thanks; I want to have a business talk with you."

"Anything wrong with the addresses?" he asked softly.

"Nothing serious; but I think it is time to make a few alterations. Two letters have been stopped in the post this week. They were both quite unimportant, and it may have been accidental; but we cannot afford to have any risks. If once the police have begun to suspect any of our addresses, they must be changed immediately."

"I will come in about that to-morrow. I am not going to talk business with you to-night; you look tired."

"I am not tired."

"Then you are depressed again."

"Oh, no; not particularly."

CHAPTER II

"Is the mistress in, Katie?"

"Yes, sir; she is dressing. If you'll just step into the parlour she will be down in a few minutes."

Katie ushered the visitor in with the cheerful friendliness of a true Devonshire girl. Martini was a special favourite of hers. He spoke English, like a foreigner, of course, but still quite respectably; and he never sat discussing politics at the top of his voice till one in the morning, when the mistress was tired, as some visitors had a way of doing. Moreover, he had come to Devonshire to help the mistress in her trouble, when her baby was dead and her husband dying there; and ever since that time the big, awkward, silent man had been to Katie as much "one of the family" as was the lazy black cat which now ensconced itself upon his knee. Pasht, for his part, regarded Martini as a useful piece of household furniture. This visitor never trod upon his tail, or puffed tobacco smoke into his eyes, or in any way obtruded upon his consciousness an aggressive biped personality. He behaved as a mere man should: provided a comfortable knee to lie upon and purr, and at table never forgot that to look on while human beings eat fish is not interesting for a cat. The friendship between them was of old date. Once, when Pasht was a kitten and his mistress too ill to think about him, he had come from England under Martini's care, tucked away in a basket. Since then, long experience had convinced him that this clumsy human bear was no fair-weather friend.

"How snug you look, you two!" said Gemma, coming into the room. "One would think you had settled yourselves for the evening."

Martini carefully lifted the cat off his knee. "I came early," he said, "in the hope that you will give me some tea before we start. There will probably be a frightful crush, and Grassini won't give us any sensible supper—they never do in those fashionable houses."

"Come now!" she said, laughing; "that's as bad as Galli! Poor Grassini has quite enough sins of his own to answer for without having his wife's imperfect housekeeping visited upon his head. As for the tea, it will be ready in a minute. Katie has been making some Devonshire cakes specially for you."

"Katie is a good soul, isn't she, Pasht? By the way, so are you to have put on that pretty dress. I was afraid you would forget."

"I promised you I would wear it, though it is rather warm for a hot evening like this."

"It will be much cooler up at Fiesole; and nothing else ever suits you so well as white cashmere. I have brought you some flowers to wear with it."

"Oh, those lovely cluster roses; I am so fond of them! But they had much better go into water. I hate to wear flowers."

"Now that's one of your superstitious fancies."

"No, it isn't; only I think they must get so bored, spending all the evening pinned to such a dull companion."

"I am afraid we shall all be bored to-night. The conversazione will be dull beyond endurance."

"Why?"

"Partly because everything Grassini touches becomes as dull as himself."

"Now don't be spiteful. It is not fair when we are going to be a man's guests."

"You are always right, Madonna. Well then, it will be dull because half the interesting people are not coming."

"How is that?"

"I don't know. Out of town, or ill, or something. Anyway, there will be two or three ambassadors and some learned Germans, and the usual nondescript crowd of tourists and Russian princes and literary club people, and a few French officers; nobody else that I know of—except, of course, the new satirist, who is to be the attraction of the evening."

"The new satirist? What, Rivarez? But I thought Grassini disapproved of him so strongly."

"Yes; but once the man is here and is sure to be talked about, of course Grassini wants his house to be the first place where the new lion will be on show. You may be sure Rivarez has heard nothing of Grassini's disapproval. He may have guessed it, though; he's sharp enough."

"I did not even know he had come."

"He only arrived yesterday. Here comes the tea. No, don't get up; let me fetch the kettle."

He was never so happy as in this little study. Gemma's friendship, her grave unconsciousness of the charm she exercised over him, her frank and simple comradeship were the brightest things for him in a life that was none too bright; and whenever he began to feel more than usually depressed he would come in here after business hours and sit with her, generally in silence, watching her as she bent over her needlework or poured out tea. She never questioned him about his troubles or expressed any sympathy in words; but he always went away stronger and calmer, feeling, as he put it to himself, that he could "trudge through another fortnight quite respectably." She possessed, without knowing it, the rare gift of consolation; and when, two years ago, his dearest friends had been betrayed in Calabria and shot down like wolves, her steady faith had been perhaps the thing which had saved him from despair.

On Sunday mornings he sometimes came in to "talk business," that expression standing for anything connected with the practical work of the Mazzinian party, of which they both were active and devoted members. She was quite a different creature then; keen, cool, and logical, perfectly accurate and perfectly neutral. Those who saw her only at her political work regarded her as a trained and disciplined conspirator, trustworthy, courageous, in every way a valuable member of the party, but somehow lacking in life and individuality. "She's a born conspirator, worth any dozen of us; and she is nothing more," Galli had said of her. The "Madonna Gemma" whom Martini knew was very difficult to get at.

"Well, and what is your 'new satirist' like?" she asked, glancing back over her shoulder as she opened the sideboard. "There, Cesare, there are barley-sugar and candied angelica for you. I wonder, by the way, why revolutionary men are always so fond of sweets."

"Other men are, too, only they think it beneath their dignity to confess it. The new satirist? Oh, the kind of man that ordinary women will rave over and you will dislike. A sort of professional dealer in sharp speeches, that goes about the world with a lackadaisical manner and a handsome ballet-girl dangling on to his coat-tails."

"Do you mean that there is really a ballet-girl, or simply that you feel cross and want to imitate the sharp speeches?"

"The Lord defend me! No; the ballet-girl is real enough and handsome enough, too, for those who like shrewish beauty. Personally, I don't. She's a Hungarian gipsy, or something of that kind, so Riccardo says; from some provincial theatre in Galicia. He seems to be rather a cool hand; he has been introducing the girl to people just as if she were his maiden aunt."

"Well, that's only fair if he has taken her away from her home."

"You may look at things that way, dear Madonna, but society won't. I think most people will very much resent being introduced to a woman whom they know to be his mistress."

"How can they know it unless he tells them so?"

"It's plain enough; you'll see if you meet her. But I should think even he would not have the audacity to bring her to the Grassinis'."

"They wouldn't receive her. Signora Grassini is not the woman to do unconventional things of that kind. But I wanted to hear about Signor Rivarez as a satirist, not as a man. Fabrizi told me he had been written to and had consented to come and take up the campaign against the Jesuits; and that is the last I have heard. There has been such a rush of work this week."

"I don't know that I can tell you much more. There doesn't seem to have been any difficulty over the money question, as we feared there would be. He's well off, it appears, and willing to work for nothing."

"Has he a private fortune, then?" "Apparently he has; though it seems rather odd—you heard that night at Fabrizi's about the state the Duprez expedition found him in. But he has got shares in mines somewhere out in Brazil; and then he has been immensely successful as a feuilleton writer in Paris and Vienna and London. He seems to have half a dozen languages at his finger-tips; and there's nothing to prevent his keeping up his newspaper connections from here. Slanging the Jesuits won't take all his time."

"That's true, of course. It's time to start, Cesare. Yes, I will wear the roses. Wait just a minute."

She ran upstairs, and came back with the roses in the bosom of her dress, and a long scarf of black Spanish lace thrown over her head. Martini surveyed her with artistic approval.

"You look like a queen, Madonna mia; like the great and wise Queen of Sheba."

"What an unkind speech!" she retorted, laughing; "when you know how hard I've been trying to mould myself into the image of the typical society lady! Who wants a conspirator to look like the Queen of Sheba? That's not the way to keep clear of spies."

"You'll never be able to personate the stupid society woman if you try for ever. But it doesn't matter, after all; you're too fair to look upon for spies to guess your opinions, even though you can't simper and hide behind your fan like Signora Grassini."

"Now Cesare, let that poor woman alone! There, take some more barley-sugar to sweeten your temper. Are you ready? Then we had better start."

Martini had been quite right in saying that the conversazione would be both crowded and dull. The literary men talked polite small-talk and looked hopelessly bored, while the "nondescript crowd of tourists and Russian princes" fluttered up and down the rooms, asking each other who were the various celebrities and trying to carry on intellectual conversation. Grassini was receiving his guests with a manner as carefully polished as his boots; but his cold face lighted up at the sight of Gemma. He did not really like her and indeed was secretly a little afraid of her; but he realized that without her his drawing room would lack a great attraction. He had risen high in his profession, and now that he was rich and well known his chief ambition was to make of his house a centre of liberal and intellectual society. He was painfully conscious that the insignificant, overdressed little woman whom in his youth he had made the mistake of marrying was not fit, with her vapid talk and faded prettiness, to be the mistress of a great literary salon. When he could prevail upon Gemma to come he always felt that the evening would be a success. Her quiet graciousness of manner set the guests at their ease, and her very presence seemed to lay the spectre of vulgarity which always, in his imagination, haunted the house.

Signora Grassini greeted Gemma affectionately, exclaiming in a loud whisper: "How charming you look to-night!" and examining the white cashmere with viciously critical eyes. She hated her visitor rancourously, for the very things for which Martini loved her; for her quiet strength of character; for her grave, sincere directness; for the steady balance of her mind; for the very expression of her face. And when Signora Grassini hated a woman, she showed it by effusive tenderness. Gemma took the compliments and endearments for what they were worth, and troubled her head no more about them. What is called "going into society" was in her eyes one of the wearisome and rather unpleasant tasks which a conspirator who wishes not to attract the notice of spies must conscientiously fulfil. She classed it together with the laborious work of writing in cipher; and, knowing how valuable a practical safeguard against suspicion is the reputation of being a well-dressed woman, studied the fashion-plates as carefully as she did the keys of her ciphers.

The bored and melancholy literary lions brightened up a little at the sound of Gemma's name; she was very popular among them; and the radical journalists, especially, gravitated at once to her end of the long room. But she was far too practised a conspirator to let them monopolize her. Radicals could be had any day; and now, when they came crowding round her, she gently sent them about their business, reminding them with a smile that they need not waste their time on converting her when there were so many tourists in need of instruction. For her part, she devoted herself to an English M. P. whose sympathies the republican party was anxious to gain; and, knowing him to be a specialist on finance, she first won his attention by asking his opinion on a technical point concerning the Austrian currency, and then deftly turned the conversation to the condition of the Lombardo-Venetian revenue. The Englishman, who had expected to be bored with small-talk, looked askance at her, evidently fearing that he had fallen into the clutches of a blue-stocking; but finding that she was both pleasant to look at and interesting to talk to, surrendered completely and plunged into as grave a discussion of Italian finance as if she had been Metternich. When Grassini brought up a Frenchman "who wishes to ask Signora Bolla something about the history of Young Italy," the M. P. rose with a bewildered sense that perhaps there was more ground for Italian discontent than he had supposed.

Later in the evening Gemma slipped out on to the terrace under the drawing-room windows to sit alone for a few moments among the great camellias and oleanders. The close air and continually shifting crowd in the rooms were beginning to give her a headache. At the further end of the terrace stood a row of palms and tree-ferns, planted in large tubs which were hidden by a bank of lilies and other flowering plants. The whole formed a complete screen, behind which was a little nook commanding a beautiful view out across the valley. The branches of a pomegranate tree, clustered with late blossoms, hung beside the narrow opening between the plants.

In this nook Gemma took refuge, hoping that no one would guess her whereabouts until she had secured herself against the threatening headache by a little rest and silence. The night was warm and beautifully still; but coming out from the hot, close rooms she felt it cool, and drew her lace scarf about her head.

Presently the sounds of voices and footsteps approaching along the terrace roused her from the dreamy state into which she had fallen. She drew back into the shadow, hoping to escape notice and get a few more precious minutes of silence before again having to rack her tired brain for conversation. To her great annoyance the footsteps paused near to the screen; then Signora Grassini's thin, piping little voice broke off for a moment in its stream of chatter.

The other voice, a man's, was remarkably soft and musical; but its sweetness of tone was marred by a peculiar, purring drawl, perhaps mere affectation, more probably the result of a habitual effort to conquer some impediment of speech, but in any case very unpleasant.

"English, did you say?" it asked. "But surely the name is quite Italian. What was it—Bolla?"

"Yes; she is the widow of poor Giovanni Bolla, who died in England about four years ago,—don't you remember? Ah, I forgot—you lead such a wandering life; we can't expect you to know of all our unhappy country's martyrs—they are so many!"

Signora Grassini sighed. She always talked in this style to strangers; the role of a patriotic mourner for the sorrows of Italy formed an effective combination with her boarding-school manner and pretty infantine pout.

"Died in England!" repeated the other voice. "Was he a refugee, then? I seem to recognize the name, somehow; was he not connected with Young Italy in its early days?"

"Yes; he was one of the unfortunate young men who were arrested in '33—you remember that sad affair? He was released in a few months; then, two or three years later, when there was a warrant out against him again, he escaped to England. The next we heard was that he was married there. It was a most romantic affair altogether, but poor Bolla always was romantic."

"And then he died in England, you say?"

"Yes, of consumption; he could not stand that terrible English climate. And she lost her only child just before his death; it caught scarlet fever. Very sad, is it not? And we are all so fond of dear Gemma! She is a little stiff, poor thing; the English always are, you know; but I think her troubles have made her melancholy, and——"

Gemma stood up and pushed back the boughs of the pomegranate tree. This retailing of her private sorrows for purposes of small-talk was almost unbearable to her, and there was visible annoyance in her face as she stepped into the light.

"Ah! here she is!" exclaimed the hostess, with admirable coolness. "Gemma, dear, I was wondering where you could have disappeared to. Signor Felice Rivarez wishes to make your acquaintance."

"So it's the Gadfly," thought Gemma, looking at him with some curiosity. He bowed to her decorously enough, but his eyes glanced over her face and figure with a look which seemed to her insolently keen and inquisitorial.

"You have found a d-d-delightful little nook here," he remarked, looking at the thick screen; "and w-w-what a charming view!"

"Yes; it's a pretty corner. I came out here to get some air."

"It seems almost ungrateful to the good God to stay indoors on such a lovely night," said the hostess, raising her eyes to the stars. (She had good eyelashes and liked to show them.) "Look, signore! Would not our sweet Italy be heaven on earth if only she were free? To think that she should be a bond-slave, with such flowers and such skies!"

"And such patriotic women!" the Gadfly murmured in his soft, languid drawl.

Gemma glanced round at him in some trepidation; his impudence was too glaring, surely, to deceive anyone. But she had underrated Signora Grassini's appetite for compliments; the poor woman cast down her lashes with a sigh.

"Ah, signore, it is so little that a woman can do! Perhaps some day I may prove my right to the name of an Italian—who knows? And now I must go back to my social duties; the French ambassador has begged me to introduce his ward to all the notabilities; you must come in presently and see her. She is a most charming girl. Gemma, dear, I brought Signor Rivarez out to show him our beautiful view; I must leave him under your care. I know you will look after him and introduce him to everyone. Ah! there is that delightful Russian prince! Have you met him? They say he is a great favourite of the Emperor Nicholas. He is military commander of some Polish town with a name that nobody can pronounce. Quelle nuit magnifique! N'est-ce-pas, mon prince?"

She fluttered away, chattering volubly to a bull-necked man with a heavy jaw and a coat glittering with orders; and her plaintive dirges for "notre malheureuse patrie," interpolated with "charmant" and "mon prince," died away along the terrace.

Gemma stood quite still beside the pomegranate tree. She was sorry for the poor, silly little woman, and annoyed at the Gadfly's languid insolence. He was watching the retreating figures with an expression of face that angered her; it seemed ungenerous to mock at such pitiable creatures.

"There go Italian and—Russian patriotism," he said, turning to her with a smile; "arm in arm and mightily pleased with each other's company. Which do you prefer?"

She frowned slightly and made no answer.

"Of c-course," he went on; "it's all a question of p-personal taste; but I think, of the two, I like the Russian variety best—it's so thorough. If Russia had to depend on flowers and skies for her supremacy instead of on powder and shot, how long do you think 'mon prince' would k-keep that Polish fortress?"

"I think," she answered coldly, "that we can hold our personal opinions without ridiculing a woman whose guests we are."

"Ah, yes! I f-forgot the obligations of hospitality here in Italy; they are a wonderfully hospitable people, these Italians. I'm sure the Austrians find them so. Won't you sit down?"

He limped across the terrace to fetch a chair for her, and placed himself opposite to her, leaning against the balustrade. The light from a window was shining full on his face; and she was able to study it at her leisure.

She was disappointed. She had expected to see a striking and powerful, if not pleasant face; but the most salient points of his appearance were a tendency to foppishness in dress and rather more than a tendency to a certain veiled insolence of expression and manner. For the rest, he was as swarthy as a mulatto, and, notwithstanding his lameness, as agile as a cat. His whole personality was oddly suggestive of a black jaguar. The forehead and left cheek were terribly disfigured by the long crooked scar of the old sabre-cut; and she had already noticed that, when he began to stammer in speaking, that side of his face was affected with a nervous twitch. But for these defects he would have been, in a certain restless and uncomfortable way, rather handsome; but it was not an attractive face.

Presently he began again in his soft, murmuring purr ("Just the voice a jaguar would talk in, if it could speak and were in a good humour," Gemma said to herself with rising irritation).

"I hear," he said, "that you are interested in the radical press, and write for the papers."

"I write a little; I have not time to do much."

"Ah, of course! I understood from Signora Grassini that you undertake other important work as well."

Gemma raised her eyebrows slightly. Signora Grassini, like the silly little woman she was, had evidently been chattering imprudently to this slippery creature, whom Gemma, for her part, was beginning actually to dislike.

"My time is a good deal taken up," she said rather stiffly; "but Signora Grassini overrates the importance of my occupations. They are mostly of a very trivial character."

"Well, the world would be in a bad way if we ALL of us spent our time in chanting dirges for Italy. I should think the neighbourhood of our host of this evening and his wife would make anybody frivolous, in self-defence. Oh, yes, I know what you're going to say; you are perfectly right, but they are both so deliciously funny with their patriotism.—Are you going in already? It is so nice out here!"

"I think I will go in now. Is that my scarf? Thank you."

He had picked it up, and now stood looking at her with wide eyes as blue and innocent as forget-me-nots in a brook.

"I know you are offended with me," he said penitently, "for fooling that painted-up wax doll; but what can a fellow do?"

"Since you ask me, I do think it an ungenerous and—well—cowardly thing to hold one's intellectual inferiors up to ridicule in that way; it is like laughing at a cripple, or———"

He caught his breath suddenly, painfully; and shrank back, glancing at his lame foot and mutilated hand. In another instant he recovered his self-possession and burst out laughing.

"That's hardly a fair comparison, signora; we cripples don't flaunt our deformities in people's faces as she does her stupidity. At least give us credit for recognizing that crooked backs are no pleasanter than crooked ways. There is a step here; will you take my arm?"

She re-entered the house in embarrassed silence; his unexpected sensitiveness had completely disconcerted her.

Directly he opened the door of the great reception room she realized that something unusual had happened in her absence. Most of the gentlemen looked both angry and uncomfortable; the ladies, with hot cheeks and carefully feigned unconsciousness, were all collected at one end of the room; the host was fingering his eye-glasses with suppressed but unmistakable fury, and a little group of tourists stood in a corner casting amused glances at the further end of the room. Evidently something was going on there which appeared to them in the light of a joke, and to most of the guests in that of an insult. Signora Grassini alone did not appear to have noticed anything; she was fluttering her fan coquettishly and chattering to the secretary of the Dutch embassy, who listened with a broad grin on his face.

Gemma paused an instant in the doorway, turning to see if the Gadfly, too, had noticed the disturbed appearance of the company. There was no mistaking the malicious triumph in his eyes as he glanced from the face of the blissfully unconscious hostess to a sofa at the end of the room. She understood at once; he had brought his mistress here under some false colour, which had deceived no one but Signora Grassini.

The gipsy-girl was leaning back on the sofa, surrounded by a group of simpering dandies and blandly ironical cavalry officers. She was gorgeously dressed in amber and scarlet, with an Oriental brilliancy of tint and profusion of ornament as startling in a Florentine literary salon as if she had been some tropical bird among sparrows and starlings. She herself seemed to feel out of place, and looked at the offended ladies with a fiercely contemptuous scowl. Catching sight of the Gadfly as he crossed the room with Gemma, she sprang up and came towards him, with a voluble flood of painfully incorrect French.

"M. Rivarez, I have been looking for you everywhere! Count Saltykov wants to know whether you can go to his villa to-morrow night. There will be dancing."

"I am sorry I can't go; but then I couldn't dance if I did. Signora Bolla, allow me to introduce to you Mme. Zita Reni."

The gipsy glanced round at Gemma with a half defiant air and bowed stiffly. She was certainly handsome enough, as Martini had said, with a vivid, animal, unintelligent beauty; and the perfect harmony and freedom of her movements were delightful to see; but her forehead was low and narrow, and the line of her delicate nostrils was unsympathetic, almost cruel. The sense of oppression which Gemma had felt in the Gadfly's society was intensified by the gypsy's presence; and when, a moment later, the host came up to beg Signora Bolla to help him entertain some tourists in the other room, she consented with an odd feeling of relief.

"Well, Madonna, and what do you think of the Gadfly?" Martini asked as they drove back to Florence late at night. "Did you ever see anything quite so shameless as the way he fooled that poor little Grassini woman?"

"About the ballet-girl, you mean?"

"Yes, he persuaded her the girl was going to be the lion of the season. Signora Grassini would do anything for a celebrity."

"I thought it an unfair and unkind thing to do; it put the Grassinis into a false position; and it was nothing less than cruel to the girl herself. I am sure she felt ill at ease."

"You had a talk with him, didn't you? What did you think of him?"

"Oh, Cesare, I didn't think anything except how glad I was to see the last of him. I never met anyone so fearfully tiring. He gave me a headache in ten minutes. He is like an incarnate demon of unrest."

"I thought you wouldn't like him; and, to tell the truth, no more do I. The man's as slippery as an eel; I don't trust him."

CHAPTER III

THE Gadfly took lodgings outside the Roman gate, near to which Zita was boarding. He was evidently somewhat of a sybarite; and, though nothing in the rooms showed any serious extravagance, there was a tendency to luxuriousness in trifles and to a certain fastidious daintiness in the arrangement of everything which surprised Galli and Riccardo. They had expected to find a man who had lived among the wildernesses of the Amazon more simple in his tastes, and wondered at his spotless ties and rows of boots, and at the masses of flowers which always stood upon his writing table. On the whole they got on very well with him. He was hospitable and friendly to everyone, especially to the local members of the Mazzinian party. To this rule Gemma, apparently, formed an exception; he seemed to have taken a dislike to her from the time of their first meeting, and in every way avoided her company. On two or three occasions he was actually rude to her, thus bringing upon himself Martini's most cordial detestation. There had been no love lost between the two men from the beginning; their temperaments appeared to be too incompatible for them to feel anything but repugnance for each other. On Martini's part this was fast developing into hostility.

"I don't care about his not liking me," he said one day to Gemma with an aggrieved air. "I don't like him, for that matter; so there's no harm done. But I can't stand the way he behaves to you. If it weren't for the scandal it would make in the party first to beg a man to come and then to quarrel with him, I should call him to account for it."

"Let him alone, Cesare; it isn't of any consequence, and after all, it's as much my fault as his."

"What is your fault?"

"That he dislikes me so. I said a brutal thing to him when we first met, that night at the Grassinis'."

"YOU said a brutal thing? That's hard to believe, Madonna."

"It was unintentional, of course, and I was very sorry. I said something about people laughing at cripples, and he took it personally. It had never occurred to me to think of him as a cripple; he is not so badly deformed."

"Of course not. He has one shoulder higher than the other, and his left arm is pretty badly disabled, but he's neither hunchbacked nor clubfooted. As for his lameness, it isn't worth talking about."

"Anyway, he shivered all over and changed colour. Of course it was horribly tactless of me, but it's odd he should be so sensitive. I wonder if he has ever suffered from any cruel jokes of that kind."

"Much more likely to have perpetrated them, I should think. There's a sort of internal brutality about that man, under all his fine manners, that is perfectly sickening to me."

"Now, Cesare, that's downright unfair. I don't like him any more than you do, but what is the use of making him out worse than he is? His manner is a little affected and irritating—I expect he has been too much lionized—and the everlasting smart speeches are dreadfully tiring; but I don't believe he means any harm."

"I don't know what he means, but there's something not clean about a man who sneers at everything. It fairly disgusted me the other day at Fabrizi's debate to hear the way he cried down the reforms in Rome, just as if he wanted to find a foul motive for everything."

Gemma sighed. "I am afraid I agreed better with him than with you on that point," she said. "All you good people are so full of the most delightful hopes and expectations; you are always ready to think that if one well-meaning middle-aged gentleman happens to get elected Pope, everything else will come right of itself. He has only got to throw open the prison doors and give his blessing to everybody all round, and we may expect the millennium within three months. You never seem able to see that he can't set things right even if he would. It's the principle of the thing that's wrong, not the behaviour of this man or that."

"What principle? The temporal power of the Pope?"

"Why that in particular? That's merely a part of the general wrong. The bad principle is that any man should hold over another the power to bind and loose. It's a false relationship to stand in towards one's fellows."

Martini held up his hands. "That will do, Madonna," he said, laughing. "I am not going to discuss with you, once you begin talking rank Antinomianism in that fashion. I'm sure your ancestors must have been English Levellers in the seventeenth century. Besides, what I came round about is this MS."

He pulled it out of his pocket.

"Another new pamphlet?"

"A stupid thing this wretched man Rivarez sent in to yesterday's committee. I knew we should come to loggerheads with him before long."

"What is the matter with it? Honestly, Cesare, I think you are a little prejudiced. Rivarez may be unpleasant, but he's not stupid."

"Oh, I don't deny that this is clever enough in its way; but you had better read the thing yourself."

The pamphlet was a skit on the wild enthusiasm over the new Pope with which Italy was still ringing. Like all the Gadfly's writing, it was bitter and vindictive; but, notwithstanding her irritation at the style, Gemma could not help recognizing in her heart the justice of the criticism.

"I quite agree with you that it is detestably malicious," she said, laying down the manuscript. "But the worst thing about it is that it's all true."

"Gemma!"

"Yes, but it is. The man's a cold-blooded eel, if you like; but he's got the truth on his side. There is no use in our trying to persuade ourselves that this doesn't hit the mark—it does!"

"Then do you suggest that we should print it?"

"Ah! that's quite another matter. I certainly don't think we ought to print it as it stands; it would hurt and alienate everybody and do no good. But if he would rewrite it and cut out the personal attacks, I think it might be made into a really valuable piece of work. As political criticism it is very fine. I had no idea he could write so well. He says things which need saying and which none of us have had the courage to say. This passage, where he compares Italy to a tipsy man weeping with tenderness on the neck of the thief who is picking his pocket, is splendidly written."

"Gemma! The very worst bit in the whole thing! I hate that ill-natured yelping at everything and everybody!"

"So do I; but that's not the point. Rivarez has a very disagreeable style, and as a human being he is not attractive; but when he says that we have made ourselves drunk with processions and embracing and shouting about love and reconciliation, and that the Jesuits and Sanfedists are the people who will profit by it all, he's right a thousand times. I wish I could have been at the committee yesterday. What decision did you finally arrive at?"

"What I have come here about: to ask you to go and talk it over with him and persuade him to soften the thing."

"Me? But I hardly know the man; and besides that, he detests me. Why should I go, of all people?"

"Simply because there's no one else to do it to-day. Besides, you are more reasonable than the rest of us, and won't get into useless arguments and quarrel with him, as we should."

"I shan't do that, certainly. Well, I will go if you like, though I have not much hope of success."

"I am sure you will be able to manage him if you try. Yes, and tell him that the committee all admired the thing from a literary point of view. That will put him into a good humour, and it's perfectly true, too."

The Gadfly was sitting beside a table covered with flowers and ferns, staring absently at the floor, with an open letter on his knee. A shaggy collie dog, lying on a rug at his feet, raised its head and growled as Gemma knocked at the open door, and the Gadfly rose hastily and bowed in a stiff, ceremonious way. His face had suddenly grown hard and expressionless.

"You are too kind," he said in his most chilling manner. "If you had let me know that you wanted to speak to me I would have called on you."

Seeing that he evidently wished her at the end of the earth, Gemma hastened to state her business. He bowed again and placed a chair for her.

"The committee wished me to call upon you," she began, "because there has been a certain difference of opinion about your pamphlet."

"So I expected." He smiled and sat down opposite to her, drawing a large vase of chrysanthemums between his face and the light.

"Most of the members agreed that, however much they may admire the pamphlet as a literary composition, they do not think that in its present form it is quite suitable for publication. They fear that the vehemence of its tone may give offence, and alienate persons whose help and support are valuable to the party."

He pulled a chrysanthemum from the vase and began slowly plucking off one white petal after another. As her eyes happened to catch the movement of the slim right hand dropping the petals, one by one, an uncomfortable sensation came over Gemma, as though she had somewhere seen that gesture before.

"As a literary composition," he remarked in his soft, cold voice, "it is utterly worthless, and could be admired only by persons who know nothing about literature. As for its giving offence, that is the very thing I intended it to do."

"That I quite understand. The question is whether you may not succeed in giving offence to the wrong people."

He shrugged his shoulders and put a torn-off petal between his teeth. "I think you are mistaken," he said. "The question is: For what purpose did your committee invite me to come here? I understood, to expose and ridicule the Jesuits. I fulfil my obligation to the best of my ability."

"And I can assure you that no one has any doubt as to either the ability or the good-will. What the committee fears is that the liberal party may take offence, and also that the town workmen may withdraw their moral support. You may have meant the pamphlet for an attack upon the Sanfedists: but many readers will construe it as an attack upon the Church and the new Pope; and this, as a matter of political tactics, the committee does not consider desirable."

"I begin to understand. So long as I keep to the particular set of clerical gentlemen with whom the party is just now on bad terms, I may speak sooth if the fancy takes me; but directly I touch upon the committee's own pet priests—'truth's a dog must to kennel; he must be whipped out, when the—Holy Father may stand by the fire and——-' Yes, the fool was right; I'd rather be any kind of a thing than a fool. Of course I must bow to the committee's decision, but I continue to think that it has pared its wit o' both sides and left—M-mon-signor M-m-montan-n-nelli in the middle."

"Montanelli?" Gemma repeated. "I don't understand you. Do you mean the Bishop of Brisighella?"

"Yes; the new Pope has just created him a Cardinal, you know. I have a letter about him here. Would you care to hear it? The writer is a friend of mine on the other side of the frontier."

"The Papal frontier?"

"Yes. This is what he writes——" He took up the letter which had been in his hand when she entered, and read aloud, suddenly beginning to stammer violently:

"'Y-o-you will s-s-s-soon have the p-pleasure of m-m-meeting one of our w-w-worst enemies, C-cardinal Lorenzo M-montan-n-nelli, the B-b-bishop of Brisig-g-hella. He int-t——'"

He broke off, paused a moment, and began again, very slowly and drawling insufferably, but no longer stammering:

~ 69 ~

"'He intends to visit Tuscany during the coming month on a mission of reconciliation. He will preach first in Florence, where he will stay for about three weeks; then will go on to Siena and Pisa, and return to the Romagna by Pistoja. He ostensibly belongs to the liberal party in the Church, and is a personal friend of the Pope and Cardinal Feretti. Under Gregory he was out of favour, and was kept out of sight in a little hole in the Apennines. Now he has come suddenly to the front. Really, of course, he is as much pulled by Jesuit wires as any Sanfedist in the country. This mission was suggested by some of the Jesuit fathers. He is one of the most brilliant preachers in the Church, and as mischievous in his way as Lambruschini himself. His business is to keep the popular enthusiasm over the Pope from subsiding, and to occupy the public attention until the Grand Duke has signed a project which the agents of the Jesuits are preparing to lay before him. What this project is I have been unable to discover.' Then, further on, it says: 'Whether Montanelli understands for what purpose he is being sent to Tuscany, or whether the Jesuits are playing on him, I cannot make out. He is either an uncommonly clever knave, or the biggest ass that was ever foaled. The odd thing is that, so far as I can discover, he neither takes bribes nor keeps mistresses—the first time I ever came across such a thing.'"

He laid down the letter and sat looking at her with half-shut eyes, waiting, apparently, for her to speak.

"Are you satisfied that your informant is correct in his facts?" she asked after a moment.

"As to the irreproachable character of Monsignor M-mon-t-tan-nelli's private life? No; but neither is he. As you will observe, he puts in the s-s-saving clause: 'So far as I c-can discover——

"I was not speaking of that," she interposed coldly, "but of the part about this mission."

"I can fully trust the writer. He is an old friend of mine—one of my comrades of '43, and he is in a position which gives him exceptional opportunities for finding out things of that kind."

"Some official at the Vatican," thought Gemma quickly. "So that's the kind of connections you have? I guessed there was something of that sort."

"This letter is, of course, a private one," the Gadfly went on; "and you understand that the information is to be kept strictly to the members of your committee."

"That hardly needs saying. Then about the pamphlet: may I tell the committee that you consent to make a few alterations and soften it a little, or that——"

"Don't you think the alterations may succeed in spoiling the beauty of the 'literary composition,' signora, as well as in reducing the vehemence of the tone?"

"You are asking my personal opinion. What I have come here to express is that of the committee as a whole."

"Does that imply that y-y-you disagree with the committee as a whole?" He had put the letter into his pocket and was now leaning forward and looking at her with an eager, concentrated expression which quite changed the character of his face. "You think———"

"If you care to know what I personally think—I disagree with the majority on both points. I do not at all admire the pamphlet from a literary point of view, and I do think it true as a presentation of facts and wise as a matter of tactics."

"That is———"

"I quite agree with you that Italy is being led away by a will-o'-the-wisp and that all this enthusiasm and rejoicing will probably land her in a terrible bog; and I should be most heartily glad to have that openly and boldly said, even at the cost of offending or alienating some of our present supporters. But as a member of a body the large majority of which holds the opposite view, I cannot insist upon my personal opinion; and I certainly think that if things of that kind are to be said at all, they should be said temperately and quietly; not in the tone adopted in this pamphlet."

"Will you wait a minute while I look through the manuscript?"

He took it up and glanced down the pages. A dissatisfied frown settled on his face.

"Yes, of course, you are perfectly right. The thing's written like a cafe chantant skit, not a political satire. But what's a man to do? If I write decently the public won't understand it; they will say it's dull if it isn't spiteful enough."

"Don't you think spitefulness manages to be dull when we get too much of it?"

He threw a keen, rapid glance at her, and burst out laughing.

"Apparently the signora belongs to the dreadful category of people who are always right! Then if I yield to the temptation to be spiteful, I may come in time to be as dull as Signora Grassini? Heavens, what a fate! No, you needn't frown. I know you don't like me, and I am going to keep to business. What it comes to, then, is practically this: if I cut out the personalities and leave the essential part of the thing as it is, the committee will very much regret that they can't take the responsibility of printing it. If I cut out the political truth and make all the hard names apply to no one but the party's enemies, the committee will praise the thing up to the skies, and you and I will know it's not worth printing. Rather a nice point of metaphysics: Which is the more desirable condition, to be printed and not be worth it, or to be worth it and not be printed? Well, signora?"

"I do not think you are tied to any such alternative. I believe that if you were to cut out the personalities the committee would consent to print the pamphlet, though the majority would, of course, not agree with it; and I am convinced that it would be very useful. But you would have to lay aside the spitefulness. If you are going to say a thing the substance of which is a big pill for your readers to swallow, there is no use in frightening them at the beginning by the form."

He sighed and shrugged his shoulders resignedly. "I submit, signora; but on one condition. If you rob me of my laugh now, I must have it out next time. When His Eminence, the irreproachable Cardinal, turns up in Florence, neither you nor your committee must object to my being as spiteful as I like. It's my due!"

He spoke in his lightest, coldest manner, pulling the chrysanthemums out of their vase and holding them up to watch the light through the translucent petals. "What an unsteady hand he has," she thought, seeing how the flowers shook and quivered. "Surely he doesn't drink!"

"You had better discuss the matter with the other members of the committee," she said, rising. "I cannot form any opinion as to what they will think about it."

"And you?" He had risen too, and was leaning against the table, pressing the flowers to his face.

She hesitated. The question distressed her, bringing up old and miserable associations. "I—hardly know," she said at last. "Many years ago I used to know something about Monsignor Montanelli. He was only a canon at that time, and Director of the theological seminary in the province where I lived as a girl. I heard a great deal about him from—someone who knew him very intimately; and I never heard anything of him that was not good. I believe that, in those days at least, he was really a most remarkable man. But that was long ago, and he may have changed. Irresponsible power corrupts so many people."

The Gadfly raised his head from the flowers, and looked at her with a steady face.

"At any rate," he said, "if Monsignor Montanelli is not himself a scoundrel, he is a tool in scoundrelly hands. It is all one to me which he is—and to my friends across the frontier. A stone in the path may have the best intentions, but it must be kicked out of the path, for all that. Allow me, signora!" He rang the bell, and, limping to the door, opened it for her to pass out.

"It was very kind of you to call, signora. May I send for a vettura? No? Good-afternoon, then! Bianca, open the hall-door, please."

Gemma went out into the street, pondering anxiously. "My friends across the frontier"—who were they? And how was the stone to be kicked out of the path? If with satire only, why had he said it with such dangerous eyes?

CHAPTER IV

MONSIGNOR MONTANELLI arrived in Florence in the first week of October. His visit caused a little flutter of excitement throughout the town. He was a famous preacher and a representative of the reformed Papacy; and people looked eagerly to him for an exposition of the "new doctrine," the gospel of love and reconciliation which was to cure the sorrows of Italy. The nomination of Cardinal Gizzi to the Roman State Secretaryship in place of the universally detested Lambruschini had raised the public enthusiasm to its highest pitch; and Montanelli was just the man who could most easily sustain it. The irreproachable strictness of his life was a phenomenon sufficiently rare among the high dignitaries of the Roman Church to attract the attention of people accustomed to regard blackmailing, peculation, and disreputable intrigues as almost invariable adjuncts to the career of a prelate. Moreover, his talent as a preacher was really great; and with his beautiful voice and magnetic personality, he would in any time and place have made his mark.

Grassini, as usual, strained every nerve to get the newly arrived celebrity to his house; but Montanelli was no easy game to catch. To all invitations he replied with the same courteous but positive refusal, saying that his health was bad and his time fully occupied, and that he had neither strength nor leisure for going into society.

"What omnivorous creatures those Grassinis are!" Martini said contemptuously to Gemma as they crossed the Signoria square one bright, cold Sunday morning. "Did you notice the way Grassini bowed when the Cardinal's carriage drove up? It's all one to them who a man is, so long as he's talked about. I never saw such lion-hunters in my life. Only last August it was the Gadfly; now it's Montanelli. I hope His Eminence feels flattered at the attention; a precious lot of adventurers have shared it with him."

They had been hearing Montanelli preach in the Cathedral; and the great building had been so thronged with eager listeners that Martini, fearing a return of Gemma's troublesome headaches, had persuaded her to come away before the Mass was over. The sunny morning, the first after a week of rain, offered him an excuse for suggesting a walk among the garden slopes by San Niccolo.

"No," she answered; "I should like a walk if you have time; but not to the hills. Let us keep along the Lung'Arno; Montanelli will pass on his way back from church and I am like Grassini—I want to see the notability."

"But you have just seen him."

"Not close. There was such a crush in the Cathedral, and his back was turned to us when the carriage passed. If we keep near to the bridge we shall be sure to see him well—he is staying on the Lung'Arno, you know."

"But what has given you such a sudden fancy to see Montanelli? You never used to care about famous preachers."

"It is not famous preachers; it is the man himself; I want to see how much he has changed since I saw him last."

"When was that?"

"Two days after Arthur's death."

Martini glanced at her anxiously. They had come out on to the Lung'Arno, and she was staring absently across the water, with a look on her face that he hated to see.

"Gemma, dear," he said after a moment; "are you going to let that miserable business haunt you all your life? We have all made mistakes when we were seventeen."

"We have not all killed our dearest friend when we were seventeen," she answered wearily; and, leaning her arm on the stone balustrade of the bridge, looked down into the river. Martini held his tongue; he was almost afraid to speak to her when this mood was on her.

"I never look down at water without remembering," she said, slowly raising her eyes to his; then with a nervous little shiver: "Let us walk on a bit, Cesare; it is chilly for standing."

They crossed the bridge in silence and walked on along the river-side. After a few minutes she spoke again.

"What a beautiful voice that man has! There is something about it that I have never heard in any other human voice. I believe it is the secret of half his influence."

"It is a wonderful voice," Martini assented, catching at a subject of conversation which might lead her away from the dreadful memory called up by the river, "and he is, apart from his voice, about the finest preacher I have ever heard. But I believe the secret of his influence lies deeper than that. It is the way his life stands out from that of almost all the other prelates. I don't know whether you could lay your hand on one other high dignitary in all the Italian Church—except the Pope himself—whose reputation is so utterly spotless. I remember, when I was in the Romagna last year, passing through his diocese and seeing those fierce mountaineers waiting in the rain to get a glimpse of him or touch his dress. He is venerated there almost as a saint; and that means a good deal among the Romagnols, who generally hate everything that wears a cassock. I remarked to one of the old peasants,—as typical a smuggler as ever I saw in my life,—that the people seemed very much devoted to their bishop, and he said: 'We don't love bishops, they are liars; we love Monsignor Montanelli. Nobody has ever known him to tell a lie or do an unjust thing.'"

"I wonder," Gemma said, half to herself, "if he knows the people think that about him."

"Why shouldn't he know it? Do you think it is not true?"

"I know it is not true."

"How do you know it?"

"Because he told me so."

"HE told you? Montanelli? Gemma, what do you mean?"

She pushed the hair back from her forehead and turned towards him. They were standing still again, he leaning on the balustrade and she slowly drawing lines on the pavement with the point of her umbrella.

"Cesare, you and I have been friends for all these years, and I have never told you what really happened about Arthur."

"There is no need to tell me, dear," he broke in hastily; "I know all about it already."

"Giovanni told you?"

"Yes, when he was dying. He told me about it one night when I was sitting up with him. He said—— Gemma, dear, I had better tell you the truth, now we have begun talking about it—he said that you were always brooding over that wretched story, and he begged me to be as good a friend to you as I could and try to keep you from thinking of it. And I have tried to, dear, though I may not have succeeded—I have, indeed."

"I know you have," she answered softly, raising her eyes for a moment; "I should have been badly off without your friendship. But—Giovanni did not tell you about Monsignor Montanelli, then?"

"No, I didn't know that he had anything to do with it. What he told me was about—all that affair with the spy, and about——"

"About my striking Arthur and his drowning himself. Well, I will tell you about Montanelli."

They turned back towards the bridge over which the Cardinal's carriage would have to pass. Gemma looked out steadily across the water as she spoke.

"In those days Montanelli was a canon; he was Director of the Theological Seminary at Pisa, and used to give Arthur lessons in philosophy and read with him after he went up to the Sapienza. They were perfectly devoted to each other; more like two lovers than teacher and pupil. Arthur almost worshipped the ground that Montanelli walked on, and I remember his once telling me that if he lost his 'Padre'—he always used to call Montanelli so—he should go and drown himself. Well, then you know what happened about the spy. The next day, my father and the Burtons—Arthur's stepbrothers, most detestable people—spent the whole day dragging the Darsena basin for the body; and I sat in my room alone and thought of what I had done——"

She paused a moment, and went on again:

"Late in the evening my father came into my room and said: 'Gemma, child, come downstairs; there's a man I want you to see.' And when we went down there was one of the students belonging to the group sitting in the consulting room, all white and shaking; and he told us about Giovanni's second letter coming from the prison to say that they had heard from the jailer about Cardi, and that Arthur had been tricked in the confessional. I remember the student saying to me: 'It is at least some consolation that we know he was innocent' My father held my hands and tried to comfort me; he did not know then about the blow. Then I went back to my room and sat there all night alone. In the morning my father went out again with the Burtons to see the harbour dragged. They had some hope of finding the body there."

"It was never found, was it?"

"No; it must have got washed out to sea; but they thought there was a chance. I was alone in my room and the servant came up to say that a 'reverendissimo padre' had called and she had told him my father was at the docks and he had gone away. I knew it must be Montanelli; so I ran out at the back door and caught him up at the garden gate. When I said: 'Canon Montanelli, I want to speak to you,' he just stopped and waited silently for me to speak. Oh, Cesare, if you had seen his face—it haunted me for months afterwards! I said: 'I am Dr. Warren's daughter, and I have come to tell you that it is I who have killed Arthur.' I told him everything, and he stood and listened, like a figure cut in stone, till I had finished; then he said: 'Set your heart at rest, my child; it is I that am a murderer, not you. I deceived him and he found it out.' And with that he turned and went out at the gate without another word."

"And then?"

"I don't know what happened to him after that; I heard the same evening that he had fallen down in the street in a kind of fit and had been carried into a house near the docks; but that is all I know. My father did everything he could for me; when I told him about it he threw up his practice and took me away to England at once, so that I should never hear anything that could remind me. He was afraid I should end in the water, too; and indeed I believe I was near it at one time. But then, you know, when we found out that my father had cancer I was obliged to come to myself—there was no one else to nurse him. And after he died I was left with the little ones on my hands until my elder brother was able to give them a home. Then there was Giovanni. Do you know, when he came to England we were almost afraid to meet each other with that frightful memory between us. He was so bitterly remorseful for his share in it all—that unhappy letter he wrote from prison. But I believe, really, it was our common trouble that drew us together."

Martini smiled and shook his head.

"It may have been so on your side," he said; "but Giovanni had made up his mind from the first time he ever saw you. I remember his coming back to Milan after that first visit to Leghorn and raving about you to me till I was perfectly sick of hearing of the English Gemma. I thought I should hate you. Ah! there it comes!"

The carriage crossed the bridge and drove up to a large house on the Lung'Arno. Montanelli was leaning back on the cushions as if too tired to care any longer for the enthusiastic crowd which had collected round the door to catch a glimpse of him. The inspired look that his face had worn in the Cathedral had faded quite away and the sunlight showed the lines of care and fatigue. When he had alighted and passed, with the heavy, spiritless tread of weary and heart-sick old age, into the house, Gemma turned away and walked slowly to the bridge. Her face seemed for a moment to reflect the withered, hopeless look of his. Martini walked beside her in silence.

"I have so often wondered," she began again after a little pause; "what he meant about the deception. It has sometimes occurred to me——"

"Yes?"

"Well, it is very strange; there was the most extraordinary personal resemblance between them."

"Between whom?"

"Arthur and Montanelli. It was not only I who noticed it. And there was something mysterious in the relationship between the members of that household. Mrs. Burton, Arthur's mother, was one of the sweetest women I ever knew. Her face had the same spiritual look as Arthur's, and I believe they were alike in character, too. But she always seemed half frightened, like a detected criminal; and her step-son's wife used to treat her as no decent person treats a dog. And then Arthur himself was such a startling contrast to all those vulgar Burtons. Of course, when one is a child one takes everything for granted; but looking back on it afterwards I have often wondered whether Arthur was really a Burton."

"Possibly he found out something about his mother—that may easily have been the cause of his death, not the Cardi affair at all," Martini interposed, offering the only consolation he could think of at the moment. Gemma shook her head.

"If you could have seen his face after I struck him, Cesare, you would not think that. It may be all true about Montanelli—very likely it is—but what I have done I have done."

They walked on a little way without speaking.

"My dear," Martini said at last; "if there were any way on earth to undo a thing that is once done, it would be worth while to brood over our old mistakes; but as it is, let the dead bury their dead. It is a terrible story, but at least the poor lad is out of it now, and luckier than some of those that are left— the ones that are in exile and in prison. You and I have them to think of, we have no right to eat out our hearts for the dead. Remember what your own Shelley says: 'The past is Death's, the future is thine own.' Take it, while it is still yours, and fix your mind, not on what you may have done long ago to hurt, but on what you can do now to help."

In his earnestness he had taken her hand. He dropped it suddenly and drew back at the sound of a soft, cold, drawling voice behind him.

"Monsignor Montan-n-nelli," murmured this languid voice, "is undoubtedly all you say, my dear doctor. In fact, he appears to be so much too good for this world that he ought to be politely escorted into the next. I am sure he would cause as great a sensation there as he has done here; there are p-p-probably many old-established ghosts who have never seen such a thing as an honest cardinal. And there is nothing that ghosts love as they do novelties——"

"How do you know that?" asked Dr. Riccardo's voice in a tone of ill-suppressed irritation.

"From Holy Writ, my dear sir. If the Gospel is to be trusted, even the most respectable of all Ghosts had a f-f-fancy for capricious alliances. Now, honesty and c-c-cardinals—that seems to me a somewhat capricious alliance, and rather an uncomfortable one, like shrimps and liquorice. Ah, Signor Martini, and Signora Bolla! Lovely weather after the rain, is it not? Have you been to hear the n-new Savonarola, too?"

Martini turned round sharply. The Gadfly, with a cigar in his mouth and a hot-house flower in his buttonhole, was holding out to him a slender, carefully-gloved hand. With the sunlight reflected in his immaculate boots and glancing back from the water on to his smiling face, he looked to Martini less lame and more conceited than usual. They were shaking hands, affably on the one side and rather sulkily on the other, when Riccardo hastily exclaimed:

"I am afraid Signora Bolla is not well!"

She was so pale that her face looked almost livid under the shadow of her bonnet, and the ribbon at her throat fluttered perceptibly from the violent beating of the heart.

"I will go home," she said faintly.

A cab was called and Martini got in with her to see her safely home. As the Gadfly bent down to arrange her cloak, which was hanging over the wheel, he raised his eyes suddenly to her face, and Martini saw that she shrank away with a look of something like terror.

"Gemma, what is the matter with you?" he asked, in English, when they had started. "What did that scoundrel say to you?"

"Nothing, Cesare; it was no fault of his. I—I—had a fright——"

"A fright?"

"Yes; I fancied——" She put one hand over her eyes, and he waited silently till she should recover her self-command. Her face was already regaining its natural colour.

"You are quite right," she said at last, turning to him and speaking in her usual voice; "it is worse than useless to look back at a horrible past. It plays tricks with one's nerves and makes one imagine all sorts of impossible things. We will NEVER talk about that subject again, Cesare, or I shall see fantastic likenesses to Arthur in every face I meet. It is a kind of hallucination, like a nightmare in broad daylight. Just now, when that odious little fop came up, I fancied it was Arthur."

CHAPTER V

THE Gadfly certainly knew how to make personal enemies. He had arrived in Florence in August, and by the end of October three-fourths of the committee which had invited him shared Martini's opinion. His savage attacks upon Montanelli had annoyed even his admirers; and Galli himself, who at first had been inclined to uphold everything the witty satirist said or did, began to acknowledge with an aggrieved air that Montanelli had better have been left in peace. "Decent cardinals are none so plenty. One might treat them politely when they do turn up."

The only person who, apparently, remained quite indifferent to the storm of caricatures and pasquinades was Montanelli himself. It seemed, as Martini said, hardly worth while to expend one's energy in ridiculing a man who took it so good-humouredly. It was said in the town that Montanelli, one day when the Archbishop of Florence was dining with him, had found in the room one of the Gadfly's bitter personal lampoons against himself, had read it through and handed the paper to the Archbishop, remarking: "That is rather cleverly put, is it not?"

One day there appeared in the town a leaflet, headed: "The Mystery of the Annunciation." Even had the author omitted his now familiar signature, a sketch of a gadfly with spread wings, the bitter, trenchant style would have left in the minds of most readers no doubt as to his identity. The skit was in the form of a dialogue between Tuscany as the Virgin Mary, and Montanelli as the angel who, bearing the lilies of purity and crowned with the olive branch of peace, was announcing the advent of the Jesuits. The whole thing was full of offensive personal allusions and hints of the most risky nature, and all Florence felt the satire to be both ungenerous and unfair. And yet all Florence laughed. There was something so irresistible in the Gadfly's grave absurdities that those who most disapproved of and disliked him laughed as immoderately at all his squibs as did his warmest partisans. Repulsive in tone as the leaflet was, it left its trace upon the popular feeling of the town. Montanelli's personal reputation stood too high for any lampoon, however witty, seriously to injure it, but for a moment the tide almost turned against him. The Gadfly had known where to sting; and, though eager crowds still collected before the Cardinal's house to see him enter or leave his carriage, ominous cries of "Jesuit!" and "Sanfedist spy!" often mingled with the cheers and benedictions.

But Montanelli had no lack of supporters. Two days after the publication of the skit, the Churchman, a leading clerical paper, brought out a brilliant article, called: "An Answer to 'The Mystery of the Annunciation,'" and signed: "A Son of the Church." It was an impassioned defence of Montanelli against the Gadfly's slanderous imputations. The anonymous writer, after expounding, with great eloquence and fervour, the doctrine of peace on earth and good will towards men, of which the new Pontiff was the evangelist, concluded by challenging the Gadfly to prove a single one of his assertions, and solemnly appealing to the public not to believe a contemptible slanderer. Both the cogency of the article as a bit of special pleading and its merit as a literary composition were sufficiently far above the average to attract much attention in the town, especially as not even the editor of the newspaper could guess the author's identity. The article was soon reprinted separately in pamphlet form; and the "anonymous defender" was discussed in every coffee-shop in Florence.

The Gadfly responded with a violent attack on the new Pontificate and all its supporters, especially on Montanelli, who, he cautiously hinted, had probably consented to the panegyric on himself. To this the anonymous defender again replied in the Churchman with an indignant denial. During the rest of Montanelli's stay the controversy raging between the two writers occupied more of the public attention than did even the famous preacher himself.

Some members of the liberal party ventured to remonstrate with the Gadfly about the unnecessary malice of his tone towards Montanelli; but they did not get much satisfaction out of him. He only smiled affably and answered with a languid little stammer: "R-really, gentlemen, you are rather unfair. I expressly stipulated, when I gave in to Signora Bolla, that I should be allowed a l-l-little chuckle all to myself now. It is so nominated in the bond!"

At the end of October Montanelli returned to his see in the Romagna, and, before leaving Florence, preached a farewell sermon in which he spoke of the controversy, gently deprecating the vehemence of both writers and begging his unknown defender to set an example of tolerance by closing a useless and unseemly war of words. On the following day the Churchman contained a notice that, at Monsignor Montanelli's publicly expressed desire, "A Son of the Church" would withdraw from the controversy.

The last word remained with the Gadfly. He issued a little leaflet, in which he declared himself disarmed and converted by Montanelli's Christian meekness and ready to weep tears of reconciliation upon the neck of the first Sanfedist he met. "I am even willing," he concluded; "to embrace my anonymous challenger himself; and if my readers knew, as his Eminence and I know, what that implies and why he remains anonymous, they would believe in the sincerity of my conversion."

In the latter part of November he announced to the literary committee that he was going for a fortnight's holiday to the seaside. He went, apparently, to Leghorn; but Dr. Riccardo, going there soon after and wishing to speak to him, searched the town for him in vain. On the 5th of December a political demonstration of the most extreme character burst out in the States of the Church, along the whole chain of the Apennines; and people began to guess the reason of the Gadfly's sudden fancy to take his holidays in the depth of winter.

He came back to Florence when the riots had been quelled, and, meeting Riccardo in the street, remarked affably:

"I hear you were inquiring for me in Leghorn; I was staying in Pisa. What a pretty old town it is! There's something quite Arcadian about it."

In Christmas week he attended an afternoon meeting of the literary committee which was held in Dr. Riccardo's lodgings near the Porta alla Croce. The meeting was a full one, and when he came in, a little late, with an apologetic bow and smile, there seemed to be no seat empty. Riccardo rose to fetch a chair from the next room, but the Gadfly stopped him. "Don't trouble about it," he said; "I shall be quite comfortable here"; and crossing the room to a window beside which Gemma had placed her chair, he sat down on the sill, leaning his head indolently back against the shutter.

As he looked down at Gemma, smiling with half-shut eyes, in the subtle, sphinx-like way that gave him the look of a Leonardo da Vinci portrait, the instinctive distrust with which he inspired her deepened into a sense of unreasoning fear.

The proposal under discussion was that a pamphlet be issued setting forth the committee's views on the dearth with which Tuscany was threatened and the measures which should be taken to meet it. The matter was a somewhat difficult one to decide, because, as usual, the committee's views upon the subject were much divided. The more advanced section, to which Gemma, Martini, and Riccardo belonged, was in favour of an energetic appeal to both government and public to take adequate measures at once for the relief of the peasantry. The moderate division—including, of course, Grassini—feared that an over-emphatic tone might irritate rather than convince the ministry.

"It is all very well, gentlemen, to want the people helped at once," he said, looking round upon the red-hot radicals with his calm and pitying air. "We most of us want a good many things that we are not likely to get; but if we start with the tone you propose to adopt, the government is very likely not to begin any relief measures at all till there is actual famine. If we could only induce the ministry to make an inquiry into the state of the crops it would be a step in advance."

Galli, in his corner by the stove, jumped up to answer his enemy.

"A step in advance—yes, my dear sir; but if there's going to be a famine, it won't wait for us to advance at that pace. The people might all starve before we got to any actual relief."

"It would be interesting to know——" Sacconi began; but several voices interrupted him.

"Speak up; we can't hear!"

"I should think not, with such an infernal row in the street," said Galli, irritably. "Is that window shut, Riccardo? One can't hear one's self speak!"

Gemma looked round. "Yes," she said, "the window is quite shut. I think there is a variety show, or some such thing, passing."

The sounds of shouting and laughter, of the tinkling of bells and trampling of feet, resounded from the street below, mixed with the braying of a villainous brass band and the unmerciful banging of a drum.

"It can't be helped these few days," said Riccardo; "we must expect noise at Christmas time. What were you saying, Sacconi?"

"I said it would be interesting to hear what is thought about the matter in Pisa and Leghorn. Perhaps Signor Rivarez can tell us something; he has just come from there."

The Gadfly did not answer. He was staring out of the window and appeared not to have heard what had been said.

"Signor Rivarez!" said Gemma. She was the only person sitting near to him, and as he remained silent she bent forward and touched him on the arm. He slowly turned his face to her, and she started as she saw its fixed and awful immobility. For a moment it was like the face of a corpse; then the lips moved in a strange, lifeless way.

"Yes," he whispered; "a variety show."

Her first instinct was to shield him from the curiosity of the others. Without understanding what was the matter with him, she realized that some frightful fancy or hallucination had seized upon him, and that, for the moment, he was at its mercy, body and soul. She rose quickly and, standing between him and the company, threw the window open as if to look out. No one but herself had seen his face.

In the street a travelling circus was passing, with mountebanks on donkeys and harlequins in parti-coloured dresses. The crowd of holiday masqueraders, laughing and shoving, was exchanging jests and showers of paper ribbon with the clowns and flinging little bags of sugar-plums to the columbine, who sat in her car, tricked out in tinsel and feathers, with artificial curls on her forehead and an artificial smile on her painted lips. Behind the car came a motley string of figures—street Arabs, beggars, clowns turning somersaults, and costermongers hawking their wares. They were jostling, pelting, and applauding a figure which at first Gemma could not see for the pushing and swaying of the crowd. The next moment, however, she saw plainly what it was—a hunchback, dwarfish and ugly, grotesquely attired in a fool's dress, with paper cap and bells. He evidently belonged to the strolling company, and was amusing the crowd with hideous grimaces and contortions.

"What is going on out there?" asked Riccardo, approaching the window. "You seem very much interested."

He was a little surprised at their keeping the whole committee waiting to look at a strolling company of mountebanks. Gemma turned round.

"It is nothing interesting," she said; "only a variety show; but they made such a noise that I thought it must be something else."

She was standing with one hand upon the window-sill, and suddenly felt the Gadfly's cold fingers press the hand with a passionate clasp. "Thank you!" he whispered softly; and then, closing the window, sat down again upon the sill.

"I'm afraid," he said in his airy manner, "that I have interrupted you, gentlemen. I was l-looking at the variety show; it is s-such a p-pretty sight."

"Sacconi was asking you a question," said Martini gruffly. The Gadfly's behaviour seemed to him an absurd piece of affectation, and he was annoyed that Gemma should have been tactless enough to follow his example. It was not like her.

The Gadfly disclaimed all knowledge of the state of feeling in Pisa, explaining that he had been there "only on a holiday." He then plunged at once into an animated discussion, first of agricultural prospects, then of the pamphlet question; and continued pouring out a flood of stammering talk till the others were quite tired. He seemed to find some feverish delight in the sound of his own voice.

When the meeting ended and the members of the committee rose to go, Riccardo came up to Martini.

"Will you stop to dinner with me? Fabrizi and Sacconi have promised to stay."

"Thanks; but I was going to see Signora Bolla home."

"Are you really afraid I can't get home by myself?" she asked, rising and putting on her wrap. "Of course he will stay with you, Dr. Riccardo; it's good for him to get a change. He doesn't go out half enough."

"If you will allow me, I will see you home," the Gadfly interposed; "I am going in that direction."

"If you really are going that way——"

"I suppose you won't have time to drop in here in the course of the evening, will you, Rivarez?" asked Riccardo, as he opened the door for them.

The Gadfly looked back over his shoulder, laughing. "I, my dear fellow? I'm going to see the variety show!"

"What a strange creature that is; and what an odd affection for mountebanks!" said Riccardo, coming back to his visitors.

"Case of a fellow-feeling, I should think," said Martini; "the man's a mountebank himself, if ever I saw one."

"I wish I could think he was only that," Fabrizi interposed, with a grave face. "If he is a mountebank I am afraid he's a very dangerous one."

"Dangerous in what way?"

"Well, I don't like those mysterious little pleasure trips that he is so fond of taking. This is the third time, you know; and I don't believe he has been in Pisa at all."

"I suppose it is almost an open secret that it's into the mountains he goes," said Sacconi. "He has hardly taken the trouble to deny that he is still in relations with the smugglers he got to know in the Savigno affair, and it's quite natural he should take advantage of their friendship to get his leaflets across the Papal frontier."

"For my part," said Riccardo; "what I wanted to talk to you about is this very question. It occurred to me that we could hardly do better than ask Rivarez to undertake the management of our own smuggling. That press at Pistoja is very inefficiently managed, to my thinking; and the way the leaflets are taken across, always rolled in those everlasting cigars, is more than primitive."

"It has answered pretty well up till now," said Martini contumaciously. He was getting wearied of hearing Galli and Riccardo always put the Gadfly forward as a model to copy, and inclined to think that the world had gone well enough before this "lackadaisical buccaneer" turned up to set everyone to rights.

"It has answered so far well that we have been satisfied with it for want of anything better; but you know there have been plenty of arrests and confiscations. Now I believe that if Rivarez undertook the business for us, there would be less of that."

"Why do you think so?"

"In the first place, the smugglers look upon us as strangers to do business with, or as sheep to fleece, whereas Rivarez is their personal friend, very likely their leader, whom they look up to and trust. You may be sure every smuggler in the Apennines will do for a man who was in the Savigno revolt what he will not do for us. In the next place, there's hardly a man among us that knows the mountains as Rivarez does. Remember, he has been a fugitive among them, and knows the smugglers' paths by heart. No smuggler would dare to cheat him, even if he wished to, and no smuggler could cheat him if he dared to try."

"Then is your proposal that we should ask him to take over the whole management of our literature on the other side of the frontier—distribution, addresses, hiding-places, everything—or simply that we should ask him to put the things across for us?"

"Well, as for addresses and hiding-places, he probably knows already all the ones that we have and a good many more that we have not. I don't suppose we should be able to teach him much in that line. As for distribution, it's as the others prefer, of course. The important question, to my mind, is the actual smuggling itself. Once the books are safe in Bologna, it's a comparatively simple matter to circulate them."

"For my part," said Martini, "I am against the plan. In the first place, all this about his skilfulness is mere conjecture; we have not actually seen him engaged in frontier work and do not know whether he keeps his head in critical moments."

"Oh, you needn't have any doubt of that!" Riccardo put in. "The history of the Savigno affair proves that he keeps his head."

"And then," Martini went on; "I do not feel at all inclined, from what little I know of Rivarez, to intrust him with all the party's secrets. He seems to me feather-brained and theatrical. To give the whole management of a party's contraband work into a man's hands is a serious matter. Fabrizi, what do you think?"

"If I had only such objections as yours, Martini," replied the professor, "I should certainly waive them in the case of a man really possessing, as Rivarez undoubtedly does, all the qualifications Riccardo speaks of. For my part, I have not the slightest doubt as to either his courage, his honesty, or his presence of mind; and that he knows both mountains and mountaineers we have had ample proof. But there is another objection. I do not feel sure that it is only for the smuggling of pamphlets he goes into the mountains. I have begun to doubt whether he has not another purpose. This is, of course, entirely between ourselves. It is a mere suspicion. It seems to me just possible that he is in connexion with some one of the 'sects,' and perhaps with the most dangerous of them."

"Which one do you mean—the 'Red Girdles'?"

"No; the 'Occoltellatori.'"

"The 'Knifers'! But that is a little body of outlaws—peasants, most of them, with neither education nor political experience."

"So were the insurgents of Savigno; but they had a few educated men as leaders, and this little society may have the same. And remember, it's pretty well known that most of the members of those more violent sects in the Romagna are survivors of the Savigno affair, who found themselves too weak to fight the Churchmen in open insurrection, and so have fallen back on assassination. Their hands are not strong enough for guns, and they take to knives instead."

"But what makes you suppose Rivarez to be connected with them?"

"I don't suppose, I merely suspect. In any case, I think we had better find out for certain before we intrust our smuggling to him. If he attempted to do both kinds of work at once he would injure our party most terribly; he would simply destroy its reputation and accomplish nothing. However, we will talk of that another time. I wanted to speak to you about the news from Rome. It is said that a commission is to be appointed to draw up a project for a municipal constitution."

CHAPTER VI

GEMMA and the Gadfly walked silently along the Lung'Arno. His feverish talkativeness seemed to have quite spent itself; he had hardly spoken a word since they left Riccardo's door, and Gemma was heartily glad of his silence. She always felt embarrassed in his company, and to-day more so than usual, for his strange behaviour at the committee meeting had greatly perplexed her.

By the Uffizi palace he suddenly stopped and turned to her.

"Are you tired?"

"No; why?"

"Nor especially busy this evening?"

"No."

"I want to ask a favour of you; I want you to come for a walk with me."

"Where to?"

"Nowhere in particular; anywhere you like."

"But what for?"

He hesitated.

"I—can't tell you—at least, it's very difficult; but please come if you can."

He raised his eyes suddenly from the ground, and she saw how strange their expression was.

"There is something the matter with you," she said gently. He pulled a leaf from the flower in his button-hole, and began tearing it to pieces. Who was it that he was so oddly like? Someone who had that same trick of the fingers and hurried, nervous gesture.

"I am in trouble," he said, looking down at his hands and speaking in a hardly audible voice. "I—don't want to be alone this evening. Will you come?"

"Yes, certainly, unless you would rather go to my lodgings."

"No; come and dine with me at a restaurant. There's one on the Signoria. Please don't refuse, now; you've promised!"

They went into a restaurant, where he ordered dinner, but hardly touched his own share, and remained obstinately silent, crumbling the bread over the cloth, and fidgeting with the fringe of his table napkin. Gemma felt thoroughly uncomfortable, and began to wish she had refused to come; the silence was growing awkward; yet she could not begin to make small-talk with a person who seemed to have forgotten her presence. At last he looked up and said abruptly:

"Would you like to see the variety show?"

She stared at him in astonishment. What had he got into his head about variety shows?

"Have you ever seen one?" he asked before she had time to speak.

"No; I don't think so. I didn't suppose they were interesting."

"They are very interesting. I don't think anyone can study the life of the people without seeing them. Let us go back to the Porta alla Croce."

When they arrived the mountebanks had set up their tent beside the town gate, and an abominable scraping of fiddles and banging of drums announced that the performance had begun.

The entertainment was of the roughest kind. A few clowns, harlequins, and acrobats, a circus-rider jumping through hoops, the painted columbine, and the hunchback performing various dull and foolish antics, represented the entire force of the company. The jokes were not, on the whole, coarse or offensive; but they were very tame and stale, and there was a depressing flatness about the whole thing. The audience laughed and clapped from their innate Tuscan courtesy; but the only part which they seemed really to enjoy was the performance of the hunchback, in which Gemma could find nothing either witty or skilful. It was merely a series of grotesque and hideous contortions, which the spectators mimicked, holding up children on their shoulders that the little ones might see the "ugly man."

"Signor Rivarez, do you really think this attractive?" said Gemma, turning to the Gadfly, who was standing beside her, his arm round one of the wooden posts of the tent. "It seems to me——"

She broke off and remained looking at him silently. Except when she had stood with Montanelli at the garden gate in Leghorn, she had never seen a human face express such fathomless, hopeless misery. She thought of Dante's hell as she watched him.

Presently the hunchback, receiving a kick from one of the clowns, turned a somersault and tumbled in a grotesque heap outside the ring. A dialogue between two clowns began, and the Gadfly seemed to wake out of a dream.

"Shall we go?" he asked; "or would you like to see more?"

"I would rather go."

They left the tent, and walked across the dark green to the river. For a few moments neither spoke.

"What did you think of the show?" the Gadfly asked presently.

"I thought it rather a dreary business; and part of it seemed to me positively unpleasant."

"Which part?"

"Well, all those grimaces and contortions. They are simply ugly; there is nothing clever about them."

"Do you mean the hunchback's performance?"

Remembering his peculiar sensitiveness on the subject of his own physical defects, she had avoided mentioning this particular bit of the entertainment; but now that he had touched upon the subject himself, she answered: "Yes; I did not like that part at all."

"That was the part the people enjoyed most."

"I dare say; and that is just the worst thing about it."

"Because it was inartistic?"

"N-no; it was all inartistic. I meant—because it was cruel."

He smiled.

"Cruel? Do you mean to the hunchback?"

"I mean—— Of course the man himself was quite indifferent; no doubt, it is to him just a way of getting a living, like the circus-rider's way or the columbine's. But the thing makes one feel unhappy. It is humiliating; it is the degradation of a human being."

"He probably is not any more degraded than he was to start with. Most of us are degraded in one way or another."

"Yes; but this—I dare say you will think it an absurd prejudice; but a human body, to me, is a sacred thing; I don't like to see it treated irreverently and made hideous."

"And a human soul?"

He had stopped short, and was standing with one hand on the stone balustrade of the embankment, looking straight at her.

"A soul?" she repeated, stopping in her turn to look at him in wonder.

He flung out both hands with a sudden, passionate gesture.

"Has it never occurred to you that that miserable clown may have a soul—a living, struggling, human soul, tied down into that crooked hulk of a body and forced to slave for it? You that are so tender-hearted to everything—you that pity the body in its fool's dress and bells—have you never thought of the wretched soul that has not even motley to cover its horrible nakedness? Think of it shivering with cold, stilled with shame and misery, before all those people—feeling their jeers that cut like a whip—their laughter, that burns like red-hot iron on the bare flesh! Think of it looking round—so helpless before them all—for the mountains that will not fall on it—for the rocks that have not the heart to cover it—envying the rats that can creep into some hole in the earth and hide; and remember that a soul is dumb—it has no voice to cry out—it must endure, and endure, and endure. Oh! I'm talking nonsense! Why on earth don't you laugh? You have no sense of humour!"

Slowly and in dead silence she turned and walked on along the river side. During the whole evening it had not once occurred to her to connect his trouble, whatever it might be, with the variety show; and now that some dim picture of his inner life had been revealed to her by this sudden outburst, she could not find, in her overwhelming pity for him, one word to say. He walked on beside her, with his head turned away, and looked into the water.

"I want you, please, to understand," he began suddenly, turning to her with a defiant air, "that everything I have just been saying to you is pure imagination. I'm rather given to romancing, but I don't like people to take it seriously."

She made no answer, and they walked on in silence. As they passed by the gateway of the Uffizi, he crossed the road and stooped down over a dark bundle that was lying against the railings.

"What is the matter, little one?" he asked, more gently than she had ever heard him speak. "Why don't you go home?"

The bundle moved, and answered something in a low, moaning voice. Gemma came across to look, and saw a child of about six years old, ragged and dirty, crouching on the pavement like a frightened animal. The Gadfly was bending down with his hand on the unkempt head.

"What is it?" he said, stooping lower to catch the unintelligible answer. "You ought to go home to bed; little boys have no business out of doors at night; you'll be quite frozen! Give me your hand and jump up like a man! Where do you live?"

He took the child's arm to raise him. The result was a sharp scream and a quick shrinking away.

"Why, what is it?" the Gadfly asked, kneeling down on the pavement. "Ah! Signora, look here!"

The child's shoulder and jacket were covered with blood.

"Tell me what has happened?" the Gadfly went on caressingly. "It wasn't a fall, was it? No? Someone's been beating you? I thought so! Who was it?"

"My uncle."

"Ah, yes! And when was it?"

"This morning. He was drunk, and I—I——"

"And you got in his way—was that it? You shouldn't get in people's way when they are drunk, little man; they don't like it. What shall we do with this poor mite, signora? Come here to the light, sonny, and let me look at that shoulder. Put your arm round my neck; I won't hurt you. There we are!"

He lifted the boy in his arms, and, carrying him across the street, set him down on the wide stone balustrade. Then, taking out a pocket-knife, he deftly ripped up the torn sleeve, supporting the child's head against his breast, while Gemma held the injured arm. The shoulder was badly bruised and grazed, and there was a deep gash on the arm.

"That's an ugly cut to give a mite like you," said the Gadfly, fastening his handkerchief round the wound to prevent the jacket from rubbing against it. "What did he do it with?"

"The shovel. I went to ask him to give me a soldo to get some polenta at the corner shop, and he hit me with the shovel."

The Gadfly shuddered. "Ah!" he said softly, "that hurts; doesn't it, little one?"

"He hit me with the shovel—and I ran away—I ran away—because he hit me."

"And you've been wandering about ever since, without any dinner?"

Instead of answering, the child began to sob violently. The Gadfly lifted him off the balustrade.

"There, there! We'll soon set all that straight. I wonder if we can get a cab anywhere. I'm afraid they'll all be waiting by the theatre; there's a grand performance going on to-night. I am sorry to drag you about so, signora; but——"

"I would rather come with you. You may want help. Do you think you can carry him so far? Isn't he very heavy?"

"Oh, I can manage, thank you."

At the theatre door they found only a few cabs waiting, and these were all engaged. The performance was over, and most of the audience had gone. Zita's name was printed in large letters on the wall-placards; she had been dancing in the ballet. Asking Gemma to wait for him a moment, the Gadfly went round to the performers' entrance, and spoke to an attendant.

"Has Mme. Reni gone yet?"

"No, sir," the man answered, staring blankly at the spectacle of a well-dressed gentleman carrying a ragged street child in his arms, "Mme. Reni is just coming out, I think; her carriage is waiting for her. Yes; there she comes."

Zita descended the stairs, leaning on the arm of a young cavalry officer. She looked superbly handsome, with an opera cloak of flame-coloured velvet thrown over her evening dress, and a great fan of ostrich plumes hanging from her waist. In the entry she stopped short, and, drawing her hand away from the officer's arm, approached the Gadfly in amazement.

"Felice!" she exclaimed under her breath, "what HAVE you got there?"

"I have picked up this child in the street. It is hurt and starving; and I want to get it home as quickly as possible. There is not a cab to be got anywhere, so I want to have your carriage."

"Felice! you are not going to take a horrid beggar-child into your rooms! Send for a policeman, and let him carry it to the Refuge or whatever is the proper place for it. You can't have all the paupers in the town——"

"It is hurt," the Gadfly repeated; "it can go to the Refuge to-morrow, if necessary, but I must see to the child first and give it some food."

Zita made a little grimace of disgust. "You've got its head right against your shirt! How CAN you? It is dirty!"

The Gadfly looked up with a sudden flash of anger.

"It is hungry," he said fiercely. "You don't know what that means, do you?"

"Signer Rivarez," interposed Gemma, coming forward, "my lodgings are quite close. Let us take the child in there. Then, if you cannot find a vettura, I will manage to put it up for the night."

He turned round quickly. "You don't mind?"

"Of course not. Good-night, Mme. Reni!"

The gipsy, with a stiff bow and an angry shrug of her shoulders, took her officer's arm again, and, gathering up the train of her dress, swept past them to the contested carriage.

"I will send it back to fetch you and the child, if you like, M. Rivarez," she said, pausing on the doorstep.

"Very well; I will give the address." He came out on to the pavement, gave the address to the driver, and walked back to Gemma with his burden.

Katie was waiting up for her mistress; and, on hearing what had happened, ran for warm water and other necessaries. Placing the child on a chair, the Gadfly knelt down beside him, and, deftly slipping off the ragged clothing, bathed and bandaged the wound with tender, skilful hands. He had just finished washing the boy, and was wrapping him in a warm blanket, when Gemma came in with a tray in her hands.

~ 90 ~

"Is your patient ready for his supper?" she asked, smiling at the strange little figure. "I have been cooking it for him."

The Gadfly stood up and rolled the dirty rags together. "I'm afraid we have made a terrible mess in your room," he said. "As for these, they had better go straight into the fire, and I will buy him some new clothes to-morrow. Have you any brandy in the house, signora? I think he ought to have a little. I will just wash my hands, if you will allow me."

When the child had finished his supper, he immediately went to sleep in the Gadfly's arms, with his rough head against the white shirt-front. Gemma, who had been helping Katie to set the disordered room tidy again, sat down at the table.

"Signor Rivarez, you must take something before you go home—you had hardly any dinner, and it's very late."

"I should like a cup of tea in the English fashion, if you have it. I'm sorry to keep you up so late."

"Oh! that doesn't matter. Put the child down on the sofa; he will tire you. Wait a minute; I will just lay a sheet over the cushions. What are you going to do with him?"

"To-morrow? Find out whether he has any other relations except that drunken brute; and if not, I suppose I must follow Mme. Reni's advice, and take him to the Refuge. Perhaps the kindest thing to do would be to put a stone round his neck and pitch him into the river there; but that would expose me to unpleasant consequences. Fast asleep! What an odd little lump of ill-luck you are, you mite—not half as capable of defending yourself as a stray cat!"

When Katie brought in the tea-tray, the boy opened his eyes and sat up with a bewildered air. Recognizing the Gadfly, whom he already regarded as his natural protector, he wriggled off the sofa, and, much encumbered by the folds of his blanket, came up to nestle against him. He was by now sufficiently revived to be inquisitive; and, pointing to the mutilated left hand, in which the Gadfly was holding a piece of cake, asked:

"What's that?"

"That? Cake; do you want some? I think you've had enough for now. Wait till to-morrow, little man."

"No—that!" He stretched out his hand and touched the stumps of the amputated fingers and the great scar on the wrist. The Gadfly put down his cake.

"Oh, that! It's the same sort of thing as what you have on your shoulder—a hit I got from someone stronger than I was."

"Didn't it hurt awfully?"

"Oh, I don't know—not more than other things. There, now, go to sleep again; you have no business asking questions at this time of night."

When the carriage arrived the boy was again asleep; and the Gadfly, without awaking him, lifted him gently and carried him out on to the stairs.

"You have been a sort of ministering angel to me to-day," he said to Gemma, pausing at the door. "But I suppose that need not prevent us from quarrelling to our heart's content in future."

"I have no desire to quarrel with anyone."

"Ah! but I have. Life would be unendurable without quarrels. A good quarrel is the salt of the earth; it's better than a variety show!"

And with that he went downstairs, laughing softly to himself, with the sleeping child in his arms.

CHAPTER VII

ONE day in the first week of January Martini, who had sent round the forms of invitation to the monthly group-meeting of the literary committee, received from the Gadfly a laconic, pencil-scrawled "Very sorry: can't come." He was a little annoyed, as a notice of "important business" had been put into the invitation; this cavalier treatment seemed to him almost insolent. Moreover, three separate letters containing bad news arrived during the day, and the wind was in the east, so that Martini felt out of sorts and out of temper; and when, at the group meeting, Dr. Riccardo asked, "Isn't Rivarez here?" he answered rather sulkily: "No; he seems to have got something more interesting on hand, and can't come, or doesn't want to."

"Really, Martini," said Galli irritably, "you are about the most prejudiced person in Florence. Once you object to a man, everything he does is wrong. How could Rivarez come when he's ill?"

"Who told you he was ill?"

"Didn't you know? He's been laid up for the last four days."

"What's the matter with him?"

"I don't know. He had to put off an appointment with me on Thursday on account of illness; and last night, when I went round, I heard that he was too ill to see anyone. I thought Riccardo would be looking after him."

"I knew nothing about it. I'll go round to-night and see if he wants anything."

The next morning Riccardo, looking very pale and tired, came into Gemma's little study. She was sitting at the table, reading out monotonous strings of figures to Martini, who, with a magnifying glass in one hand and a finely pointed pencil in the other, was making tiny marks in the pages of a book. She made with one hand a gesture requesting silence. Riccardo, knowing that a person who is writing in cipher must not be interrupted, sat down on the sofa behind her and yawned like a man who can hardly keep awake.

"2, 4; 3, 7; 6, 1; 3, 5; 4, 1;" Gemma's voice went on with machine-like evenness. "8, 4; 7, 2; 5, 1; that finishes the sentence, Cesare."

She stuck a pin into the paper to mark the exact place, and turned round.

"Good-morning, doctor; how fagged you look! Are you well?"

"Oh, I'm well enough—only tired out. I've had an awful night with Rivarez."

"With Rivarez?"

"Yes; I've been up with him all night, and now I must go off to my hospital patients. I just came round to know whether you can think of anyone that could look after him a bit for the next few days. He's in a devil of a state. I'll do my best, of course; but I really haven't the time; and he won't hear of my sending in a nurse."

"What is the matter with him?"

"Well, rather a complication of things. First of all——"

"First of all, have you had any breakfast?"

"Yes, thank you. About Rivarez—no doubt, it's complicated with a lot of nerve trouble; but the main cause of disturbance is an old injury that seems to have been disgracefully neglected. Altogether, he's in a frightfully knocked-about state; I suppose it was that war in South America—and he certainly didn't get proper care when the mischief was done. Probably things were managed in a very rough-and-ready fashion out there; he's lucky to be alive at all. However, there's a chronic tendency to inflammation, and any trifle may bring on an attack——"

"Is that dangerous?"

"N-no; the chief danger in a case of that kind is of the patient getting desperate and taking a dose of arsenic."

"It is very painful, of course?"

"It's simply horrible; I don't know how he manages to bear it. I was obliged to stupefy him with opium in the night—a thing I hate to do with a nervous patient; but I had to stop it somehow."

"He is nervous, I should think."

"Very, but splendidly plucky. As long as he was not actually light-headed with the pain last night, his coolness was quite wonderful. But I had an awful job with him towards the end. How long do you suppose this thing has been going on? Just five nights; and not a soul within call except that stupid landlady, who wouldn't wake if the house tumbled down, and would be no use if she did."

"But what about the ballet-girl?"

"Yes; isn't that a curious thing? He won't let her come near him. He has a morbid horror of her. Altogether, he's one of the most incomprehensible creatures I ever met—a perfect mass of contradictions."

He took out his watch and looked at it with a preoccupied face. "I shall be late at the hospital; but it can't be helped. The junior will have to begin without me for once. I wish I had known of all this before—it ought not to have been let go on that way night after night."

"But why on earth didn't he send to say he was ill?" Martini interrupted. "He might have guessed we shouldn't have left him stranded in that fashion."

"I wish, doctor," said Gemma, "that you had sent for one of us last night, instead of wearing yourself out like this."

"My dear lady, I wanted to send round to Galli; but Rivarez got so frantic at the suggestion that I didn't dare attempt it. When I asked him whether there was anyone else he would like fetched, he looked at me for a minute, as if he were scared out of his wits, and then put up both hands to his eyes and said: 'Don't tell them; they will laugh!' He seemed quite possessed with some fancy about people laughing at something. I couldn't make out what; he kept talking Spanish; but patients do say the oddest things sometimes."

"Who is with him now?" asked Gemma.

"No one except the landlady and her maid."

"I'll go to him at once," said Martini.

"Thank you. I'll look round again in the evening. You'll find a paper of written directions in the table-drawer by the large window, and the opium is on the shelf in the next room. If the pain comes on again, give him another dose—not more than one; but don't leave the bottle where he can get at it, whatever you do; he might be tempted to take too much."

When Martini entered the darkened room, the Gadfly turned his head round quickly, and, holding out to him a burning hand, began, in a bad imitation of his usual flippant manner:

"Ah, Martini! You have come to rout me out about those proofs. It's no use swearing at me for missing the committee last night; the fact is, I have not been quite well, and——"

"Never mind the committee. I have just seen Riccardo, and have come to know if I can be of any use."

The Gadfly set his face like a flint.

"Oh, really! that is very kind of you; but it wasn't worth the trouble. I'm only a little out of sorts."

"So I understood from Riccardo. He was up with you all night, I believe."

The Gadfly bit his lip savagely.

"I am quite comfortable, thank you, and don't want anything."

"Very well; then I will sit in the other room; perhaps you would rather be alone. I will leave the door ajar, in case you call me."

"Please don't trouble about it; I really shan't want anything. I should be wasting your time for nothing."

"Nonsense, man!" Martini broke in roughly. "What's the use of trying to fool me that way? Do you think I have no eyes? Lie still and go to sleep, if you can."

He went into the adjoining room, and, leaving the door open, sat down with a book. Presently he heard the Gadfly move restlessly two or three times. He put down his book and listened. There was a short silence, then another restless movement; then the quick, heavy, panting breath of a man clenching his teeth to suppress a groan. He went back into the room.

"Can I do anything for you, Rivarez?"

There was no answer, and he crossed the room to the bed-side. The Gadfly, with a ghastly, livid face, looked at him for a moment, and silently shook his head.

"Shall I give you some more opium? Riccardo said you were to have it if the pain got very bad."

"No, thank you; I can bear it a bit longer. It may be worse later on."

Martini shrugged his shoulders and sat down beside the bed. For an interminable hour he watched in silence; then he rose and fetched the opium.

"Rivarez, I won't let this go on any longer; if you can stand it, I can't. You must have the stuff."

The Gadfly took it without speaking. Then he turned away and closed his eyes. Martini sat down again, and listened as the breathing became gradually deep and even.

The Gadfly was too much exhausted to wake easily when once asleep. Hour after hour he lay absolutely motionless. Martini approached him several times during the day and evening, and looked at the still figure; but, except the breathing, there was no sign of life. The face was so wan and colourless that at last a sudden fear seized upon him; what if he had given too much opium? The injured left arm lay on the coverlet, and he shook it gently to rouse the sleeper. As he did so, the unfastened sleeve fell back, showing a series of deep and fearful scars covering the arm from wrist to elbow.

"That arm must have been in a pleasant condition when those marks were fresh," said Riccardo's voice behind him.

"Ah, there you are at last! Look here, Riccardo; ought this man to sleep forever? I gave him a dose about ten hours ago, and he hasn't moved a muscle since."

Riccardo stooped down and listened for a moment.

"No; he is breathing quite properly; it's nothing but sheer exhaustion— what you might expect after such a night. There may be another paroxysm before morning. Someone will sit up, I hope?"

"Galli will; he has sent to say he will be here by ten."

"It's nearly that now. Ah, he's waking! Just see the maidservant gets that broth hot. Gently—gently, Rivarez! There, there, you needn't fight, man; I'm not a bishop!"

The Gadfly started up with a shrinking, scared look. "Is it my turn?" he said hurriedly in Spanish. "Keep the people amused a minute; I—— Ah! I didn't see you, Riccardo."

He looked round the room and drew one hand across his forehead as if bewildered. "Martini! Why, I thought you had gone away. I must have been asleep."

"You have been sleeping like the beauty in the fairy story for the last ten hours; and now you are to have some broth and go to sleep again."

"Ten hours! Martini, surely you haven't been here all that time?"

"Yes; I was beginning to wonder whether I hadn't given you an overdose of opium."

The Gadfly shot a sly glance at him.

"No such luck! Wouldn't you have nice quiet committee-meetings? What the devil do you want, Riccardo? Do for mercy's sake leave me in peace, can't you? I hate being mauled about by doctors."

"Well then, drink this and I'll leave you in peace. I shall come round in a day or two, though, and give you a thorough overhauling. I think you have pulled through the worst of this business now; you don't look quite so much like a death's head at a feast."

"Oh, I shall be all right soon, thanks. Who's that—Galli? I seem to have a collection of all the graces here to-night."

"I have come to stop the night with you."

"Nonsense! I don't want anyone. Go home, all the lot of you. Even if the thing should come on again, you can't help me; I won't keep taking opium. It's all very well once in a way."

"I'm afraid you're right," Riccardo said. "But that's not always an easy resolution to stick to."

The Gadfly looked up, smiling. "No fear! If I'd been going in for that sort of thing, I should have done it long ago."

"Anyway, you are not going to be left alone," Riccardo answered drily. "Come into the other room a minute, Galli; I want to speak to you. Good-night, Rivarez; I'll look in to-morrow."

Martini was following them out of the room when he heard his name softly called. The Gadfly was holding out a hand to him.

"Thank you!"

"Oh, stuff! Go to sleep."

When Riccardo had gone, Martini remained a few minutes in the outer room, talking with Galli. As he opened the front door of the house he heard a carriage stop at the garden gate and saw a woman's figure get out and come up the path. It was Zita, returning, evidently, from some evening entertainment. He lifted his hat and stood aside to let her pass, then went out into the dark lane leading from the house to the Poggio Imperiale. Presently the gate clicked and rapid footsteps came down the lane.

"Wait a minute!" she said.

When he turned back to meet her she stopped short, and then came slowly towards him, dragging one hand after her along the hedge. There was a single street-lamp at the corner, and he saw by its light that she was hanging her head down as though embarrassed or ashamed.

"How is he?" she asked without looking up.

"Much better than he was this morning. He has been asleep most of the day and seems less exhausted. I think the attack is passing over."

She still kept her eyes on the ground.

"Has it been very bad this time?"

"About as bad as it can well be, I should think."

"I thought so. When he won't let me come into the room, that always means it's bad."

"Does he often have attacks like this?"

"That depends—— It's so irregular. Last summer, in Switzerland, he was quite well; but the winter before, when we were in Vienna, it was awful. He wouldn't let me come near him for days together. He hates to have me about when he's ill."

She glanced up for a moment, and, dropping her eyes again, went on:

"He always used to send me off to a ball, or concert, or something, on one pretext or another, when he felt it coming on. Then he would lock himself into his room. I used to slip back and sit outside the door—he would have been furious if he'd known. He'd let the dog come in if it whined, but not me. He cares more for it, I think."

There was a curious, sullen defiance in her manner.

"Well, I hope it won't be so bad any more," said Martini kindly. "Dr. Riccardo is taking the case seriously in hand. Perhaps he will be able to make a permanent improvement. And, in any case, the treatment gives relief at the moment. But you had better send to us at once, another time. He would have suffered very much less if we had known of it earlier. Good-night!"

He held out his hand, but she drew back with a quick gesture of refusal.

"I don't see why you want to shake hands with his mistress."

"As you like, of course," he began in embarrassment.

She stamped her foot on the ground. "I hate you!" she cried, turning on him with eyes like glowing coals. "I hate you all! You come here talking politics to him; and he lets you sit up the night with him and give him things to stop the pain, and I daren't so much as peep at him through the door! What is he to you? What right have you to come and steal him away from me? I hate you! I hate you! I HATE you!"

She burst into a violent fit of sobbing, and, darting back into the garden, slammed the gate in his face.

"Good Heavens!" said Martini to himself, as he walked down the lane. "That girl is actually in love with him! Of all the extraordinary things——"

CHAPTER VIII

THE Gadfly's recovery was rapid. One afternoon in the following week Riccardo found him lying on the sofa in a Turkish dressing-gown, chatting with Martini and Galli. He even talked about going downstairs; but Riccardo merely laughed at the suggestion and asked whether he would like a tramp across the valley to Fiesole to start with.

"You might go and call on the Grassinis for a change," he added wickedly. "I'm sure madame would be delighted to see you, especially now, when you look so pale and interesting."

The Gadfly clasped his hands with a tragic gesture.

"Bless my soul! I never thought of that! She'd take me for one of Italy's martyrs, and talk patriotism to me. I should have to act up to the part, and tell her I've been cut to pieces in an underground dungeon and stuck together again rather badly; and she'd want to know exactly what the process felt like. You don't think she'd believe it, Riccardo? I'll bet you my Indian dagger against the bottled tape-worm in your den that she'll swallow the biggest lie I can invent. That's a generous offer, and you'd better jump at it."

"Thanks, I'm not so fond of murderous tools as you are."

"Well, a tape-worm is as murderous as a dagger, any day, and not half so pretty."

"But as it happens, my dear fellow, I don't want the dagger and I do want the tape-worm. Martini, I must run off. Are you in charge of this obstreperous patient?"

"Only till three o'clock. Galli and I have to go to San Miniato, and Signora Bolla is coming till I can get back."

"Signora Bolla!" the Gadfly repeated in a tone of dismay. "Why, Martini, this will never do! I can't have a lady bothered over me and my ailments. Besides, where is she to sit? She won't like to come in here."

"Since when have you gone in so fiercely for the proprieties?" asked Riccardo, laughing. "My good man, Signora Bolla is head nurse in general to all of us. She has looked after sick people ever since she was in short frocks, and does it better than any sister of mercy I know. Won't like to come into your room! Why, you might be talking of the Grassini woman! I needn't leave any directions if she's coming, Martini. Heart alive, it's half-past two; I must be off!"

"Now, Rivarez, take your physic before she comes," said Galli, approaching the sofa with a medicine glass.

"Damn the physic!" The Gadfly had reached the irritable stage of convalescence, and was inclined to give his devoted nurses a bad time. "W-what do you want to d-d-dose me with all sorts of horrors for now the pain is gone?"

"Just because I don't want it to come back. You wouldn't like it if you collapsed when Signora Bolla is here and she had to give you opium."

"My g-good sir, if that pain is going to come back it will come; it's not a t-toothache to be frightened away with your trashy mixtures. They are about as much use as a t-toy squirt for a house on fire. However, I suppose you must have your way."

He took the glass with his left hand, and the sight of the terrible scars recalled Galli to the former subject of conversation.

"By the way," he asked; "how did you get so much knocked about? In the war, was it?"

"Now, didn't I just tell you it was a case of secret dungeons and——"

"Yes, that version is for Signora Grassini's benefit. Really, I suppose it was in the war with Brazil?"

"Yes, I got a bit hurt there; and then hunting in the savage districts and one thing and another."

"Ah, yes; on the scientific expedition. You can fasten your shirt; I have quite done. You seem to have had an exciting time of it out there."

"Well, of course you can't live in savage countries without getting a few adventures once in a way," said the Gadfly lightly; "and you can hardly expect them all to be pleasant."

"Still, I don't understand how you managed to get so much knocked about unless in a bad adventure with wild beasts—those scars on your left arm, for instance."

"Ah, that was in a puma-hunt. You see, I had fired——"

There was a knock at the door.

"Is the room tidy, Martini? Yes? Then please open the door. This is really most kind, signora; you must excuse my not getting up."

"Of course you mustn't get up; I have not come as a caller. I am a little early, Cesare. I thought perhaps you were in a hurry to go."

"I can stop for a quarter of an hour. Let me put your cloak in the other room. Shall I take the basket, too?"

"Take care; those are new-laid eggs. Katie brought them in from Monte Oliveto this morning. There are some Christmas roses for you, Signor Rivarez; I know you are fond of flowers."

She sat down beside the table and began clipping the stalks of the flowers and arranging them in a vase.

"Well, Rivarez," said Galli; "tell us the rest of the puma-hunt story; you had just begun."

"Ah, yes! Galli was asking me about life in South America, signora; and I was telling him how I came to get my left arm spoiled. It was in Peru. We had been wading a river on a puma-hunt, and when I fired at the beast the powder wouldn't go off; it had got splashed with water. Naturally the puma didn't wait for me to rectify that; and this is the result."

"That must have been a pleasant experience."

"Oh, not so bad! One must take the rough with the smooth, of course; but it's a splendid life on the whole. Serpent-catching, for instance——"

He rattled on, telling anecdote after anecdote; now of the Argentine war, now of the Brazilian expedition, now of hunting feats and adventures with savages or wild beasts. Galli, with the delight of a child hearing a fairy story, kept interrupting every moment to ask questions. He was of the impressionable Neapolitan temperament and loved everything sensational. Gemma took some knitting from her basket and listened silently, with busy fingers and downcast eyes. Martini frowned and fidgeted. The manner in which the anecdotes were told seemed to him boastful and self-conscious; and, notwithstanding his unwilling admiration for a man who could endure physical pain with the amazing fortitude which he had seen the week before, he genuinely disliked the Gadfly and all his works and ways.

"It must have been a glorious life!" sighed Galli with naive envy. "I wonder you ever made up your mind to leave Brazil. Other countries must seem so flat after it!"

"I think I was happiest in Peru and Ecuador," said the Gadfly. "That really is a magnificent tract of country. Of course it is very hot, especially the coast district of Ecuador, and one has to rough it a bit; but the scenery is superb beyond imagination."

"I believe," said Galli, "the perfect freedom of life in a barbarous country would attract me more than any scenery. A man must feel his personal, human dignity as he can never feel it in our crowded towns."

"Yes," the Gadfly answered; "that is——"

Gemma raised her eyes from her knitting and looked at him. He flushed suddenly scarlet and broke off. There was a little pause.

"Surely it is not come on again?" asked Galli anxiously.

"Oh, nothing to speak of, thanks to your s-s-soothing application that I b-b-blasphemed against. Are you going already, Martini?"

"Yes. Come along, Galli; we shall be late."

Gemma followed the two men out of the room, and presently returned with an egg beaten up in milk.

"Take this, please," she said with mild authority; and sat down again to her knitting. The Gadfly obeyed meekly.

For half an hour, neither spoke. Then the Gadfly said in a very low voice: "Signora Bolla!"

She looked up. He was tearing the fringe of the couch-rug, and kept his eyes lowered.

"You didn't believe I was speaking the truth just now," he began.

"I had not the smallest doubt that you were telling falsehoods," she answered quietly.

"You were quite right. I was telling falsehoods all the time."

"Do you mean about the war?"

"About everything. I was not in that war at all; and as for the expedition, I had a few adventures, of course, and most of those stories are true, but it was not that way I got smashed. You have detected me in one lie, so I may as well confess the lot, I suppose."

"Does it not seem to you rather a waste of energy to invent so many falsehoods?" she asked. "I should have thought it was hardly worth the trouble."

"What would you have? You know your own English proverb: 'Ask no questions and you'll be told no lies.' It's no pleasure to me to fool people that way, but I must answer them somehow when they ask what made a cripple of me; and I may as well invent something pretty while I'm about it. You saw how pleased Galli was."

"Do you prefer pleasing Galli to speaking the truth?"

"The truth!" He looked up with the torn fringe in his hand. "You wouldn't have me tell those people the truth? I'd cut my tongue out first!" Then with an awkward, shy abruptness:

"I have never told it to anybody yet; but I'll tell you if you care to hear."

She silently laid down her knitting. To her there was something grievously pathetic in this hard, secret, unlovable creature, suddenly flinging his personal confidence at the feet of a woman whom he barely knew and whom he apparently disliked.

A long silence followed, and she looked up. He was leaning his left arm on the little table beside him, and shading his eyes with the mutilated hand, and she noticed the nervous tension of the fingers and the throbbing of the scar on the wrist. She came up to him and called him softly by name. He started violently and raised his head.

"I f-forgot," he stammered apologetically. "I was g-going to t-tell you about——"

"About the—accident or whatever it was that caused your lameness. But if it worries you——"

"The accident? Oh, the smashing! Yes; only it wasn't an accident, it was a poker."

She stared at him in blank amazement. He pushed back his hair with a hand that shook perceptibly, and looked up at her, smiling.

"Won't you sit down? Bring your chair close, please. I'm so sorry I can't get it for you. R-really, now I come to think of it, the case would have been a p-perfect t-treasure-trove for Riccardo if he had had me to treat; he has the true surgeon's love for broken bones, and I believe everything in me that was breakable was broken on that occasion—except my neck."

"And your courage," she put in softly. "But perhaps you count that among your unbreakable possessions."

He shook his head. "No," he said; "my courage has been mended up after a fashion, with the rest of me; but it was fairly broken then, like a smashed tea-cup; that's the horrible part of it. Ah—— Yes; well, I was telling you about the poker.

"It was—let me see—nearly thirteen years ago, in Lima. I told you Peru was a delightful country to live in; but it's not quite so nice for people that happen to be at low water, as I was. I had been down in the Argentine, and then in Chili, tramping the country and starving, mostly; and had come up from Valparaiso as odd-man on a cattle-boat. I couldn't get any work in Lima itself, so I went down to the docks,—they're at Callao, you know,—to try there. Well of course in all those shipping-ports there are low quarters where the seafaring people congregate; and after some time I got taken on as servant in one of the gambling hells there. I had to do the cooking and billiard-marking, and fetch drink for the sailors and their women, and all that sort of thing. Not very pleasant work; still I was glad to get it; there was at least food and the sight of human faces and sound of human tongues—of a kind. You may think that was no advantage; but I had just been down with yellow fever, alone in the outhouse of a wretched half-caste shanty, and the thing had given me the horrors. Well, one night I was told to put out a tipsy Lascar who was making himself obnoxious; he had come ashore and lost all his money and was in a bad temper. Of course I had to obey if I didn't want to lose my place and starve; but the man was twice as strong as I—I was not twenty-one and as weak as a cat after the fever. Besides, he had the poker."

He paused a moment, glancing furtively at her; then went on:

"Apparently he intended to put an end to me altogether; but somehow he managed to scamp his work—Lascars always do if they have a chance; and left just enough of me not smashed to go on living with."

"Yes, but the other people, could they not interfere? Were they all afraid of one Lascar?"

He looked up and burst out laughing.

"THE OTHER PEOPLE? The gamblers and the people of the house? Why, you don't understand! They were negroes and Chinese and Heaven knows what; and I was their servant—THEIR PROPERTY. They stood round and enjoyed the fun, of course. That sort of thing counts for a good joke out there. So it is if you don't happen to be the subject practised on."

She shuddered.

"Then what was the end of it?"

"That I can't tell you much about; a man doesn't remember the next few days after a thing of that kind, as a rule. But there was a ship's surgeon near, and it seems that when they found I was not dead, somebody called him in. He patched me up after a fashion—Riccardo seems to think it was rather badly done, but that may be professional jealousy. Anyhow, when I came to my senses, an old native woman had taken me in for Christian charity—that sounds queer, doesn't it? She used to sit huddled up in the corner of the hut, smoking a black pipe and spitting on the floor and crooning to herself. However, she meant well, and she told me I might die in peace and nobody should disturb me. But the spirit of contradiction was strong in me and I elected to live. It was rather a difficult job scrambling back to life, and sometimes I am inclined to think it was a great deal of cry for very little wool. Anyway that old woman's patience was wonderful; she kept me—how long was it?—nearly four months lying in her hut, raving like a mad thing at intervals, and as vicious as a bear with a sore ear between-whiles. The pain was pretty bad, you see, and my temper had been spoiled in childhood with overmuch coddling."

"And then?"

"Oh, then—I got up somehow and crawled away. No, don't think it was any delicacy about taking a poor woman's charity—I was past caring for that; it was only that I couldn't bear the place any longer. You talked just now about my courage; if you had seen me then! The worst of the pain used to come on every evening, about dusk; and in the afternoon I used to lie alone, and watch the sun get lower and lower—— Oh, you can't understand! It makes me sick to look at a sunset now!"

A long pause.

"Well, then I went up country, to see if I could get work anywhere—it would have driven me mad to stay in Lima. I got as far as Cuzco, and there—— — Really I don't know why I'm inflicting all this ancient history on you; it hasn't even the merit of being funny."

She raised her head and looked at him with deep and serious eyes. "PLEASE don't talk that way," she said.

He bit his lip and tore off another piece of the rug-fringe.

"Shall I go on?" he asked after a moment.

"If—if you will. I am afraid it is horrible to you to remember."

"Do you think I forget when I hold my tongue? It's worse then. But don't imagine it's the thing itself that haunts me so. It is the fact of having lost the power over myself."

"I—don't think I quite understand."

"I mean, it is the fact of having come to the end of my courage, to the point where I found myself a coward."

"Surely there is a limit to what anyone can bear."

"Yes; and the man who has once reached that limit never knows when he may reach it again."

"Would you mind telling me," she asked, hesitating, "how you came to be stranded out there alone at twenty?"

"Very simply: I had a good opening in life, at home in the old country, and ran away from it."

"Why?"

He laughed again in his quick, harsh way.

"Why? Because I was a priggish young cub, I suppose. I had been brought up in an over-luxurious home, and coddled and faddled after till I thought the world was made of pink cotton-wool and sugared almonds. Then one fine day I found out that someone I had trusted had deceived me. Why, how you start! What is it?"

"Nothing. Go on, please."

"I found out that I had been tricked into believing a lie; a common bit of experience, of course; but, as I tell you, I was young and priggish, and thought that liars go to hell. So I ran away from home and plunged into South America to sink or swim as I could, without a cent in my pocket or a word of Spanish in my tongue, or anything but white hands and expensive habits to get my bread with. And the natural result was that I got a dip into the real hell to cure me of imagining sham ones. A pretty thorough dip, too—it was just five years before the Duprez expedition came along and pulled me out."

"Five years! Oh, that is terrible! And had you no friends?"

"Friends! I"—he turned on her with sudden fierceness—"I have NEVER had a friend!"

The next instant he seemed a little ashamed of his vehemence, and went on quickly:

"You mustn't take all this too seriously; I dare say I made the worst of things, and really it wasn't so bad the first year and a half; I was young and strong and I managed to scramble along fairly well till the Lascar put his mark on me. But after that I couldn't get work. It's wonderful what an effectual tool a poker is if you handle it properly; and nobody cares to employ a cripple."

"What sort of work did you do?"

"What I could get. For some time I lived by odd-jobbing for the blacks on the sugar plantations, fetching and carrying and so on. It's one of the curious things in life, by the way, that slaves always contrive to have a slave of their own, and there's nothing a negro likes so much as a white fag to bully. But it was no use; the overseers always turned me off. I was too lame to be quick; and I couldn't manage the heavy loads. And then I was always getting these attacks of inflammation, or whatever the confounded thing is.

"After some time I went down to the silver-mines and tried to get work there; but it was all no good. The managers laughed at the very notion of taking me on, and as for the men, they made a dead set at me."

"Why was that?"

"Oh, human nature, I suppose; they saw I had only one hand that I could hit back with. They're a mangy, half-caste lot; negroes and Zambos mostly. And then those horrible coolies! So at last I got enough of that, and set off to tramp the country at random; just wandering about, on the chance of something turning up."

"To tramp? With that lame foot!"

He looked up with a sudden, piteous catching of the breath.

"I—I was hungry," he said.

She turned her head a little away and rested her chin on one hand. After a moment's silence he began again, his voice sinking lower and lower as he spoke:

"Well, I tramped, and tramped, till I was nearly mad with tramping, and nothing came of it. I got down into Ecuador, and there it was worse than ever. Sometimes I'd get a bit of tinkering to do,—I'm a pretty fair tinker,—or an errand to run, or a pigstye to clean out; sometimes I did—oh, I hardly know what. And then at last, one day———"

The slender, brown hand clenched itself suddenly on the table, and Gemma, raising her head, glanced at him anxiously. His side-face was turned towards her, and she could see a vein on the temple beating like a hammer, with quick, irregular strokes. She bent forward and laid a gentle hand on his arm.

"Never mind the rest; it's almost too horrible to talk about."

He stared doubtfully at the hand, shook his head, and went on steadily:

"Then one day I met a travelling variety show. You remember that one the other night; well, that sort of thing, only coarser and more indecent. The Zambos are not like these gentle Florentines; they don't care for anything that is not foul or brutal. There was bull-fighting, too, of course. They had camped out by the roadside for the night; and I went up to their tent to beg. Well, the weather was hot and I was half starved, and so—I fainted at the door of the tent. I had a trick of fainting suddenly at that time, like a boarding-school girl with tight stays. So they took me in and gave me brandy, and food, and so on; and then—the next morning—they offered me——"

Another pause.

"They wanted a hunchback, or monstrosity of some kind; for the boys to pelt with orange-peel and banana-skins—something to set the blacks laughing——— You saw the clown that night—well, I was that—for two years. I suppose you have a humanitarian feeling about negroes and Chinese. Wait till you've been at their mercy!

"Well, I learned to do the tricks. I was not quite deformed enough; but they set that right with an artificial hump and made the most of this foot and arm—— And the Zambos are not critical; they're easily satisfied if only they can get hold of some live thing to torture—the fool's dress makes a good deal of difference, too.

"The only difficulty was that I was so often ill and unable to play. Sometimes, if the manager was out of temper, he would insist on my coming into the ring when I had these attacks on; and I believe the people liked those evenings best. Once, I remember, I fainted right off with the pain in the middle of the performance—— When I came to my senses again, the audience had got round me—hooting and yelling and pelting me with———"

"Don't! I can't hear any more! Stop, for God's sake!"

She was standing up with both hands over her ears. He broke off, and, looking up, saw the glitter of tears in her eyes.

"Damn it all, what an idiot I am!" he said under his breath.

She crossed the room and stood for a little while looking out of the window. When she turned round, the Gadfly was again leaning on the table and covering his eyes with one hand. He had evidently forgotten her presence, and she sat down beside him without speaking. After a long silence she said slowly:

"I want to ask you a question."

"Yes?" without moving.

"Why did you not cut your throat?"

He looked up in grave surprise. "I did not expect YOU to ask that," he said. "And what about my work? Who would have done it for me?"

"Your work—— Ah, I see! You talked just now about being a coward;

well, if you have come through that and kept to your purpose, you are the very bravest man that I have ever met."

He covered his eyes again, and held her hand in a close passionate clasp. A silence that seemed to have no end fell around them.

Suddenly a clear and fresh soprano voice rang out from the garden below, singing a verse of a doggerel French song:

"Eh, Pierrot! Danse, Pierrot!
Danse un peu, mon pauvre Jeannot!
Vive la danse et l'allegresse!
Jouissons de notre bell' jeunesse!
Si moi je pleure ou moi je soupire,
Si moi je fais la triste figure—
Monsieur, ce n'est que pour rire!
Ha! Ha, ha, ha!
Monsieur, ce n'est que pour rire!"

At the first words the Gadfly tore his hand from Gemma's and shrank away with a stifled groan. She clasped both hands round his arm and pressed it firmly, as she might have pressed that of a person undergoing a surgical operation. When the song broke off and a chorus of laughter and applause came from the garden, he looked up with the eyes of a tortured animal.

"Yes, it is Zita," he said slowly; "with her officer friends. She tried to come in here the other night, before Riccardo came. I should have gone mad if she had touched me!"

"But she does not know," Gemma protested softly. "She cannot guess that she is hurting you."

"She is like a Creole," he answered, shuddering. "Do you remember her face that night when we brought in the beggar-child? That is how the half-castes look when they laugh."

Another burst of laughter came from the garden. Gemma rose and opened the window. Zita, with a gold-embroidered scarf wound coquettishly round her head, was standing in the garden path, holding up a bunch of violets, for the possession of which three young cavalry officers appeared to be competing.

"Mme. Reni!" said Gemma.

Zita's face darkened like a thunder-cloud. "Madame?" she said, turning and raising her eyes with a defiant look.

"Would your friends mind speaking a little more softly? Signor Rivarez is very unwell."

The gipsy flung down her violets. "Allez-vous en!" she said, turning sharply on the astonished officers. "Vous m'embetez, messieurs!"

She went slowly out into the road. Gemma closed the window.

"They have gone away," she said, turning to him.

"Thank you. I—I am sorry to have troubled you."

"It was no trouble." He at once detected the hesitation in her voice.

"'But?'" he said. "That sentence was not finished, signora; there was an unspoken 'but' in the back of your mind."

"If you look into the backs of people's minds, you mustn't be offended at what you read there. It is not my affair, of course, but I cannot understand——"

"My aversion to Mme. Reni? It is only when——"

"No, your caring to live with her when you feel that aversion. It seems to me an insult to her as a woman and as——"

"A woman!" He burst out laughing harshly. "Is THAT what you call a woman? 'Madame, ce n'est que pour rire!'"

"That is not fair!" she said. "You have no right to speak of her in that way to anyone—especially to another woman!"

He turned away, and lay with wide-open eyes, looking out of the window at the sinking sun. She lowered the blind and closed the shutters, that he might not see it set; then sat down at the table by the other window and took up her knitting again.

"Would you like the lamp?" she asked after a moment.

He shook his head.

When it grew too dark to see, Gemma rolled up her knitting and laid it in the basket. For some time she sat with folded hands, silently watching the Gadfly's motionless figure. The dim evening light, falling on his face, seemed to soften away its hard, mocking, self-assertive look, and to deepen the tragic lines about the mouth. By some fanciful association of ideas her memory went vividly back to the stone cross which her father had set up in memory of Arthur, and to its inscription:

"All thy waves and billows have gone over me."

An hour passed in unbroken silence. At last she rose and went softly out of the room. Coming back with a lamp, she paused for a moment, thinking that the Gadfly was asleep. As the light fell on his face he turned round.

"I have made you a cup of coffee," she said, setting clown the lamp.

"Put it down a minute. Will you come here, please."

He took both her hands in his.

"I have been thinking," he said. "You are quite right; it is an ugly tangle I have got my life into. But remember, a man does not meet every day a woman whom he can—love; and I—I have been in deep waters. I am afraid——"

"Afraid——"

"Of the dark. Sometimes I DARE not be alone at night. I must have something living—something solid beside me. It is the outer darkness, where shall be—— No, no! It's not that; that's a sixpenny toy hell;—it's the INNER darkness. There's no weeping or gnashing of teeth there; only silence—silence——"

His eyes dilated. She was quite still, hardly breathing till he spoke again.

"This is all mystification to you, isn't it? You can't understand—luckily for you. What I mean is that I have a pretty fair chance of going mad if I try to live quite alone—— Don't think too hardly of me, if you can help it; I am not altogether the vicious brute you perhaps imagine me to be."

"I cannot try to judge for you," she answered. "I have not suffered as you have. But—I have been in rather deep water too, in another way; and I think—I am sure—that if you let the fear of anything drive you to do a really cruel or unjust or ungenerous thing, you will regret it afterwards. For the rest—if you have failed in this one thing, I know that I, in your place, should have failed altogether,—should have cursed God and died."

He still kept her hands in his.

"Tell me," he said very softly; "have you ever in your life done a really cruel thing?"

She did not answer, but her head sank down, and two great tears fell on his hand.

"Tell me!" he whispered passionately, clasping her hands tighter. "Tell me! I have told you all my misery."

"Yes,—once,—long ago. And I did it to the person I loved best in the world."

The hands that clasped hers were trembling violently; but they did not loosen their hold.

"He was a comrade," she went on; "and I believed a slander against him,—a common glaring lie that the police had invented. I struck him in the face for a traitor; and he went away and drowned himself. Then, two days later, I found out that he had been quite innocent. Perhaps that is a worse memory than any of yours. I would cut off my right hand to undo what it has done."

Something swift and dangerous—something that she had not seen before,—flashed into his eyes. He bent his head down with a furtive, sudden gesture and kissed the hand.

She drew back with a startled face. "Don't!" she cried out piteously. "Please don't ever do that again! You hurt me!"

"Do you think you didn't hurt the man you killed?"

"The man I—killed—— Ah, there is Cesare at the gate at last! I—I must go!"

When Martini came into the room he found the Gadfly lying alone with the untouched coffee beside him, swearing softly to himself in a languid, spiritless way, as though he got no satisfaction out of it.

CHAPTER IX

A FEW days later, the Gadfly, still rather pale and limping more than usual, entered the reading room of the public library and asked for Cardinal Montanelli's sermons. Riccardo, who was reading at a table near him, looked up. He liked the Gadfly very much, but could not digest this one trait in him—this curious personal maliciousness.

"Are you preparing another volley against that unlucky Cardinal?" he asked half irritably.

"My dear fellow, why do you a-a-always attribute evil m-m-motives to people? It's m-most unchristian. I am preparing an essay on contemporary theology for the n-n-new paper."

"What new paper?" Riccardo frowned. It was perhaps an open secret that a new press-law was expected and that the Opposition was preparing to astonish the town with a radical newspaper; but still it was, formally, a secret.

"The Swindlers' Gazette, of course, or the Church Calendar."

"Sh-sh! Rivarez, we are disturbing the other readers."

"Well then, stick to your surgery, if that's your subject, and l-l-leave me to th-theology—that's mine. I d-d-don't interfere with your treatment of broken bones, though I know a p-p-precious lot more about them than you do."

He sat down to his volume of sermons with an intent and preoccupied face. One of the librarians came up to him.

"Signor Rivarez! I think you were in the Duprez expedition, exploring the tributaries of the Amazon? Perhaps you will kindly help us in a difficulty. A lady has been inquiring for the records of the expedition, and they are at the binder's."

"What does she want to know?"

"Only in what year the expedition started and when it passed through Ecuador."

"It started from Paris in the autumn of 1837, and passed through Quito in April, 1838. We were three years in Brazil; then went down to Rio and got back to Paris in the summer of 1841. Does the lady want the dates of the separate discoveries?"

"No, thank you; only these. I have written them down. Beppo, take this paper to Signora Bolla, please. Many thanks, Signor Rivarez. I am sorry to have troubled you."

The Gadfly leaned back in his chair with a perplexed frown. What did she want the dates for? When they passed through Ecuador——

Gemma went home with the slip of paper in her hand. April, 1838—and Arthur had died in May, 1833. Five years—

She began pacing up and down her room. She had slept badly the last few nights, and there were dark shadows under her eyes.

Five years;—and an "overluxurious home"—and "someone he had trusted had deceived him"—had deceived him—and he had found it out——

She stopped and put up both hands to her head. Oh, this was utterly mad—it was not possible—it was absurd——

And yet, how they had dragged that harbour!

Five years—and he was "not twenty-one" when the Lascar—— Then he must have been nineteen when he ran away from home. Had he not said: "A year and a half——" Where did he get those blue eyes from, and that nervous restlessness of the fingers? And why was he so bitter against Montanelli? Five years—five years———

If she could but know that he was drowned—if she could but have seen the body; some day, surely, the old wound would have left off aching, the old memory would have lost its terrors. Perhaps in another twenty years she would have learned to look back without shrinking.

All her youth had been poisoned by the thought of what she had done. Resolutely, day after day and year after year, she had fought against the demon of remorse. Always she had remembered that her work lay in the future; always had shut her eyes and ears to the haunting spectre of the past. And day after day, year after year, the image of the drowned body drifting out to sea had never left her, and the bitter cry that she could not silence had risen in her heart: "I have killed Arthur! Arthur is dead!" Sometimes it had seemed to her that her burden was too heavy to be borne.

Now she would have given half her life to have that burden back again. If she had killed him—that was a familiar grief; she had endured it too long to sink under it now. But if she had driven him, not into the water but into—— She sat down, covering her eyes with both hands. And her life had been darkened for his sake, because he was dead! If she had brought upon him nothing worse than death——

Steadily, pitilessly she went back, step by step, through the hell of his past life. It was as vivid to her as though she had seen and felt it all; the helpless shivering of the naked soul, the mockery that was bitterer than death, the horror of loneliness, the slow, grinding, relentless agony. It was as vivid as if she had sat beside him in the filthy Indian hut; as if she had suffered with him in the silver-mines, the coffee fields, the horrible variety show—

The variety show—— No, she must shut out that image, at least; it was enough to drive one mad to sit and think of it.

She opened a little drawer in her writing-desk. It contained the few personal relics which she could not bring herself to destroy. She was not given to the hoarding up of sentimental trifles; and the preservation of these keepsakes was a concession to that weaker side of her nature which she kept under with so steady a hand. She very seldom allowed herself to look at them.

Now she took them out, one after another: Giovanni's first letter to her, and the flowers that had lain in his dead hand; a lock of her baby's hair and a withered leaf from her father's grave. At the back of the drawer was a miniature portrait of Arthur at ten years old—the only existing likeness of him.

She sat down with it in her hands and looked at the beautiful childish head, till the face of the real Arthur rose up afresh before her. How clear it was in every detail! The sensitive lines of the mouth, the wide, earnest eyes, the seraphic purity of expression—they were graven in upon her memory, as though he had died yesterday. Slowly the blinding tears welled up and hid the portrait.

Oh, how could she have thought such a thing! It was like sacrilege even to dream of this bright, far-off spirit, bound to the sordid miseries of life. Surely the gods had loved him a little, and had let him die young! Better a thousand times that he should pass into utter nothingness than that he should live and be the Gadfly—the Gadfly, with his faultless neckties and his doubtful witticisms, his bitter tongue and his ballet girl! No, no! It was all a horrible, senseless fancy; and she had vexed her heart with vain imaginings. Arthur was dead.

"May I come in?" asked a soft voice at the door.

She started so that the portrait fell from her hand, and the Gadfly, limping across the room, picked it up and handed it to her.

"How you startled me!" she said.

"I am s-so sorry. Perhaps I am disturbing you?"

"No. I was only turning over some old things."

She hesitated for a moment; then handed him back the miniature.

"What do you think of that head?"

While he looked at it she watched his face as though her life depended upon its expression; but it was merely negative and critical.

"You have set me a difficult task," he said. "The portrait is faded, and a child's face is always hard to read. But I should think that child would grow into an unlucky man, and the wisest thing he could do would be to abstain from growing into a man at all."

"Why?"

"Look at the line of the under-lip. Th-th-that is the sort of nature that feels pain as pain and wrong as wrong; and the world has no r-r-room for such people; it needs people who feel nothing but their work."

"Is it at all like anyone you know?"

He looked at the portrait more closely.

"Yes. What a curious thing! Of course it is; very like."

"Like whom?"

"C-c-cardinal Montan-nelli. I wonder whether his irreproachable Eminence has any nephews, by the way? Who is it, if I may ask?"

"It is a portrait, taken in childhood, of the friend I told you about the other day——"

"Whom you killed?"

She winced in spite of herself. How lightly, how cruelly he used that dreadful word!

"Yes, whom I killed—if he is really dead."

"If?"

She kept her eyes on his face.

"I have sometimes doubted," she said. "The body was never found. He may have run away from home, like you, and gone to South America."

"Let us hope not. That would be a bad memory to carry about with you. I have d-d-done some hard fighting in my t-time, and have sent m-more than one man to Hades, perhaps; but if I had it on my conscience that I had sent any l-living thing to South America, I should sleep badly——"

"Then do you believe," she interrupted, coming nearer to him with clasped hands, "that if he were not drowned,—if he had been through your experience instead,—he would never come back and let the past go? Do you believe he would NEVER forget? Remember, it has cost me something, too. Look!"

She pushed back the heavy waves of hair from her forehead. Through the black locks ran a broad white streak.

There was a long silence.

"I think," the Gadfly said slowly, "that the dead are better dead. Forgetting some things is a difficult matter. And if I were in the place of your dead friend, I would s-s-stay dead. The REVENANT is an ugly spectre."

She put the portrait back into its drawer and locked the desk.

"That is hard doctrine," she said. "And now we will talk about something else."

"I came to have a little business talk with you, if I may—a private one, about a plan that I have in my head."

She drew a chair to the table and sat down. "What do you think of the projected press-law?" he began, without a trace of his usual stammer.

"What I think of it? I think it will not be of much value, but half a loaf is better than no bread."

"Undoubtedly. Then do you intend to work on one of the new papers these good folk here are preparing to start?"

"I thought of doing so. There is always a great deal of practical work to be done in starting any paper—printing and circulation arrangements and——"

"How long are you going to waste your mental gifts in that fashion?"

"Why 'waste'?"

"Because it is waste. You know quite well that you have a far better head than most of the men you are working with, and you let them make a regular drudge and Johannes factotum of you. Intellectually you are as far ahead of Grassini and Galli as if they were schoolboys; yet you sit correcting their proofs like a printer's devil."

"In the first place, I don't spend all my time in correcting proofs; and moreover it seems to me that you exaggerate my mental capacities. They are by no means so brilliant as you think."

"I don't think them brilliant at all," he answered quietly; "but I do think them sound and solid, which I s of much more importance. At those dreary committee meetings it is always you who put your finger on the weak spot in everybody's logic."

"You are not fair to the others. Martini, for instance, has a very logical head, and there is no doubt about the capacities of Fabrizi and Lega. Then Grassini has a sounder knowledge of Italian economic statistics than any official in the country, perhaps."

"Well, that's not saying much; but let us lay them and their capacities aside. The fact remains that you, with such gifts as you possess, might do more important work and fill a more responsible post than at present."

"I am quite satisfied with my position. The work I am doing is not of very much value, perhaps, but we all do what we can."

"Signora Bolla, you and I have gone too far to play at compliments and modest denials now. Tell me honestly, do you recognize that you are using up your brain on work which persons inferior to you could do as well?"

"Since you press me for an answer—yes, to some extent."

"Then why do you let that go on?"

No answer.

"Why do you let it go on?"

"Because—I can't help it."

"Why?"

She looked up reproachfully. "That is unkind—it's not fair to press me so."

"But all the same you are going to tell me why."

"If you must have it, then—because my life has been smashed into pieces, and I have not the energy to start anything REAL, now. I am about fit to be a revolutionary cab-horse, and do the party's drudge-work. At least I do it conscientiously, and it must be done by somebody."

"Certainly it must be done by somebody; but not always by the same person."

"It's about all I'm fit for."

He looked at her with half-shut eyes, inscrutably. Presently she raised her head.

"We are returning to the old subject; and this was to be a business talk. It is quite useless, I assure you, to tell me I might have done all sorts of things. I shall never do them now. But I may be able to help you in thinking out your plan. What is it?"

"You begin by telling me that it is useless for me to suggest anything, and then ask what I want to suggest. My plan requires your help in action, not only in thinking out."

"Let me hear it and then we will discuss."

"Tell me first whether you have heard anything about schemes for a rising in Venetia."

"I have heard of nothing but schemes for risings and Sanfedist plots ever since the amnesty, and I fear I am as sceptical about the one as about the other."

"So am I, in most cases; but I am speaking of really serious preparations for a rising of the whole province against the Austrians. A good many young fellows in the Papal States—particularly in the Four Legations—are secretly preparing to get across there and join as volunteers. And I hear from my friends in the Romagna——"

"Tell me," she interrupted, "are you quite sure that these friends of yours can be trusted?"

"Quite sure. I know them personally, and have worked with them."

"That is, they are members of the 'sect' to which you belong? Forgive my scepticism, but I am always a little doubtful as to the accuracy of information received from secret societies. It seems to me that the habit——"

"Who told you I belonged to a 'sect'?" he interrupted sharply.

"No one; I guessed it."

"Ah!" He leaned back in his chair and looked at her, frowning. "Do you always guess people's private affairs?" he said after a moment.

"Very often. I am rather observant, and have a habit of putting things together. I tell you that so that you may be careful when you don't want me to know a thing."

"I don't mind your knowing anything so long as it goes no further. I suppose this has not——"

She lifted her head with a gesture of half-offended surprise. "Surely that is an unnecessary question!" she said.

"Of course I know you would not speak of anything to outsiders; but I thought that perhaps, to the members of your party——"

"The party's business is with facts, not with my personal conjectures and fancies. Of course I have never mentioned the subject to anyone."

"Thank you. Do you happen to have guessed which sect I belong to?"

"I hope—you must not take offence at my frankness; it was you who started this talk, you know—— I do hope it is not the 'Knifers.'"

"Why do you hope that?"

"Because you are fit for better things."

"We are all fit for better things than we ever do. There is your own answer back again. However, it is not the 'Knifers' that I belong to, but the 'Red Girdles.' They are a steadier lot, and take their work more seriously."

"Do you mean the work of knifing?"

"That, among other things. Knives are very useful in their way; but only when you have a good, organized propaganda behind them. That is what I dislike in the other sect. They think a knife can settle all the world's difficulties; and that's a mistake. It can settle a good many, but not all."

"Do you honestly believe that it settles any?"

He looked at her in surprise.

"Of course," she went on, "it eliminates, for the moment, the practical difficulty caused by the presence of a clever spy or objectionable official; but whether it does not create worse difficulties in place of the one removed is another question. It seems to me like the parable of the swept and garnished house and the seven devils. Every assassination only makes the police more vicious and the people more accustomed to violence and brutality, and the last state of the community may be worse than the first."

"What do you think will happen when the revolution comes? Do you suppose the people won't have to get accustomed to violence then? War is war."

"Yes, but open revolution is another matter. It is one moment in the people's life, and it is the price we have to pay for all our progress. No doubt fearful things will happen; they must in every revolution. But they will be isolated facts—exceptional features of an exceptional moment. The horrible thing about this promiscuous knifing is that it becomes a habit. The people get to look upon it as an every-day occurrence, and their sense of the sacredness of human life gets blunted. I have not been much in the Romagna, but what little I have seen of the people has given me the impression that they have got, or are getting, into a mechanical habit of violence."

"Surely even that is better than a mechanical habit of obedience and submission."

"I don't think so. All mechanical habits are bad and slavish, and this one is ferocious as well. Of course, if you look upon the work of the revolutionist as the mere wresting of certain definite concessions from the government, then the secret sect and the knife must seem to you the best weapons, for there is nothing else which all governments so dread. But if you think, as I do, that to force the government's hand is not an end in itself, but only a means to an end, and that what we really need to reform is the relation between man and man, then you must go differently to work. Accustoming ignorant people to the sight of blood is not the way to raise the value they put on human life."

"And the value they put on religion?"

"I don't understand."

He smiled.

"I think we differ as to where the root of the mischief lies. You place it in a lack of appreciation of the value of human life."

"Rather of the sacredness of human personality."

"Put it as you like. To me the great cause of our muddles and mistakes seems to lie in the mental disease called religion."

"Do you mean any religion in particular?"

"Oh, no! That is a mere question of external symptoms. The disease itself is what is called a religious attitude of mind. It is the morbid desire to set up a fetich and adore it, to fall down and worship something. It makes little difference whether the something be Jesus or Buddha or a tum-tum tree. You don't agree with me, of course. You may be atheist or agnostic or anything you like, but I could feel the religious temperament in you at five yards. However, it is of no use for us to discuss that. But you are quite mistaken in thinking that I, for one, look upon the knifing as merely a means of removing objectionable officials—it is, above all, a means, and I think the best means, of undermining the prestige of the Church and of accustoming people to look upon clerical agents as upon any other vermin."

"And when you have accomplished that; when you have roused the wild beast that sleeps in the people and set it on the Church; then——"

"Then I shall have done the work that makes it worth my while to live."

"Is THAT the work you spoke of the other day?"

"Yes, just that."

She shivered and turned away.

"You are disappointed in me?" he said, looking up with a smile.

"No; not exactly that. I am—I think—a little afraid of you."

She turned round after a moment and said in her ordinary business voice:

"This is an unprofitable discussion. Our standpoints are too different. For my part, I believe in propaganda, propaganda, and propaganda; and when you can get it, open insurrection."

"Then let us come back to the question of my plan; it has something to do with propaganda and more with insurrection."

"Yes?"

"As I tell you, a good many volunteers are going from the Romagna to join the Venetians. We do not know yet how soon the insurrection will break out. It may not be till the autumn or winter; but the volunteers in the Apennines must be armed and ready, so that they may be able to start for the plains directly they are sent for. I have undertaken to smuggle the firearms and ammunition on to Papal territory for them——"

"Wait a minute. How do you come to be working with that set? The revolutionists in Lombardy and Venetia are all in favour of the new Pope. They are going in for liberal reforms, hand in hand with the progressive movement in the Church. How can a 'no-compromise' anti-clerical like you get on with them?"

He shrugged his shoulders. "What is it to me if they like to amuse themselves with a rag-doll, so long as they do their work? Of course they will take the Pope for a figurehead. What have I to do with that, if only the insurrection gets under way somehow? Any stick will do to beat a dog with, I suppose, and any cry to set the people on the Austrians."

"What is it you want me to do?"

"Chiefly to help me get the firearms across."

"But how could I do that?"

"You are just the person who could do it best. I think of buying the arms in England, and there is a good deal of difficulty about bringing them over. It's impossible to get them through any of the Pontifical sea-ports; they must come by Tuscany, and go across the Apennines."

"That makes two frontiers to cross instead of one."

"Yes; but the other way is hopeless; you can't smuggle a big transport in at a harbour where there is no trade, and you know the whole shipping of Civita Vecchia amounts to about three row-boats and a fishing smack. If we once get the things across Tuscany, I can manage the Papal frontier; my men know every path in the mountains, and we have plenty of hiding-places. The transport must come by sea to Leghorn, and that is my great difficulty; I am not in with the smugglers there, and I believe you are."

"Give me five minutes to think."

She leaned forward, resting one elbow on her knee, and supporting the chin on the raised hand. After a few moments' silence she looked up.

"It is possible that I might be of some use in that part of the work," she said; "but before we go any further, I want to ask you a question. Can you give me your word that this business is not connected with any stabbing or secret violence of any kind?"

"Certainly. It goes without saying that I should not have asked you to join in a thing of which I know you disapprove."

"When do you want a definite answer from me?"

"There is not much time to lose; but I can give you a few days to decide in."

"Are you free next Saturday evening?"

"Let me see—to-day is Thursday; yes."

"Then come here. I will think the matter over and give you a final answer."

On the following Sunday Gemma sent in to the committee of the Florentine branch of the Mazzinian party a statement that she wished to undertake a special work of a political nature, which would for a few months prevent her from performing the functions for which she had up till now been responsible to the party.

Some surprise was felt at this announcement, but the committee raised no objection; she had been known in the party for several years as a person whose judgment might be trusted; and the members agreed that if Signora Bolla took an unexpected step, she probably had good reasons for it.

To Martini she said frankly that she had undertaken to help the Gadfly with some "frontier work." She had stipulated for the right to tell her old friend this much, in order that there might be no misunderstanding or painful sense of doubt and mystery between them. It seemed to her that she owed him this proof of confidence. He made no comment when she told him; but she saw, without knowing why, that the news had wounded him deeply.

They were sitting on the terrace of her lodging, looking out over the red roofs to Fiesole. After a long silence, Martini rose and began tramping up and down with his hands in his pockets, whistling to himself—a sure sign with him of mental agitation. She sat looking at him for a little while.

"Cesare, you are worried about this affair," she said at last. "I am very sorry you feel so despondent over it; but I could decide only as seemed right to me."

"It is not the affair," he answered, sullenly; "I know nothing about it, and it probably is all right, once you have consented to go into it. It's the MAN I distrust."

"I think you misunderstand him; I did till I got to know him better. He is far from perfect, but there is much more good in him than you think."

"Very likely." For a moment he tramped to and fro in silence, then suddenly stopped beside her.

"Gemma, give it up! Give it up before it is too late! Don't let that man drag you into things you will repent afterwards."

"Cesare," she said gently, "you are not thinking what you are saying. No one is dragging me into anything. I have made this decision of my own will, after thinking the matter well over alone. You have a personal dislike to Rivarez, I know; but we are talking of politics now, not of persons."

"Madonna! Give it up! That man is dangerous; he is secret, and cruel, and unscrupulous—and he is in love with you!"

She drew back.

"Cesare, how can you get such fancies into your head?"

"He is in love with you," Martini repeated. "Keep clear of him, Madonna!"

"Dear Cesare, I can't keep clear of him; and I can't explain to you why. We are tied together—not by any wish or doing of our own."

"If you are tied, there is nothing more to say," Martini answered wearily.

He went away, saying that he was busy, and tramped for hours up and down the muddy streets. The world looked very black to him that evening. One poor ewe-lamb—and this slippery creature had stepped in and stolen it away.

CHAPTER X

TOWARDS the middle of February the Gadfly went to Leghorn. Gemma had introduced him to a young Englishman there, a shipping-agent of liberal views, whom she and her husband had known in England. He had on several occasions performed little services for the Florentine radicals: had lent money to meet an unforeseen emergency, had allowed his business address to be used for the party's letters, etc.; but always through Gemma's mediumship, and as a private friend of hers. She was, therefore, according to party etiquette, free to make use of the connexion in any way that might seem good to her. Whether any use could be got out of it was quite another question. To ask a friendly sympathizer to lend his address for letters from Sicily or to keep a few documents in a corner of his counting-house safe was one thing; to ask him to smuggle over a transport of firearms for an insurrection was another; and she had very little hope of his consenting.

"You can but try," she had said to the Gadfly; "but I don't think anything will come of it. If you were to go to him with that recommendation and ask for five hundred scudi, I dare say he'd give them to you at once—he's exceedingly generous,—and perhaps at a pinch he would lend you his passport or hide a fugitive in his cellar; but if you mention such a thing as rifles he will stare at you and think we're both demented."

"Perhaps he may give me a few hints, though, or introduce me to a friendly sailor or two," the Gadfly had answered. "Anyway, it's worth while to try."

One day at the end of the month he came into her study less carefully dressed than usual, and she saw at once from his face that he had good news to tell.

"Ah, at last! I was beginning to think something must have happened to you!"

"I thought it safer not to write, and I couldn't get back sooner."

"You have just arrived?"

"Yes; I am straight from the diligence; I looked in to tell you that the affair is all settled."

"Do you mean that Bailey has really consented to help?"

"More than to help; he has undertaken the whole thing,—packing, transports,—everything. The rifles will be hidden in bales of merchandise and will come straight through from England. His partner, Williams, who is a great friend of his, has consented to see the transport off from Southampton, and

Bailey will slip it through the custom house at Leghorn. That is why I have been such a long time; Williams was just starting for Southampton, and I went with him as far as Genoa."

"To talk over details on the way?"

"Yes, as long as I wasn't too sea-sick to talk about anything."

"Are you a bad sailor?" she asked quickly, remembering how Arthur had suffered from sea-sickness one day when her father had taken them both for a pleasure-trip.

"About as bad as is possible, in spite of having been at sea so much. But we had a talk while they were loading at Genoa. You know Williams, I think? He's a thoroughly good fellow, trustworthy and sensible; so is Bailey, for that matter; and they both know how to hold their tongues."

"It seems to me, though, that Bailey is running a serious risk in doing a thing like this."

"So I told him, and he only looked sulky and said: 'What business is that of yours?' Just the sort of thing one would expect him to say. If I met Bailey in Timbuctoo, I should go up to him and say: 'Good-morning, Englishman.'"

"But I can't conceive how you managed to get their consent; Williams, too; the last man I should have thought of."

"Yes, he objected strongly at first; not on the ground of danger, though, but because the thing is 'so unbusiness-like.' But I managed to win him over after a bit. And now we will go into details."

When the Gadfly reached his lodgings the sun had set, and the blossoming pyrus japonica that hung over the garden wall looked dark in the fading light. He gathered a few sprays and carried them into the house. As he opened the study door, Zita started up from a chair in the corner and ran towards him.

"Oh, Felice; I thought you were never coming!"

His first impulse was to ask her sharply what business she had in his study; but, remembering that he had not seen her for three weeks, he held out his hand and said, rather frigidly:

"Good-evening, Zita; how are you?"

She put up her face to be kissed, but he moved past as though he had not seen the gesture, and took up a vase to put the pyrus in. The next instant the door was flung wide open, and the collie, rushing into the room, performed an ecstatic dance round him, barking and whining with delight. He put down the flowers and stooped to pat the dog.

"Well, Shaitan, how are you, old man? Yes, it's really I. Shake hands, like a good dog!"

The hard, sullen look came into Zita's face.

"Shall we go to dinner?" she asked coldly. "I ordered it for you at my place, as you wrote that you were coming this evening."

He turned round quickly.

"I am v-v-very sorry; you sh-should not have waited for me! I will just get a bit tidy and come round at once. P-perhaps you would not mind putting these into water."

When he came into Zita's dining room she was standing before a mirror, fastening one of the sprays into her dress. She had apparently made up her mind to be good-humoured, and came up to him with a little cluster of crimson buds tied together.

"Here is a buttonhole for you; let me put it in your coat."

All through dinner-time he did his best to be amiable, and kept up a flow of small-talk, to which she responded with radiant smiles. Her evident joy at his return somewhat embarrassed him; he had grown so accustomed to the idea that she led her own life apart from his, among such friends and companions as were congenial to her, that it had never occurred to him to imagine her as missing him. And yet she must have felt dull to be so much excited now.

"Let us have coffee up on the terrace," she said; "it is quite warm this evening."

"Very well. Shall I take your guitar? Perhaps you will sing."

She flushed with delight; he was critical about music and did not often ask her to sing.

On the terrace was a broad wooden bench running round the walls. The Gadfly chose a corner with a good view of the hills, and Zita, seating herself on the low wall with her feet on the bench, leaned back against a pillar of the roof. She did not care much for scenery; she preferred to look at the Gadfly.

"Give me a cigarette," she said. "I don't believe I have smoked once since you went away."

"Happy thought! It's just s-s-smoke I want to complete my bliss."

She leaned forward and looked at him earnestly.

"Are you really happy?"

The Gadfly's mobile brows went up.

"Yes; why not? I have had a good dinner; I am looking at one of the m-most beautiful views in Europe; and now I'm going to have coffee and hear a Hungarian folk-song. There is nothing the matter with either my conscience or my digestion; what more can man desire?"

"I know another thing you desire."

"What?"

"That!" She tossed a little cardboard box into his hand.

"B-burnt almonds! Why d-didn't you tell me before I began to s-smoke?" he cried reproachfully.

"Why, you baby! you can eat them when you have done smoking. There comes the coffee."

The Gadfly sipped his coffee and ate his burnt almonds with the grave and concentrated enjoyment of a cat drinking cream.

"How nice it is to come back to d-decent coffee, after the s-s-stuff one gets at Leghorn!" he said in his purring drawl.

"A very good reason for stopping at home now you are here."

"Not much stopping for me; I'm off again to-morrow."

The smile died on her face.

"To-morrow! What for? Where are you going to?"

"Oh! two or three p-p-places, on business."

It had been decided between him and Gemma that he must go in person into the Apennines to make arrangements with the smugglers of the frontier region about the transporting of the firearms. To cross the Papal frontier was for him a matter of serious danger; but it had to be done if the work was to succeed.

"Always business!" Zita sighed under her breath; and then asked aloud: "Shall you be gone long?"

"No; only a fortnight or three weeks, p-p-probably."

"I suppose it's some of THAT business?" she asked abruptly.

"'That' business?"

"The business you're always trying to get your neck broken over—the everlasting politics."

"It has something to do with p-p-politics."

Zita threw away her cigarette.

"You are fooling me," she said. "You are going into some danger or other."

"I'm going s-s-straight into the infernal regions," he answered languidly. "D-do you happen to have any friends there you want to send that ivy to? You n-needn't pull it all down, though."

She had fiercely torn off a handful of the climber from the pillar, and now flung it down with vehement anger.

"You are going into danger," she repeated; "and you won't even say so honestly! Do you think I am fit for nothing but to be fooled and joked with? You will get yourself hanged one of these days, and never so much as say good-bye. It's always politics and politics—I'm sick of politics!"

"S-so am I," said the Gadfly, yawning lazily; "and therefore we'll talk about something else—unless you will sing."

"Well, give me the guitar, then. What shall I sing?"

"The ballad of the lost horse; it suits your voice so well."

She began to sing the old Hungarian ballad of the man who loses first his horse, then his home, and then his sweetheart, and consoles himself with the reflection that "more was lost at Mohacz field." The song was one of the Gadfly's especial favourites; its fierce and tragic melody and the bitter stoicism of the refrain appealed to him as no softer music ever did.

Zita was in excellent voice; the notes came from her lips strong and clear, full of the vehement desire of life. She would have sung Italian or Slavonic music badly, and German still worse; but she sang the Magyar folk-songs splendidly.

The Gadfly listened with wide-open eyes and parted lips; he had never heard her sing like this before. As she came to the last line, her voice began suddenly to shake.

"Ah, no matter! More was lost——"

She broke down with a sob and hid her face among the ivy leaves.

"Zita!" The Gadfly rose and took the guitar from her hand. "What is it?"

She only sobbed convulsively, hiding her face in both hands. He touched her on the arm.

"Tell me what is the matter," he said caressingly.

"Let me alone!" she sobbed, shrinking away. "Let me alone!"

He went quietly back to his seat and waited till the sobs died away. Suddenly he felt her arms about his neck; she was kneeling on the floor beside him.

"Felice—don't go! Don't go away!"

"We will talk about that afterwards," he said, gently extricating himself from the clinging arms. "Tell me first what has upset you so. Has anything been frightening you?"

She silently shook her head.

"Have I done anything to hurt you?"

"No." She put a hand up against his throat.

"What, then?"

"You will get killed," she whispered at last. "I heard one of those men that come here say the other day that you will get into trouble—and when I ask you about it you laugh at me!"

"My dear child," the Gadfly said, after a little pause of astonishment, "you have got some exaggerated notion into your head. Very likely I shall get killed some day—that is the natural consequence of being a revolutionist. But there is no reason to suppose I am g-g-going to get killed just now. I am running no more risk than other people."

"Other people—what are other people to me? If you loved me you wouldn't go off this way and leave me to lie awake at night, wondering whether you're arrested, or dream you are dead whenever I go to sleep. You don't care as much for me as for that dog there!"

The Gadfly rose and walked slowly to the other end of the terrace. He was quite unprepared for such a scene as this and at a loss how to answer her. Yes, Gemma was right; he had got his life into a tangle that he would have hard work to undo.

"Sit down and let us talk about it quietly," he said, coming back after a moment. "I think we have misunderstood each other; of course I should not have laughed if I had thought you were serious. Try to tell me plainly what is troubling you; and then, if there is any misunderstanding, we may be able to clear it up."

"There's nothing to clear up. I can see you don't care a brass farthing for me."

"My dear child, we had better be quite frank with each other. I have always tried to be honest about our relationship, and I think I have never deceived you as to——"

"Oh, no! you have been honest enough; you have never even pretended to think of me as anything else but a prostitute,—a trumpery bit of second-hand finery that plenty of other men have had before you—"

"Hush, Zita! I have never thought that way about any living thing."

"You have never loved me," she insisted sullenly.

"No, I have never loved you. Listen to me, and try to think as little harm of me as you can."

"Who said I thought any harm of you? I——"

"Wait a minute. This is what I want to say: I have no belief whatever in conventional moral codes, and no respect for them. To me the relations between men and women are simply questions of personal likes and dislikes———"

"And of money," she interrupted with a harsh little laugh. He winced and hesitated a moment.

"That, of course, is the ugly part of the matter. But believe me, if I had thought that you disliked me, or felt any repulsion to the thing, I would never have suggested it, or taken advantage of your position to persuade you to it. I have never done that to any woman in my life, and I have never told a woman a lie about my feeling for her. You may trust me that I am speaking the truth——"

He paused a moment, but she did not answer.

"I thought," he went on; "that if a man is alone in the world and feels the need of—of a woman's presence about him, and if he can find a woman who is attractive to him and to whom he is not repulsive, he has a right to accept, in a grateful and friendly spirit, such pleasure as that woman is willing to give him, without entering into any closer bond. I saw no harm in the thing, provided only there is no unfairness or insult or deceit on either side. As for your having been in that relation with other men before I met you, I did not think about that. I merely thought that the connexion would be a pleasant and harmless one for both of us, and that either was free to break it as soon as it became irksome. If I was mistaken—if you have grown to look upon it differently—then——"

He paused again.

"Then?" she whispered, without looking up.

"Then I have done you a wrong, and I am very sorry. But I did not mean to do it."

"You 'did not mean' and you 'thought'——Felice, are you made of cast iron? Have you never been in love with a woman in your life that you can't see I love you?"

A sudden thrill went through him; it was so long since anyone had said to him: "I love you." Instantly she started up and flung her arms round him.

"Felice, come away with me! Come away from this dreadful country and all these people and their politics! What have we got to do with them? Come away, and we will be happy together. Let us go to South America, where you used to live."

The physical horror of association startled him back into self-control; he unclasped her hands from his neck and held them in a steady grasp.

"Zita! Try to understand what I am saying to you. I do not love you; and if I did I would not come away with you. I have my work in Italy, and my comrades——"

"And someone else that you love better than me!" she cried out fiercely.

"Oh, I could kill you! It is not your comrades you care about; it's—— I know who it is!"

"Hush!" he said quietly. "You are excited and imagining things that are not true."

"You suppose I am thinking of Signora Bolla? I'm not so easily duped! You only talk politics with her; you care no more for her than you do for me. It's that Cardinal!"

The Gadfly started as if he had been shot.

"Cardinal?" he repeated mechanically.

"Cardinal Montanelli, that came here preaching in the autumn. Do you think I didn't see your face when his carriage passed? You were as white as my pocket-handkerchief! Why, you're shaking like a leaf now because I mentioned his name!"

He stood up.

"You don't know what you are talking about," he said very slowly and softly. "I—hate the Cardinal. He is the worst enemy I have."

"Enemy or no, you love him better than you love anyone else in the world. Look me in the face and say that is not true, if you can!"

He turned away, and looked out into the garden. She watched him furtively, half-scared at what she had done; there was something terrifying in his silence. At last she stole up to him, like a frightened child, and timidly pulled his sleeve. He turned round.

"It is true," he said.

CHAPTER XI

"BUT c-c-can't I meet him somewhere in the hills? Brisighella is a risky place for me."

"Every inch of ground in the Romagna is risky for you; but just at this moment Brisighella is safer for you than any other place."

"Why?"

"I'll tell you in a minute. Don't let that man with the blue jacket see your face; he's dangerous. Yes; it was a terrible storm; I don't remember to have seen the vines so bad for a long time."

The Gadfly spread his arms on the table, and laid his face upon them, like a man overcome with fatigue or wine; and the dangerous new-comer in the blue jacket, glancing swiftly round, saw only two farmers discussing their crops over a flask of wine and a sleepy mountaineer with his head on the table. It was the usual sort of thing to see in little places like Marradi; and the owner of the blue jacket apparently made up his mind that nothing could be gained by listening; for he drank his wine at a gulp and sauntered into the outer room. There he stood leaning on the counter and gossiping lazily with the landlord, glancing every now and then out of the corner of one eye through the open door, beyond which sat the three figures at the table. The two farmers went on sipping their wine and discussing the weather in the local dialect, and the Gadfly snored like a man whose conscience is sound.

At last the spy seemed to make up his mind that there was nothing in the wine-shop worth further waste of his time. He paid his reckoning, and, lounging out of the house, sauntered away down the narrow street. The Gadfly, yawning and stretching, lifted himself up and sleepily rubbed the sleeve of his linen blouse across his eyes.

"Pretty sharp practice that," he said, pulling a clasp-knife out of his pocket and cutting off a chunk from the rye-loaf on the table. "Have they been worrying you much lately, Michele?"

"They've been worse than mosquitos in August. There's no getting a minute's peace; wherever one goes, there's always a spy hanging about. Even right up in the hills, where they used to be so shy about venturing, they have taken to coming in bands of three or four—haven't they, Gino? That's why we arranged for you to meet Domenichino in the town."

"Yes; but why Brisighella? A frontier town is always full of spies."

"Brisighella just now is a capital place. It's swarming with pilgrims from all parts of the country."

"But it's not on the way to anywhere."

"It's not far out of the way to Rome, and many of the Easter Pilgrims are going round to hear Mass there."

"I d-d-didn't know there was anything special in Brisighella."

"There's the Cardinal. Don't you remember his going to Florence to preach last December? It's that same Cardinal Montanelli. They say he made a great sensation."

"I dare say; I don't go to hear sermons."

"Well, he has the reputation of being a saint, you see."

"How does he manage that?"

"I don't know. I suppose it's because he gives away all his income, and lives like a parish priest with four or five hundred scudi a year."

"Ah!" interposed the man called Gino; "but it's more than that. He doesn't only give away money; he spends his whole life in looking after the poor, and seeing the sick are properly treated, and hearing complaints and grievances from morning till night. I'm no fonder of priests than you are, Michele, but Monsignor Montanelli is not like other Cardinals."

"Oh, I dare say he's more fool than knave!" said Michele. "Anyhow, the people are mad after him, and the last new freak is for the pilgrims to go round that way to ask his blessing. Domenichino thought of going as a pedlar, with a basket of cheap crosses and rosaries. The people like to buy those things and ask the Cardinal to touch them; then they put them round their babies' necks to keep off the evil eye."

"Wait a minute. How am I to go—as a pilgrim? This make-up suits me p-pretty well, I think; but it w-won't do for me to show myself in Brisighella in the same character that I had here; it would be ev-v-vidence against you if I get taken."

"You won't get taken; we have a splendid disguise for you, with a passport and all complete."

"What is it?"

"An old Spanish pilgrim—a repentant brigand from the Sierras. He fell ill in Ancona last year, and one of our friends took him on board a trading-vessel out of charity, and set him down in Venice, where he had friends, and he left his papers with us to show his gratitude. They will just do for you."

"A repentant b-b-brigand? But w-what about the police?"

"Oh, that's all right! He finished his term of the galleys some years ago, and has been going about to Jerusalem and all sorts of places saving his soul ever since. He killed his son by mistake for somebody else, and gave himself up to the police in a fit of remorse."

"Was he quite old?"

"Yes; but a white beard and wig will set that right, and the description suits you to perfection in every other respect. He was an old soldier, with a lame foot and a sabre-cut across the face like yours; and then his being a Spaniard, too—you see, if you meet any Spanish pilgrims, you can talk to them all right."

"Where am I to meet Domenichino?"

"You join the pilgrims at the cross-road that we will show you on the map, saying you had lost your way in the hills. Then, when you reach the town, you go with the rest of them into the marketplace, in front of the Cardinal's palace."

"Oh, he manages to live in a p-palace, then, in s-spite of being a saint?"

"He lives in one wing of it, and has turned the rest into a hospital. Well, you all wait there for him to come out and give his benediction, and Domenichino will come up with his basket and say: 'Are you one of the pilgrims, father?' and you answer: 'I am a miserable sinner.' Then he puts down his basket and wipes his face with his sleeve, and you offer him six soldi for a rosary."

"Then, of course, he arranges where we can talk?"

"Yes; he will have plenty of time to give you the address of the meeting-place while the people are gaping at Montanelli. That was our plan; but if you don't like it, we can let Domenichino know and arrange something else."

"No; it will do; only see that the beard and wig look natural."

"Are you one of the pilgrims, father?"

The Gadfly, sitting on the steps of the episcopal palace, looked up from under his ragged white locks, and gave the password in a husky, trembling voice, with a strong foreign accent. Domenichino slipped the leather strap from his shoulder, and set down his basket of pious gewgaws on the step. The crowd of peasants and pilgrims sitting on the steps and lounging about the market-place was taking no notice of them, but for precaution's sake they kept up a desultory conversation, Domenichino speaking in the local dialect and the Gadfly in broken Italian, intermixed with Spanish words.

"His Eminence! His Eminence is coming out!" shouted the people by the door. "Stand aside! His Eminence is coming!"

They both stood up.

"Here, father," said Domenichino, putting into the Gadfly's hand a little image wrapped in paper; "take this, too, and pray for me when you get to Rome."

The Gadfly thrust it into his breast, and turned to look at the figure in the violet Lenten robe and scarlet cap that was standing on the upper step and blessing the people with outstretched arms.

Montanelli came slowly down the steps, the people crowding about him to kiss his hands. Many knelt down and put the hem of his cassock to their lips as he passed.

"Peace be with you, my children!"

At the sound of the clear, silvery voice, the Gadfly bent his head, so that the white hair fell across his face; and Domenichino, seeing the quivering of the pilgrim's staff in his hand, said to himself with admiration: "What an actor!"

A woman standing near to them stooped down and lifted her child from the step. "Come, Cecco," she said. "His Eminence will bless you as the dear Lord blessed the children."

The Gadfly moved a step forward and stopped. Oh, it was hard! All these outsiders—these pilgrims and mountaineers—could go up and speak to him, and he would lay his hand on their children's hair. Perhaps he would say "Carino" to that peasant boy, as he used to say——

The Gadfly sank down again on the step, turning away that he might not see. If only he could shrink into some corner and stop his ears to shut out the sound! Indeed, it was more than any man should have to bear—to be so close, so close that he could have put out his arm and touched the dear hand.

"Will you not come under shelter, my friend?" the soft voice said. "I am afraid you are chilled."

The Gadfly's heart stood still. For a moment he was conscious of nothing but the sickening pressure of the blood that seemed as if it would tear his breast asunder; then it rushed back, tingling and burning through all his body, and he looked up. The grave, deep eyes above him grew suddenly tender with divine compassion at the sight of his face.

"Stand bark a little, friends," Montanelli said, turning to the crowd; "I want to speak to him."

The people fell slowly back, whispering to each other, and the Gadfly, sitting motionless, with teeth clenched and eyes on the ground, felt the gentle touch of Montanelli's hand upon his shoulder.

"You have had some great trouble. Can I do anything to help you?"

The Gadfly shook his head in silence.

"Are you a pilgrim?"

"I am a miserable sinner."

The accidental similarity of Montanelli's question to the password came like a chance straw, that the Gadfly, in his desperation, caught at, answering automatically. He had begun to tremble under the soft pressure of the hand that seemed to burn upon his shoulder.

The Cardinal bent down closer to him.

"Perhaps you would care to speak to me alone? If I can be any help to you——"

For the first time the Gadfly looked straight and steadily into Montanelli's eyes; he was already recovering his self-command.

"It would be no use," he said; "the thing is hopeless."

A police official stepped forward out of the crowd.

"Forgive my intruding, Your Eminence. I think the old man is not quite sound in his mind. He is perfectly harmless, and his papers are in order, so we don't interfere with him. He has been in penal servitude for a great crime, and is now doing penance."

"A great crime," the Gadfly repeated, shaking his head slowly.

"Thank you, captain; stand aside a little, please. My friend, nothing is hopeless if a man has sincerely repented. Will you not come to me this evening?"

"Would Your Eminence receive a man who is guilty of the death of his own son?"

The question had almost the tone of a challenge, and Montanelli shrank and shivered under it as under a cold wind.

"God forbid that I should condemn you, whatever you have done!" he said solemnly. "In His sight we are all guilty alike, and our righteousness is as filthy rags. If you will come to me I will receive you as I pray that He may one day receive me."

The Gadfly stretched out his hands with a sudden gesture of passion.

"Listen!" he said; "and listen all of you, Christians! If a man has killed his only son—his son who loved and trusted him, who was flesh of his flesh and bone of his bone; if he has led his son into a death-trap with lies and deceit—is there hope for that man in earth or heaven? I have confessed my sin before God and man, and I have suffered the punishment that men have laid on me, and they have let me go; but when will God say, 'It is enough'? What benediction will take away His curse from my soul? What absolution will undo this thing that I have done?"

In the dead silence that followed the people looked at Montanelli, and saw the heaving of the cross upon his breast.

He raised his eyes at last, and gave the benediction with a hand that was not quite steady.

"God is merciful," he said. "Lay your burden before His throne; for it is written: 'A broken and contrite heart shalt thou not despise.'"

He turned away and walked through the market-place, stopping everywhere to speak to the people, and to take their children in his arms.

In the evening the Gadfly, following the directions written on the wrapping of the image, made his way to the appointed meeting-place. It was the house of a local doctor, who was an active member of the "sect." Most of the conspirators were already assembled, and their delight at the Gadfly's arrival gave him a new proof, if he had needed one, of his popularity as a leader.

"We're glad enough to see you again," said the doctor; "but we shall be gladder still to see you go. It's a fearfully risky business, and I, for one, was against the plan. Are you quite sure none of those police rats noticed you in the market-place this morning?"

"Oh, they n-noticed me enough, but they d-didn't recognize me. Domenichino m-managed the thing capitally. But where is he? I don't see him."

"He has not come yet. So you got on all smoothly? Did the Cardinal give you his blessing?"

"His blessing? Oh, that's nothing," said Domenichino, coming in at the door. "Rivarez, you're as full of surprises as a Christmas cake. How many more talents are you going to astonish us with?"

"What is it now?" asked the Gadfly languidly. He was leaning back on a sofa, smoking a cigar. He still wore his pilgrim's dress, but the white beard and wig lay beside him.

"I had no idea you were such an actor. I never saw a thing done so magnificently in my life. You nearly moved His Eminence to tears."

"How was that? Let us hear, Rivarez."

The Gadfly shrugged his shoulders. He was in a taciturn and laconic mood, and the others, seeing that nothing was to be got out of him, appealed to Domenichino to explain. When the scene in the market-place had been related, one young workman, who had not joined in the laughter of the rest, remarked abruptly:

"It was very clever, of course; but I don't see what good all this play-acting business has done to anybody."

"Just this much," the Gadfly put in; "that I can go where I like and do what I like anywhere in this district, and not a single man, woman, or child will ever think of suspecting me. The story will be all over the place by to-morrow, and when I meet a spy he will only think: 'It's mad Diego, that confessed his sins in the market-place.' That is an advantage gained, surely."

"Yes, I see. Still, I wish the thing could have been done without fooling the Cardinal. He's too good to have that sort of trick played on him."

"I thought myself he seemed fairly decent," the Gadfly lazily assented.

"Nonsense, Sandro! We don't want Cardinals here!" said Domenichino. "And if Monsignor Montanelli had taken that post in Rome when he had the chance of getting it, Rivarez couldn't have fooled him."

"He wouldn't take it because he didn't want to leave his work here."

"More likely because he didn't want to get poisoned off by Lambruschini's agents. They've got something against him, you may depend upon it. When a Cardinal, especially such a popular one, 'prefers to stay' in a God-forsaken little hole like this, we all know what that means—don't we, Rivarez?"

The Gadfly was making smoke-rings. "Perhaps it is a c-c-case of a 'b-b-broken and contrite heart,'" he remarked, leaning his head back to watch them float away. "And now, men, let us get to business."

They began to discuss in detail the various plans which had been formed for the smuggling and concealment of weapons. The Gadfly listened with keen attention, interrupting every now and then to correct sharply some inaccurate statement or imprudent proposal. When everyone had finished speaking, he made a few practical suggestions, most of which were adopted without discussion. The meeting then broke up. It had been resolved that, at least until he was safely back in Tuscany, very late meetings, which might attract the notice of the police, should be avoided. By a little after ten o'clock all had dispersed except the doctor, the Gadfly, and Domenichino, who remained as a sub-committee for the discussion of special points. After a long and hot dispute, Domenichino looked up at the clock.

"Half-past eleven; we mustn't stop any longer or the night-watchman may see us."

"When does he pass?" asked the Gadfly.

"About twelve o'clock; and I want to be home before he comes. Good-night, Giordani. Rivarez, shall we walk together?"

"No; I think we are safer apart. Then I shall see you again?"

"Yes; at Castel Bolognese. I don't know yet what disguise I shall be in, but you have the password. You leave here to-morrow, I think?"

The Gadfly was carefully putting on his beard and wig before the looking-glass.

"To-morrow morning, with the pilgrims. On the next day I fall ill and stop behind in a shepherd's hut, and then take a short cut across the hills. I shall be down there before you will. Good-night!"

Twelve o'clock was striking from the Cathedral bell-tower as the Gadfly looked in at the door of the great empty barn which had been thrown open as a lodging for the pilgrims. The floor was covered with clumsy figures, most of which were snoring lustily, and the air was insufferably close and foul. He drew back with a little shudder of repugnance; it would be useless to attempt to sleep in there; he would take a walk, and then find some shed or haystack which would, at least, be clean and quiet.

It was a glorious night, with a great full moon gleaming in a purple sky. He began to wander through the streets in an aimless way, brooding miserably over the scene of the morning, and wishing that he had never consented to Domenichino's plan of holding the meeting in Brisighella. If at the beginning he had declared the project too dangerous, some other place would have been chosen; and both he and Montanelli would have been spared this ghastly, ridiculous farce.

How changed the Padre was! And yet his voice was not changed at all; it was just the same as in the old days, when he used to say: "Carino."

The lantern of the night-watchman appeared at the other end of the street, and the Gadfly turned down a narrow, crooked alley. After walking a few yards he found himself in the Cathedral Square, close to the left wing of the episcopal palace. The square was flooded with moonlight, and there was no one in sight; but he noticed that a side door of the Cathedral was ajar. The sacristan must have forgotten to shut it. Surely nothing could be going on there so late at night. He might as well go in and sleep on one of the benches instead of in the stifling barn; he could slip out in the morning before the sacristan came; and even if anyone did find him, the natural supposition would be that mad Diego had been saying his prayers in some corner, and had got shut in.

He listened a moment at the door, and then entered with the noiseless step that he had retained notwithstanding his lameness. The moonlight streamed through the windows, and lay in broad bands on the marble floor. In the chancel, especially, everything was as clearly visible as by daylight. At the foot of the altar steps Cardinal Montanelli knelt alone, bare-headed, with clasped hands.

The Gadfly drew back into the shadow. Should he slip away before Montanelli saw him? That, no doubt, would be the wisest thing to do—perhaps the most merciful. And yet, what harm could it do for him to go just a little nearer—to look at the Padre's face once more, now that the crowd was gone, and there was no need to keep up the hideous comedy of the morning? Perhaps it would be his last chance—and the Padre need not see him; he would steal up softly and look—just this once. Then he would go back to his work.

Keeping in the shadow of the pillars, he crept softly up to the chancel rails, and paused at the side entrance, close to the altar. The shadow of the episcopal throne was broad enough to cover him, and he crouched down in the darkness, holding his breath.

"My poor boy! Oh, God; my poor boy!"

The broken whisper was full of such endless despair that the Gadfly shuddered in spite of himself. Then came deep, heavy, tearless sobs; and he saw Montanelli wring his hands together like a man in bodily pain.

He had not thought it would be so bad as this. How often had he said to himself with bitter assurance: "I need not trouble about it; that wound was healed long ago." Now, after all these years, it was laid bare before him, and he saw it bleeding still. And how easy it would be to heal it now at last! He need only lift his hand—only step forward and say: "Padre, it is I." There was Gemma, too, with that white streak across her hair. Oh, if he could but forgive! If he could but cut out from his memory the past that was burned into it so deep—the Lascar, and the sugar-plantation, and the variety show! Surely there was no other misery like this—to be willing to forgive, to long to forgive; and to know that it was hopeless—that he could not, dared not forgive.

Montanelli rose at last, made the sign of the cross, and turned away from the altar. The Gadfly shrank further back into the shadow, trembling with fear lest he should be seen, lest the very beating of his heart should betray him; then he drew a long breath of relief. Montanelli had passed him, so close that the violet robe had brushed against his cheek,—had passed and had not seen him.

Had not seen him—— Oh, what had he done? This had been his last chance—this one precious moment—and he had let it slip away. He started up and stepped into the light.

"Padre!"

The sound of his own voice, ringing up and dying away along the arches of the roof, filled him with fantastic terror. He shrank back again into the shadow. Montanelli stood beside the pillar, motionless, listening with wide-open eyes, full of the horror of death. How long the silence lasted the Gadfly could not tell; it might have been an instant, or an eternity. He came to his senses with a sudden shock. Montanelli was beginning to sway as though he would fall, and his lips moved, at first silently.

"Arthur!" the low whisper came at last; "yes, the water is deep——"

The Gadfly came forward.

"Forgive me, Your Eminence! I thought it was one of the priests."

"Ah, it is the pilgrim?" Montanelli had at once recovered his self-control, though the Gadfly could see, from the restless glitter of the sapphire on his hand, that he was still trembling. "Are you in need of anything, my friend? It is late, and the Cathedral is closed at night."

"I beg pardon, Your Eminence, if I have done wrong. I saw the door open, and came in to pray, and when I saw a priest, as I thought, in meditation, I waited to ask a blessing on this."

He held up the little tin cross that he had bought from Domenichino. Montanelli took it from his hand, and, re-entering the chancel, laid it for a moment on the altar.

"Take it, my son," he said, "and be at rest, for the Lord is tender and pitiful. Go to Rome, and ask the blessing of His minister, the Holy Father. Peace be with you!"

The Gadfly bent his head to receive the benediction, and turned slowly away.

"Stop!" said Montanelli.

He was standing with one hand on the chancel rail.

"When you receive the Holy Eucharist in Rome," he said, "pray for one in deep affliction—for one on whose soul the hand of the Lord is heavy."

There were almost tears in his voice, and the Gadfly's resolution wavered. Another instant and he would have betrayed himself. Then the thought of the variety-show came up again, and he remembered, like Jonah, that he did well to be angry.

"Who am I, that He should hear my prayers? A leper and an outcast! If I could bring to His throne, as Your Eminence can, the offering of a holy life—of a soul without spot or secret shame———"

Montanelli turned abruptly away.

"I have only one offering to give," he said; "a broken heart."

A few days later the Gadfly returned to Florence in the diligence from Pistoja. He went straight to Gemma's lodgings, but she was out. Leaving a message that he would return in the morning he went home, sincerely hoping that he should not again find his study invaded by Zita. Her jealous reproaches would act on his nerves, if he were to hear much of them to-night, like the rasping of a dentist's file.

"Good-evening, Bianca," he said when the maid-servant opened the door. "Has Mme. Reni been here to-day?"

She stared at him blankly

"Mme. Reni? Has she come back, then, sir?"

"What do you mean?" he asked with a frown, stopping short on the mat.

"She went away quite suddenly, just after you did, and left all her things behind her. She never so much as said she was going."

"Just after I did? What, a f-fortnight ago?"

"Yes, sir, the same day; and her things are lying about higgledy-piggledy. All the neighbours are talking about it."

He turned away from the door-step without speaking, and went hastily down the lane to the house where Zita had been lodging. In her rooms nothing had been touched; all the presents that he had given her were in their usual places; there was no letter or scrap of writing anywhere.

"If you please, sir," said Bianca, putting her head in at the door, "there's an old woman———"

He turned round fiercely.

"What do you want here—following me about?"

"An old woman wishes to see you."

"What does she want? Tell her I c-can't see her; I'm busy."

"She has been coming nearly every evening since you went away, sir, always asking when you would come back."

"Ask her w-what her business is. No; never mind; I suppose I must go myself."

The old woman was waiting at his hall door. She was very poorly dressed, with a face as brown and wrinkled as a medlar, and a bright-coloured scarf twisted round her head. As he came in she rose and looked at him with keen black eyes.

"You are the lame gentleman," she said, inspecting him critically from head to foot. "I have brought you a message from Zita Reni."

He opened the study door, and held it for her to pass in; then followed her and shut the door, that Bianca might not hear.

"Sit down, please. N-now, tell me who you are."

"It's no business of yours who I am. I have come to tell you that Zita Reni has gone away with my son."

"With—your—son?"

"Yes, sir; if you don't know how to keep your mistress when you've got her, you can't complain if other men take her. My son has blood in his veins, not milk and water; he comes of the Romany folk."

"Ah, you are a gipsy! Zita has gone back to her own people, then?"

She looked at him in amazed contempt. Apparently, these Christians had not even manhood enough to be angry when they were insulted.

"What sort of stuff are you made of, that she should stay with you? Our women may lend themselves to you a bit for a girl's fancy, or if you pay them well; but the Romany blood comes back to the Romany folk."

The Gadfly's face remained as cold and steady as before.

"Has she gone away with a gipsy camp, or merely to live with your son?"

The woman burst out laughing.

"Do you think of following her and trying to win her back? It's too late, sir; you should have thought of that before!"

"No; I only want to know the truth, if you will tell it to me."

She shrugged her shoulders; it was hardly worth while to abuse a person who took it so meekly.

"The truth, then, is that she met my son in the road the day you left her, and spoke to him in the Romany tongue; and when he saw she was one of our folk, in spite of her fine clothes, he fell in love with her bonny face, as OUR men fall in love, and took her to our camp. She told us all her trouble, and sat crying and sobbing, poor lassie, till our hearts were sore for her. We comforted her as best we could; and at last she took off her fine clothes and put on the things our lasses wear, and gave herself to my son, to be his woman and to have him for her man. He won't say to her: 'I don't love you,' and: 'I've other things to do.' When a woman is young, she wants a man; and what sort of man are you, that you can't even kiss a handsome girl when she puts her arms round your neck?"

"You said," he interrupted, "that you had brought me a message from her."

"Yes; I stopped behind when the camp went on, so as to give it. She told me to say that she has had enough of your folk and their hair-splitting and their sluggish blood; and that she wants to get back to her own people and be free. 'Tell him,' she said, 'that I am a woman, and that I loved him; and that is why I would not be his harlot any longer.' The lassie was right to come away. There's no harm in a girl getting a bit of money out of her good looks if she can—that's what good looks are for; but a Romany lass has nothing to do with LOVING a man of your race."

The Gadfly stood up.

"Is that all the message?" he said. "Then tell her, please, that I think she has done right, and that I hope she will be happy. That is all I have to say. Good-night!"

He stood perfectly still until the garden gate closed behind her; then he sat down and covered his face with both hands.

Another blow on the cheek! Was no rag of pride to be left him—no shred of self-respect? Surely he had suffered everything that man can endure; his very heart had been dragged in the mud and trampled under the feet of the passers-by; there was no spot in his soul where someone's contempt was not branded in, where someone's mockery had not left its iron trace. And now this gipsy girl, whom he had picked up by the wayside—even she had the whip in her hand.

Shaitan whined at the door, and the Gadfly rose to let him in. The dog rushed up to his master with his usual frantic manifestations of delight, but soon, understanding that something was wrong, lay down on the rug beside him, and thrust a cold nose into the listless hand.

An hour later Gemma came up to the front door. No one appeared in answer to her knock; Bianca, finding that the Gadfly did not want any dinner, had slipped out to visit a neighbour's cook. She had left the door open, and a light burning in the hall. Gemma, after waiting for some time, decided to enter and try if she could find the Gadfly, as she wished to speak to him about an important message which had come from Bailey. She knocked at the study door, and the Gadfly's voice answered from within: "You can go away, Bianca. I don't want anything."

She softly opened the door. The room was quite dark, but the passage lamp threw a long stream of light across it as she entered, and she saw the Gadfly sitting alone, his head sunk on his breast, and the dog asleep at his feet.

"It is I," she said.

He started up. "Gemma,—— Gemma! Oh, I have wanted you so!"

Before she could speak he was kneeling on the floor at her feet and hiding his face in the folds of her dress. His whole body was shaken with a convulsive tremor that was worse to see than tears.

She stood still. There was nothing she could do to help him—nothing. This was the bitterest thing of all. She must stand by and look on passively—she who would have died to spare him pain. Could she but dare to stoop and clasp her arms about him, to hold him close against her heart and shield him, were it with her own body, from all further harm or wrong; surely then he would be Arthur to her again; surely then the day would break and the shadows flee away.

Ah, no, no! How could he ever forget? Was it not she who had cast him into hell—she, with her own right hand?

She had let the moment slip by. He rose hastily and sat down by the table, covering his eyes with one hand and biting his lip as if he would bite it through.

Presently he looked up and said quietly:

"I am afraid I startled you."

She held out both her hands to him. "Dear," she said, "are we not friends enough by now for you to trust me a little bit? What is it?"

"Only a private trouble of my own. I don't see why you should be worried over it."

"Listen a moment," she went on, taking his hand in both of hers to steady its convulsive trembling. "I have not tried to lay hands on a thing that is not mine to touch. But now that you have given me, of your own free will, so much of your confidence, will you not give me a little more—as you would do if I were your sister. Keep the mask on your face, if it is any consolation to you, but don't wear a mask on your soul, for your own sake."

He bent his head lower. "You must be patient with me," he said. "I am an unsatisfactory sort of brother to have, I'm afraid; but if you only knew—— I have been nearly mad this last week. It has been like South America again. And somehow the devil gets into me and——" He broke off.

"May I not have my share in your trouble?" she whispered at last.

His head sank down on her arm. "The hand of the Lord is heavy."

PART III

CHAPTER I

THE next five weeks were spent by Gemma and the Gadfly in a whirl of excitement and overwork which left them little time or energy for thinking about their personal affairs. When the arms had been safely smuggled into Papal territory there remained a still more difficult and dangerous task: that of conveying them unobserved from the secret stores in the mountain caverns and ravines to the various local centres and thence to the separate villages. The whole district was swarming with spies; and Domenichino, to whom the Gadfly had intrusted the ammunition, sent into Florence a messenger with an urgent appeal for either help or extra time. The Gadfly had insisted that the work should be finished by the middle of June; and what with the difficulty of conveying heavy transports over bad roads, and the endless hindrances and delays caused by the necessity of continually evading observation, Domenichino was growing desperate. "I am between Scylla and Charybdis," he wrote. "I dare not work quickly, for fear of detection, and I must not work slowly if we are to be ready in time. Either send me efficient help at once, or let the Venetians know that we shall not be ready till the first week in July."

The Gadfly carried the letter to Gemma and, while she read it, sat frowning at the floor and stroking the cat's fur the wrong way.

"This is bad," she said. "We can hardly keep the Venetians waiting for three weeks."

"Of course we can't; the thing is absurd. Domenichino m-might unders-s-stand that. We must follow the lead of the Venetians, not they ours."

"I don't see that Domenichino is to blame; he has evidently done his best, and he can't do impossibilities."

"It's not in Domenichino that the fault lies; it's in the fact of his being one person instead of two. We ought to have at least one responsible man to guard the store and another to see the transports off. He is quite right; he must have efficient help."

"But what help are we going to give him? We have no one in Florence to send."

"Then I m-must go myself."

She leaned back in her chair and looked at him with a little frown.

"No, that won't do; it's too risky."

"It will have to do if we can't f-f-find any other way out of the difficulty."

"Then we must find another way, that's all. It's out of the question for you to go again just now."

An obstinate line appeared at the corners of his under lip.

"I d-don't see that it's out of the question."

"You will see if you think about the thing calmly for a minute. It is only five weeks since you got back; the police are on the scent about that pilgrim business, and scouring the country to find a clue. Yes, I know you are clever at disguises; but remember what a lot of people saw you, both as Diego and as the countryman; and you can't disguise your lameness or the scar on your face."

"There are p-plenty of lame people in the world."

"Yes, but there are not plenty of people in the Romagna with a lame foot and a sabre-cut across the cheek and a left arm injured like yours, and the combination of blue eyes with such dark colouring."

"The eyes don't matter; I can alter them with belladonna."

"You can't alter the other things. No, it won't do. For you to go there just now, with all your identification-marks, would be to walk into a trap with your eyes open. You would certainly be taken."

"But s-s-someone must help Domenichino."

"It will be no help to him to have you caught at a critical moment like this. Your arrest would mean the failure of the whole thing."

But the Gadfly was difficult to convince, and the discussion went on and on without coming nearer to any settlement. Gemma was beginning to realize how nearly inexhaustible was the fund of quiet obstinacy in his character; and, had the matter not been one about which she felt strongly, she would probably have yielded for the sake of peace. This, however, was a case in which she could not conscientiously give way; the practical advantage to be gained from the proposed journey seemed to her not sufficiently important to be worth the risk, and she could not help suspecting that his desire to go was prompted less by a conviction of grave political necessity than by a morbid craving for the excitement of danger. He had got into the habit of risking his neck, and his tendency to run into unnecessary peril seemed to her a form of intemperance which should be quietly but steadily resisted. Finding all her arguments unavailing against his dogged resolve to go his own way, she fired her last shot.

"Let us be honest about it, anyway," she said; "and call things by their true names. It is not Domenichino's difficulty that makes you so determined to go. It is your own personal passion for——"

"It's not true!" he interrupted vehemently. "He is nothing to me; I don't care if I never see him again."

He broke off, seeing in her face that he had betrayed himself. Their eyes met for an instant, and dropped; and neither of them uttered the name that was in both their minds.

"It—it is not Domenichino I want to save," he stammered at last, with his face half buried in the cat's fur; "it is that I—I understand the danger of the work failing if he has no help."

She passed over the feeble little subterfuge, and went on as if there had been no interruption:

"It is your passion for running into danger which makes you want to go there. You have the same craving for danger when you are worried that you had for opium when you were ill."

"It was not I that asked for the opium," he said defiantly; "it was the others who insisted on giving it to me."

"I dare say. You plume yourself a little on your stoicism, and to ask for physical relief would have hurt your pride; but it is rather flattered than otherwise when you risk your life to relieve the irritation of your nerves. And yet, after all, the distinction is a merely conventional one."

He drew the cat's head back and looked down into the round, green eyes. "Is it true, Pasht?" he said. "Are all these unkind things true that your mistress is s-saying about me? Is it a case of mea culpa; mea m-maxima culpa? You wise beast, you never ask for opium, do you? Your ancestors were gods in Egypt, and no man t-trod on their tails. I wonder, though, what would become of your calm superiority to earthly ills if I were to take this paw of yours and hold it in the c-candle. Would you ask me for opium then? Would you? Or perhaps—for death? No, pussy, we have no right to die for our personal convenience. We may spit and s-swear a bit, if it consoles us; but we mustn't pull the paw away."

"Hush!" She took the cat off his knee and put it down on a footstool. "You and I will have time for thinking about those things later on. What we have to think of now is how to get Domenichino out of his difficulty. What is it, Katie; a visitor? I am busy."

"Miss Wright has sent you this, ma'am, by hand."

The packet, which was carefully sealed, contained a letter, addressed to Miss Wright, but unopened and with a Papal stamp. Gemma's old school friends still lived in Florence, and her more important letters were often received, for safety, at their address.

"It is Michele's mark," she said, glancing quickly over the letter, which seemed to be about the summer-terms at a boarding house in the Apennines, and pointing to two little blots on a corner of the page. "It is in chemical ink; the reagent is in the third drawer of the writing-table. Yes; that is it."

He laid the letter open on the desk and passed a little brush over its pages. When the real message stood out on the paper in a brilliant blue line, he leaned back in his chair and burst out laughing.

"What is it?" she asked hurriedly. He handed her the paper.

"DOMENICHINO HAS BEEN ARRESTED. COME AT ONCE."

She sat down with the paper in her hand and stared hopelessly at the Gadfly.

"W-well?" he said at last, with his soft, ironical drawl; "are you satisfied now that I must go?"

"Yes, I suppose you must," she answered, sighing. "And I too."

He looked up with a little start. "You too? But——"

"Of course. It will be very awkward, I know, to be left without anyone here in Florence; but everything must go to the wall now except the providing of an extra pair of hands."

"There are plenty of hands to be got there."

"They don't belong to people whom you can trust thoroughly, though. You said yourself just now that there must be two responsible persons in charge; and if Domenichino couldn't manage alone it is evidently impossible for you to do so. A person as desperately compromised as you are is very much handicapped, remember, in work of that kind, and more dependent on help than anyone else would be. Instead of you and Domenichino, it must be you and I."

He considered for a moment, frowning.

"Yes, you are quite right," he said; "and the sooner we go the better. But we must not start together. If I go off to-night, you can take, say, the afternoon coach to-morrow."

"Where to?"

"That we must discuss. I think I had b-b-better go straight in to Faenza. If I start late to-night and ride to Borgo San Lorenzo I can get my disguise arranged there and go straight on."

"I don't see what else we can do," she said, with an anxious little frown; "but it is very risky, your going off in such a hurry and trusting to the smugglers finding you a disguise at Borgo. You ought to have at least three clear days to double on your trace before you cross the frontier."

"You needn't be afraid," he answered, smiling; "I may get taken further on, but not at the frontier. Once in the hills I am as safe as here; there's not a smuggler in the Apennines that would betray me. What I am not quite sure about is how you are to get across."

"Oh, that is very simple! I shall take Louisa Wright's passport and go for a holiday. No one knows me in the Romagna, but every spy knows you."

"F-fortunately, so does every smuggler."

She took out her watch.

"Half-past two. We have the afternoon and evening, then, if you are to start to-night."

"Then the best thing will be for me to go home and settle everything now, and arrange about a good horse. I shall ride in to San Lorenzo; it will be safer."

"But it won't be safe at all to hire a horse. The owner will——-"

"I shan't hire one. I know a man that will lend me a horse, and that can be trusted. He has done things for me before. One of the shepherds will bring it back in a fortnight. I shall be here again by five or half-past, then; and while I am gone, I w-want you to go and find Martini and exp-plain everything to him."

"Martini!" She turned round and looked at him in astonishment.

"Yes; we must take him into confidence—unless you can think of anyone else."

"I don't quite understand what you mean."

"We must have someone here whom we can trust, in case of any special difficulty; and of all the set here Martini is the man in whom I have most confidence. Riccardo would do anything he could for us, of course; but I think Martini has a steadier head. Still, you know him better than I do; it is as you think."

"I have not the slightest doubt as to Martini's trustworthiness and efficiency in every respect; and I think he would probably consent to give us any help he could. But——"

He understood at once.

"Gemma, what would you feel if you found out that a comrade in bitter need had not asked you for help you might have given, for fear of hurting or distressing you? Would you say there was any true kindness in that?"

"Very well," she said, after a little pause; "I will send Katie round at once and ask him to come; and while she is gone I will go to Louisa for her passport; she promised to lend it whenever I want one. What about money? Shall I draw some out of the bank?"

"No; don't waste time on that; I can draw enough from my account to last us for a bit. We will fall back on yours later on if my balance runs short. Till half-past five, then; I shall be sure to find you here, of course?"

"Oh, yes! I shall be back long before then."

Half an hour after the appointed time he returned, and found Gemma and Martini sitting on the terrace together. He saw at once that their conversation had been a distressing one; the traces of agitation were visible in both of them, and Martini was unusually silent and glum.

"Have you arranged everything?" she asked, looking up.

"Yes; and I have brought you some money for the journey. The horse will be ready for me at the Ponte Rosso barrier at one in the night."

"Is not that rather late? You ought to get into San Lorenzo before the people are up in the morning."

"So I shall; it's a very fast horse; and I don't want to leave here when there's a chance of anyone noticing me. I shan't go home any more; there's a spy watching at the door, and he thinks me in."

"How did you get out without his seeing you?"

"Out of the kitchen window into the back garden and over the neighbour's orchard wall; that's what makes me so late; I had to dodge him. I left the owner of the horse to sit in the study all the evening with the lamp lighted. When the spy sees the light in the window and a shadow on the blind he will be quite satisfied that I am writing at home this evening."

"Then you will stay here till it is time to go to the barrier?"

"Yes; I don't want to be seen in the street any more to-night. Have a cigar, Martini? I know Signora Bolla doesn't mind smoke."

"I shan't be here to mind; I must go downstairs and help Katie with the dinner."

When she had gone Martini got up and began to pace to and fro with his hands behind his back. The Gadfly sat smoking and looking silently out at the drizzling rain.

"Rivarez!" Martini began, stopping in front of him, but keeping his eyes on the ground; "what sort of thing are you going to drag her into?"

The Gadfly took the cigar from his mouth and blew away a long trail of smoke.

"She has chosen for herself," he said, "without compulsion on anyone's part."

"Yes, yes—I know. But tell me——"

He stopped.

"I will tell you anything I can."

"Well, then—I don't know much about the details of these affairs in the hills,—are you going to take her into any very serious danger?"

"Do you want the truth?"

"Yes."

"Then—yes."

Martini turned away and went on pacing up and down. Presently he stopped again.

"I want to ask you another question. If you don't choose to answer it, you needn't, of course; but if you do answer, then answer honestly. Are you in love with her?"

The Gadfly deliberately knocked the ash from his cigar and went on smoking in silence.

"That means—that you don't choose to answer?"

"No; only that I think I have a right to know why you ask me that."

"Why? Good God, man, can't you see why?"

"Ah!" He laid down his cigar and looked steadily at Martini. "Yes," he said at last, slowly and softly. "I am in love with her. But you needn't think I am going to make love to her, or worry about it. I am only going to——"

His voice died away in a strange, faint whisper. Martini came a step nearer.

"Only going—to——"

"To die."

He was staring straight before him with a cold, fixed look, as if he were dead already. When he spoke again his voice was curiously lifeless and even.

"You needn't worry her about it beforehand," he said; "but there's not the ghost of a chance for me. It's dangerous for everyone; that she knows as well as I do; but the smugglers will do their best to prevent her getting taken. They are good fellows, though they are a bit rough. As for me, the rope is round my neck, and when I cross the frontier I pull the noose."

"Rivarez, what do you mean? Of course it's dangerous, and particularly so for you; I understand that; but you have often crossed the frontier before and always been successful."

"Yes, and this time I shall fail."

"But why? How can you know?"

The Gadfly smiled drearily.

"Do you remember the German legend of the man that died when he met his own Double? No? It appeared to him at night in a lonely place, wringing its hands in despair. Well, I met mine the last time I was in the hills; and when I cross the frontier again I shan't come back."

Martini came up to him and put a hand on the back of his chair.

"Listen, Rivarez; I don't understand a word of all this metaphysical stuff, but I do understand one thing: If you feel about it that way, you are not in a fit state to go. The surest way to get taken is to go with a conviction that you will be taken. You must be ill, or out of sorts somehow, to get maggots of that kind into your head. Suppose I go instead of you? I can do any practical work there is to be done, and you can send a message to your men, explaining———"

"And let you get killed instead? That would be very clever."

"Oh, I'm not likely to get killed! They don't know me as they do you. And, besides, even if I did———"

He stopped, and the Gadfly looked up with a slow, inquiring gaze. Martini's hand dropped by his side.

"She very likely wouldn't miss me as much as she would you," he said in his most matter-of-fact voice. "And then, besides, Rivarez, this is public business, and we have to look at it from the point of view of utility—the greatest good of the greatest number. Your 'final value'—isn't that what the economists call it?—is higher than mine; I have brains enough to see that, though I haven't any cause to be particularly fond of you. You are a bigger man than I am; I'm not sure that you are a better one, but there's more of you, and your death would be a greater loss than mine."

From the way he spoke he might have been discussing the value of shares on the Exchange. The Gadfly looked up, shivering as if with cold.

"Would you have me wait till my grave opens of itself to swallow me up?
"If I must die,
I will encounter darkness as a bride——
Look here, Martini, you and I are talking nonsense."

"You are, certainly," said Martini gruffly.

"Yes, and so are you. For Heaven's sake, don't let's go in for romantic self-sacrifice, like Don Carlos and Marquis Posa. This is the nineteenth century; and if it's my business to die, I have got to do it."

"And if it's my business to live, I have got to do that, I suppose. You're the lucky one, Rivarez."

"Yes," the Gadfly assented laconically; "I was always lucky."

They smoked in silence for a few minutes, and then began to talk of business details. When Gemma came up to call them to dinner, neither of them betrayed in face or manner that their conversation had been in any way unusual. After dinner they sat discussing plans and making necessary arrangements till eleven o'clock, when Martini rose and took his hat.

"I will go home and fetch that riding-cloak of mine, Rivarez. I think you will be less recognizable in it than in your light suit. I want to reconnoitre a bit, too, and make sure there are no spies about before we start."

"Are you coming with me to the barrier?"

"Yes; it's safer to have four eyes than two in case of anyone following you. I'll be back by twelve. Be sure you don't start without me. I had better take the key, Gemma, so as not to wake anyone by ringing."

She raised her eyes to his face as he took the keys. She understood that he had invented a pretext in order to leave her alone with the Gadfly.

"You and I will talk to-morrow," she said. "We shall have time in the morning, when my packing is finished."

"Oh, yes! Plenty of time. There are two or three little things I want to ask you about, Rivarez; but we can talk them over on our way to the barrier. You had better send Katie to bed, Gemma; and be as quiet as you can, both of you. Good-bye till twelve, then."

He went away with a little nod and smile, banging the door after him to let the neighbours hear that Signora Bolla's visitor was gone.

Gemma went out into the kitchen to say good-night to Katie, and came back with black coffee on a tray.

"Would you like to lie down a bit?" she said. "You won't have any sleep the rest of the night."

"Oh, dear no! I shall sleep at San Lorenzo while the men are getting my disguise ready."

"Then have some coffee. Wait a minute; I will get you out the biscuits."

As she knelt down at the side-board he suddenly stooped over her shoulder.

"Whatever have you got there? Chocolate creams and English toffee! Why, this is l-luxury for a king!"

She looked up, smiling faintly at his enthusiastic tone.

"Are you fond of sweets? I always keep them for Cesare; he is a perfect baby over any kind of lollipops."

"R-r-really? Well, you must get him s-some more to-morrow and give me these to take with me. No, let me p-p-put the toffee in my pocket; it will console me for all the lost joys of life. I d-do hope they'll give me a bit of toffee to suck the day I'm hanged."

"Oh, do let me find a cardboard box for it, at least, before you put it in your pocket! You will be so sticky! Shall I put the chocolates in, too?"

"No, I want to eat them now, with you."

"But I don't like chocolate, and I want you to come and sit down like a reasonable human being. We very likely shan't have another chance to talk quietly before one or other of us is killed, and———"

"She d-d-doesn't like chocolate!" he murmured under his breath. "Then I must be greedy all by myself. This is a case of the hangman's supper, isn't it? You are going to humour all my whims to-night. First of all, I want you to sit on this easy-chair, and, as you said I might lie down, I shall lie here and be comfortable."

He threw himself down on the rug at her feet, leaning his elbow on the chair and looking up into her face.

"How pale you are!" he said. "That's because you take life sadly, and don't like chocolate——"

"Do be serious for just five minutes! After all, it is a matter of life and death."

"Not even for two minutes, dear; neither life nor death is worth it."

He had taken hold of both her hands and was stroking them with the tips of his fingers.

"Don't look so grave, Minerva! You'll make me cry in a minute, and then you'll be sorry. I do wish you'd smile again; you have such a d-delightfully unexpected smile. There now, don't scold me, dear! Let us eat our biscuits together, like two good children, without quarrelling over them—for to-morrow we die."

He took a sweet biscuit from the plate and carefully halved it, breaking the sugar ornament down the middle with scrupulous exactness.

"This is a kind of sacrament, like what the goody-goody people have in church. 'Take, eat; this is my body.' And we must d-drink the wine out of the s-s-same glass, you know—yes, that is right. 'Do this in remembrance——'"

She put down the glass.

"Don't!" she said, with almost a sob. He looked up, and took her hands again.

"Hush, then! Let us be quiet for a little bit. When one of us dies, the other will remember this. We will forget this loud, insistent world that howls about our ears; we will go away together, hand in hand; we will go away into the secret halls of death, and lie among the poppy-flowers. Hush! We will be quite still."

He laid his head down against her knee and covered his face. In the silence she bent over him, her hand on the black head. So the time slipped on and on; and they neither moved nor spoke.

"Dear, it is almost twelve," she said at last. He raised his head.

"We have only a few minutes more; Martini will be back presently. Perhaps we shall never see each other again. Have you nothing to say to me?"

He slowly rose and walked away to the other side of the room. There was a moment's silence.

"I have one thing to say," he began in a hardly audible voice; "one thing—to tell you——"

He stopped and sat down by the window, hiding his face in both hands.

"You have been a long time deciding to be merciful," she said softly.

"I have not seen much mercy in my life; and I thought—at first—you wouldn't care——"

"You don't think that now."

She waited a moment for him to speak and then crossed the room and stood beside him.

"Tell me the truth at last," she whispered. "Think, if you are killed and I not—I should have to go through all my life and never know—never be quite sure——"

He took her hands and clasped them tightly.

"If I am killed—— You see, when I went to South America—— Ah, Martini!"

He broke away with a violent start and threw open the door of the room. Martini was rubbing his boots on the mat.

"Punctual to the m-m-minute, as usual! You're an an-n-nimated chronometer, Martini. Is that the r-r-riding-cloak?"

"Yes; and two or three other things. I have kept them as dry as I could, but it's pouring with rain. You will have a most uncomfortable ride, I'm afraid."

"Oh, that's no matter. Is the street clear?"

"Yes; all the spies seem to have gone to bed. I don't much wonder either, on such a villainous night. Is that coffee, Gemma? He ought to have something hot before he goes out into the wet, or he will catch cold."

"It is black coffee, and very strong. I will boil some milk."

She went into the kitchen, passionately clenching her teeth and hands to keep from breaking down. When she returned with the milk the Gadfly had put on the riding-cloak and was fastening the leather gaiters which Martini had brought. He drank a cup of coffee, standing, and took up the broad-brimmed riding hat.

"I think it's time to start, Martini; we must make a round before we go to the barrier, in case of anything. Good-bye, for the present, signora; I shall meet you at Forli on Friday, then, unless anything special turns up. Wait a minute; th-this is the address."

He tore a leaf out of his pocket-book and wrote a few words in pencil.

"I have it already," she said in a dull, quiet voice.

"H-have you? Well, there it is, anyway. Come, Martini. Sh-sh-sh! Don't let the door creak!"

They crept softly downstairs. When the street door clicked behind them she went back into the room and mechanically unfolded the paper he had put into her hand. Underneath the address was written:

"I will tell you everything there."

CHAPTER II

IT was market-day in Brisighella, and the country folk had come in from the villages and hamlets of the district with their pigs and poultry, their dairy produce and droves of half-wild mountain cattle. The market-place was thronged with a perpetually shifting crowd, laughing, joking, bargaining for dried figs, cheap cakes, and sunflower seeds. The brown, bare-footed children sprawled, face downward, on the pavement in the hot sun, while their mothers sat under the trees with their baskets of butter and eggs.

Monsignor Montanelli, coming out to wish the people "Good-morning," was at once surrounded by a clamourous throng of children, holding up for his acceptance great bunches of irises and scarlet poppies and sweet white narcissus from the mountain slopes. His passion for wild flowers was affectionately tolerated by the people, as one of the little follies which sit gracefully on very wise men. If anyone less universally beloved had filled his house with weeds and grasses they would have laughed at him; but the "blessed Cardinal" could afford a few harmless eccentricities.

"Well, Mariuccia," he said, stopping to pat one of the children on the head; "you have grown since I saw you last. And how is the grandmother's rheumatism?"

"She's been better lately, Your Eminence; but mother's bad now."

"I'm sorry to hear that; tell the mother to come down here some day and see whether Dr. Giordani can do anything for her. I will find somewhere to put her up; perhaps the change will do her good. You are looking better, Luigi; how are your eyes?"

He passed on, chatting with the mountaineers. He always remembered the names and ages of the children, their troubles and those of their parents; and would stop to inquire, with sympathetic interest, for the health of the cow that fell sick at Christmas, or of the rag-doll that was crushed under a cart-wheel last market-day.

When he returned to the palace the marketing began. A lame man in a blue shirt, with a shock of black hair hanging into his eyes and a deep scar across the left cheek, lounged up to one of the booths and, in very bad Italian, asked for a drink of lemonade.

"You're not from these parts," said the woman who poured it out, glancing up at him.

"No. I come from Corsica."

"Looking for work?"

"Yes; it will be hay-cutting time soon, and a gentleman that has a farm near Ravenna came across to Bastia the other day and told me there's plenty of work to be got there."

"I hope you'll find it so, I'm sure, but times are bad hereabouts."

"They're worse in Corsica, mother. I don't know what we poor folk are coming to."

"Have you come over alone?"

"No, my mate is with me; there he is, in the red shirt. Hola, Paolo!"

Michele hearing himself called, came lounging up with his hands in his pockets. He made a fairly good Corsican, in spite of the red wig which he had put on to render himself unrecognizable. As for the Gadfly, he looked his part to perfection.

They sauntered through the market-place together, Michele whistling between his teeth, and the Gadfly trudging along with a bundle over his shoulder, shuffling his feet on the ground to render his lameness less observable. They were waiting for an emissary, to whom important directions had to be given.

"There's Marcone, on horseback, at that corner," Michele whispered suddenly. The Gadfly, still carrying his bundle, shuffled towards the horseman.

"Do you happen to be wanting a hay-maker, sir?" he said, touching his ragged cap and running one finger along the bridle. It was the signal agreed upon, and the rider, who from his appearance might have been a country squire's bailiff, dismounted and threw the reins on the horse's neck.

"What sort of work can you do, my man?"

The Gadfly fumbled with his cap.

"I can cut grass, sir, and trim hedges"—he began; and without any break in his voice, went straight on: "At one in the morning at the mouth of the round cave. You must have two good horses and a cart. I shall be waiting inside the cave—— And then I can dig, sir, and——"

"That will do, I only want a grass-cutter. Have you ever been out before?"

"Once, sir. Mind, you must come well-armed; we may meet a flying squadron. Don't go by the wood-path; you're safer on the other side. If you meet a spy, don't stop to argue with him; fire at once—— I should be very glad of work, sir."

"Yes, I dare say, but I want an experienced grass-cutter. No, I haven't got any coppers to-day."

A very ragged beggar had slouched up to them, with a doleful, monotonous whine.

"Have pity on a poor blind man, in the name of the Blessed Virgin——— Get out of this place at once; there's a flying squadron coming along——Most Holy Queen of Heaven, Maiden undefiled—It's you they're after, Rivarez; they'll be here in two minutes—— And so may the saints reward you—— You'll have to make a dash for it; there are spies at all the corners. It's no use trying to slip away without being seen."

Marcone slipped the reins into the Gadfly's hand.

"Make haste! Ride out to the bridge and let the horse go; you can hide in the ravine. We're all armed; we can keep them back for ten minutes."

"No. I won't have you fellows taken. Stand together, all of you, and fire after me in order. Move up towards our horses; there they are, tethered by the palace steps; and have your knives ready. We retreat fighting, and when I throw my cap down, cut the halters and jump every man on the nearest horse. We may all reach the wood that way."

They had spoken in so quiet an undertone that even the nearest bystanders had not supposed their conversation to refer to anything more dangerous than grass-cutting. Marcone, leading his own mare by the bridle, walked towards the tethered horses, the Gadfly slouching along beside him, and the beggar following them with an outstretched hand and a persistent whine. Michele came up whistling; the beggar had warned him in passing, and he quietly handed on the news to three countrymen who were eating raw onions under a tree. They immediately rose and followed him; and before anyone's notice had been attracted to them, the whole seven were standing together by the steps of the palace, each man with one hand on the hidden pistol, and the tethered horses within easy reach.

"Don't betray yourselves till I move," the Gadfly said softly and clearly. "They may not recognize us. When I fire, then begin in order. Don't fire at the men; lame their horses—then they can't follow us. Three of you fire, while the other three reload. If anyone comes between you and our horses, kill him. I take the roan. When I throw down my cap, each man for himself; don't stop for anything."

"Here they come," said Michele; and the Gadfly turned round, with an air of naive and stupid wonder, as the people suddenly broke off in their bargaining.

Fifteen armed men rode slowly into the marketplace. They had great difficulty to get past the throng of people at all, and, but for the spies at the corners of the square, all the seven conspirators could have slipped quietly away while the attention of the crowd was fixed upon the soldiers. Michele moved a little closer to the Gadfly.

"Couldn't we get away now?"

"No; we're surrounded with spies, and one of them has recognized me. He has just sent a man to tell the captain where I am. Our only chance is to lame their horses."

"Which is the spy?"

"The first man I fire at. Are you all ready? They have made a lane to us; they are going to come with a rush."

"Out of the way there!" shouted the captain. "In the name of His Holiness!"

The crowd had drawn back, startled and wondering; and the soldiers made a quick dash towards the little group standing by the palace steps. The Gadfly drew a pistol from his blouse and fired, not at the advancing troops, but at the spy, who was approaching the horses, and who fell back with a broken collar-bone. Immediately after the report, six more shots were fired in quick succession, as the conspirators moved steadily closer to the tethered horses.

One of the cavalry horses stumbled and plunged; another fell to the ground with a fearful cry. Then, through the shrieking of the panic-stricken people, came the loud, imperious voice of the officer in command, who had risen in the stirrups and was holding a sword above his head.

"This way, men!"

He swayed in the saddle and sank back; the Gadfly had fired again with his deadly aim. A little stream of blood was trickling down the captain's uniform; but he steadied himself with a violent effort, and, clutching at his horse's mane, cried out fiercely:

"Kill that lame devil if you can't take him alive! It's Rivarez!"

"Another pistol, quick!" the Gadfly called to his men; "and go!"

He flung down his cap. It was only just in time, for the swords of the now infuriated soldiers were flashing close in front of him.

"Put down your weapons, all of you!"

Cardinal Montanelli had stepped suddenly between the combatants; and one of the soldiers cried out in a voice sharp with terror:

"Your Eminence! My God, you'll be murdered!"

Montanelli only moved a step nearer, and faced the Gadfly's pistol.

Five of the conspirators were already on horseback and dashing up the hilly street. Marcone sprang on to the back of his mare. In the moment of riding away, he glanced back to see whether his leader was in need of help. The roan was close at hand, and in another instant all would have been safe; but as the figure in the scarlet cassock stepped forward, the Gadfly suddenly wavered and the hand with the pistol sank down. The instant decided everything. Immediately he was surrounded and flung violently to the ground, and the weapon was dashed out of his hand by a blow from the flat of a soldier's sword. Marcone struck his mare's flank with the stirrup; the hoofs of the cavalry horses were thundering up the hill behind him; and it would have been worse than useless to stay and be taken too. Turning in the saddle as he galloped away, to fire a last shot in the teeth of the nearest pursuer, he saw the Gadfly, with blood on his face, trampled under the feet of horses and soldiers and spies; and heard the savage curses of the captors, the yells of triumph and rage.

Montanelli did not notice what had happened; he had moved away from the steps, and was trying to calm the terrified people. Presently, as he stooped over the wounded spy, a startled movement of the crowd made him look up. The soldiers were crossing the square, dragging their prisoner after them by the rope with which his hands were tied. His face was livid with pain and exhaustion, and he panted fearfully for breath; but he looked round at the Cardinal, smiling with white lips, and whispered:

"I c-cong-gratulate your Eminence."

Five days later Martini reached Forli. He had received from Gemma by post a bundle of printed circulars, the signal agreed upon in case of his being needed in any special emergency; and, remembering the conversation on the terrace, he guessed the truth at once. All through the journey he kept repeating to himself that there was no reason for supposing anything to have happened to the Gadfly, and that it was absurd to attach any importance to the childish superstitions of so nervous and fanciful a person; but the more he reasoned with himself against the idea, the more firmly did it take possession of his mind.

"I have guessed what it is: Rivarez is taken, of course?" he said, as he came into Gemma's room.

"He was arrested last Thursday, at Brisighella. He defended himself desperately and wounded the captain of the squadron and a spy."

"Armed resistance; that's bad!"

"It makes no difference; he was too deeply compromised already for a pistol-shot more or less to affect his position much."

"What do you think they are going to do with him?"

She grew a shade paler even than before.

"I think," she said; "that we must not wait to find out what they mean to do."

"You think we shall be able to effect a rescue?"

"We MUST."

He turned away and began to whistle, with his hands behind his back. Gemma let him think undisturbed. She was sitting still, leaning her head against the back of the chair, and looking out into vague distance with a fixed and tragic absorption. When her face wore that expression, it had a look of Durer's "Melancolia."

"Have you seen him?" Martini asked, stopping for a moment in his tramp.

"No; he was to have met me here the next morning."

"Yes, I remember. Where is he?"

"In the fortress; very strictly guarded, and, they say, in chains."

He made a gesture of indifference.

"Oh, that's no matter; a good file will get rid of any number of chains. If only he isn't wounded——"

"He seems to have been slightly hurt, but exactly how much we don't know. I think you had better hear the account of it from Michele himself; he was present at the arrest."

"How does he come not to have been taken too? Did he run away and leave Rivarez in the lurch?"

"It's not his fault; he fought as long as anybody did, and followed the directions given him to the letter. For that matter, so did they all. The only person who seems to have forgotten, or somehow made a mistake at the last minute, is Rivarez himself. There's something inexplicable about it altogether. Wait a moment; I will call Michele."

She went out of the room, and presently came back with Michele and a broad-shouldered mountaineer.

"This is Marco," she said. "You have heard of him; he is one of the smugglers. He has just got here, and perhaps will be able to tell us more.

Michele, this is Cesare Martini, that I spoke to you about. Will you tell him what happened, as far as you saw it?"

Michele gave a short account of the skirmish with the squadron.

"I can't understand how it happened," he concluded. "Not one of us would have left him if we had thought he would be taken; but his directions were quite precise, and it never occurred to us, when he threw down his cap, that he would wait to let them surround him. He was close beside the roan—I saw him cut the tether—and I handed him a loaded pistol myself before I mounted. The only thing I can suppose is that he missed his footing,—being lame,—in trying to mount. But even then, he could have fired."

"No, it wasn't that," Marcone interposed. "He didn't attempt to mount. I was the last one to go, because my mare shied at the firing; and I looked round to see whether he was safe. He would have got off clear if it hadn't been for the Cardinal."

"Ah!" Gemma exclaimed softly; and Martini repeated in amazement: "The Cardinal?"

"Yes; he threw himself in front of the pistol—confound him! I suppose Rivarez must have been startled, for he dropped his pistol-hand and put the other one up like this"—laying the back of his left wrist across his eyes—"and of course they all rushed on him."

"I can't make that out," said Michele. "It's not like Rivarez to lose his head at a crisis."

"Probably he lowered his pistol for fear of killing an unarmed man," Martini put in. Michele shrugged his shoulders.

"Unarmed men shouldn't poke their noses into the middle of a fight. War is war. If Rivarez had put a bullet into His Eminence, instead of letting himself be caught like a tame rabbit, there'd be one honest man the more and one priest the less."

He turned away, biting his moustache. His anger was very near to breaking down in tears.

"Anyway," said Martini, "the thing's done, and there's no use wasting time in discussing how it happened. The question now is how we're to arrange an escape for him. I suppose you're all willing to risk it?"

Michele did not even condescend to answer the superfluous question, and the smuggler only remarked with a little laugh: "I'd shoot my own brother, if he weren't willing."

"Very well, then—— First thing; have you got a plan of the fortress?"

Gemma unlocked a drawer and took out several sheets of paper.

"I have made out all the plans. Here is the ground floor of the fortress; here are the upper and lower stories of the towers, and here the plan of the ramparts. These are the roads leading to the valley, and here are the paths and hiding-places in the mountains, and the underground passages."

"Do you know which of the towers he is in?"

"The east one, in the round room with the grated window. I have marked it on the plan."

"How did you get your information?"

"From a man nicknamed 'The Cricket,' a soldier of the guard. He is cousin to one of our men—Gino."

"You have been quick about it."

"There's no time to lose. Gino went into Brisighella at once; and some of the plans we already had. That list of hiding-places was made by Rivarez himself; you can see by the handwriting."

"What sort of men are the soldiers of the guard?"

"That we have not been able to find out yet; the Cricket has only just come to the place, and knows nothing about the other men."

"We must find out from Gino what the Cricket himself is like. Is anything known of the government's intentions? Is Rivarez likely to be tried in Brisighella or taken in to Ravenna?"

"That we don't know. Ravenna, of course, is the chief town of the Legation and by law cases of importance can be tried only there, in the Tribunal of First Instance. But law doesn't count for much in the Four Legations; it depends on the personal fancy of anybody who happens to be in power."

"They won't take him in to Ravenna," Michele interposed.

"What makes you think so?"

"I am sure of it. Colonel Ferrari, the military Governor at Brisighella, is uncle to the officer that Rivarez wounded; he's a vindictive sort of brute and won't give up a chance to spite an enemy."

"You think he will try to keep Rivarez here?"

"I think he will try to get him hanged."

Martini glanced quickly at Gemma. She was very pale, but her face had not changed at the words. Evidently the idea was no new one to her.

"He can hardly do that without some formality," she said quietly; "but he might possibly get up a court-martial on some pretext or other, and justify himself afterwards by saying that the peace of the town required it."

"But what about the Cardinal? Would he consent to things of that kind?"

"He has no jurisdiction in military affairs."

"No, but he has great influence. Surely the Governor would not venture on such a step without his consent?"

"He'll never get that," Marcone interrupted. "Montanelli was always against the military commissions, and everything of the kind. So long as they keep him in Brisighella nothing serious can happen; the Cardinal will always take the part of any prisoner. What I am afraid of is their taking him to Ravenna. Once there, he's lost."

"We shouldn't let him get there," said Michele. "We could manage a rescue on the road; but to get him out of the fortress here is another matter."

"I think," said Gemma; "that it would be quite useless to wait for the chance of his being transferred to Ravenna. We must make the attempt at Brisighella, and we have no time to lose. Cesare, you and I had better go over the plan of the fortress together, and see whether we can think out anything. I have an idea in my head, but I can't get over one point."

"Come, Marcone," said Michele, rising; "we will leave them to think out their scheme. I have to go across to Fognano this afternoon, and I want you to come with me. Vincenzo hasn't sent those cartridges, and they ought to have been here yesterday."

When the two men had gone, Martini went up to Gemma and silently held out his hand. She let her fingers lie in his for a moment.

"You were always a good friend, Cesare," she said at last; "and a very present help in trouble. And now let us discuss plans."

CHAPTER III

"AND I once more most earnestly assure Your Eminence that your refusal is endangering the peace of the town."

The Governor tried to preserve the respectful tone due to a high dignitary of the Church; but there was audible irritation in his voice. His liver was out of order, his wife was running up heavy bills, and his temper had been sorely tried during the last three weeks. A sullen, disaffected populace, whose dangerous mood grew daily more apparent; a district honeycombed with plots and bristling with hidden weapons; an inefficient garrison, of whose loyalty he was more than doubtful, and a Cardinal whom he had pathetically described to his adjutant as the "incarnation of immaculate pig-headedness," had already reduced him to the verge of desperation. Now he was saddled with the Gadfly, an animated quintessence of the spirit of mischief.

Having begun by disabling both the Governor's favourite nephew and his most valuable spy, the "crooked Spanish devil" had followed up his exploits in the market-place by suborning the guards, browbeating the interrogating officers, and "turning the prison into a bear-garden." He had now been three weeks in the fortress, and the authorities of Brisighella were heartily sick of their bargain. They had subjected him to interrogation upon interrogation; and after employing, to obtain admissions from him, every device of threat, persuasion, and stratagem which their ingenuity could suggest, remained just as wise as on the day of his capture. They had begun to realize that it would perhaps have been better to send him into Ravenna at once. It was, however, too late to rectify the mistake. The Governor, when sending in to the Legate his report of the arrest, had begged, as a special favour, permission to superintend personally the investigation of this case; and, his request having been graciously acceded to, he could not now withdraw without a humiliating confession that he was overmatched.

The idea of settling the difficulty by a courtmartial had, as Gemma and Michele had foreseen, presented itself to him as the only satisfactory solution; and Cardinal Montanelli's stubborn refusal to countenance this was the last drop which made the cup of his vexations overflow.

"I think," he said, "that if Your Eminence knew what I and my assistants have put up with from this man you would feel differently about the matter. I fully understand and respect the conscientious objection to irregularities in judicial proceedings; but this is an exceptional case and calls for exceptional measures."

"There is no case," Montanelli answered, "which calls for injustice; and to condemn a civilian by the judgment of a secret military tribunal is both unjust and illegal."

"The case amounts to this, Your Eminence: The prisoner is manifestly guilty of several capital crimes. He joined the infamous attempt of Savigno, and the military commission nominated by Monsignor Spinola would certainly have had him shot or sent to the galleys then, had he not succeeded in escaping to Tuscany. Since that time he has never ceased plotting. He is known to be an influential member of one of the most pestilent secret societies in the country. He is gravely suspected of having consented to, if not inspired, the assassination of no less than three confidential police agents. He has been caught—one might almost say—in the act of smuggling firearms into the Legation. He has offered armed resistance to authority and seriously wounded two officials in the discharge of their duty, and he is now a standing menace to the peace and order of the town. Surely, in such a case, a court-martial is justifiable."

"Whatever the man has done," Montanelli replied, "he has the right to be judged according to law."

"The ordinary course of law involves delay, Your Eminence, and in this case every moment is precious. Besides everything else, I am in constant terror of his escaping."

"If there is any danger of that, it rests with you to guard him more closely."

"I do my best, Your Eminence, but I am dependent upon the prison staff, and the man seems to have bewitched them all. I have changed the guard four times within three weeks; I have punished the soldiers till I am tired of it, and nothing is of any use. I can't prevent their carrying letters backwards and forwards. The fools are in love with him as if he were a woman."

"That is very curious. There must be something remarkable about him."

"There's a remarkable amount of devilry—I beg pardon, Your Eminence, but really this man is enough to try the patience of a saint. It's hardly credible, but I have to conduct all the interrogations myself, for the regular officer cannot stand it any longer."

"How is that?"

"It's difficult to explain. Your Eminence, but you would understand if you had once heard the way he goes on. One might think the interrogating officer were the criminal and he the judge."

"But what is there so terrible that he can do? He can refuse to answer your questions, of course; but he has no weapon except silence."

"And a tongue like a razor. We are all mortal, Your Eminence, and most of us have made mistakes in our time that we don't want published on the house-tops. That's only human nature, and it's hard on a man to have his little slips of twenty years ago raked up and thrown in his teeth——"

"Has Rivarez brought up some personal secret of the interrogating officer?"

"Well, really—the poor fellow got into debt when he was a cavalry officer, and borrowed a little sum from the regimental funds——"

"Stole public money that had been intrusted to him, in fact?"

"Of course it was very wrong, Your Eminence; but his friends paid it back at once, and the affair was hushed up,—he comes of a good family,—and ever since then he has been irreproachable. How Rivarez found out about it I can't conceive; but the first thing he did at interrogation was to bring up this old scandal—before the subaltern, too! And with as innocent a face as if he were saying his prayers! Of course the story's all over the Legation by now. If Your Eminence would only be present at one of the interrogations, I am sure you would realize—— He needn't know anything about it. You might overhear him from———"

Montanelli turned round and looked at the Governor with an expression which his face did not often wear.

"I am a minister of religion," he said; "not a police-spy; and eavesdropping forms no part of my professional duties."

"I—I didn't mean to give offence———"

"I think we shall not get any good out of discussing this question further. If you will send the prisoner here, I will have a talk with him."

"I venture very respectfully to advise Your Eminence not to attempt it. The man is perfectly incorrigible. It would be both safer and wiser to overstep the letter of the law for this once, and get rid of him before he does any more mischief. It is with great diffidence that I venture to press the point after what Your Eminence has said; but after all I am responsible to Monsignor the Legate for the order of the town———"

"And I," Montanelli interrupted, "am responsible to God and His Holiness that there shall be no underhand dealing in my diocese. Since you press me in the matter, colonel, I take my stand upon my privilege as Cardinal. I will not allow a secret court-martial in this town in peace-time. I will receive the prisoner here, and alone, at ten to-morrow morning."

"As Your Eminence pleases," the Governor replied with sulky respectfulness; and went away, grumbling to himself: "They're about a pair, as far as obstinacy goes."

He told no one of the approaching interview till it was actually time to knock off the prisoner's chains and start for the palace. It was quite enough, as he remarked to his wounded nephew, to have this Most Eminent son of Balaam's ass laying down the law, without running any risk of the soldiers plotting with Rivarez and his friends to effect an escape on the way.

When the Gadfly, strongly guarded, entered the room where Montanelli was writing at a table covered with papers, a sudden recollection came over him, of a hot midsummer afternoon when he had sat turning over manuscript sermons in a study much like this. The shutters had been closed, as they were here, to keep out the heat, and a fruitseller's voice outside had called: "Fragola! Fragola!"

He shook the hair angrily back from his eyes and set his mouth in a smile.

Montanelli looked up from his papers.

"You can wait in the hall," he said to the guards.

"May it please Your Eminence," began the sergeant, in a lowered voice and with evident nervousness, "the colonel thinks that this prisoner is dangerous and that it would be better————"

A sudden flash came into Montanelli's eyes.

"You can wait in the hall," he repeated quietly; and the sergeant, saluting and stammering excuses with a frightened face, left the room with his men.

"Sit down, please," said the Cardinal, when the door was shut. The Gadfly obeyed in silence.

"Signor Rivarez," Montanelli began after a pause, "I wish to ask you a few questions, and shall be very much obliged to you if you will answer them."

The Gadfly smiled. "My ch-ch-chief occupation at p-p-present is to be asked questions."

"And—not to answer them? So I have heard; but these questions are put by officials who are investigating your case and whose duty is to use your answers as evidence."

"And th-those of Your Eminence?" There was a covert insult in the tone more than in the words, and the Cardinal understood it at once; but his face did not lose its grave sweetness of expression.

"Mine," he said, "whether you answer them or not, will remain between you and me. If they should trench upon your political secrets, of course you will not answer. Otherwise, though we are complete strangers to each other, I hope that you will do so, as a personal favour to me."

"I am ent-t-tirely at the service of Your Eminence." He said it with a little bow, and a face that would have taken the heart to ask favours out of the daughters of the horse-leech.

"First, then, you are said to have been smuggling firearms into this district. What are they wanted for?"

"T-t-to k-k-kill rats with."

"That is a terrible answer. Are all your fellow-men rats in your eyes if they cannot think as you do?"

"S-s-some of them."

Montanelli leaned back in his chair and looked at him in silence for a little while.

"What is that on your hand?" he asked suddenly.

The Gadfly glanced at his left hand. "Old m-m-marks from the teeth of some of the rats."

"Excuse me; I was speaking of the other hand. That is a fresh hurt."

The slender, flexible right hand was badly cut and grazed. The Gadfly held it up. The wrist was swollen, and across it ran a deep and long black bruise.

"It is a m-m-mere trifle, as you see," he said. "When I was arrested the other day,—thanks to Your Eminence,"—he made another little bow,—"one of the soldiers stamped on it."

Montanelli took the wrist and examined it closely. "How does it come to be in such a state now, after three weeks?" he asked. "It is all inflamed."

"Possibly the p-p-pressure of the iron has not done it much good."

The Cardinal looked up with a frown.

"Have they been putting irons on a fresh wound?"

"N-n-naturally, Your Eminence; that is what fresh wounds are for. Old wounds are not much use. They will only ache; you c-c-can't make them burn properly."

Montanelli looked at him again in the same close, scrutinizing way; then rose and opened a drawer full of surgical appliances.

"Give me the hand," he said.

The Gadfly, with a face as hard as beaten iron, held out the hand, and Montanelli, after bathing the injured place, gently bandaged it. Evidently he was accustomed to such work.

"I will speak about the irons," he said. "And now I want to ask you another question: What do you propose to do?"

"Th-th-that is very simply answered, Your Eminence. To escape if I can, and if I can't, to die."

"Why 'to die'?"

"Because if the Governor doesn't succeed in getting me shot, I shall be sent to the galleys, and for me that c-c-comes to the same thing. I have not got the health to live through it."

Montanelli rested his arm on the table and pondered silently. The Gadfly did not disturb him. He was leaning back with half-shut eyes, lazily enjoying the delicious physical sensation of relief from the chains.

"Supposing," Montanelli began again, "that you were to succeed in escaping; what should you do with your life?"

"I have already told Your Eminence; I should k-k-kill rats."

"You would kill rats. That is to say, that if I were to let you escape from here now,—supposing I had the power to do so,—you would use your freedom to foster violence and bloodshed instead of preventing them?"

The Gadfly raised his eyes to the crucifix on the wall. "'Not peace, but a sword';—at l-least I should be in good company. For my own part, though, I prefer pistols."

"Signor Rivarez," said the Cardinal with unruffled composure, "I have not insulted you as yet, or spoken slightingly of your beliefs or friends. May I not expect the same courtesy from you, or do you wish me to suppose that an atheist cannot be a gentleman?"

"Ah, I q-quite forgot. Your Eminence places courtesy high among the Christian virtues. I remember your sermon in Florence, on the occasion of my c-controversy with your anonymous defender."

"That is one of the subjects about which I wished to speak to you. Would you mind explaining to me the reason of the peculiar bitterness you seem to feel against me? If you have simply picked me out as a convenient target, that is another matter. Your methods of political controversy are your own affair, and we are not discussing politics now. But I fancied at the time that there was some personal animosity towards me; and if so, I should be glad to know whether I have ever done you wrong or in any way given you cause for such a feeling."

Ever done him wrong! The Gadfly put up the bandaged hand to his throat. "I must refer Your Eminence to Shakspere," he said with a little laugh. "It's as with the man who can't endure a harmless, necessary cat. My antipathy is a priest. The sight of the cassock makes my t-t-teeth ache."

"Oh, if it is only that——" Montanelli dismissed the subject with an indifferent gesture.

"Still," he added, "abuse is one thing and perversion of fact is another. When you stated, in answer to my sermon, that I knew the identity of the anonymous writer, you made a mistake,—I do not accuse you of wilful falsehood,—and stated what was untrue. I am to this day quite ignorant of his name."

The Gadfly put his head on one side, like an intelligent robin, looked at him for a moment gravely, then suddenly threw himself back and burst into a peal of laughter.

"S-s-sancta simplicitas! Oh, you, sweet, innocent, Arcadian people—and you never guessed! You n-never saw the cloven hoof?"

Montanelli stood up. "Am I to understand, Signor Rivarez, that you wrote both sides of the controversy yourself?"

"It was a shame, I know," the Gadfly answered, looking up with wide, innocent blue eyes. "And you s-s-swallowed everything whole; just as if it had been an oyster. It was very wrong; but oh, it w-w-was so funny!"

Montanelli bit his lip and sat down again. He had realized from the first that the Gadfly was trying to make him lose his temper, and had resolved to keep it whatever happened; but he was beginning to find excuses for the Governor's exasperation. A man who had been spending two hours a day for the last three weeks in interrogating the Gadfly might be pardoned an occasional swear-word.

"We will drop that subject," he said quietly. "What I wanted to see you for particularly is this: My position here as Cardinal gives me some voice, if I choose to claim my privilege, in the question of what is to be done with you. The only use to which I should ever put such a privilege would be to interfere in case of any violence to you which was not necessary to prevent you from doing violence to others. I sent for you, therefore, partly in order to ask whether you have anything to complain of,—I will see about the irons; but perhaps there is something else,—and partly because I felt it right, before giving my opinion, to see for myself what sort of man you are."

"I have nothing to complain of, Your Eminence. 'A la guerre comme a la guerre.' I am not a schoolboy, to expect any government to pat me on the head for s-s-smuggling firearms onto its territory. It's only natural that they should hit as hard as they can. As for what sort of man I am, you have had a romantic confession of my sins once. Is not that enough; or w-w-would you like me to begin again?"

"I don't understand you," Montanelli said coldly, taking up a pencil and twisting it between his fingers.

"Surely Your Eminence has not forgotten old Diego, the pilgrim?" He suddenly changed his voice and began to speak as Diego: "I am a miserable sinner———"

The pencil snapped in Montanelli's hand. "That is too much!" he said.

The Gadfly leaned his head back with a soft little laugh, and sat watching while the Cardinal paced silently up and down the room.

"Signor Rivarez," said Montanelli, stopping at last in front of him, "you have done a thing to me that a man who was born of a woman should hesitate to do to his worst enemy. You have stolen in upon my private grief and have made for yourself a mock and a jest out of the sorrow of a fellow-man. I once more beg you to tell me: Have I ever done you wrong? And if not, why have you played this heartless trick on me?"

The Gadfly, leaning back against the chair-cushions, looked up with his subtle, chilling, inscrutable smile.

"It am-m-mused me, Your Eminence; you took it all so much to heart, and it rem-m-minded me—a little bit—of a variety show——"

Montanelli, white to the very lips, turned away and rang the bell.

"You can take back the prisoner," he said when the guards came in.

After they had gone he sat down at the table, still trembling with unaccustomed indignation, and took up a pile of reports which had been sent in to him by the parish priests of his diocese.

Presently he pushed them away, and, leaning on the table, hid his face in both hands. The Gadfly seemed to have left some terrible shadow of himself, some ghostly trail of his personality, to haunt the room; and Montanelli sat trembling and cowering, not daring to look up lest he should see the phantom presence that he knew was not there. The spectre hardly amounted to a hallucination. It was a mere fancy of overwrought nerves; but he was seized with an unutterable dread of its shadowy presence—of the wounded hand, the smiling, cruel mouth, the mysterious eyes, like deep sea water——

He shook off the fancy and settled to his work. All day long he had scarcely a free moment, and the thing did not trouble him; but going into his bedroom late at night, he stopped on the threshold with a sudden shock of fear. What if he should see it in a dream? He recovered himself immediately and knelt down before the crucifix to pray.

But he lay awake the whole night through.

CHAPTER IV

MONTANELLI'S anger did not make him neglectful of his promise. He protested so emphatically against the manner in which the Gadfly had been chained that the unfortunate Governor, who by now was at his wit's end, knocked off all the fetters in the recklessness of despair. "How am I to know," he grumbled to the adjutant, "what His Eminence will object to next? If he calls a simple pair of handcuffs 'cruelty,' he'll be exclaiming against the window-bars presently, or wanting me to feed Rivarez on oysters and truffles. In my young days malefactors were malefactors and were treated accordingly, and nobody thought a traitor any better than a thief. But it's the fashion to be seditious nowadays; and His Eminence seems inclined to encourage all the scoundrels in the country."

"I don't see what business he has got to interfere at all," the adjutant remarked. "He is not a Legate and has no authority in civil and military affairs. By law———"

"What is the use of talking about law? You can't expect anyone to respect laws after the Holy Father has opened the prisons and turned the whole crew of Liberal scamps loose on us! It's a positive infatuation! Of course Monsignor Montanelli will give himself airs; he was quiet enough under His Holiness the late Pope, but he's cock of the walk now. He has jumped into favour all at once and can do as he pleases. How am I to oppose him? He may have secret authorization from the Vatican, for all I know. Everything's topsy-turvy now; you can't tell from day to day what may happen next. In the good old times one knew what to be at, but nowadays———"

The Governor shook his head ruefully. A world in which Cardinals troubled themselves over trifles of prison discipline and talked about the "rights" of political offenders was a world that was growing too complex for him.

The Gadfly, for his part, had returned to the fortress in a state of nervous excitement bordering on hysteria. The meeting with Montanelli had strained his endurance almost to breaking-point; and his final brutality about the variety show had been uttered in sheer desperation, merely to cut short an interview which, in another five minutes, would have ended in tears.

Called up for interrogation in the afternoon of the same day, he did nothing but go into convulsions of laughter at every question put to him; and when the Governor, worried out of all patience, lost his temper and began to swear, he only laughed more immoderately than ever. The unlucky Governor fumed and stormed and threatened his refractory prisoner with impossible punishments; but finally came, as James Burton had come long ago, to the conclusion that it was mere waste of breath and temper to argue with a person in so unreasonable a state of mind.

The Gadfly was once more taken back to his cell; and there lay down upon the pallet, in the mood of black and hopeless depression which always succeeded to his boisterous fits. He lay till evening without moving, without even thinking; he had passed, after the vehement emotion of the morning, into a strange, half-apathetic state, in which his own misery was hardly more to him than a dull and mechanical weight, pressing on some wooden thing that had forgotten to be a soul. In truth, it was of little consequence how all ended; the one thing that mattered to any sentient being was to be spared unbearable pain, and whether the relief came from altered conditions or from the deadening of the power to feel, was a question of no moment. Perhaps he would succeed in escaping; perhaps they would kill him; in any case he should never see the Padre again, and it was all vanity and vexation of spirit.

One of the warders brought in supper, and the Gadfly looked up with heavy-eyed indifference.

"What time is it?"

"Six o'clock. Your supper, sir."

He looked with disgust at the stale, foul-smelling, half-cold mess, and turned his head away. He was feeling bodily ill as well as depressed; and the sight of the food sickened him.

"You will be ill if you don't eat," said the soldier hurriedly. "Take a bit of bread, anyway; it'll do you good."

The man spoke with a curious earnestness of tone, lifting a piece of sodden bread from the plate and putting it down again. All the conspirator awoke in the Gadfly; he had guessed at once that there was something hidden in the bread.

"You can leave it; I'll eat a bit by and by," he said carelessly. The door was open, and he knew that the sergeant on the stairs could hear every word spoken between them.

When the door was locked on him again, and he had satisfied himself that no one was watching at the spy-hole, he took up the piece of bread and carefully crumbled it away. In the middle was the thing he had expected, a bundle of small files. It was wrapped in a bit of paper, on which a few words were written. He smoothed the paper out carefully and carried it to what little light there was. The writing was crowded into so narrow a space, and on such thin paper, that it was very difficult to read.

"The door is unlocked, and there is no moon. Get the filing done as fast as possible, and come by the passage between two and three. We are quite ready and may not have another chance."

He crushed the paper feverishly in his hand. All the preparations were ready, then, and he had only to file the window bars; how lucky it was that the chains were off! He need not stop about filing them. How many bars were there? Two, four; and each must be filed in two places: eight. Oh, he could manage that in the course of the night if he made haste—— How had Gemma and Martini contrived to get everything ready so quickly—disguises, passports, hiding-places? They must have worked like cart-horses to do it—— And it was her plan that had been adopted after all. He laughed a little to himself at his own foolishness; as if it mattered whether the plan was hers or not, once it was a good one! And yet he could not help being glad that it was she who had struck on the idea of his utilizing the subterranean passage, instead of letting himself down by a rope-ladder, as the smugglers had at first suggested. Hers was the more complex and difficult plan, but did not involve, as the other did, a risk to the life of the sentinel on duty outside the east wall. Therefore, when the two schemes had been laid before him, he had unhesitatingly chosen Gemma's.

The arrangement was that the friendly guard who went by the nickname of "The Cricket" should seize the first opportunity of unlocking, without the knowledge of his fellows, the iron gate leading from the courtyard into the subterranean passage underneath the ramparts, and should then replace the key on its nail in the guard-room. The Gadfly, on receiving information of this, was to file through the bars of his window, tear his shirt into strips and plait them into a rope, by means of which he could let himself down on to the broad east wall of the courtyard. Along this wall he was to creep on hands and knees while the sentinel was looking in the opposite direction, lying flat upon the masonry whenever the man turned towards him. At the southeast corner was a half-ruined turret. It was upheld, to some extent, by a thick growth of ivy; but great masses of crumbling stone had fallen inward and lay in the courtyard, heaped against the wall. From this turret he was to climb down by the ivy and the heaps of stone into the courtyard; and, softly opening the unlocked gate, to make his way along the passage to a subterranean tunnel communicating with it. Centuries ago this tunnel had formed a secret corridor between the fortress and a tower on the neighbouring hill; now it was quite disused and blocked in many places by the falling in of the rocks. No one but the smugglers knew of a certain carefully-hidden hole in the mountain-side which they had bored through to the tunnel; no one suspected that stores of forbidden merchandise were often kept, for weeks together, under the very ramparts of the fortress itself, while the customs-officers were vainly searching the houses of the sullen, wrathful-eyed mountaineers. At this hole the Gadfly was to creep out on to the hillside, and make his way in the dark to a lonely spot where Martini and a smuggler would be waiting for him. The one great difficulty was that opportunities to unlock the gate after the evening patrol did not occur every night, and the descent from the window could not be made in very clear weather without too great a risk of being observed by the sentinel. Now that there was really a fair chance of success, it must not be missed.

He sat down and began to eat some of the bread. It at least did not disgust him like the rest of the prison food, and he must eat something to keep up his strength.

He had better lie down a bit, too, and try to get a little sleep; it would not be safe to begin filing before ten o'clock, and he would have a hard night's work.

And so, after all, the Padre had been thinking of letting him escape! That was like the Padre. But he, for his part, would never consent to it. Anything rather than that! If he escaped, it should be his own doing and that of his comrades; he would have no favours from priests.

How hot it was! Surely it must be going to thunder; the air was so close and oppressive. He moved restlessly on the pallet and put the bandaged right hand behind his head for a pillow; then drew it away again. How it burned and throbbed! And all the old wounds were beginning to ache, with a dull, faint persistence. What was the matter with them? Oh, absurd! It was only the thundery weather. He would go to sleep and get a little rest before beginning his filing.

Eight bars, and all so thick and strong! How many more were there left to file? Surely not many. He must have been filing for hours,—interminable hours—yes, of course, that was what made his arm ache—— And how it ached; right through to the very bone! But it could hardly be the filing that made his side ache so; and the throbbing, burning pain in the lame leg—was that from filing?

He started up. No, he had not been asleep; he had been dreaming with open eyes—dreaming of filing, and it was all still to do. There stood the window-bars, untouched, strong and firm as ever. And there was ten striking from the clock-tower in the distance. He must get to work.

He looked through the spy-hole, and, seeing that no one was watching, took one of the files from his breast.

No, there was nothing the matter with him—nothing! It was all imagination. The pain in his side was indigestion, or a chill, or some such thing; not much wonder, after three weeks of this insufferable prison food and air. As for the aching and throbbing all over, it was partly nervous trouble and partly want of exercise. Yes, that was it, no doubt; want of exercise. How absurd not to have thought of that before!

He would sit down a little bit, though, and let it pass before he got to work. It would be sure to go over in a minute or two.

To sit still was worse than all. When he sat still he was at its mercy, and his face grew gray with fear. No, he must get up and set to work, and shake it off. It should depend upon his will to feel or not to feel; and he would not feel, he would force it back.

He stood up again and spoke to himself, aloud and distinctly:

"I am not ill; I have no time to be ill. I have those bars to file, and I am not going to be ill."

Then he began to file.

A quarter-past ten—half-past ten—a quarter to eleven—— He filed and filed, and every grating scrape of the iron was as though someone were filing on his body and brain. "I wonder which will be filed through first," he said to himself with a little laugh; "I or the bars?" And he set his teeth and went on filing.

Half-past eleven. He was still filing, though the hand was stiff and swollen and would hardly grasp the tool. No, he dared not stop to rest; if he once put the horrible thing down he should never have the courage to begin again.

The sentinel moved outside the door, and the butt end of his carbine scratched against the lintel. The Gadfly stopped and looked round, the file still in his lifted hand. Was he discovered?

A little round pellet had been shot through the spy-hole and was lying on the floor. He laid down the file and stooped to pick up the round thing. It was a bit of rolled paper.

It was a long way to go down and down, with the black waves rushing about him—how they roared——!

Ah, yes! He was only stooping down to pick up the paper. He was a bit giddy; many people are when they stoop. There was nothing the matter with him—nothing.

He picked it up, carried it to the light, and unfolded it steadily.

"Come to-night, whatever happens; the Cricket will be transferred to-morrow to another service. This is our only chance."

He destroyed the paper as he had done the former one, picked up his file again, and went back to work, dogged and mute and desperate.

One o'clock. He had been working for three hours now, and six of the eight bars were filed. Two more, and then, to climb———

He began to recall the former occasions when these terrible attacks had come on. The last had been the one at New Year; and he shuddered as he remembered those five nights. But that time it had not come on so suddenly; he had never known it so sudden.

He dropped the file and flung out both hands blindly, praying, in his utter desperation, for the first time since he had been an atheist; praying to anything—to nothing—to everything.

"Not to-night! Oh, let me be ill to-morrow! I will bear anything to-morrow—only not to-night!"

He stood still for a moment, with both hands up to his temples; then he took up the file once more, and once more went back to his work.

Half-past one. He had begun on the last bar. His shirt-sleeve was bitten to rags; there was blood on his lips and a red mist before his eyes, and the sweat poured from his forehead as he filed, and filed, and filed——

After sunrise Montanelli fell asleep. He was utterly worn out with the restless misery of the night and slept for a little while quietly; then he began to dream.

At first he dreamed vaguely, confusedly; broken fragments of images and fancies followed each other, fleeting and incoherent, but all filled with the same dim sense of struggle and pain, the same shadow of indefinable dread. Presently he began to dream of sleeplessness; the old, frightful, familiar dream that had been a terror to him for years. And even as he dreamed he recognized that he had been through it all before.

He was wandering about in a great empty place, trying to find some quiet spot where he could lie down and sleep. Everywhere there were people, walking up and down; talking, laughing, shouting; praying, ringing bells, and clashing metal instruments together. Sometimes he would get away to a little distance from the noise, and would lie down, now on the grass, now on a wooden bench, now on some slab of stone. He would shut his eyes and cover them with both hands to keep out the light; and would say to himself: "Now I will get to sleep." Then the crowds would come sweeping up to him, shouting, yelling, calling him by name, begging him: "Wake up! Wake up, quick; we want you!"

Again: he was in a great palace, full of gorgeous rooms, with beds and couches and low soft lounges. It was night, and he said to himself: "Here, at last, I shall find a quiet place to sleep." But when he chose a dark room and lay down, someone came in with a lamp, flashing the merciless light into his eyes, and said: "Get up; you are wanted."

He rose and wandered on, staggering and stumbling like a creature wounded to death; and heard the clocks strike one, and knew that half the night was gone already—the precious night that was so short. Two, three, four, five—by six o'clock the whole town would wake up and there would be no more silence.

He went into another room and would have lain down on a bed, but someone started up from the pillows, crying out: "This bed is mine!" and he shrank away with despair in his heart.

Hour after hour struck, and still he wandered on and on, from room to room, from house to house, from corridor to corridor. The horrible gray dawn was creeping near and nearer; the clocks were striking five; the night was gone and he had found no rest. Oh, misery! Another day—another day!

He was in a long, subterranean corridor, a low, vaulted passage that seemed to have no end. It was lighted with glaring lamps and chandeliers; and through its grated roof came the sounds of dancing and laughter and merry music. Up there, in the world of the live people overhead, there was some festival, no doubt. Oh, for a place to hide and sleep; some little place, were it even a grave! And as he spoke he stumbled over an open grave. An open grave, smelling of death and rottenness—— Ah, what matter, so he could but sleep!

"This grave is mine!" It was Gladys; and she raised her head and stared at him over the rotting shroud. Then he knelt down and stretched out his arms to her.

"Gladys! Gladys! Have a little pity on me; let me creep into this narrow space and sleep. I do not ask you for your love; I will not touch you, will not speak to you; only let me lie down beside you and sleep! Oh, love, it is so long since I have slept! I cannot bear another day. The light glares in upon my soul; the noise is beating my brain to dust. Gladys, let me come in here and sleep!"

And he would have drawn her shroud across his eyes. But she shrank away, screaming:

"It is sacrilege; you are a priest!"

On and on he wandered, and came out upon the sea-shore, on the barren rocks where the fierce light struck down, and the water moaned its low, perpetual wail of unrest. "Ah!" he said; "the sea will be more merciful; it, too, is wearied unto death and cannot sleep."

Then Arthur rose up from the deep, and cried aloud:

"This sea is mine!"

"Your Eminence! Your Eminence!"

Montanelli awoke with a start. His servant was knocking at the door. He rose mechanically and opened it, and the man saw how wild and scared he looked.

"Your Eminence—are you ill?"

He drew both hands across his forehead.

"No; I was asleep, and you startled me."

"I am very sorry; I thought I had heard you moving early this morning, and I supposed———"

"Is it late now?"

"It is nine o'clock, and the Governor has called. He says he has very important business, and knowing Your Eminence to be an early riser———"

"Is he downstairs? I will come presently."

He dressed and went downstairs.

"I am afraid this is an unceremonious way to call upon Your Eminence," the Governor began.

"I hope there is nothing the matter?"

"There is very much the matter. Rivarez has all but succeeded in escaping."

"Well, so long as he has not quite succeeded there is no harm done. How was it?"

"He was found in the courtyard, right against the little iron gate. When the patrol came in to inspect the courtyard at three o'clock this morning one of the men stumbled over something on the ground; and when they brought the light up they found Rivarez lying across the path unconscious. They raised an alarm at once and called me up; and when I went to examine his cell I found all the window-bars filed through and a rope made of torn body-linen hanging from one of them. He had let himself down and climbed along the wall. The iron gate, which leads into the subterranean tunnels, was found to be unlocked. That looks as if the guards had been suborned."

"But how did he come to be lying across the path? Did he fall from the rampart and hurt himself?"

"That is what I thought at first. Your Eminence; but the prison surgeon can't find any trace of a fall. The soldier who was on duty yesterday says that Rivarez looked very ill last night when he brought in the supper, and did not eat anything. But that must be nonsense; a sick man couldn't file those bars through and climb along that roof. It's not in reason."

"Does he give any account of himself?"

"He is unconscious, Your Eminence."

"Still?"

"He just half comes to himself from time to time and moans, and then goes off again."

~ 170 ~

"That is very strange. What does the doctor think?"

"He doesn't know what to think. There is no trace of heart-disease that he can find to account for the thing; but whatever is the matter with him, it is something that must have come on suddenly, just when he had nearly managed to escape. For my part, I believe he was struck down by the direct intervention of a merciful Providence."

Montanelli frowned slightly.

"What are you going to do with him?" he asked.

"That is a question I shall settle in a very few days. In the meantime I have had a good lesson. That is what comes of taking off the irons—with all due respect to Your Eminence."

"I hope," Montanelli interrupted, "that you will at least not replace the fetters while he is ill. A man in the condition you describe can hardly make any more attempts to escape."

"I shall take good care he doesn't," the Governor muttered to himself as he went out. "His Eminence can go hang with his sentimental scruples for all I care. Rivarez is chained pretty tight now, and is going to stop so, ill or not."

"But how can it have happened? To faint away at the last moment, when everything was ready; when he was at the very gate! It's like some hideous joke."

"I tell you," Martini answered, "the only thing I can think of is that one of these attacks must have come on, and that he must have struggled against it as long as his strength lasted and have fainted from sheer exhaustion when he got down into the courtyard."

Marcone knocked the ashes savagely from his pipe.

"Well, anyhow, that's the end of it; we can't do anything for him now, poor fellow."

"Poor fellow!" Martini echoed, under his breath. He was beginning to realise that to him, too, the world would look empty and dismal without the Gadfly.

"What does she think?" the smuggler asked, glancing towards the other end of the room, where Gemma sat alone, her hands lying idly in her lap, her eyes looking straight before her into blank nothingness.

"I have not asked her; she has not spoken since I brought her the news. We had best not disturb her just yet."

She did not appear to be conscious of their presence, but they both spoke with lowered voices, as though they were looking at a corpse. After a dreary little pause, Marcone rose and put away his pipe.

"I will come back this evening," he said; but Martini stopped him with a gesture.

"Don't go yet; I want to speak to you." He dropped his voice still lower and continued in almost a whisper:

"Do you believe there is really no hope?"

"I don't see what hope there can be now. We can't attempt it again. Even if he were well enough to manage his part of the thing, we couldn't do our share. The sentinels are all being changed, on suspicion. The Cricket won't get another chance, you may be sure."

"Don't you think," Martini asked suddenly; "that, when he recovers, something might be done by calling off the sentinels?"

"Calling off the sentinels? What do you mean?"

"Well, it has occurred to me that if I were to get in the Governor's way when the procession passes close by the fortress on Corpus Domini day and fire in his face, all the sentinels would come rushing to get hold of me, and some of you fellows could perhaps help Rivarez out in the confusion. It really hardly amounts to a plan; it only came into my head."

"I doubt whether it could be managed," Marcone answered with a very grave face. "Certainly it would want a lot of thinking out for anything to come of it. But"—he stopped and looked at Martini—"if it should be possible—would you do it?"

Martini was a reserved man at ordinary times; but this was not an ordinary time. He looked straight into the smuggler's face.

"Would I do it?" he repeated. "Look at her!"

There was no need for further explanations; in saying that he had said all. Marcone turned and looked across the room.

She had not moved since their conversation began. There was no doubt, no fear, even no grief in her face; there was nothing in it but the shadow of death. The smuggler's eyes filled with tears as he looked at her.

"Make haste, Michele!" he said, throwing open the verandah door and looking out. "Aren't you nearly done, you two? There are a hundred and fifty things to do!"

Michele, followed by Gino, came in from the verandah.

"I am ready now," he said. "I only want to ask the signora——"

He was moving towards her when Martini caught him by the arm.

"Don't disturb her; she's better alone."

"Let her be!" Marcone added. "We shan't do any good by meddling. God knows, it's hard enough on all of us; but it's worse for her, poor soul!"

CHAPTER V

FOR a week the Gadfly lay in a fearful state. The attack was a violent one, and the Governor, rendered brutal by fear and perplexity, had not only chained him hand and foot, but had insisted on his being bound to his pallet with leather straps, drawn so tight that he could not move without their cutting into the flesh. He endured everything with his dogged, bitter stoicism till the end of the sixth day. Then his pride broke down, and he piteously entreated the prison doctor for a dose of opium. The doctor was quite willing to give it; but the Governor, hearing of the request, sharply forbade "any such foolery."

"How do you know what he wants it for?" he said. "It's just as likely as not that he's shamming all the time and wants to drug the sentinel, or some such devilry. Rivarez is cunning enough for anything."

"My giving him a dose would hardly help him to drug the sentinel," replied the doctor, unable to suppress a smile. "And as for shamming—there's not much fear of that. He is as likely as not to die."

"Anyway, I won't have it given. If a man wants to be tenderly treated, he should behave accordingly. He has thoroughly deserved a little sharp discipline. Perhaps it will be a lesson to him not to play tricks with the window-bars again."

"The law does not admit of torture, though," the doctor ventured to say; "and this is coming perilously near it."

"The law says nothing about opium, I think," said the Governor snappishly.

"It is for you to decide, of course, colonel; but I hope you will let the straps be taken off at any rate. They are a needless aggravation of his misery. There's no fear of his escaping now. He couldn't stand if you let him go free."

"My good sir, a doctor may make a mistake like other people, I suppose. I have got him safe strapped now, and he's going to stop so."

"At least, then, have the straps a little loosened. It is downright barbarity to keep them drawn so tight."

"They will stop exactly as they are; and I will thank you, sir, not to talk about barbarity to me. If I do a thing, I have a reason for it."

So the seventh night passed without any relief, and the soldier stationed on guard at the cell door crossed himself, shuddering, over and over again, as he listened all night long to heart-rending moans. The Gadfly's endurance was failing him at last.

At six in the morning the sentinel, just before going off duty, unlocked the door softly and entered the cell. He knew that he was committing a serious breach of discipline, but could not bear to go away without offering the consolation of a friendly word.

He found the Gadfly lying still, with closed eyes and parted lips. He stood silent for a moment; then stooped down and asked:

"Can I do anything for you, sir? I have only a minute."

The Gadfly opened his eyes. "Let me alone!" he moaned. "Let me alone—"

He was asleep almost before the soldier had slipped back to his post.

Ten days afterwards the Governor called again at the palace, but found that the Cardinal had gone to visit a sick man at Pieve d'Ottavo, and was not expected home till the afternoon. That evening, just as he was sitting down to dinner, his servant came in to announce:

"His Eminence would like to speak to you."

The Governor, with a hasty glance into the looking glass, to make sure that his uniform was in order, put on his most dignified air, and went into the reception room, where Montanelli was sitting, beating his hand gently on the arm of the chair and looking out of the window with an anxious line between his brows.

"I heard that you called to-day," he said, cutting short the Governor's polite speeches with a slightly imperious manner which he never adopted in speaking to the country folk. "It was probably on the business about which I have been wishing to speak to you."

"It was about Rivarez, Your Eminence."

"So I supposed. I have been thinking the matter over these last few days. But before we go into that, I should like to hear whether you have anything new to tell me."

The Governor pulled his moustaches with an embarrassed air.

"The fact is, I came to know whether Your Eminence had anything to tell me. If you still have an objection to the course I proposed taking, I should be sincerely glad of your advice in the matter; for, honestly, I don't know what to do."

"Is there any new difficulty?"

"Only that next Thursday is the 3d of June,—Corpus Domini,—and somehow or other the matter must be settled before then."

"Thursday is Corpus Domini, certainly; but why must it be settled especially before then?"

"I am exceedingly sorry, Your Eminence, if I seem to oppose you, but I can't undertake to be responsible for the peace of the town if Rivarez is not got rid of before then. All the roughest set in the hills collects here for that day, as Your Eminence knows, and it is more than probable that they may attempt to break open the fortress gates and take him out. They won't succeed; I'll take care of that, if I have to sweep them from the gates with powder and shot. But we are very likely to have something of that kind before the day is over. Here in the Romagna there is bad blood in the people, and when once they get out their knives——"

"I think with a little care we can prevent matters going as far as knives. I have always found the people of this district easy to get on with, if they are reasonably treated. Of course, if you once begin to threaten or coerce a Romagnol he becomes unmanageable. But have you any reason for supposing a new rescue scheme is intended?"

"I heard, both this morning and yesterday, from confidential agents of mine, that a great many rumours are circulating all over the district and that the people are evidently up to some mischief or other. But one can't find out the details; if one could it would be easier to take precautions. And for my part, after the fright we had the other day, I prefer to be on the safe side. With such a cunning fox as Rivarez one can't be too careful."

"The last I heard about Rivarez was that he was too ill to move or speak. Is he recovering, then?"

"He seems much better now, Your Eminence. He certainly has been very ill—unless he was shamming all the time."

"Have you any reason for supposing that likely?"

"Well, the doctor seems convinced that it was all genuine; but it's a very mysterious kind of illness. Any way, he is recovering, and more intractable than ever."

"What has he done now?"

"There's not much he can do, fortunately," the Governor answered, smiling as he remembered the straps. "But his behaviour is something indescribable. Yesterday morning I went into the cell to ask him a few questions; he is not well enough yet to come to me for interrogation—and indeed, I thought it best not to run any risk of the people seeing him until he recovers. Such absurd stories always get about at once."

"So you went there to interrogate him?"

"Yes, Your Eminence. I hoped he would be more amenable to reason now."

Montanelli looked him over deliberately, almost as if he had been inspecting a new and disagreeable animal. Fortunately, however, the Governor was fingering his sword-belt, and did not see the look. He went on placidly:

"I have not subjected him to any particular severities, but I have been obliged to be rather strict with him—especially as it is a military prison—and I thought that perhaps a little indulgence might have a good effect. I offered to relax the discipline considerably if he would behave in a reasonable manner; and how does Your Eminence suppose he answered me? He lay looking at me a minute, like a wolf in a cage, and then said quite softly: 'Colonel, I can't get up and strangle you; but my teeth are pretty good; you had better take your throat a little further off.' He is as savage as a wild-cat."

"I am not surprised to hear it," Montanelli answered quietly. "But I came to ask you a question. Do you honestly believe that the presence of Rivarez in the prison here constitutes a serious danger to the peace of the district?"

"Most certainly I do, Your Eminence."

"You think that, to prevent the risk of bloodshed, it is absolutely necessary that he should somehow be got rid of before Corpus Domini?"

"I can only repeat that if he is here on Thursday, I do not expect the festival to pass over without a fight, and I think it likely to be a serious one."

"And you think that if he were not here there would be no such danger?"

"In that case, there would either be no disturbance at all, or at most a little shouting and stone-throwing. If Your Eminence can find some way of getting rid of him, I will undertake that the peace shall be kept. Otherwise, I expect most serious trouble. I am convinced that a new rescue plot is on hand, and Thursday is the day when we may expect the attempt. Now, if on that very morning they suddenly find that he is not in the fortress at all, their plan fails of itself, and they have no occasion to begin fighting. But if we have to repulse them, and the daggers once get drawn among such throngs of people, we are likely to have the place burnt down before nightfall."

"Then why do you not send him in to Ravenna?"

"Heaven knows, Your Eminence, I should be thankful to do it! But how am I to prevent the people rescuing him on the way? I have not soldiers enough to resist an armed attack; and all these mountaineers have got knives or flint-locks or some such thing."

"You still persist, then, in wishing for a court-martial, and in asking my consent to it?"

"Pardon me, Your Eminence; I ask you only one thing—to help me prevent riots and bloodshed. I am quite willing to admit that the military commissions, such as that of Colonel Freddi, were sometimes unnecessarily severe, and irritated instead of subduing the people; but I think that in this case a court-martial would be a wise measure and in the long run a merciful one. It would prevent a riot, which in itself would be a terrible disaster, and which very likely might cause a return of the military commissions His Holiness has abolished."

The Governor finished his little speech with much solemnity, and waited for the Cardinal's answer. It was a long time coming; and when it came was startlingly unexpected.

"Colonel Ferrari, do you believe in God?"

"Your Eminence!" the colonel gasped in a voice full of exclamation-stops.

"Do you believe in God?" Montanelli repeated, rising and looking down at him with steady, searching eyes. The colonel rose too.

"Your Eminence, I am a Christian man, and have never yet been refused absolution."

Montanelli lifted the cross from his breast.

"Then swear on the cross of the Redeemer Who died for you, that you have been speaking the truth to me."

The colonel stood still and gazed at it blankly. He could not quite make up his mind which was mad, he or the Cardinal.

"You have asked me," Montanelli went on, "to give my consent to a man's death. Kiss the cross, if you dare, and tell me that you believe there is no other way to prevent greater bloodshed. And remember that if you tell me a lie you are imperilling your immortal soul."

After a little pause, the Governor bent down and put the cross to his lips.

"I believe it," he said.

Montanelli turned slowly away.

"I will give you a definite answer to-morrow. But first I must see Rivarez and speak to him alone."

"Your Eminence—if I might suggest—I am sure you will regret it. For that matter, he sent me a message yesterday, by the guard, asking to see Your Eminence; but I took no notice of it, because——"

"Took no notice!" Montanelli repeated. "A man in such circumstances sent you a message, and you took no notice of it?"

"I am sorry if Your Eminence is displeased. I did not wish to trouble you over a mere impertinence like that; I know Rivarez well enough by now to feel sure that he only wanted to insult you. And, indeed, if you will allow me to say so, it would be most imprudent to go near him alone; he is really dangerous— so much so, in fact, that I have thought it necessary to use some physical restraint of a mild kind———"

"And you really think there is much danger to be apprehended from one sick and unarmed man, who is under physical restraint of a mild kind?" Montanelli spoke quite gently, but the colonel felt the sting of his quiet contempt, and flushed under it resentfully.

"Your Eminence will do as you think best," he said in his stiffest manner. "I only wished to spare you the pain of hearing this man's awful blasphemies."

"Which do you think the more grievous misfortune for a Christian man; to hear a blasphemous word uttered, or to abandon a fellow-creature in extremity?"

The Governor stood erect and stiff, with his official face, like a face of wood. He was deeply offended at Montanelli's treatment of him, and showed it by unusual ceremoniousness.

"At what time does Your Eminence wish to visit the prisoner?" he asked.

"I will go to him at once."

"As Your Eminence pleases. If you will kindly wait a few moments, I will send someone to prepare him."

The Governor had come down from his official pedestal in a great hurry. He did not want Montanelli to see the straps.

"Thank you; I would rather see him as he is, without preparation. I will go straight up to the fortress. Good-evening, colonel; you may expect my answer to-morrow morning."

CHAPTER VI

HEARING the cell-door unlocked, the Gadfly turned away his eyes with languid indifference. He supposed that it was only the Governor, coming to worry him with another interrogation. Several soldiers mounted the narrow stair, their carbines clanking against the wall; then a deferential voice said: "It is rather steep here, Your Eminence."

He started convulsively, and then shrank down, catching his breath under the stinging pressure of the straps.

Montanelli came in with the sergeant and three guards.

"If Your Eminence will kindly wait a moment," the sergeant began nervously, "one of my men will bring a chair. He has just gone to fetch it. Your Eminence will excuse us—if we had been expecting you, we should have been prepared."

"There is no need for any preparation. Will you kindly leave us alone, sergeant; and wait at the foot of the stairs with your men?"

"Yes, Your Eminence. Here is the chair; shall I put it beside him?"

The Gadfly was lying with closed eyes; but he felt that Montanelli was looking at him.

"I think he is asleep, Your Eminence," the sergeant was beginning, but the Gadfly opened his eyes.

"No," he said.

As the soldiers were leaving the cell they were stopped by a sudden exclamation from Montanelli; and, turning back, saw that he was bending down to examine the straps.

"Who has been doing this?" he asked. The sergeant fumbled with his cap.

"It was by the Governor's express orders, Your Eminence."

"I had no idea of this, Signer Rivarez," Montanelli said in a voice of great distress.

"I told Your Eminence," the Gadfly answered, with his hard smile, "that I n-n-never expected to be patted on the head."

"Sergeant, how long has this been going on?"

"Since he tried to escape, Your Eminence."

"That is, nearly a week? Bring a knife and cut these off at once."

"May it please Your Eminence, the doctor wanted to take them off, but Colonel Ferrari wouldn't allow it."

"Bring a knife at once." Montanelli had not raised his voice, but the soldiers could see that he was white with anger. The sergeant took a clasp-knife from his pocket, and bent down to cut the arm-strap. He was not a skilful-fingered man; and he jerked the strap tighter with an awkward movement, so that the Gadfly winced and bit his lip in spite of all his self-control. Montanelli came forward at once.

"You don't know how to do it; give me the knife."

"Ah-h-h!" The Gadfly stretched out his arms with a long, rapturous sigh as the strap fell off. The next instant Montanelli had cut the other one, which bound his ankles.

"Take off the irons, too, sergeant; and then come here. I want to speak to you."

He stood by the window, looking on, till the sergeant threw down the fetters and approached him.

"Now," he said, "tell me everything that has been happening."

The sergeant, nothing loath, related all that he knew of the Gadfly's illness, of the "disciplinary measures," and of the doctor's unsuccessful attempt to interfere.

"But I think, Your Eminence," he added, "that the colonel wanted the straps kept on as a means of getting evidence."

"Evidence?"

"Yes, Your Eminence; the day before yesterday I heard him offer to have them taken off if he"—with a glance at the Gadfly—"would answer a question he had asked."

Montanelli clenched his hand on the window-sill, and the soldiers glanced at one another: they had never seen the gentle Cardinal angry before. As for the Gadfly, he had forgotten their existence; he had forgotten everything except the physical sensation of freedom. He was cramped in every limb; and now stretched, and turned, and twisted about in a positive ecstasy of relief.

"You can go now, sergeant," the Cardinal said. "You need not feel anxious about having committed a breach of discipline; it was your duty to tell me when I asked you. See that no one disturbs us. I will come out when I am ready."

When the door had closed behind the soldiers, he leaned on the window-sill and looked for a while at the sinking sun, so as to leave the Gadfly a little more breathing time.

"I have heard," he said presently, leaving the window, and sitting down beside the pallet, "that you wish to speak to me alone. If you feel well enough to tell me what you wanted to say, I am at your service."

He spoke very coldly, with a stiff, imperious manner that was not natural to him. Until the straps were off, the Gadfly was to him simply a grievously wronged and tortured human being; but now he recalled their last interview, and the deadly insult with which it had closed. The Gadfly looked up, resting his head lazily on one arm. He possessed the gift of slipping into graceful attitudes; and when his face was in shadow no one would have guessed through what deep waters he had been passing. But, as he looked up, the clear evening light showed how haggard and colourless he was, and how plainly the trace of the last few days was stamped on him. Montanelli's anger died away.

"I am afraid you have been terribly ill," he said. "I am sincerely sorry that I did not know of all this. I would have put a stop to it before."

The Gadfly shrugged his shoulders. "All's fair in war," he said coolly. "Your Eminence objects to straps theoretically, from the Christian standpoint; but it is hardly fair to expect the colonel to see that. He, no doubt, would prefer not to try them on his own skin—which is j-j-just my case. But that is a matter of p-p-personal convenience. At this moment I am undermost—w-w-what would you have? It is very kind of Your Eminence, though, to call here; but perhaps that was done from the C-c-christian standpoint, too. Visiting prisoners—ah, yes! I forgot. 'Inasmuch as ye did it unto one of the l-least of these'—it's not very complimentary, but one of the least is duly grateful."

"Signor Rivarez," the Cardinal interrupted, "I have come here on your account—not on my own. If you had not been 'undermost,' as you call it, I should never have spoken to you again after what you said to me last week; but you have the double privilege of a prisoner and a sick man, and I could not refuse to come. Have you anything to say to me, now I am here; or have you sent for me merely to amuse yourself by insulting an old man?"

There was no answer. The Gadfly had turned away, and was lying with one hand across his eyes.

"I am—very sorry to trouble you," he said at last, huskily; "but could I have a little water?"

There was a jug of water standing by the window, and Montanelli rose and fetched it. As he slipped his arm round the Gadfly to lift him, he suddenly felt the damp, cold fingers close over his wrist like a vice.

"Give me your hand—quick—just a moment," the Gadfly whispered. "Oh, what difference does it make to you? Only one minute!"

He sank down, hiding his face on Montanelli's arm, and quivering from head to foot.

"Drink a little water," Montanelli said after a moment. The Gadfly obeyed silently; then lay back on the pallet with closed eyes. He himself could have given no explanation of what had happened to him when Montanelli's hand had touched his cheek; he only knew that in all his life there had been nothing more terrible.

Montanelli drew his chair closer to the pallet and sat down. The Gadfly was lying quite motionless, like a corpse, and his face was livid and drawn. After a long silence, he opened his eyes, and fixed their haunting, spectral gaze on the Cardinal.

"Thank you," he said. "I—am sorry. I think—you asked me something?"

"You are not fit to talk. If there is anything you want to say to me, I will try to come again to-morrow."

"Please don't go, Your Eminence—indeed, there is nothing the matter with me. I—I have been a little upset these few days; it was half of it malingering, though—the colonel will tell you so if you ask him."

"I prefer to form my own conclusions," Montanelli answered quietly.

"S-so does the colonel. And occasionally, do you know, they are rather witty. You w-w-wouldn't think it to look at him; but s-s-sometimes he gets hold of an or-r-riginal idea. On Friday night, for instance—I think it was Friday, but I got a l-little mixed as to time towards the end—anyhow, I asked for a d-dose of opium—I remember that quite distinctly; and he came in here and said I m-might h-h-have it if I would tell him who un-l-l-locked the gate. I remember his saying: 'If it's real, you'll consent; if you don't, I shall look upon it as a p-proof that you are shamming.' It n-n-never oc-c-curred to me before how comic that is; it's one of the f-f-funniest things——"

He burst into a sudden fit of harsh, discordant laughter; then, turning sharply on the silent Cardinal, went on, more and more hurriedly, and stammering so that the words were hardly intelligible:

"You d-d-don't see that it's f-f-funny? Of c-course not; you r-religious people n-n-never have any s-sense of humour—you t-take everything t-t-tragically. F-for instance, that night in the Cath-thedral—how solemn you were! By the way—w-what a path-thetic figure I must have c-cut as the pilgrim! I d-don't believe you e-even see anything c-c-comic in the b-business you have c-come about this evening."

Montanelli rose.

"I came to hear what you have to say; but I think you are too much excited to say it to-night. The doctor had better give you a sedative, and we will talk to-morrow, when you have had a night's sleep."

"S-sleep? Oh, I shall s-sleep well enough, Your Eminence, when you g-give your c-consent to the colonel's plan—an ounce of l-lead is a s-splendid sedative."

"I don't understand you," Montanelli said, turning to him with a startled look.

The Gadfly burst out laughing again.

"Your Eminence, Your Eminence, t-t-truth is the c-chief of the Christian virtues! D-d-do you th-th-think I d-d-don't know how hard the Governor has been trying to g-get your consent to a court-martial? You had b-better by half g-give it, Your Eminence; it's only w-what all your b-brother prelates would do in your place. 'Cosi fan tutti;' and then you would be doing s-such a lot of good, and so l-little harm! Really, it's n-not worth all the sleepless nights you have been spending over it!"

"Please stop laughing a minute," Montanelli interrupted, "and tell me how you heard all this. Who has been talking to you about it?"

"H-hasn't the colonel e-e-ever told you I am a d-d-devil—not a man? No? He has t-told me so often enough! Well, I am devil enough to f-find out a little bit what p-people are thinking about. Your E-eminence is thinking that I'm a conf-founded nuisance, and you wish s-somebody else had to settle what's to be done with me, without disturbing your s-sensitive conscience. That's a p-pretty fair guess, isn't it?"

"Listen to me," the Cardinal said, sitting down again beside him, with a very grave face. "However you found out all this, it is quite true. Colonel Ferrari fears another rescue attempt on the part of your friends, and wishes to forestall it in—the way you speak of. You see, I am quite frank with you."

"Your E-eminence was always f-f-famous for truthfulness," the Gadfly put in bitterly.

"You know, of course," Montanelli went on, "that legally I have no jurisdiction in temporal matters; I am a bishop, not a legate. But I have a good deal of influence in this district; and the colonel will not, I think, venture to take so extreme a course unless he can get, at least, my tacit consent to it. Up till now I have unconditionally opposed the scheme; and he has been trying very hard to conquer my objection by assuring me that there is great danger of an armed attempt on Thursday when the crowd collects for the procession—an attempt which probably would end in bloodshed. Do you follow me?"

The Gadfly was staring absently out of the window. He looked round and answered in a weary voice:

"Yes, I am listening."

"Perhaps you are really not well enough to stand this conversation to-night. Shall I come back in the morning? It is a very serious matter, and I want your whole attention."

"I would rather get it over now," the Gadfly answered in the same tone. "I follow everything you say."

"Now, if it be true," Montanelli went on, "that there is any real danger of riots and bloodshed on account of you, I am taking upon myself a tremendous responsibility in opposing the colonel; and I believe there is at least some truth in what he says. On the other hand, I am inclined to think that his judgment is warped, to a certain extent, by his personal animosity against you, and that he probably exaggerates the danger. That seems to me the more likely since I have seen this shameful brutality." He glanced at the straps and chains lying on the floor, and went on:

"If I consent, I kill you; if I refuse, I run the risk of killing innocent persons. I have considered the matter earnestly, and have sought with all my heart for a way out of this dreadful alternative. And now at last I have made up my mind."

"To kill me and s-save the innocent persons, of course—the only decision a Christian man could possibly come to. 'If thy r-right hand offend thee,' etc. I have n-not the honour to be the right hand of Your Eminence, and I have offended you; the c-c-conclusion is plain. Couldn't you tell me that without so much preamble?"

The Gadfly spoke with languid indifference and contempt, like a man weary of the whole subject.

"Well?" he added after a little pause. "Was that the decision, Your Eminence?"

"No."

The Gadfly shifted his position, putting both hands behind his head, and looked at Montanelli with half-shut eyes. The Cardinal, with his head sunk down as in deep thought, was softly beating one hand on the arm of his chair. Ah, that old, familiar gesture!

"I have decided," he said, raising his head at last, "to do, I suppose, an utterly unprecedented thing. When I heard that you had asked to see me, I resolved to come here and tell you everything, as I have done, and to place the matter in your own hands."

"In—my hands?"

"Signor Rivarez, I have not come to you as cardinal, or as bishop, or as judge; I have come to you as one man to another. I do not ask you to tell me whether you know of any such scheme as the colonel apprehends. I understand quite well that, if you do, it is your secret and you will not tell it. But I do ask you to put yourself in my place. I am old, and, no doubt, have not much longer to live. I would go down to my grave without blood on my hands."

"Is there none on them as yet, Your Eminence?"

Montanelli grew a shade paler, but went on quietly:

"All my life I have opposed repressive measures and cruelty wherever I have met with them. I have always disapproved of capital punishment in all its forms; I have protested earnestly and repeatedly against the military commissions in the last reign, and have been out of favour on account of doing so. Up till now such influence and power as I have possessed have always been employed on the side of mercy. I ask you to believe me, at least, that I am speaking the truth. Now, I am placed in this dilemma. By refusing, I am exposing the town to the danger of riots and all their consequences; and this to save the life of a man who blasphemes against my religion, who has slandered and wronged and insulted me personally (though that is comparatively a trifle), and who, as I firmly believe, will put that life to a bad use when it is given to him. But—it is to save a man's life."

He paused a moment, and went on again:

"Signor Rivarez, everything that I know of your career seems to me bad and mischievous; and I have long believed you to be reckless and violent and unscrupulous. To some extent I hold that opinion of you still. But during this last fortnight you have shown me that you are a brave man and that you can be faithful to your friends. You have made the soldiers love and admire you, too; and not every man could have done that. I think that perhaps I have misjudged you, and that there is in you something better than what you show outside. To that better self in you I appeal, and solemnly entreat you, on your conscience, to tell me truthfully—in my place, what would you do?"

A long silence followed; then the Gadfly looked up.

"At least, I would decide my own actions for myself, and take the consequences of them. I would not come sneaking to other people, in the cowardly Christian way, asking them to solve my problems for me!"

The onslaught was so sudden, and its extraordinary vehemence and passion were in such startling contrast to the languid affectation of a moment before, that it was as though he had thrown off a mask.

"We atheists," he went on fiercely, "understand that if a man has a thing to bear, he must bear it as best he can; and if he sinks under it—why, so much the worse for him. But a Christian comes whining to his God, or his saints; or, if they won't help him, to his enemies—he can always find a back to shift his burdens on to. Isn't there a rule to go by in your Bible, or your Missal, or any of your canting theology books, that you must come to me to tell you what to do? Heavens and earth, man! Haven't I enough as it is, without your laying your responsibilities on my shoulders? Go back to your Jesus; he exacted the uttermost farthing, and you'd better do the same. After all, you'll only be killing an atheist—a man who boggles over 'shibboleth'; and that's no great crime, surely!"

He broke off, panting for breath, and then burst out again:

"And YOU to talk of cruelty! Why, that p-p-pudding-headed ass couldn't hurt me as much as you do if he tried for a year; he hasn't got the brains. All he can think of is to pull a strap tight, and when he can't get it any tighter he's at the end of his resources. Any fool can do that! But you—— 'Sign your own death sentence, please; I'm too tender-hearted to do it myself.' Oh! it would take a Christian to hit on that—a gentle, compassionate Christian, that turns pale at the sight of a strap pulled too tight! I might have known when you came in, like an angel of mercy—so shocked at the colonel's 'barbarity'—that the real thing was going to begin! Why do you look at me that way? Consent, man, of course, and go home to your dinner; the thing's not worth all this fuss. Tell your colonel he can have me shot, or hanged, or whatever comes handiest— roasted alive, if it's any amusement to him—and be done with it!"

The Gadfly was hardly recognizable; he was beside himself with rage and desperation, panting and quivering, his eyes glittering with green reflections like the eyes of an angry cat.

Montanelli had risen, and was looking down at him silently. He did not understand the drift of the frenzied reproaches, but he understood out of what extremity they were uttered; and, understanding that, forgave all past insults.

"Hush!" he said. "I did not want to hurt you so. Indeed, I never meant to shift my burden on to you, who have too much already. I have never consciously done that to any living creature——"

"It's a lie!" the Gadfly cried out with blazing eyes. "And the bishopric?"

"The—bishopric?"

"Ah! you've forgotten that? It's so easy to forget! 'If you wish it, Arthur, I will say I cannot go. I was to decide your life for you—I, at nineteen! If it weren't so hideous, it would be funny."

"Stop!" Montanelli put up both hands to his head with a desperate cry. He let them fall again, and walked slowly away to the window. There he sat down on the sill, resting one arm on the bars, and pressing his forehead against it. The Gadfly lay and watched him, trembling.

Presently Montanelli rose and came back, with lips as pale as ashes.

"I am very sorry," he said, struggling piteously to keep up his usual quiet manner, "but I must go home. I—am not quite well."

He was shivering as if with ague. All the Gadfly's fury broke down.

"Padre, can't you see——"

Montanelli shrank away, and stood still.

"Only not that!" he whispered at last. "My God, anything but that! If I am going mad——"

The Gadfly raised himself on one arm, and took the shaking hands in his.

"Padre, will you never understand that I am not really drowned?"

The hands grew suddenly cold and stiff. For a moment everything was dead with silence, and then Montanelli knelt down and hid his face on the Gadfly's breast.

When he raised his head the sun had set, and the red glow was dying in the west. They had forgotten time and place, and life and death; they had forgotten, even, that they were enemies.

"Arthur," Montanelli whispered, "are you real? Have you come back to me from the dead?"

"From the dead——" the Gadfly repeated, shivering. He was lying with his head on Montanelli's arm, as a sick child might lie in its mother's embrace.

"You have come back—you have come back at last!"

The Gadfly sighed heavily. "Yes," he said; "and you have to fight me, or to kill me."

"Oh, hush, carino! What is all that now? We have been like two children lost in the dark, mistaking one another for phantoms. Now we have found each other, and have come out into the light. My poor boy, how changed you are— how changed you are! You look as if all the ocean of the world's misery had passed over your head—you that used to be so full of the joy of life! Arthur, is it really you? I have dreamed so often that you had come back to me; and then have waked and seen the outer darkness staring in upon an empty place. How can I know I shall not wake again and find it all a dream? Give me something tangible—tell me how it all happened."

"It happened simply enough. I hid on a goods vessel, as stowaway, and got out to South America."

"And there?"

"There I—lived, if you like to call it so, till—oh, I have seen something else besides theological seminaries since you used to teach me philosophy! You say you have dreamed of me—yes, and much! You say you have dreamed of me—yes, and I of you——"

He broke off, shuddering.

"Once," he began again abruptly, "I was working at a mine in Ecuador—"

"Not as a miner?"

"No, as a miner's fag—odd-jobbing with the coolies. We had a barrack to sleep in at the pit's mouth; and one night—I had been ill, the same as lately, and carrying stones in the blazing sun—I must have got light-headed, for I saw you come in at the door-way. You were holding a crucifix like that one on the wall. You were praying, and brushed past me without turning. I cried out to you to help me—to give me poison or a knife—something to put an end to it all before I went mad. And you—ah———!"

He drew one hand across his eyes. Montanelli was still clasping the other.

"I saw in your face that you had heard, but you never looked round; you went on with your prayers. When you had finished, and kissed the crucifix, you glanced round and whispered: 'I am very sorry for you, Arthur; but I daren't show it; He would be angry.' And I looked at Him, and the wooden image was laughing.

"Then, when I came to my senses, and saw the barrack and the coolies with their leprosy, I understood. I saw that you care more to curry favour with that devilish God of yours than to save me from any hell. And I have remembered that. I forgot just now when you touched me; I—have been ill, and I used to love you once. But there can be nothing between us but war, and war, and war. What do you want to hold my hand for? Can't you see that while you believe in your Jesus we can't be anything but enemies?"

Montanelli bent his head and kissed the mutilated hand.

"Arthur, how can I help believing in Him? If I have kept my faith through all these frightful years, how can I ever doubt Him any more, now that He has given you back to me? Remember, I thought I had killed you."

"You have that still to do."

"Arthur!" It was a cry of actual terror; but the Gadfly went on, unheeding:

"Let us be honest, whatever we do, and not shilly-shally. You and I stand on two sides of a pit, and it's hopeless trying to join hands across it. If you have decided that you can't, or won't, give up that thing"—he glanced again at the crucifix on the wall—"you must consent to what the colonel——"

"Consent! My God—consent—Arthur, but I love you!"

The Gadfly's face contracted fearfully.

"Which do you love best, me or that thing?"

Montanelli slowly rose. The very soul in him withered with dread, and he seemed to shrivel up bodily, and to grow feeble, and old, and wilted, like a leaf that the frost has touched. He had awaked out of his dream, and the outer darkness was staring in upon an empty place.

"Arthur, have just a little mercy on me——"

"How much had you for me when your lies drove me out to be slave to the blacks on the sugar-plantations? You shudder at that—ah, these tender-hearted saints! This is the man after God's own heart—the man that repents of his sin and lives. No one dies but his son. You say you love me,—your love has cost me dear enough! Do you think I can blot out everything, and turn back into Arthur at a few soft words—I, that have been dish-washer in filthy half-caste brothels and stable-boy to Creole farmers that were worse brutes than their own cattle? I, that have been zany in cap and bells for a strolling variety show—drudge and Jack-of-all-trades to the matadors in the bull-fighting ring; I, that have been slave to every black beast who cared to set his foot on my neck; I, that have been starved and spat upon and trampled under foot; I, that have begged for mouldy scraps and been refused because the dogs had the first right? Oh, what is the use of all this! How can I TELL you what you have brought on me? And now—you love me! How much do you love me? Enough to give up your God for me? Oh, what has He done for you, this everlasting Jesus,—what has He suffered for you, that you should love Him more than me? Is it for the pierced hands He is so dear to you? Look at mine! Look here, and here, and here——"

He tore open his shirt and showed the ghastly scars.

"Padre, this God of yours is an impostor, His wounds are sham wounds, His pain is all a farce! It is I that have the right to your heart! Padre, there is no torture you have not put me to; if you could only know what my life has been! And yet I would not die! I have endured it all, and have possessed my soul in patience, because I would come back and fight this God of yours. I have held this purpose as a shield against my heart, and it has saved me from madness, and from the second death. And now, when I come back, I find Him still in my place—this sham victim that was crucified for six hours, forsooth, and rose again from the dead! Padre, I have been crucified for five years, and I, too, have risen from the dead. What are you going to do with me? What are you going to do with me?"

He broke down. Montanelli sat like some stone image, or like a dead man set upright. At first, under the fiery torrent of the Gadfly's despair, he had quivered a little, with the automatic shrinking of the flesh, as under the lash of a whip; but now he was quite still. After a long silence he looked up and spoke, lifelessly, patiently:

"Arthur, will you explain to me more clearly? You confuse and terrify me so, I can't understand. What is it you demand of me?"

The Gadfly turned to him a spectral face.

"I demand nothing. Who shall compel love? You are free to choose between us two the one who is most dear to you. If you love Him best, choose Him."

"I can't understand," Montanelli repeated wearily. "What is there I can choose? I cannot undo the past."

"You have to choose between us. If you love me, take that cross off your neck and come away with me. My friends are arranging another attempt, and with your help they could manage it easily. Then, when we are safe over the frontier, acknowledge me publicly. But if you don't love me enough for that,—if this wooden idol is more to you than I,—then go to the colonel and tell him you consent. And if you go, then go at once, and spare me the misery of seeing you. I have enough without that."

Montanelli looked up, trembling faintly. He was beginning to understand.

"I will communicate with your friends, of course. But—to go with you—it is impossible—I am a priest."

"And I accept no favours from priests. I will have no more compromises, Padre; I have had enough of them, and of their consequences. You must give up your priesthood, or you must give up me."

"How can I give you up? Arthur, how can I give you up?"

"Then give up Him. You have to choose between us. Would you offer me a share of your love—half for me, half for your fiend of a God? I will not take His leavings. If you are His, you are not mine."

"Would you have me tear my heart in two? Arthur! Arthur! Do you want to drive me mad?"

The Gadfly struck his hand against the wall.

"You have to choose between us," he repeated once more.

Montanelli drew from his breast a little case containing a bit of soiled and crumpled paper.

"Look!" he said.

"I believed in you, as I believed in God. God is a thing made of clay, that I can smash with a hammer; and you have fooled me with a lie."

The Gadfly laughed and handed it back. "How d-d-delightfully young one is at nineteen! To take a hammer and smash things seems so easy. It's that now—only it's I that am under the hammer. As for you, there are plenty of other people you can fool with lies—and they won't even find you out."

"As you will," Montanelli said. "Perhaps in your place I should be as merciless as you—God knows. I can't do what you ask, Arthur; but I will do what I can. I will arrange your escape, and when you are safe I will have an accident in the mountains, or take the wrong sleeping-draught by mistake—whatever you like to choose. Will that content you? It is all I can do. It is a great sin; but I think He will forgive me. He is more merciful———"

The Gadfly flung out both hands with a sharp cry.

"Oh, that is too much! That is too much! What have I done that you should think of me that way? What right have you—— As if I wanted to be revenged on you! Can't you see that I only want to save you? Will you never understand that I love you?"

He caught hold of Montanelli's hands and covered them with burning kisses and tears.

"Padre, come away with us! What have you to do with this dead world of priests and idols? They are full of the dust of bygone ages; they are rotten; they are pestilent and foul! Come out of this plague-stricken Church—come away with us into the light! Padre, it is we that are life and youth; it is we that are the everlasting springtime; it is we that are the future! Padre, the dawn is close upon us—will you miss your part in the sunrise? Wake up, and let us forget the horrible nightmares,—wake up, and we will begin our life again! Padre, I have always loved you—always, even when you killed me—will you kill me again?"

Montanelli tore his hands away. "Oh, God have mercy on me!" he cried out. "YOU HAVE YOUR MOTHER'S EYES!"

A strange silence, long and deep and sudden, fell upon them both. In the gray twilight they looked at each other, and their hearts stood still with fear.

"Have you anything more to say?" Montanelli whispered. "Any—hope to give me?"

"No. My life is of no use to me except to fight priests. I am not a man; I am a knife. If you let me live, you sanction knives."

Montanelli turned to the crucifix. "God! Listen to this——"

His voice died away into the empty stillness without response. Only the mocking devil awoke again in the Gadfly.

"'C-c-call him louder; perchance he s-s-sleepeth'——"

Montanelli started up as if he had been struck. For a moment he stood looking straight before him;—then he sat down on the edge of the pallet, covered his face with both hands, and burst into tears. A long shudder passed through the Gadfly, and the damp cold broke out on his body. He knew what the tears meant.

He drew the blanket over his head that he might not hear. It was enough that he had to die—he who was so vividly, magnificently alive. But he could not shut out the sound; it rang in his ears, it beat in his brain, it throbbed in all his pulses. And still Montanelli sobbed and sobbed, and the tears dripped down between his fingers.

He left off sobbing at last, and dried his eyes with his handkerchief, like a child that has been crying. As he stood up the handkerchief slipped from his knee and fell to the floor.

"There is no use in talking any more," he said. "You understand?"

"I understand," the Gadfly answered, with dull submission. "It's not your fault. Your God is hungry, and must be fed."

Montanelli turned towards him. The grave that was to be dug was not more still than they were. Silent, they looked into each other's eyes, as two lovers, torn apart, might gaze across the barrier they cannot pass.

It was the Gadfly whose eyes sank first. He shrank down, hiding his face; and Montanelli understood that the gesture meant "Go!" He turned, and went out of the cell. A moment later the Gadfly started up.

"Oh, I can't bear it! Padre, come back! Come back!"

The door was shut. He looked around him slowly, with a wide, still gaze, and understood that all was over. The Galilean had conquered.

All night long the grass waved softly in the courtyard below—the grass that was so soon to wither, uprooted by the spade; and all night long the Gadfly lay alone in the darkness, and sobbed.

CHAPTER VII

THE court-martial was held on Tuesday morning. It was a very short and simple affair; a mere formality, occupying barely twenty minutes. There was, indeed, nothing to spend much time over; no defence was allowed, and the only witnesses were the wounded spy and officer and a few soldiers. The sentence was drawn up beforehand; Montanelli had sent in the desired informal consent; and the judges (Colonel Ferrari, the local major of dragoons, and two officers of the Swiss guards) had little to do. The indictment was read aloud, the witnesses gave their evidence, and the signatures were affixed to the sentence, which was then read to the condemned man with befitting solemnity. He listened in silence; and when asked, according to the usual form, whether he had anything to say, merely waved the question aside with an impatient movement of his hand. Hidden on his breast was the handkerchief which Montanelli had let fall. It had been kissed and wept over all night, as though it were a living thing. Now he looked wan and spiritless, and the traces of tears were still about his eyelids; but the words: "to be shot," did not seem to affect him much. When they were uttered, the pupils of his eyes dilated, but that was all.

"Take him back to his cell," the Governor said, when all the formalities were over; and the sergeant, who was evidently near to breaking down, touched the motionless figure on the shoulder. The Gadfly looked round him with a little start.

"Ah, yes!" he said. "I forgot."

There was something almost like pity in the Governor's face. He was not a cruel man by nature, and was secretly a little ashamed of the part he had been playing during the last month. Now that his main point was gained he was willing to make every little concession in his power.

"You needn't put the irons on again," he said, glancing at the bruised and swollen wrists. "And he can stay in his own cell. The condemned cell is wretchedly dark and gloomy," he added, turning to his nephew; "and really the thing's a mere formality."

He coughed and shifted his feet in evident embarrassment; then called back the sergeant, who was leaving the room with his prisoner.

"Wait, sergeant; I want to speak to him."

The Gadfly did not move, and the Governor's voice seemed to fall on unresponsive ears.

"If you have any message you would like conveyed to your friends or relatives—— You have relatives, I suppose?"

There was no answer.

"Well, think it over and tell me, or the priest. I will see it is not neglected. You had better give your messages to the priest; he shall come at once, and stay the night with you. If there is any other wish——"

The Gadfly looked up.

"Tell the priest I would rather be alone. I have no friends and no messages."

"But you will want to confess."

"I am an atheist. I want nothing but to be left in peace."

He said it in a dull, quiet voice, without defiance or irritation; and turned slowly away. At the door he stopped again.

"I forgot, colonel; there is a favour I wanted to ask. Don't let them tie me or bandage my eyes to-morrow, please. I will stand quite still."

At sunrise on Wednesday morning they brought him out into the courtyard. His lameness was more than usually apparent, and he walked with evident difficulty and pain, leaning heavily on the sergeant's arm; but all the weary submission had gone out of his face. The spectral terrors that had crushed him down in the empty silence, the visions and dreams of the world of shadows, were gone with the night which gave them birth; and once the sun was shining and his enemies were present to rouse the fighting spirit in him, he was not afraid.

The six carabineers who had been told off for the execution were drawn up in line against the ivied wall; the same crannied and crumbling wall down which he had climbed on the night of his unlucky attempt. They could hardly refrain from weeping as they stood together, each man with his carbine in his hand. It seemed to them a horror beyond imagination that they should be called out to kill the Gadfly. He and his stinging repartees, his perpetual laughter, his bright, infectious courage, had come into their dull and dreary lives like a wandering sunbeam; and that he should die, and at their hands, was to them as the darkening of the clear lamps of heaven.

Under the great fig-tree in the courtyard, his grave was waiting for him. It had been dug in the night by unwilling hands; and tears had fallen on the spade. As he passed he looked down, smiling, at the black pit and the withering grass beside it; and drew a long breath, to smell the scent of the freshly turned earth.

Near the tree the sergeant stopped short, and the Gadfly looked round with his brightest smile.

"Shall I stand here, sergeant?"

The man nodded silently; there was a lump in his throat, and he could not have spoken to save his life. The Governor, his nephew, the lieutenant of carabineers who was to command, a doctor and a priest were already in the courtyard, and came forward with grave faces, half abashed under the radiant defiance of the Gadfly's laughing eyes.

"G-good morning, gentlemen! Ah, and his reverence is up so early, too! How do you do, captain? This is a pleasanter occasion for you than our former meeting, isn't it? I see your arm is still in a sling; that's because I bungled my work. These good fellows will do theirs better—won't you, lads?"

He glanced round at the gloomy faces of the carabineers.

"There'll be no need of slings this time, any way. There, there, you needn't look so doleful over it! Put your heels together and show how straight you can shoot. Before long there'll be more work cut out for you than you'll know how to get through, and there's nothing like practice beforehand."

"My son," the priest interrupted, coming forward, while the others drew back to leave them alone together; "in a few minutes you must enter into the presence of your Maker. Have you no other use but this for these last moments that are left you for repentance? Think, I entreat you, how dreadful a thing it is to die without absolution, with all your sins upon your head. When you stand before your Judge it will be too late to repent. Will you approach His awful throne with a jest upon your lips?"

"A jest, your reverence? It is your side that needs that little homily, I think. When our turn comes we shall use field-guns instead of half a dozen second-hand carbines, and then you'll see how much we're in jest."

"YOU will use field-guns! Oh, unhappy man! Have you still not realized on what frightful brink you stand?"

The Gadfly glanced back over his shoulder at the open grave.

"And s-s-so your reverence thinks that, when you have put me down there, you will have done with me? Perhaps you will lay a stone on the top to pre-v-vent a r-resurrection 'after three days'? No fear, your reverence! I shan't poach on the monopoly in cheap theatricals; I shall lie as still as a m-mouse, just where you put me. And all the same, WE shall use field-guns."

"Oh, merciful God," the priest cried out; "forgive this wretched man!"

"Amen!" murmured the lieutenant of carabineers, in a deep bass growl, while the colonel and his nephew crossed themselves devoutly.

As there was evidently no hope of further insistence producing any effect, the priest gave up the fruitless attempt and moved aside, shaking his head and murmuring a prayer. The short and simple preparations were made without more delay, and the Gadfly placed himself in the required position, only turning his head to glance up for a moment at the red and yellow splendour of the sunrise. He had repeated the request that his eyes might not be bandaged, and his defiant face had wrung from the colonel a reluctant consent. They had both forgotten what they were inflicting on the soldiers.

He stood and faced them, smiling, and the carbines shook in their hands.

"I am quite ready," he said.

The lieutenant stepped forward, trembling a little with excitement. He had never given the word of command for an execution before.

"Ready—present—fire!"

The Gadfly staggered a little and recovered his balance. One unsteady shot had grazed his cheek, and a little blood fell on to the white cravat. Another ball had struck him above the knee. When the smoke cleared away the soldiers looked and saw him smiling still and wiping the blood from his cheek with the mutilated hand

"A bad shot, men!" he said; and his voice cut in, clear and articulate, upon the dazed stupor of the wretched soldiers. "Have another try."

A general groan and shudder passed through the row of carabineers. Each man had aimed aside, with a secret hope that the death-shot would come from his neighbour's hand, not his; and there the Gadfly stood and smiled at them; they had only turned the execution into a butchery, and the whole ghastly business was to do again. They were seized with sudden terror, and, lowering their carbines, listened hopelessly to the furious curses and reproaches of the officers, staring in dull horror at the man whom they had killed and who somehow was not dead.

The Governor shook his fist in their faces, savagely shouting to them to stand in position, to present arms, to make haste and get the thing over. He had become as thoroughly demoralized as they were, and dared not look at the terrible figure that stood, and stood, and would not fall. When the Gadfly spoke to him he started and shuddered at the sound of the mocking voice.

"You have brought out the awkward squad this morning, colonel! Let me see if I can manage them better. Now, men! Hold your tool higher there, you to the left. Bless your heart, man, it's a carbine you've got in your hand, not a frying-pan! Are you all straight? Now then! Ready—present——"

"Fire!" the colonel interrupted, starting forward. It was intolerable that this man should give the command for his own death.

There was another confused, disorganized volley, and the line broke up into a knot of shivering figures, staring before them with wild eyes. One of the soldiers had not even discharged his carbine; he had flung it away, and crouched down, moaning under his breath: "I can't—I can't!"

The smoke cleared slowly away, floating up into the glimmer of the early sunlight; and they saw that the Gadfly had fallen; and saw, too, that he was still not dead. For the first moment soldiers and officials stood as if they had been turned to stone, and watched the ghastly thing that writhed and struggled on the ground; then both doctor and colonel rushed forward with a cry, for he had dragged himself up on one knee and was still facing the soldiers, and still laughing.

"Another miss! Try—again, lads—see—if you can't——"

He suddenly swayed and fell over sideways on the grass.

"Is he dead?" the colonel asked under his breath; and the doctor, kneeling down, with a hand on the bloody shirt, answered softly:

"I think so—God be praised!"

"God be praised!" the colonel repeated. "At last!"

His nephew was touching him on the arm.

"Uncle! It's the Cardinal! He's at the gate and wants to come in."

"What? He can't come in—I won't have it! What are the guards about? Your Eminence——"

The gate had opened and shut, and Montanelli was standing in the courtyard, looking before him with still and awful eyes.

"Your Eminence! I must beg of you—this is not a fit sight for you! The execution is only just over; the body is not yet——"

"I have come to look at him," Montanelli said. Even at the moment it struck the Governor that his voice and bearing were those of a sleep-walker.

"Oh, my God!" one of the soldiers cried out suddenly; and the Governor glanced hastily back. Surely———

The blood-stained heap on the grass had once more begun to struggle and moan. The doctor flung himself down and lifted the head upon his knee.

"Make haste!" he cried in desperation. "You savages, make haste! Get it over, for God's sake! There's no bearing this!"

Great jets of blood poured over his hands, and the convulsions of the figure that he held in his arms shook him, too, from head to foot. As he looked frantically round for help, the priest bent over his shoulder and put a crucifix to the lips of the dying man.

"In the name of the Father and of the Son——"

The Gadfly raised himself against the doctor's knee, and, with wide-open eyes, looked straight upon the crucifix.

Slowly, amid hushed and frozen stillness, he lifted the broken right hand and pushed away the image. There was a red smear across its face.

"Padre—is your—God—satisfied?"

His head fell back on the doctor's arm.

"Your Eminence!"

As the Cardinal did not awake from his stupor, Colonel Ferrari repeated, louder:

"Your Eminence!"

Montanelli looked up.

"He is dead."

"Quite dead, your Eminence. Will you not come away? This is a horrible sight."

"He is dead," Montanelli repeated, and looked down again at the face. "I touched him; and he is dead."

"What does he expect a man to be with half a dozen bullets in him?" the lieutenant whispered contemptuously; and the doctor whispered back. "I think the sight of the blood has upset him."

The Governor put his hand firmly on Montanelli's arm.

"Your Eminence—you had better not look at him any longer. Will you allow the chaplain to escort you home?"

"Yes—I will go."

He turned slowly from the blood-stained spot and walked away, the priest and sergeant following. At the gate he paused and looked back, with a ghostlike, still surprise.

"He is dead."

A few hours later Marcone went up to a cottage on the hillside to tell Martini that there was no longer any need for him to throw away his life.

All the preparations for a second attempt at rescue were ready, as the plot was much more simple than the former one. It had been arranged that on the following morning, as the Corpus Domini procession passed along the fortress hill, Martini should step forward out of the crowd, draw a pistol from his breast, and fire in the Governor's face. In the moment of wild confusion which would follow twenty armed men were to make a sudden rush at the gate, break into the tower, and, taking the turnkey with them by force, to enter the prisoner's cell and carry him bodily away, killing or overpowering everyone who interfered with them. From the gate they were to retire fighting, and cover the retreat of a second band of armed and mounted smugglers, who would carry him off into a safe hiding-place in the hills. The only person in the little group who knew nothing of the plan was Gemma; it had been kept from her at Martini's special desire. "She will break her heart over it soon enough," he had said.

As the smuggler came in at the garden gate Martini opened the glass door and stepped out on to the verandah to meet him.

"Any news, Marcone? Ah!"

The smuggler had pushed back his broad-brimmed straw hat.

They sat down together on the verandah. Not a word was spoken on either side. From the instant when Martini had caught sight of the face under the hat-brim he had understood.

"When was it?" he asked after a long pause; and his own voice, in his ears, was as dull and wearisome as everything else.

"This morning, at sunrise. The sergeant told me. He was there and saw it."

Martini looked down and flicked a stray thread from his coat-sleeve.

Vanity of vanities; this also is vanity. He was to have died to-morrow. And now the land of his heart's desire had vanished, like the fairyland of golden sunset dreams that fades away when the darkness comes; and he was driven back into the world of every day and every night—the world of Grassini and Galli, of ciphering and pamphleteering, of party squabbles between comrades and dreary intrigues among Austrian spies—of the old revolutionary mill-round that maketh the heart sick. And somewhere down at the bottom of his consciousness there was a great empty place; a place that nothing and no one would fill any more, now that the Gadfly was dead.

Someone was asking him a question, and he raised his head, wondering what could be left that was worth the trouble of talking about.

"What did you say?"

"I was saying that of course you will break the news to her."

Life, and all the horror of life, came back into Martini's face.

"How can I tell her?" he cried out. "You might as well ask me to go and stab her. Oh, how can I tell her—how can I!"

He had clasped both hands over his eyes; but, without seeing, he felt the smuggler start beside him, and looked up. Gemma was standing in the doorway.

"Have you heard, Cesare?" she said. "It is all over. They have shot him."

CHAPTER VIII

"INTROIBO ad altare Dei." Montanelli stood before the high altar among his ministers and acolytes and read the Introit aloud in steady tones. All the Cathedral was a blaze of light and colour; from the holiday dresses of the congregation to the pillars with their flaming draperies and wreaths of flowers there was no dull spot in it. Over the open spaces of the doorway fell great scarlet curtains, through whose folds the hot June sunlight glowed, as through the petals of red poppies in a corn-field. The religious orders with their candles and torches, the companies of the parishes with their crosses and flags, lighted up the dim side-chapels; and in the aisles the silken folds of the processional banners drooped, their gilded staves and tassels glinting under the arches. The surplices of the choristers gleamed, rainbow-tinted, beneath the coloured windows; the sunlight lay on the chancel floor in chequered stains of orange and purple and green. Behind the altar hung a shimmering veil of silver tissue; and against the veil and the decorations and the altar-lights the Cardinal's figure stood out in its trailing white robes like a marble statue that had come to life.

As was customary on processional days, he was only to preside at the Mass, not to celebrate, so at the end of the Indulgentiam he turned from the altar and walked slowly to the episcopal throne, celebrant and ministers bowing low as he passed.

"I'm afraid His Eminence is not well," one of the canons whispered to his neighbour; "he seems so strange."

Montanelli bent his head to receive the jewelled mitre. The priest who was acting as deacon of honour put it on, looked at him for an instant, then leaned forward and whispered softly:

"Your Eminence, are you ill?"

Montanelli turned slightly towards him. There was no recognition in his eyes.

"Pardon, Your Eminence!" the priest whispered, as he made a genuflexion and went back to his place, reproaching himself for having interrupted the Cardinal's devotions.

The familiar ceremony went on; and Montanelli sat erect and still, his glittering mitre and gold-brocaded vestments flashing back the sunlight, and the heavy folds of his white festival mantle sweeping down over the red carpet. The light of a hundred candles sparkled among the sapphires on his breast, and shone into the deep, still eyes that had no answering gleam; and when, at the words: "Benedicite, pater eminentissime," he stooped to bless the incense, and the sunbeams played among the diamonds, he might have recalled some splendid and fearful ice-spirit of the mountains, crowned with rainbows and robed in drifted snow, scattering, with extended hands, a shower of blessings or of curses.

At the elevation of the Host he descended from his throne and knelt before the altar. There was a strange, still evenness about all his movements; and as he rose and went back to his place the major of dragoons, who was sitting in gala uniform behind the Governor, whispered to the wounded captain: "The old Cardinal's breaking, not a doubt of it. He goes through his work like a machine."

"So much the better!" the captain whispered back. "He's been nothing but a mill-stone round all our necks ever since that confounded amnesty."

"He did give in, though, about the court-martial."

"Yes, at last; but he was a precious time making up his mind to. Heavens, how close it is! We shall all get sun-stroke in the procession. It's a pity we're not Cardinals, to have a canopy held over our heads all the way—— Sh-sh-sh! There's my uncle looking at us!"

Colonel Ferrari had turned round to glance severely at the two younger officers. After the solemn event of yesterday morning he was in a devout and serious frame of mind, and inclined to reproach them with a want of proper feeling about what he regarded as "a painful necessity of state."

The masters of the ceremonies began to assemble and place in order those who were to take part in the procession. Colonel Ferrari rose from his place and moved up to the chancel-rail, beckoning to the other officers to accompany him. When the Mass was finished, and the Host had been placed behind the crystal shield in the processional sun, the celebrant and his ministers retired to the sacristy to change their vestments, and a little buzz of whispered conversation broke out through the church. Montanelli remained seated on his throne, looking straight before him, immovably. All the sea of human life and motion seemed to surge around and below him, and to die away into stillness about his feet. A censer was brought to him; and he raised his hand with the action of an automaton, and put the incense into the vessel, looking neither to the right nor to the left.

The clergy had come back from the sacristy, and were waiting in the chancel for him to descend; but he remained utterly motionless. The deacon of honour, bending forward to take off the mitre, whispered again, hesitatingly:

"Your Eminence!"

The Cardinal looked round.

"What did you say?"

"Are you quite sure the procession will not be too much for you? The sun is very hot."

"What does the sun matter?"

Montanelli spoke in a cold, measured voice, and the priest again fancied that he must have given offence.

"Forgive me, Your Eminence. I thought you seemed unwell."

Montanelli rose without answering. He paused a moment on the upper step of the throne, and asked in the same measured way:

"What is that?"

The long train of his mantle swept down over the steps and lay spread out on the chancel-floor, and he was pointing to a fiery stain on the white satin.

"It's only the sunlight shining through a coloured window, Your Eminence."

"The sunlight? Is it so red?"

He descended the steps, and knelt before the altar, swinging the censer slowly to and fro. As he handed it back, the chequered sunlight fell on his bared head and wide, uplifted eyes, and cast a crimson glow across the white veil that his ministers were folding round him.

He took from the deacon the sacred golden sun; and stood up, as choir and organ burst into a peal of triumphal melody.

"Pange, lingua, gloriosi
Corporis mysterium,
Sanguinisque pretiosi
Quem in mundi pretium,
Fructus ventris generosi
Rex effudit gentium."

The bearers came slowly forward, and raised the silken canopy over his head, while the deacons of honour stepped to their places at his right and left and drew back the long folds of the mantle. As the acolytes stooped to lift his robe from the chancel-floor, the lay fraternities heading the procession started to pace down the nave in stately double file, with lighted candles held to left and right.

He stood above them, by the altar, motionless under the white canopy, holding the Eucharist aloft with steady hands, and watched them as they passed. Two by two, with candles and banners and torches, with crosses and images and flags, they swept slowly down the chancel steps, along the broad nave between the garlanded pillars, and out under the lifted scarlet curtains into the blazing sunlight of the street; and the sound of their chanting died into a rolling murmur, drowned in the pealing of new and newer voices, as the unending stream flowed on, and yet new footsteps echoed down the nave.

The companies of the parishes passed, with their white shrouds and veiled faces; then the brothers of the Misericordia, black from head to foot, their eyes faintly gleaming through the holes in their masks. Next came the monks in solemn row: the mendicant friars, with their dusky cowls and bare, brown feet; the white-robed, grave Dominicans. Then followed the lay officials of the district; dragoons and carabineers and the local police-officials; the Governor in gala uniform, with his brother officers beside him. A deacon followed, holding up a great cross between two acolytes with gleaming candles; and as the curtains were lifted high to let them pass out at the doorway, Montanelli caught a momentary glimpse, from where he stood under the canopy, of the sunlit blaze of carpeted street and flag-hung walls and white-robed children scattering roses. Ah, the roses; how red they were!

On and on the procession paced in order; form succeeding to form and colour to colour. Long white surplices, grave and seemly, gave place to gorgeous vestments and embroidered pluvials. Now passed a tall and slender golden cross, borne high above the lighted candles; now the cathedral canons, stately in their dead white mantles. A chaplain paced down the chancel, with the crozier between two flaring torches; then the acolytes moved forward in step, their censers swinging to the rhythm of the music; the bearers raised the canopy higher, counting their steps: "One, two; one, two!" and Montanelli started upon the Way of the Cross.

Down the chancel steps and all along the nave he passed; under the gallery where the organ pealed and thundered; under the lifted curtains that were so red—so fearfully red; and out into the glaring street, where the blood-red roses lay and withered, crushed into the red carpet by the passing of many feet. A moment's pause at the door, while the lay officials came forward to replace the canopy-bearers; then the procession moved on again, and he with it, his hands clasping the Eucharistic sun, and the voices of the choristers swelling and dying around him, with the rhythmical swaying of censers and the rolling tramp of feet.

"Verbum caro, panem verum,
Verbo carnem efficit;
Sitque sanguis Christi merum——"

Always blood and always blood! The carpet stretched before him like a red river; the roses lay like blood splashed on the stones—— Oh, God! Is all Thine earth grown red, and all Thy heaven? Ah, what is it to Thee, Thou mighty God——Thou, whose very lips are smeared with blood!

"Tantum ergo Sacramentum,
Veneremur cernui."

He looked through the crystal shield at the Eucharist. What was that oozing from the wafer—dripping down between the points of the golden sun—down on to his white robe? What had he seen dripping down—dripping from a lifted hand?

The grass in the courtyard was trampled and red,—all red,—there was so much blood. It was trickling down the cheek, and dripping from the pierced right hand, and gushing in a hot red torrent from the wounded side. Even a lock of the hair was dabbled in it,—the hair that lay all wet and matted on the forehead—ah, that was the death-sweat; it came from the horrible pain.

The voices of the choristers rose higher, triumphantly:

"Genitori, genitoque,
Laus et jubilatio,
Salus, honor, virtus quoque,
Sit et benedictio."

Oh, that is more than any patience can endure! God, Who sittest on the brazen heavens enthroned, and smilest with bloody lips, looking down upon agony and death, is it not enough? Is it not enough, without this mockery of praise and blessing? Body of Christ, Thou that wast broken for the salvation of men; blood of Christ, Thou that wast shed for the remission of sins; is it not enough?

"Ah, call Him louder; perchance He sleepeth!

"Dost Thou sleep indeed, dear love; and wilt Thou never wake again? Is the grave so jealous of its victory; and will the black pit under the tree not loose Thee even for a little, heart's delight?"

Then the Thing behind the crystal shield made answer, and the blood dripped down as It spoke:

"Hast thou chosen, and wilt repent of thy choice? Is thy desire not fulfilled? Look upon these men that walk in the light and are clad in silk and in gold: for their sake was I laid in the black pit. Look upon the children scattering roses, and hearken to their singing if it be sweet: for their sake is my mouth filled with dust, and the roses are red from the well-springs of my heart. See where the people kneel to drink the blood that drips from thy garment-hem: for their sake was it shed, to quench their ravening thirst. For it is written: 'Greater love hath no man than this, if a man lay down his life for his friends.'"

"Oh, Arthur, Arthur; there is greater love than this! If a man lay down the life of his best beloved, is not that greater?"

And It answered again:

"Who is thy best beloved? In sooth, not I."

And when he would have spoken the words froze on his tongue, for the singing of the choristers passed over them, as the north wind over icy pools, and hushed them into silence:

> "Dedit fragilibus corporis ferculum,
> Dedit et tristibus sanguinis poculum,
> Dicens: Accipite, quod trado vasculum
> Omnes ex eo bibite."

Drink of it, Christians; drink of it, all of you! Is it not yours? For you the red stream stains the grass; for you the living flesh is seared and torn. Eat of it, cannibals; eat of it, all of you! This is your feast and your orgy; this is the day of your joy! Haste you and come to the festival; join the procession and march with us; women and children, young men and old men—come to the sharing of flesh! Come to the pouring of blood-wine and drink of it while it is red; take and eat of the Body——

Ah, God; the fortress! Sullen and brown, with crumbling battlements and towers dark among the barren hills, it scowled on the procession sweeping past in the dusty road below. The iron teeth of the portcullis were drawn down over the mouth of the gate; and as a beast crouched on the mountain-side, the fortress guarded its prey. Yet, be the teeth clenched never so fast, they shall be broken and riven asunder; and the grave in the courtyard within shall yield up her dead. For the Christian hosts are marching, marching in mighty procession to their sacramental feast of blood, as marches an army of famished rats to the gleaning; and their cry is: "Give! Give!" and they say not: "It is enough."

"Wilt thou not be satisfied? For these men was I sacrificed; thou hast destroyed me that they might live; and behold, they march everyone on his ways, and they shall not break their ranks.

"This is the army of Christians, the followers of thy God; a great people and a strong. A fire devoureth before them, and behind them a flame burneth;

the land is as the garden of Eden before them, and behind them a desolate wilderness; yea, and nothing shall escape them."

"Oh, yet come back, come back to me, beloved; for I repent me of my choice! Come back, and we will creep away together, to some dark and silent grave where the devouring army shall not find us; and we will lay us down there, locked in one another's arms, and sleep, and sleep, and sleep. And the hungry Christians shall pass by in the merciless daylight above our heads; and when they howl for blood to drink and for flesh to eat, their cry shall be faint in our ears; and they shall pass on their ways and leave us to our rest."

And It answered yet again:

"Where shall I hide me? Is it not written: 'They shall run to and fro in the city; they shall run upon the wall; they shall climb up upon the houses; they shall enter in at the windows like a thief?' If I build me a tomb on the mountain-top, shall they not break it open? If I dig me a grave in the river-bed, shall they not tear it up? Verily, they are keen as blood-hounds to seek out their prey; and for them are my wounds red, that they may drink. Canst thou not hear them, what they sing?"

And they sang, as they went in between the scarlet curtains of the Cathedral door; for the procession was over, and all the roses were strewn:

"Ave, verum Corpus, natum
De Maria Virgine:
Vere passum, immolatum
In cruce pro homine!
Cujus latus perforatum
Undam fluxit cum sanguinae;
Esto nobis praegustatum
Mortis in examinae."

And when they had left off singing, he entered at the doorway, and passed between the silent rows of monks and priests, where they knelt, each man in his place, with the lighted candles uplifted. And he saw their hungry eyes fixed on the sacred Body that he bore; and he knew why they bowed their heads as he passed. For the dark stream ran down the folds of his white vestments; and on the stones of the Cathedral floor his footsteps left a deep, red stain.

So he passed up the nave to the chancel rails; and there the bearers paused, and he went out from under the canopy and up to the altar steps. To left and right the white-robed acolytes knelt with their censers and the chaplains with their torches; and their eyes shone greedily in the flaring light as they watched the Body of the Victim.

And as he stood before the altar, holding aloft with blood-stained hands the torn and mangled body of his murdered love, the voices of the guests bidden to the Eucharistic feast rang out in another peal of song:

"Oh salutaris Hostia,
Quae coeli pandis ostium;
Bella praemunt hostilia,
Da robur, fer, auxilium!"

Ah, and now they come to take the Body——Go then, dear heart, to thy bitter doom, and open the gates of heaven for these ravening wolves that will not be denied. The gates that are opened for me are the gates of the nethermost hell.

And as the deacon of honour placed the sacred vessel on the altar, Montanelli sank down where he had stood, and knelt upon the step; and from the white altar above him the blood flowed down and dripped upon his head. And the voices of the singers rang on, pealing under the arches and echoing along the vaulted roof:

"Uni trinoque Domino
Sit sempiterna gloria:
Qui vitam sine termino
Nobis donet in patria."

"Sine termino—sine termino!" Oh, happy Jesus, Who could sink beneath His cross! Oh, happy Jesus, Who could say: "It is finished!" This doom is never ended; it is eternal as the stars in their courses. This is the worm that dieth not and the fire that is not quenched. "Sine termino, sine termino!"

Wearily, patiently, he went through his part in the remaining ceremonies, fulfilling mechanically, from old habit, the rites that had no longer any meaning for him. Then, after the benediction, he knelt down again before the altar and covered his face; and the voice of the priest reading aloud the list of indulgences swelled and sank like a far-off murmur from a world to which he belonged no more.

The voice broke off, and he stood up and stretched out his hand for silence. Some of the congregation were moving towards the doors; and they turned back with a hurried rustle and murmur, as a whisper went through the Cathedral:

"His Eminence is going to speak."

His ministers, startled and wondering, drew closer to him and one of them whispered hastily: "Your Eminence, do you intend to speak to the people now?"

Montanelli silently waved him aside. The priests drew back, whispering together; the thing was unusual, even irregular; but it was within the Cardinal's prerogative if he chose to do it. No doubt, he had some statement of exceptional importance to make; some new reform from Rome to announce or a special communication from the Holy Father.

Montanelli looked down from the altar-steps upon the sea of upturned faces. Full of eager expectancy they looked up at him as he stood above them, spectral and still and white.

"Sh-sh! Silence!" the leaders of the procession called softly; and the murmuring of the congregation died into stillness, as a gust of wind dies among whispering tree-tops. All the crowd gazed up, in breathless silence, at the white figure on the altar-steps. Slowly and steadily he began to speak:

"It is written in the Gospel according to St. John: 'God so loved the world, that He gave His only begotten Son that the world through Him might be saved.'

"This is the festival of the Body and Blood of the Victim who was slain for your salvation; the Lamb of God, which taketh away the sins of the world; the Son of God, Who died for your transgressions. And you are assembled here in solemn festival array, to eat of the sacrifice that was given for you, and to render thanks for this great mercy. And I know that this morning, when you came to share in the banquet, to eat of the Body of the Victim, your hearts were filled with joy, as you remembered the Passion of God the Son, Who died, that you might be saved.

"But tell me, which among you has thought of that other Passion—of the Passion of God the Father, Who gave His Son to be crucified? Which of you has remembered the agony of God the Father, when He bent from His throne in the heavens above, and looked down upon Calvary?

"I have watched you to-day, my people, as you walked in your ranks in solemn procession; and I have seen that your hearts are glad within you for the remission of your sins, and that you rejoice in your salvation. Yet I pray you that you consider at what price that salvation was bought. Surely it is very precious, and the price of it is above rubies; it is the price of blood."

A faint, long shudder passed through the listening crowd. In the chancel the priests bent forward and whispered to one another; but the preacher went on speaking, and they held their peace.

"Therefore it is that I speak with you this day: I AM THAT I AM. For I looked upon your weakness and your sorrow, and upon the little children about your feet; and my heart was moved to compassion for their sake, that they must die. Then I looked into my dear son's eyes; and I knew that the Atonement of Blood was there. And I went my way, and left him to his doom.

"This is the remission of sins. He died for you, and the darkness has swallowed him up; he is dead, and there is no resurrection; he is dead, and I have no son. Oh, my boy, my boy!"

The Cardinal's voice broke in a long, wailing cry; and the voices of the terrified people answered it like an echo. All the clergy had risen from their places, and the deacons of honour started forward to lay their hands on the preacher's arm. But he wrenched it away, and faced them suddenly, with the eyes of an angry wild beast.

"What is this? Is there not blood enough? Wait your turn, jackals; you shall all be fed!"

They shrank away and huddled shivering together, their panting breath thick and loud, their faces white with the whiteness of chalk. Montanelli turned again to the people, and they swayed and shook before him, as a field of corn before a hurricane.

"You have killed him! You have killed him! And I suffered it, because I would not let you die. And now, when you come about me with your lying praises and your unclean prayers, I repent me—I repent me that I have done this thing! It were better that you all should rot in your vices, in the bottomless filth of damnation, and that he should live. What is the worth of your plague-spotted souls, that such a price should be paid for them? But it is too late—too late! I cry aloud, but he does not hear me; I beat at the door of the grave, but he will not wake; I stand alone, in desert space, and look around me, from the blood-stained earth where the heart of my heart lies buried, to the void and awful heaven that is left unto me, desolate. I have given him up; oh, generation of vipers, I have given him up for you!

"Take your salvation, since it is yours! I fling it to you as a bone is flung to a pack of snarling curs! The price of your banquet is paid for you; come, then, and gorge yourselves, cannibals, bloodsuckers—carrion beasts that feed on the dead! See where the blood streams down from the altar, foaming and hot from my darling's heart—the blood that was shed for you! Wallow and lap it and smear yourselves red with it! Snatch and fight for the flesh and devour it—and trouble me no more! This is the body that was given for you—look at it, torn and bleeding, throbbing still with the tortured life, quivering from the bitter death-agony; take it, Christians, and eat!"

He had caught up the sun with the Host and lifted it above his head; and now flung it crashing down upon the floor. At the ring of the metal on stone the clergy rushed forward together, and twenty hands seized the madman.

Then, and only then, the silence of the people broke in a wild, hysterical scream; and, overturning chairs and benches, beating at the doorways, trampling one upon another, tearing down curtains and garlands in their haste, the surging, sobbing human flood poured out upon the street.

EPILOGUE

"GEMMA, there's a man downstairs who wants to see you." Martini spoke in the subdued tone which they had both unconsciously adopted during these last ten days. That, and a certain slow evenness of speech and movement, were the sole expression which either of them gave to their grief.

Gemma, with bare arms and an apron over her dress, was standing at a table, putting up little packages of cartridges for distribution. She had stood over the work since early morning; and now, in the glaring afternoon, her face looked haggard with fatigue.

"A man, Cesare? What does he want?"

"I don't know, dear. He wouldn't tell me. He said he must speak to you alone."

"Very well." She took off her apron and pulled down the sleeves of her dress. "I must go to him, I suppose; but very likely it's only a spy."

"In any case, I shall be in the next room, within call. As soon as you get rid of him you had better go and lie down a bit. You have been standing too long to-day."

"Oh, no! I would rather go on working."

She went slowly down the stairs, Martini following in silence. She had grown to look ten years older in these few days, and the gray streak across her hair had widened into a broad band. She mostly kept her eyes lowered now; but when, by chance, she raised them, he shivered at the horror in their shadows.

In the little parlour she found a clumsy-looking man standing with his heels together in the middle of the floor. His whole figure and the half-frightened way he looked up when she came in, suggested to her that he must be one of the Swiss guards. He wore a countryman's blouse, which evidently did not belong to him, and kept glancing round as though afraid of detection.

"Can you speak German?" he asked in the heavy Zurich patois.

"A little. I hear you want to see me."

"You are Signora Bolla? I've brought you a letter."

"A—letter?" She was beginning to tremble, and rested one hand on the table to steady herself.

"I'm one of the guard over there." He pointed out of the window to the fortress on the hill. "It's from—the man that was shot last week. He wrote it the night before. I promised him I'd give it into your own hand myself."

She bent her head down. So he had written after all.

"That's why I've been so long bringing it," the soldier went on. "He said I was not to give it to anyone but you, and I couldn't get off before—they watched me so. I had to borrow these things to come in."

He was fumbling in the breast of his blouse. The weather was hot, and the sheet of folded paper that he pulled out was not only dirty and crumpled, but damp. He stood for a moment shuffling his feet uneasily; then put up one hand and scratched the back of his head.

"You won't say anything," he began again timidly, with a distrustful glance at her. "It's as much as my life's worth to have come here."

"Of course I shall not say anything. No, wait a minute——"

As he turned to go, she stopped him, feeling for her purse; but he drew back, offended.

"I don't want your money," he said roughly. "I did it for him—because he asked me to. I'd have done more than that for him. He'd been good to me—God help me!"

The little catch in his voice made her look up. He was slowly rubbing a grimy sleeve across his eyes.

"We had to shoot," he went on under his breath; "my mates and I. A man must obey orders. We bungled it, and had to fire again—and he laughed at us—he called us the awkward squad—and he'd been good to me——"

There was silence in the room. A moment later he straightened himself up, made a clumsy military salute, and went away.

She stood still for a little while with the paper in her hand; then sat down by the open window to read. The letter was closely written in pencil, and in some parts hardly legible. But the first two words stood out quite clear upon the page; and they were in English:

"Dear Jim."

The writing grew suddenly blurred and misty. And she had lost him again—had lost him again! At the sight of the familiar childish nickname all the hopelessness of her bereavement came over her afresh, and she put out her hands in blind desperation, as though the weight of the earth-clods that lay above him were pressing on her heart.

Presently she took up the paper again and went on reading:

"I am to be shot at sunrise to-morrow. So if I am to keep at all my promise to tell you everything, I must keep it now. But, after all, there is not much need of explanations between you and me. We always understood each other without many words, even when we were little things.

"And so, you see, my dear, you had no need to break your heart over that old story of the blow. It was a hard hit, of course; but I have had plenty of others as hard, and yet I have managed to get over them,—even to pay back a few of them,—and here I am still, like the mackerel in our nursery-book (I forget its name), 'Alive and kicking, oh!' This is my last kick, though; and then, to-morrow morning, and—'Finita la Commedia!' You and I will translate that: 'The variety show is over'; and will give thanks to the gods that they have had, at least, so much mercy on us. It is not much, but it is something; and for this and all other blessings may we be truly thankful!

"About that same to-morrow morning, I want both you and Martini to understand clearly that I am quite happy and satisfied, and could ask no better thing of Fate. Tell that to Martini as a message from me; he is a good fellow and a good comrade, and he will understand. You see, dear, I know that the stick-in-the-mud people are doing us a good turn and themselves a bad one by going back to secret trials and executions so soon, and I know that if you who are left stand together steadily and hit hard, you will see great things. As for me, I shall go out into the courtyard with as light a heart as any child starting home for the holidays. I have done my share of the work, and this death-sentence is the proof that I have done it thoroughly. They kill me because they are afraid of me; and what more can any man's heart desire?

"It desires just one thing more, though. A man who is going to die has a right to a personal fancy, and mine is that you should see why I have always been such a sulky brute to you, and so slow to forget old scores. Of course, though, you understand why, and I tell you only for the pleasure of writing the words. I loved you, Gemma, when you were an ugly little girl in a gingham frock, with a scratchy tucker and your hair in a pig-tail down your back; and I love you still. Do you remember that day when I kissed your hand, and when you so piteously begged me 'never to do that again'? It was a scoundrelly trick to play, I know; but you must forgive that; and now I kiss the paper where I have written your name. So I have kissed you twice, and both times without your consent.

"That is all. Good-bye, my dear."

There was no signature, but a verse which they had learned together as children was written under the letter:
"Then am I
A happy fly,
If I live
Or if I die."

Half an hour later Martini entered the room, and, startled out of the silence of half a life-time, threw down the placard he was carrying and flung his arms about her.

"Gemma! What is it, for God's sake? Don't sob like that—you that never cry! Gemma! Gemma, my darling!"

"Nothing, Cesare; I will tell you afterwards—I—can't talk about it just now."

She hurriedly slipped the tear-stained letter into her pocket; and, rising, leaned out of the window to hide her face. Martini held his tongue and bit his moustache. After all these years he had betrayed himself like a schoolboy—and she had not even noticed it!

"The Cathedral bell is tolling," she said after a little while, looking round with recovered self-command. "Someone must be dead."

"That is what I came to show you," Martini answered in his everyday voice. He picked up the placard from the floor and handed it to her. Hastily printed in large type was a black-bordered announcement that: "Our dearly beloved Bishop, His Eminence the Cardinal, Monsignor Lorenzo Montanelli," had died suddenly at Ravenna, "from the rupture of an aneurism of the heart."

She glanced up quickly from the paper, and Martini answered the unspoken suggestion in her eyes with a shrug of his shoulders.

"What would you have, Madonna? Aneurism is as good a word as any other."